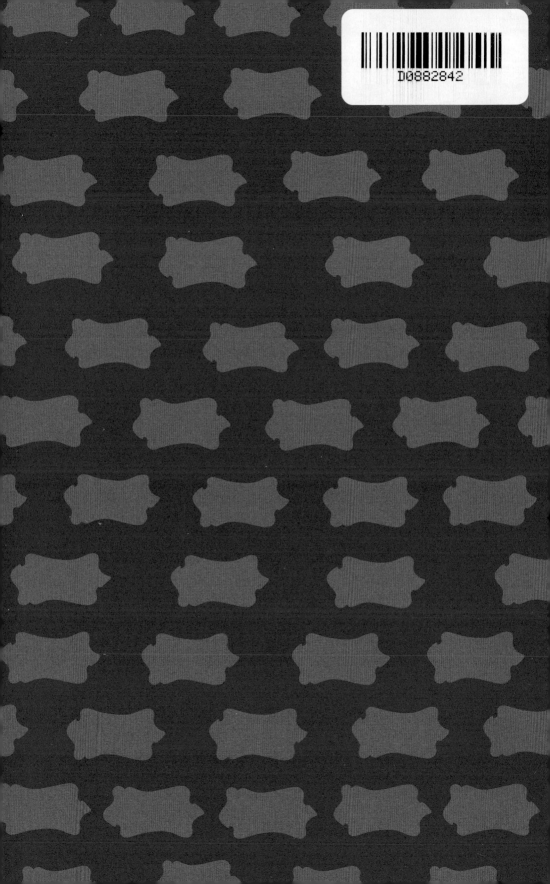

'[*A Season on Earth* is] an ideal jumping-off point for readers new to Murnane and his particular way of looking at the world.'
Books+Publishing (five-star review)

'No living Australian writer…has higher claims to permanence or a richer sense of distinction.'
Sydney Morning Herald

'Unquestionably one of the most original writers working in Australia today.'
Australian

'A writer of the greatest skill and tonal control.'
Financial Times

'Reading Murnane, one cares less about what is happening in the story and more about what one is thinking about as one reads. The effect of his writing is to induce images in the reader's own mind, and to hold the reader inside a world in which the reader is at every turn encouraged to turn his or her attention to those fast flocking images.'
New York Times

'Murnane's is a vision that blesses and beatifies every detail.'
Washington Post

'A careful stylist and a slyly comic writer with large ideas.'
Robyn Cresswell, *Paris Review*

'*The Plains* is a bizarre masterpiece that can feel less like something you've read than something you've dreamed.'
Ben Lerner, *New Yorker*

'Murnane, a genius, is a worthy heir to Beckett.'
Teju Cole, *Guardian*

A SEASON ON EARTH

A SEASON ON EARTH
GERALD MURNANE

TEXT PUBLISHING MELBOURNE AUSTRALIA

textpublishing.com.au

The Text Publishing Company

Swann House, 22 William Street, Melbourne, Victoria 3000, Australia

Published by The Text Publishing Company, 2019 (*A Lifetime on Clouds* first published by William Heinemann, Australia, 1976)

Jacket design by W. H. Chong
Front-cover image by Neville Bowler / Fairfax Syndication
Page design by Text
Typeset by Midland Typesetters

Printed and bound in Australia by Griffin Press, an accredited ISO/NZS 14001:2004 Environmental Management System printer

ISBN: 9781925773347 (hardback)
ISBN: 9781925774160 (ebook)

A catalogue record for this book is available from the National Library of Australia.

A SEASON ON EARTH

FOREWORD

According to my records, I sat with Hilary McPhee of Heinemann Australia in her office in Inkerman Street, St Kilda, in July 1973 and handed over to her the typescript of *Tamarisk Row*, which I had worked at intermittently for the previous nine years. I've always counted myself fortunate to have been able to submit my first work of fiction in person and with a recommendation. When I had finished *Tamarisk Row* nearly a year earlier, I knew no one in publishing and little about the ways of publishers. My only source of advice was the author Barry Oakley, who was a friend of mine at the time. Barry was good enough to look over my typescript and to tell Hilary McPhee, his own editor, that my work was well worth her consideration.

The typescript that I handed to Hilary was overly long, and I had had the typed pages bound by a bookbinder into two volumes, which made the text seem even longer. I took the monstrous item out of my literary archive just now and estimated that it comprises at least 140,000 words. To have written such a thing, let alone to have submitted it to a publisher, seems to me now sheer folly, but I don't recall myself feeling the least embarrassment when I handed my two thick volumes to Hilary, nor her making any comment on their size.

She was not long in doing so, however. A few weeks later she told me she was prepared to publish *Tamarisk Row* if I would first remove at least half the original text.

This I did willingly. It was by no means a hard task, given that the book consisted of numerous short sections, most of which could be wholly removed without leaving scar tissue.

All of the above is most relevant to the history of *A Season on Earth*, my second work of fiction, which is now published in its original format forty-three years after it was mutilated at the request of a publisher's editor. My records tell me that I wrote the first notes for my second work in August 1973, *in the very month* when I was told by Hilary McPhee that my first work was at least twice too long for publication. Of course, I had no intention, while I was planning my second work, that it should grow to the size of its bulky sibling. (I had likewise never intended, in the beginning, that *Tamarisk Row* should be much longer than the average first novel.) But can I truly offer the excuse that my second work simply outgrew its original plan while I wrote it? Should I not have had continually in mind while writing *A Season on Earth* the fate of *Tamarisk Row*? I cannot recall having any such concern during the two years when I was bringing *A Season on Earth* to its final length: about 142,000 words.

According to my notes from those days, I took from August 1973 until February 1974 to work out what I called my Final Plan. My slow progress would have been partly the result of my having to work at the very same time on reducing *Tamarisk Row* to its required length.

In more recent decades, I've kept detailed records of my dealings with publishers, but I can find few written records of Heinemann Australia's turning my four-part work *A Season on Earth* into the two-part work *A Lifetime on Clouds*, which is what took place in 1976. According to a brief summary that I made at the time, a first handwritten draft of the four-part work was finished in June 1975. I then hand-wrote a second draft and sent this to a professional typist in September 1975. I collected the finished typescript in December 1975. I then had the typescript bound into two volumes and delivered these to Heinemann Australia in March 1976.

Hilary McPhee was no longer the editor at Heinemann. She had left to found her own publishing company, the successful firm of McPhee Gribble. No full-time editor had been appointed in her place. Instead, the services of a freelance editor, Edward Kynaston, seemed much in use. Even I could see that my publisher was languishing. Kynaston could hardly be said to have replaced Hilary. She had been a dynamic presence around the place and an active commissioning editor. Kynaston worked from his home, assessing some of the unsolicited submissions and marking up typescripts for the printer. The head of the firm, John Burchall, was a likeable man but what I would have called a functioning alcoholic. A few years earlier, when *Tamarisk Row* had been in the pipeline, my publishers were a lively bunch; now, they seemed adrift, but I was bound by my earlier contract to offer them my latest work.

The best that I can say for Edward Kynaston is that he was prompt and decisive. Only a few weeks after I had delivered my typescript, my new editor told me in John Burchall's office that he and John were delighted with my work. I've forgotten most of what was said at the meeting but I can never forget Kynaston's calling my latest work a comic masterpiece. I may have been briefly flattered by the word 'masterpiece', but I was disappointed that my editor had such a narrow view of a work that was much more than a comic romp. I soon learned that he was softening me up for a proposal that I might not like. The proposal was that my typescript should be neatly bisected. It was really two books, I was told. They would publish the first half as soon as possible and the second half soon afterwards as a sequel.

I straightaway opposed the idea. I tried to appeal to Burchall, but he was firmly with Kynaston. Clearly, they had discussed the matter at length beforehand. All I could do was to ask for time.

I worked frantically at home for a few weeks. (I was supported at the time by a one-year fellowship from the Australia Council.) I shortened my typescript as I had previously shortened *Tamarisk Row* for Hilary McPhee—by stapling blank sheets over the sequences of pages meant for discarding. My aim was to severely prune the whole and to have Heinemann publish only one book of four much-shortened sections. I would have done better to save my time—Kynaston and Burchall would not budge; my so-called masterpiece was to be neatly halved.

I've sometimes wondered what might have happened if I had taken the whole typescript to McPhee Gribble at that point, but I've never been any sort of tactician, and the thought seems never to have occurred to me. I was in my thirties, and my two advisers or opponents were in their fifties. I knew they had misread my work, but if I gave way to them I was at least assured of having a second book of mine in print, and so I gave way.

My next task was to rewrite the last few pages of the second of the four sections of the original work. I seem to have done this skilfully enough, given that no reader or reviewer has ever claimed to find the ending of *A Lifetime on Clouds* hasty, contrived or unconvincing. A much harder task awaited me if the plan for publishing a sequel to *A Lifetime on Clouds* was to be effected. I understood that many a reader of the sequel would not previously have read *A Lifetime on Clouds*. I had to write a new block of fiction for these readers. I had to rewrite completely the beginning of the third of the four sections in order to explain why Adrian Sherd was travelling, early in his final year of secondary school, from his home in Melbourne to a junior seminary in New South Wales.

I wasted perhaps six months trying to perform the impossible. I can still recollect the mood of dejection that overcame me on many of the days while I struggled to summarise in a few pages the peculiar emotional history of the young man who was set on joining the Charleroi Fathers. I suspect I knew from the first that my task was hopeless. Worse, I suspect I knew from the first that the second book—the sequel—would never be published. *A Lifetime on Clouds* was rather well received but it was far from being the raging success that would have assured the success of its sequel. I don't even recall any discussion of a possible sequel after the publication of *A Lifetime on Clouds*. I certainly never raised the matter with Heinemann. Burchall, Kynaston and I seemed, for once, in agreement.

The six years between the publication of *A Lifetime on Clouds* and of *The Plains* were the bleakest of my writing career. There were several other causes for this, but I've never doubted that my writerly misfortunes during those years were mostly the result of the butchering of *A Season on Earth*. The third and fourth sections rested in my literary archive for decades, and few of my growing number of readers would have known of their existence. I could seldom bring myself to look at them, and if I sometimes dared to think of their being published in the future, I could only imagine the two lost sections being published as a sort of literary curiosity with a long introduction to explain their context and history. I seem never to have supposed that some enterprising and courageous publisher would one day publish the original four-part work.

When Michael Heyward was visiting me in Goroke in 2012, I showed him the original four-part typescript during a tour of my archives and told him its history. Michael was eager to read the unpublished sections but I denied him the opportunity. Once again, I seemed to suppose that any talk of publication involved only the as-yet-unpublished sections. Finally, in late 2017, Michael gave me to understand that he would consider publishing the original four-part work, and I willingly gave him a copy of the third and fourth sections.

I'm overjoyed to see this book in print, more than forty years after I first submitted it for publication. I've sometimes heard or read that *A Lifetime on Clouds* is markedly different from the rest of my published fiction, or that my second book seems to lack something when compared with the others. These statements are well and truly justified. *A Lifetime on Clouds is* different; it's only *half* a book and Adrian Sherd is only *half* a character. Now that my original text has been published at last, *A Season on Earth*, wholly restored, can take its rightful place among my other titles.

I'm truly grateful to Text Publishing for performing a literary miracle.

Gerald Murnane, Goroke, 2018

PART ONE

He was driving a station wagon towards a lonely beach in Florida—an immense arc of untrodden white sand sloping down to the warm, sapphire-blue waters of the Gulf of Mexico. His name was Adrian Sherd. His friends in the car with him were Jayne and Marilyn and Susan. They were going on a picnic together.

They were almost at the beach when Jayne said, 'Oh damn! I've left my bathers behind. Has anyone got a spare pair?'

No one had. Jayne was very disappointed.

The sea came into view. The women gasped at the beauty of it under the cloudless sky. Jayne said, 'I can't resist that glorious water. I'm going to have my swim anyway.'

'Will you swim in your scanties and brassiere?' asked Marilyn.

'No. The saltwater would ruin them.'

Sherd pretended not to be listening. But his stomach was weak with excitement.

'You mean you'll swim in the—?' Susan began.

Jayne tossed back her long dark hair and glanced at Sherd. 'Why not? Adrian won't be shocked—will you, Adrian?'

'Of course not. I've always believed the human body is nothing to be ashamed of.'

The grass above the sand was lush and green like a lawn. Sherd and Jayne spread out the picnic lunch. The other two hung back and whispered together.

Susan came over and spoke. 'It won't be fair for Jayne if she goes swimming with nothing on and Adrian is allowed to peer at her all day. Adrian will have to strip off too. That's a fair exchange.'

They all looked at Sherd. He said, 'That wouldn't be fair either. Susan and Marilyn will see me in the raw without having to take their own bathers off.'

Jayne agreed with Sherd that the only fair thing would be for all four of them to leave their bathers off. But Susan and Marilyn refused.

After lunch Susan and Marilyn went into the trees and came back wearing their twopiece bathers. Jayne and Sherd waited until the others were in the water. Then they slipped out of their clothes with their backs turned to each other and ran down the sand staring straight ahead of them.

In the water Jayne dived and splashed so much that it was some time before Sherd saw even the tops of her breasts. At first he thought she was teasing him. Then he realised he was behaving so calmly and naturally himself that she didn't know how anxious he was to see her.

Jayne ran out of the water at last and Sherd followed her back to the car. She stood side-on to him and dried herself, bending and twisting her flawless body to meet the towel.

Sherd couldn't pretend any longer that he saw this sort of thing every day. He stood in front of her and admired her. Then, while she sat beside him with only a towel draped round her shoulders, he made a long speech praising every part of her body in turn. And when she still made no effort to cover herself, he was moved to confess the real reason why he had brought them to the lonely beach.

Jayne was not alarmed. She even smiled a little as though she might have suspected already what was in his mind.

Susan and Marilyn came out of the water and went behind the trees to change. They both stared hard at Sherd as they passed.

Jayne said, 'I still think it's unfair, those two seeing you in the nude and hiding their own bodies. I'm sure you'd like to look at them, wouldn't you?'

She bent her lovely compassionate face close to his and said, 'Listen, Adrian. I've got a plan.'

After this, events happened so fast that he barely had time to enjoy them properly. Jayne tiptoed up behind the other two women. Sherd followed, trembling. Jayne tore the towels away from their naked bodies, pushed Susan into the car and locked the door. Marilyn squealed and tried to cover herself with her hands, but Jayne grabbed her arms from behind and held her for Adrian to admire. Then, while Marilyn walked around swearing and looking for her clothes, Jayne dragged Susan out of the car and showed her to Adrian.

Adrian lost control of himself. He looked just once more at Jayne. Her eyes met his. She seemed to know what he was going to do. She couldn't help feeling a little disappointed that he preferred another's charms to her own. But she saw he was overcome by his passions.

Jayne leaned back resignedly against the car and watched. Even Susan forgot to cover herself, and watched too. And the two of them stood smiling provocatively while he grappled with Marilyn's naked body and finally subdued her and copulated with her.

Next morning Adrian Sherd was sitting in the Form Four classroom in St Carthage's College in Swindon, a south-eastern suburb of Melbourne.

The day started with forty minutes of Christian Doctrine. The brother in charge was taking them through one of the Gospels. A boy would read a few lines and then the brother would start a discussion. 'It will pay us to look very closely at this parable, boys. Robert Carmody, what do you think it means?'

Adrian Sherd had a sheet of paper hidden under his Gospel and a packet of coloured pencils on the seat beside him. He was looking for a way to make the Christian Doctrine period pass more quickly. Instead of drawing his usual map of America showing the main railways and places of interest, he decided to sketch a rough plan of his classroom. He drew twenty-nine rectangles for the desks and marked in each rectangle the initials of the two boys who sat there.

He thought of several ways of decorating his sketch. Because it was a Christian Doctrine period, he chose a spiritual colour scheme. He took a yellow pencil and drew little spears of light radiating outwards from the boys whose souls were in the state of grace.

Adrian awarded his golden rays to about twenty boys. These fellows spent all their lunch hour bowling at the cricket nets or playing handball against the side of the school. Most of them were crazy about some hobby—stamp collecting or chemistry sets or model railways. They talked freely to the brothers out of the classroom. And they made a show of turning their backs and walking away from anyone who started to tell a dirty joke.

Next Adrian edged with black the initials of the boys who were in the state of mortal sin. He started with himself and his three friends, Michael Cornthwaite, Stan Seskis and Terry O'Mullane. The four of them admitted they were sex maniacs. Every day they met beside the handball courts. Someone would tell a new dirty joke or discuss the sex appeal of a film star or interpret an adult conversation he had overheard or simply report that he had done it the night before.

Adrian blackened the initials of other fellows who were not friends of his but had let slip something that betrayed them. Once, for instance, Adrian had overheard a quiet boy named Gourlay telling a joke to his friend.

> GOURLAY: Every night after cricket practice I pull a muscle.
> FRIEND: After practice? How come?
> GOURLAY: Oh, it happens when I'm lying in bed with nothing to do before I go to sleep.

Adrian marked both Gourlay and his friend in black—the friend because of the guilty way he had laughed at Gourlay's joke.

He took only a few minutes to colour all the mortal

sinners. There were about a dozen. This still left nearly thirty boys unmarked. Adrian puzzled over some of these. They were well grown with pimply faces and they shaved every second or third day. They had been seen to smile at dirty jokes and they always looked bored during Christian Doctrine periods. Adrian would have liked to colour them black to boost the numbers of his own group, but he had no definite evidence that they were habitual sinners.

In the end he put a pale grey shadow over the initials of all the remaining boys as a sign that their souls were discoloured by venial sins.

The Christian Doctrine period was still not finished. Adrian drew a yellow cloud above his chart to represent heaven. Down below he drew a black tunnel leading to hell. There was room at each side of his page for more of the universe, so he put a grey zone at one side for purgatory and a green zone opposite for limbo.

He sat back and admired his work. The colours around the initials indicated clearly where each boy's soul would go if the world ended suddenly that morning before any of them could get to confession or even murmur an act of perfect contrition.

None of them could go to limbo, of course, because that was a place of perfect natural happiness reserved for the souls of babies who had died before baptism or adult pagans who had never been baptised but had lived sinless lives according to their lights. But Adrian had included limbo in his chart because it had always attracted him. A brother had once said that some theologians believed limbo might be the earth itself after the General Judgement. They meant that, after the end of the world, God would remake the whole planet as a place of perfect natural happiness.

Sometimes when Adrian realised how unlikely it was that he would get to heaven, he would willingly have traded his right to heaven for safe conduct to limbo. But because he had been baptised he had to choose between heaven and hell.

He slipped his chart into his desk and looked around the room at the fellows he had marked with black. They were an odd assortment, with not much in common apart from the sin that enslaved them. They even differed in the way they committed their secret sin.

Cornthwaite only did it in total darkness—usually late at night with a pillow over his head. He claimed that the sight of it disgusted him. His inspiration was always the same—the memory of a few afternoons with his twelve-year-old cousin Patricia when her parents were out of the house. The girl's parents had told Cornthwaite afterwards that he needn't bother coming to the house again.

Adrian often asked Cornthwaite what he had done to the girl. But Cornthwaite would only say it was nothing like people imagined and he didn't want bastards like Sherd even thinking dirty thoughts about his young cousin.

O'Mullane preferred to do it in broad daylight. He swore he didn't need to think of women or girls. He got his excitement from the feel of whichever lubricant he was using. He was always experimenting with butter or hair oil or soap or his mother's cosmetics. Sometimes he stung or burnt himself and had to give up doing it for a few days.

Seskis only used film stars. He didn't care whether they wore bathing suits or street clothes so long as their lips were red and moist. He sometimes went to an afternoon show in a theatre in Melbourne where he could sit in an empty row and do it quietly through a hole in the lining of his trousers pocket while some woman parted her lips close to the camera.

Ullathorne looked at *National Geographic* magazines with pictures of bare-breasted women from remote parts of the world. He had once offered to lend Adrian one of his best magazines. Adrian admired some bare-breasted girls from the island of Yap until he read in a caption under a photo that Yap women sometimes had spiders and scorpions living in their voluminous grass skirts.

Froude used a set of photographs. The man who came to his house to teach him violin used to slip a photo into Froude's pocket after each lesson. Each photo showed a different boy standing or sitting or lying down naked with his penis erect. The boys were all about thirteen or fourteen years old. Froude had no idea who they were. He had asked his music teacher and been told he would find out in good time.

Adrian had seen some of Froude's photos. They were so clear and well lit that he told Froude to ask the music teacher if he had any similar pictures of girls or women.

Purcell used the nude scene from the film *Ecstasy* starring Hedy Lamarr when she was very young. He had read about the film in an old copy of *Pix* magazine and torn out the picture of Hedy Lamarr floating on her back in a murky river. He admitted it was hard to make out Hedy's breasts in the photo, and the rest of her body was out of sight under the water. But he said he got a colossal thrill just from having a picture of one of the only nude films ever made.

The other habitual sinners were mostly unimaginative fellows who simply made up adventures about themselves and some of the girls they knew. Adrian considered himself luckier than any of them, because he used the whole of the USA for his love life.

The Christian Doctrine period ended at last and the class stood and recited the Prayer Between Lessons. The boys in mortal sin looked no less devout than the others. Perhaps they believed, like Adrian, that one day they would find a cure that really worked.

Adrian and his friends sometimes discussed cures for their habit. One day Seskis had turned up at school with the story of a novel cure.

SESKIS: I was reading this little booklet my father gave me. It was full of advice to young men and it said to avoid irritation and stimulation during the night you should wash and soap well around the genitals in the bath or shower.

CORNTHWAITE: Whoever wrote that must be crazy. Did you try it?

SESKIS: Two or three times in the bath. I soaped the thing until I couldn't see it for suds and bubbles. It stood up the whole time and nearly drove me mad. So I had to finish it off right there in the bath.

O'MULLANE: Like the time a priest told me in confession not to eat hot spicy foods for tea or supper. So I only had a slice of toast and a glass of milk for tea to see what happened. Next thing I woke up starving in the night and had to do it to put myself back to sleep.

SHERD: Sometimes I think the only cure is to get married as soon as you're old enough. But I reckon I could stop it now if I had to sleep in a room with someone else so they'd hear the mattress squeaking if I did anything at night.

O'MULLANE: Bullshit. When our parish tennis club went to Bendigo for the big Catholic Easter Tournament, Casamento and me and two big bastards were in bunks in this little room. One of the big bastards tried to get us all to throw two shillings on the floor and make it a race to do it over the edge of the bunks. Winner takes all.

CORNTHWAITE: Filthy bastards.

O'MULLANE: Of course the one who wanted the race was the bastard they call Horse from the size of his tool. He would have won by a mile.

SHERD: Tell the truth and say you were too embarrassed to do it with other people in the room. It proves what I said about my cure for it.

O'MULLANE: I would have backed myself with any money against bastards my own size.

CORNTHWAITE: The only cure is to get hold of a tart and do the real thing to her. O'Mullane will end up a homo the way he's going. And Sherd will still be looking for a cure when he's a dirty old bachelor.

After school each day Adrian Sherd walked from St Carthage's College half a mile along the Swindon Road tramline to Swindon railway station. Then he travelled five miles by electric train to his own suburb of Accrington.

From the Accrington station Adrian walked nearly a mile along a dirt track beside the main road. It was 1953, and outer suburbs like Accrington had few made roads

12

or footpaths. He passed factories whose names were familiar—PLASDIP PRODUCTS, WOBURN COMPONENTS, AUSTRALIAN CARD CLOTHING, EZIFOLD FURNITURE— but whose products were a mystery to him.

Adrian's street, Riviera Grove, was a chain of water-holes between clumps of manuka and wattle scrub. Each winter, builders and delivery men drove their trucks over the low scrub, looking for a safe route, but the only people in the street who owned a car left it parked each night on the main road, two hundred yards from their house.

On one side of the Sherds' house was a dense stand of tea-tree scrub thirty feet tall with only one narrow track winding into it. On the other side was the wooden frame of a house and behind it the fibrocement bungalow, twenty feet by ten, where the New Australian Andy Horvath lived with his wife and small son and mother-in-law.

The Sherds' house was a two-year-old double-fronted weatherboard, painted cream with dark-green trimmings. It had a lawn with borders of geraniums and pelargoniums at the front, but the backyard was nearly all native grass and watsonia lilies. Along the back fence was a fowl run with a shed of palings at one end. Near one of the side fences was a weatherboard lavatory (cream with a dark-green door) with a trapdoor at the back where the night man dragged out the pan each week and shoved an empty pan in. Sometimes the pan filled up a few days before the night man's visit. Then Adrian's father would dig a deep hole in the fowl run and empty half the pan into it. He did it furtively after dark while Adrian held a torch for him.

On the opposite side of the yard was a fibrocement shed with a cement floor and a small louvre window at one end. One half of the shed was filled with bags of fowl feed, garden tools and odd pieces of broken furniture. The other half was left clear. Leaning against one wall of the shed was a plywood door left over after the Sherds' house had been built. A model-railway layout was screwed onto one side of the door. It was a Hornby Clockwork layout—a main track with a loop and two sidings.

The Sherds' house had three bedrooms, a lounge, a kitchen, a bathroom and a laundry. The kitchen floor was covered with linoleum. All the other floors were polished boards. The lounge room had an open fireplace, two armchairs and a couch of faded floral-patterned velvet, and a small bookcase. The kitchen had a wood stove and a small electric cooker with a hotplate and a griller. There was an ice chest in a corner and a mantel radio over the fireplace. The table and chairs were wooden.

The only other pieces of furniture were the beds and wardrobes and dressing tables—a walnut-veneer suite in the front bedroom and oddments in the boys' rooms. Adrian's two younger brothers slept in the middle bedroom. Adrian had the back bedroom, which was called the sleepout because it had louvre windows.

As soon as Adrian got home from school he had to take off his school suit to save it from wear. Then he put on the only other clothes he had—the shirt and trousers and jumper that had been his previous school uniform but were now too patched for school.

Adrian's young brothers had been home from school for an hour already. (They travelled a mile and a half by bus to Our Lady of Good Counsel's parish school.) Adrian found and cleaned their school shoes as well as his own.

He filled the woodbox in the kitchen with split logs that his father had left under a sheet of corrugated iron behind the lavatory. He filled a cardboard box in the laundry with briquettes for the hot-water system. Then he split kindling wood and stacked it on the kitchen hearth for his mother to use next morning. If his father was still not home, Adrian fed the fowls and collected the eggs.

Sometimes before tea Adrian climbed over the side fence and looked around in the tea-tree scrub. He visited a bull-ants' nest and tapped a stick near the entrance. The ants came storming out to look for the enemy. Adrian dropped leaves and twigs on them to tease them.

There were possums' nests high up in the branches of the tea-tree. Adrian knew the possums were hiding inside, but he had never been able to scare them out. The tea-tree had no branches strong enough for climbing, and the sticks that he threw got tangled in the twigs and foliage.

When Adrian had first discovered the ants and possums he decided to observe their habits like a scientist. For a few days he kept a diary describing the ants' habits and drew maps to show how far they travelled from their nest. He thought of becoming a famous naturalist and talking on the radio like Crosbie Morrison with his program, *Wild Life*. He even planned to dig away the side of the ants' nest and put a sheet of glass inside so he could study them in their tunnels. But he didn't know where to buy glass and he found he couldn't dig a hole with straight sides anyway.

If he walked on through the scrub he came to the Gaffneys' side fence. The Sherds knew very little about the few other households in Riviera Grove. They were all what Adrian's parents called young couples, with two or

15

three small children. Adrian sometimes saw a mother in gumboots pushing a load of kids in a pram through the muddy street or chasing a child that had waded too far into a puddle. One day he had spied on Mrs Gaffney through a hole in her fence. She was wearing something that he knew was called a playsuit and hanging out nappies on the line. He had a good view of her face and legs but he decided it was useless to compare her with any film star or pin-up girl.

After he had set the table for tea, Adrian read the sporting pages of the *Argus* and then glanced through the front pages for the cheesecake picture that was always somewhere among the important news. It was usually a photograph of a young woman in bathers leaning far forward and smiling at the camera.

If the woman was an American film star he studied her carefully. He was always looking for photogenic starlets to play small roles in his American adventures.

If she was only a young Australian woman he read the caption ('Attractive Julie Starr found Melbourne's autumn sunshine yesterday too tempting to resist. The breeze was chilly but Julie, a telephonist aged eighteen, braved the shallows at Elwood in her lunch hour and brought back memories of summer') and spent a few minutes trying to work out the size and shape of her breasts. Then he folded up the paper and forgot about her. He wanted no Melbourne typists and telephonists on his American journeys. He would feel uncomfortable if he saw on the train one morning some woman who had shared his American secrets only the night before.

When tea was over Adrian stacked up the dishes and washed them for his brothers to dry and put away. At six-thirty

16

he turned on the wireless to 3KZ. For half an hour while he finished the dishes or played Ludo or Snakes and Ladders with his brothers, he heard the latest hit tunes, interrupted only by brief advertisements for films showing at Hoyts Suburban Theatres.

Adrian always made a show of being busy at something else while hit tunes were playing. If his parents had thought he was listening to the words they might have switched the wireless off or even banned him from hearing the program again. Too many of the hit tunes were love songs about kisses like wine or memories of charms or touches that thrilled.

But Adrian was not really interested in the words. Nearly every night on 3KZ he heard a few short passages of music that seemed to describe the landscape of America. The opening notes of a romantic ballad might have just the right blend of vagueness and loneliness to suggest the Great Plains states. Or the last hectic chorus of a Mitch Miller record might put him in mind of the sensual Deep South where it was always summer.

The wireless was switched off again at seven. No one wanted to hear the news or the serials and musical programs that followed it. Mr Sherd went to bed early to finish one of the stack of books that his wife borrowed each week from the library behind the children's-wear shop in Accrington (Romance, Crime, Historical Romance, New Titles). Mrs Sherd sat by the kitchen stove knitting. Adrian's brothers played with their Meccano set or traced through lunch-wrap paper some pictures from the small stack of old *National Geographic* magazines in the lounge room. Adrian began his homework.

The house was quiet. There was rarely the sound of a car or truck in Riviera Grove or the streets around it. Every half-hour an electric train passed along the line between Melbourne and Coroke. It was nearly a mile from the Sherds' house, but on windless nights they heard clearly the rattling of the bogeys and the whining of the motor. As the noise died away, Adrian's brothers called out 'Up!' or 'Down!' and argued over which way the train had been heading.

Adrian worked at his homework until nearly ten o'clock. Every day at school three or four boys were strapped for not doing their homework. Their excuses astonished Adrian. They had gone out, or started listening to the wireless and forgotten the time, or been told by their parents to sit up and talk to the visitors. Or they had been sent to bed because there was a party going on at their house.

In the two years since the Sherds had moved to Accrington, they had almost never gone out after dark. And Adrian could not remember anyone visiting them at night. The boys who had other things to do instead of home-work came from the suburbs close to Swindon—places with made roads and footpaths and front gardens full of shrubs. The suburbs had dignified names such as Luton and Glen Iris and Woodstock. Adrian imagined the houses in these suburbs full of merry laughter every night of the week.

When his homework was finished Adrian went out for a few minutes to the back shed. He switched on the light and lowered his model railway track to the floor. On the wood beneath the tracks was a faint pencilled outline of the United States of America. Adrian wound up his clockwork engine. He lowered it onto the rails near New York City and hooked two passenger coaches behind it. The train sped south-west

18

towards Texas then around past California to Idaho and on across the prairies to the Great Lakes. At Chicago there was a set of points. Adrian switched them so that the train travelled first around the perimeter of the country (Pennsylvania, New York state, New England and back to New York City) and then, on each alternate lap, down through the Midwest and the Ozarks to rejoin the main line near Florida.

After four or five laps of the track the train slowed down and came to a stop. Adrian noted carefully the exact place where its journey ended. Then he put the engine and coaches away and went back to the house and got ready for bed.

The map in Adrian's shed was crudely drawn. The proportions of America were all wrong. The country had been twisted out of shape to make its most beautiful landscapes no more than stages in an endless journey. But Adrian knew his map by heart. Each few inches of railway track gave access to some picturesque scene from American films or magazines. No matter where the train might stop, it brought him to familiar country.

Nearly every night Adrian made an American journey and found himself in some pleasant part of the American outdoors. Sometimes he was content to wander there alone. But usually he went in search of American women. There were dozens to choose from. He had seen their pictures in Australian newspapers and magazines. Some of them he had even watched in films. And all of them were just as beautiful as he had imagined them.

In the weeks before the coronation of the new Queen, Adrian and his mother made a scrapbook out of cuttings from the *Argus* and the *Australian Women's Weekly*. On the night when the coronation was broadcast direct from London, the Sherds sat round the wireless with the scrapbook open on the kitchen table. They followed the exact route of the procession on a large map of London. When the commentator described the scene in Westminster Abbey they tried to find each of the places mentioned on a labelled diagram, although some of the Protestant terms like transept and nave confused them a little.

When nothing much was happening in the abbey, Adrian feasted on the choicest items in the scrapbook—the coloured illustrations of the crown jewels and Her Majesty's robes and regalia. They were the most beautiful things he had ever seen. He delighted in every sumptuous fold of the robes and every winking highlight of the jewels. Then, to appreciate their splendour still more, he compared them with other things he had once thought beautiful.

A few years before, when he was an altar boy, he used to stare each morning at the patterns on the back of the priest's chasuble. There was one with the shape of a lamb outlined in amber-coloured stones on a background of white. The lamb held in its upraised foreleg a silver staff with a golden scroll unfurled at the top. The whole design was topped by the disc of an enormous Host with rays beaming from it and the letters IHS across it in beads the colour of blood.

Adrian had once asked the priest after mass whether the stones and beads on the chasuble were proper jewels. The priest had looked a little apologetic and said no, the parish wasn't wealthy enough for that. They were (he paused) semi-precious stones. Adrian was not at all disappointed. Any sort of precious stones appealed to him.

On coronation night Adrian studied the picture in the *Argus* of Her Majesty's robe and saw that no chasuble could rival it.

The solemn ceremony of the coronation itself was too much for Adrian to visualise with only the wireless broadcast to help him. But two days later when the *Argus* published its full-colour souvenir supplement, he saw the scene in the abbey in all its splendour. He compared all that magnificence with two scenes that he had once thought would never be surpassed for beauty.

Years before, he had watched a film about the *Arabian Nights*. It was the first Technicolor film he had seen. Evelyn Keyes was a princess guarded by black slaves in her father's palace. Cornel Wilde was the man who fell in love with her and tried to elope with her. At one point in the film, the slaves were carrying Evelyn Keyes through the streets of Baghdad in a sedan chair. She was inside her private compartment, concealed by thick purple and gold drapery. Cornel Wilde stopped the slaves and tried to fight them. Evelyn Keyes peeped out for a few seconds and smiled shyly at him.

Adrian never forgot that brief glimpse of her. She was dressed in pastel-coloured satins. A white silk veil covered part of her face, but anyone could see she was breathtakingly beautiful. Her complexion was a radiant pinkish-gold, and the gorgeously coloured fabrics around her set it off to perfection.

In one of his adventures, Mandrake the Magician (in the comic strip at the back of the *Women's Weekly*) found a race of people like Ancient Romans living on the far side of the moon. When they were ready for sleep at night, the Moonlings climbed onto filmy envelopes inflated with a special light gas. All night long the handsome moon-dwellers, in long white robes, sprawled on their transparent cushions and wafted from room to room of their spacious houses.

But the glamour of Evelyn Keyes could not match the simple beauty of the young Queen, and the Moonlings on their floating beds were not half so graceful and dignified as the lords and ladies of England in Westminster Abbey.

For a few days after the coronation, Adrian was restless and agitated. Picking his way through the puddles in his street or carving railway sidings and points into his wooden ruler in school, he thought how little pageantry there was in his life. At night he stared at the coloured souvenir pictures and wondered how to bring the splendour of the coronation to Accrington.

One night when he arrived with Lauren and Rita and Linda in the Bluegrass Country of Kentucky, the women started to whisper and smile together. He realised they were planning a little surprise for him.

They told him to wait while they went behind some bushes. Lauren and Linda came back first. They wore brief twopiece bathing suits that dazzled him. The fabric was cloth-of-gold studded with semi-precious copies of all the emeralds and rubies and diamonds in the crown jewels.

Behind them came Rita, draped in a replica of the coronation robe itself. And when the other two lifted her train he saw just enough to tell him that under the extravagant ermine-tipped robe she was stark naked.

Some mornings when Adrian Sherd stood in the bathroom waiting for the hot water to come through the pipes and fingering the latest pimples on his face, he remembered his

American journey of the previous night and wondered if he was going mad.

Each night his adventures became a little more outrageous. On his first trips to America he had walked for hours hand in hand with film stars through scenic landscapes. He had undressed them and gone the whole way with them afterwards but always politely and considerately. But as the American countryside became more familiar he found he needed more than one woman to excite him. Instead of admiring the scenery he had begun to spend his time talking coarsely to the women and encouraging them to join in all kinds of obscene games.

Some of these games seemed so absurd afterwards that Adrian decided only a lunatic could have invented them. He could not imagine any men or women in real life doing such things together.

He thought of his own parents. Every night they left their bedroom door ajar to prove they had nothing to hide. And Mrs Sherd always bolted the bathroom door when she went to have a bath so that not even her husband could look in at her.

In all the backyards around Riviera Grove there was no place where a couple could even sunbathe together unobserved. And in most of the houses there were young children running round all day. Perhaps the parents waited for the children to go to sleep and then frolicked together late at night. But from what Adrian heard of their conversations in the local bus, it seemed they had no time for fun.

The men worked on their houses and gardens. 'I stayed up till all hours last night trying to put up an extra cupboard in the laundry,' a man would say.

The women were often sick. 'Bev's still in hospital. Her mother's stopping with us to mind the nippers.'

Even their annual holidays were innocent. 'Our in-laws lent us their caravan at Safety Beach. It's a bit of a madhouse with the two of us and the three littlies all in bunks, but it's worth it for their sakes.'

Adrian divided Melbourne into three regions—slums, garden suburbs and outer suburbs. The slums were all the inner suburbs where the houses were joined together and had no front gardens. East Melbourne, Richmond, Carlton—Adrian was not at all curious about the people who lived in these slums. They were criminals or dirty and poor, and he couldn't bear to think of their pale grubby skin naked or sticking out of bathing suits.

The garden suburbs formed a great arc around the east and south-east of Melbourne. Swindon, where Adrian went to school, was in the heart of them, and most of the boys at his school lived in leafy streets. The people of the garden suburbs had full-grown trees brushing against their windows. They spread a tablecloth before every meal and poured their tomato sauce from little glass jugs. The women always wore stockings when they went shopping.

Most of the houses and gardens in these suburbs were ideal for sexual games, but Adrian doubted if they were ever used for that purpose. The people of the garden suburbs were too dignified and serious. The men sat with suits on all day in offices or banks and brought home important papers to work on after tea. The women looked so sternly at schoolboys and schoolgirls giggling together on the Swindon Road trams that Adrian thought they would have slapped their husbands' faces at the very mention of lewd games.

The outer suburbs were the ones that Adrian knew best. Whenever he tried to imagine the city of Melbourne as a whole, he saw it shaped like a great star with the outer suburbs its distinctive arms. Their miles of pinkish-brown tiled roofs reached far out into the farmlands and market gardens and bush or scrub as a sign that the modern age had come to Australia.

When Adrian read in the newspaper about a typical Melbourne family, he saw their white or cream weather-board house in a treeless yard surrounded by fences of neatly sawn palings. From articles and cartoons in the *Argus* he had learned a lot about these people, but nothing to suggest they did the things he was interested in.

The women of the outer suburbs were not beautiful (although occasionally one was described as attractive or vivacious). They wore dressing gowns all morning, and frilly aprons over their clothes for the rest of the day. They wore their hair in curlers under scarves knotted above the forehead. When they talked over their back fences it was mostly about their husbands' stupid habits.

The husbands still had sexual thoughts occasionally. They liked to stare at pictures of film stars or beauty contestants. But the wives apparently were sick of sex (perhaps because they had too many children or because they had run out of ideas to make it interesting). They were always snatching the pictures from their husbands' hands. On the beach in summer a wife would bury her husband's head in the sand or chain his feet to an umbrella to keep him from following some beautiful young woman.

Adrian was reassured to learn that some husbands dreamed (like himself) of doing things with film stars and bathing beauties. But he would have liked to know that someone in Melbourne was actually making his dreams come true.

The little that Adrian learned from the radio was more confusing than helpful. Sometimes he heard in a radio play a conversation like this.

> YOUNG WIFE: I saw the doctor today.
> HUSBAND (only half-listening): Oh?
> YOUNG WIFE: He told me…(a pause)…I'm going to have a baby.
> HUSBAND (amazed): What? You're joking! It can't be!

Adrian had even watched a scene like this in an American film. He could only conclude that many husbands fathered their children while they were dozing off late at night, or even in their sleep. Or perhaps what they did with their wives was so dull and perfunctory that they forgot about it soon afterwards. Either way it was more evidence that the kind of sexual activity Adrian preferred was not common in real life.

Even after watching an American film, Adrian still thought he might have been a very rare kind of sex maniac. The men and women in films seemed to want nothing more than to fall in love. They struggled against misfortunes and risked their lives only for the joy of holding each other and declaring their love. At the end of each film Adrian stared at the heroine. She closed her eyes and leaned back in a kind of swoon. All that her lover could do was to support her in his arms and kiss her tenderly. She was in no condition to play American sex games.

Adrian read books by R. L. Stevenson, D. K. Broster, Sir Walter Scott, Charles Kingsley, Alexandre Dumas and

Ion L. Idriess. But he never expected to find in literature any proof that grown men and women behaved as he and his women friends did in America. Somewhere in the Vatican was an Index of Banned Books. Some of these books might have told him what he wanted to know. But it was impossible that any of them would ever fall into his hands. And even if they did, he would probably not dare to read them, since the penalty was automatic excommunication.

But an innocent-looking library book eventually proved to Adrian that at least some adults enjoyed the pleasures that he devised on his American journeys.

Adrian borrowed books from a children's library run by a women's committee of the Liberal Party over a shop in Swindon Road. (There was no library at St Carthage's College.) One afternoon he was looking through the books on the few shelves marked Australia.

In a book by Ion L. Idriess Adrian found a picture of a naked man lolling on the ground against a backdrop of tropical vegetation while his eight wives (naked except for tiny skirts between their legs) waited to do his bidding. The man was Parajoulta, King of the Blue Mud Bay tribe in the Northern Territory. Although he and his wives were Aborigines, there was a look in his eye that cheered Adrian.

The people of Accrington and the outer suburbs might have thought Adrian was crazy if they could have seen him with his women beside some beach or trout stream in America. But King Parajoulta would probably have understood. He sometimes played the very same games in the lush groves around Blue Mud Bay.

On the first Thursday of every month Adrian's form walked by twos from St Carthage's College to the Swindon parish church. First Thursday was confession day for the hundreds of boys at the college. The four confessionals built into the walls of the church were not enough. Extra priests sat in comfortable chairs just inside the altar rails and heard confessions with their heads bowed and their eyes averted from the boys kneeling at their elbows.

Adrian always chose the longest queue and knelt down to wait with his face in his hands as though he was examining his conscience.

The examination of conscience was supposed to be a long careful search for all the sins committed since your last confession. Adrian's *Sunday Missal* had a list of questions to assist the penitent in his examination. Adrian often read the questions to cheer himself up. He might have been a great sinner but at least he had never believed in fortune tellers or consulted them; gone to places of worship belonging to other denominations; sworn oaths in slight or trivial matters; talked, gazed or laughed in church; oppressed anyone; been guilty of lascivious dressing or painting.

Adrian had no need to examine his conscience. There was only one kind of mortal sin that he committed. All he had to do before confession was to work out his total for the month. For this he had a simple formula. 'Let x be the number of days since my last confession.

'Then the total of sins $= \frac{2x}{5} + 4$ (for weekends, public holidays or days of unusual excitement).'

Yet he could never bring himself to confess this total. He could have admitted easily that he had lied twenty times or lost his temper fifty times or disobeyed his parents a hundred times. But he had never been brave enough to walk into confession and say, 'It is one month since my last confession, Father, and I accuse myself of committing an impure action by myself sixteen times.'

To reduce his total to a more respectable size Adrian used his knowledge of moral theology. The three conditions necessary for mortal sin were grave matter, full knowledge and full consent. In his case the matter was certainly grave. And he could hardly deny that he knew exactly what he was doing when he sinned. (Some of his American adventures lasted for nearly half an hour.) But did he always consent fully to what took place?

Any act of consent must be performed by the Will. Sometimes just before a trip to America, Adrian caught sight of his Will. It appeared as a crusader in armour with his sword upraised—the same crusader that Adrian had seen as a child in advertisements for Hearns Bronchitis Mixture. The Will was struggling against a pack of little imps with bald grinning heads and spidery limbs. These were the Passions. (In the old advertisements the crusader had worn the word Hearns on his breast and the imps had been labelled Catarrh, Influenza, Tonsilitis, Sore Throat and Cough.) The battle took place in some vague arena in the region of Adrian Sherd's soul. The Passions were always too many and too strong for the Will, and the last thing that Adrian saw before he arrived in America was the crusader going down beneath the exultant imps.

But the important thing was that he had gone down fighting. The Will had offered some resistance to the Passions. Adrian had not gone to America with the full consent of his Will.

In the last moments before entering the confessional Adrian tried to estimate how many times he had seen this vision of his Will. He arrived at a figure, subtracted it from his gross total and confessed to a net total of six or seven mortal sins of impurity.

Adrian often wondered how the other regular sinners got through their confessions. He questioned them discreetly whenever he could.

Cornthwaite never confessed impure actions—only impure thoughts. He tried to convince Adrian that the thought was the essential part of any sin, and therefore the only part that had to be confessed and forgiven.

Seskis had a trick of faltering in the middle of his confession as though he couldn't find the right words to describe his sin. The priest usually took him for a first offender and treated him lightly.

O'Mullane sometimes told the priest that his sins happened late at night when he didn't know whether he was asleep or awake. But one priest cross-examined him and got him confused and then refused him absolution for trying to tell a lie to the Holy Ghost. O'Mullane was so scared that he gave up the sin altogether for nearly a month.

Carolan used to confess just four sins each month, although he might have committed ten or twelve in that time. He kept a careful record of the unconfessed sins and swore he would confess every one of them before he died. He intended to wipe them out four at a time each month after he had finally given up the habit.

A fellow named Di Nuzzo boasted one day that a certain priest in his parish never asked any questions or made any comment no matter how many sins of impurity you confessed.

30

Di Nuzzo said, 'I'll never go to any other priest again until I'm married. You just tell him your monthly total and he sighs a bit and gives you your penance.'

Adrian envied Di Nuzzo until the day when the priest was transferred to another parish. On the first Saturday of every month Di Nuzzo had to ride his bike nearly five miles to East St Kilda just to have an easy confession. Two years later, when Di Nuzzo had left school, Adrian saw him one Saturday morning in the city waiting for a West Coburg tram.

Di Nuzzo grinned and said, 'It had to happen. They've posted him to a new parish on the far side of Melbourne. I have to take a bus for two miles from the tram terminus. But I'm saving up to buy a motorbike.'

On the first Thursday of every month, when he came out of the confessional, Adrian knelt in front of Our Lady's altar and prayed for the gift of Holy Purity. Then he said a special prayer of thanksgiving to God for preserving his life during the past month while his soul had been in a state of mortal sin. (If he had died suddenly during that time he would have spent eternity in hell.)

For most of that day he told himself he had finished with impurity. He even kept away from Cornthwaite and his friends in the school ground. But when he arrived home he saw his model railroad leaning against the wall in the shed. He whispered the names of landscapes he had still not explored—Great Smoky Mountains, Sun Valley, Grand Rapids—and he knew he would soon go back to America.

But he was not free to go back yet. On the following Sunday morning he would be at mass with his family. His parents would know that he had been to confession on the Thursday. They would expect him to go to communion with them. If he did not go, they would know for certain that some time between Thursday and Sunday he had committed a mortal sin. His father would start asking questions. If Mr Sherd even suspected the truth about the American journey, Adrian would die of shame or run away from home.

For the sake of his future, Adrian had to avoid mortal sin from Thursday until Sunday morning. And it was not enough just to stay away from America. Any impure thought, if he wilfully entertained it, was a mortal sin. Such thoughts could appear in his mind at any hour of the day or night. It would be a desperate struggle.

The Thursday night was the easiest. Adrian needed a rest. The last few nights before his monthly confession usually wore him out. On those nights he knew he would not be visiting America again for some time, and he tried to enjoy every minute in the country as though it was his last.

On Friday at school he kept away again from Cornthwaite and the others. For as long as Adrian was in the state of grace, his former friends were what the church called bad companions.

On Friday night he did all his weekend homework and stayed up as late as possible to tire himself. In bed he remembered the advice a priest had once given him in confession: 'Take your pleasure from good and holy things.'

He closed his eyes and thought of good and holy landscapes. He saw the vineyards on the hills of Italy, where ninety-nine per cent of the people were Catholics. He crossed the golden plateaus of Spain, the only country in the world where the Communists had been fought and beaten to a standstill. The whole of Latin America was safe to explore, but he usually fell asleep before he reached there.

On Saturday morning he read the sporting section of the *Argus* but was careful not to open the other pages. They were sure to have some picture that would torment him all day.

After lunch he went for a ride on his father's old bike to tire himself out. He chose a route with plenty of hills and made sure he would have to ride the last few miles into the wind. On the steepest climbs, when he could hardly keep the pedals moving, he hissed to the rhythm of his straining thighs, 'Chastise the body. Chastise the body.'

There were still temptations even in the bleakest suburbs. Sometimes he saw the backs of a woman's thighs as she bent forward in her garden, or the shapes of her breasts bouncing under her sweater as she pushed a mower. When this happened he slowed down and waited for a glimpse of the woman's face. It was nearly always so plain that he was glad to forget all about her.

He came home exhausted and had a shower before tea. (On other Saturdays he had a bath late at night. He lay back with his organ submerged and thought foul thoughts to make it break the surface like the periscope of a submarine.) The taps in the shower recess were so hard to regulate that he had no time to stand still. He came out shivering with cold. His organ was a wrinkled stub. He flicked the towel at it and whispered, 'Bring the body into subjection.'

After tea he listened to the *London Stores Show* on the wireless to hear the football results. Then he played a game of football he had invented. He arranged thirty-six coloured scraps of paper on the table for men and threw dice to decide the path of the ball. He played the game until nearly midnight. Then he went to bed and thought about football until he fell asleep.

On Sunday morning the Sherd family caught the bus to nine o'clock mass at Our Lady of Good Counsel's, Accrington. The people in the bus were nearly always the same from week to week. They even sat in the same seats. A young woman sat opposite the Sherds. Most Sundays Adrian took no notice of her. She had a pasty face and a dumpy figure. But on the first Sunday of each month the sight of her legs gave him no peace.

Adrian believed in the devil. It could only have been the devil who arranged for a pair of legs to lie in wait for him on the first Sunday of the month when he was within an hour of reaching the altar rails without sinning. To defeat this last temptation he recited over and over to himself from the Prayers after Mass, 'Thrust Satan down into hell and with him the other wicked spirits who wander through the world seeking the ruin of souls.'

He never looked at the legs for more than a second at a time. And he never looked anywhere near them when his parents or the young woman's parents or the woman herself or any other passenger might have caught him at it. Sometimes he only saw the legs once or twice on the whole trip. But he knew by heart every curve and undulation on them, the freckles on the lower parts of the kneecaps, the mole on one shin, the tension of the stockings over the ankle bones.

The legs talked to him. They whispered that he still had to wait more than an hour until he was safe at the altar

34

rails. They urged him to close his eyes during the sermon and visualise them in all their naked beauty and wilfully consent to enjoy the pleasure he got.

When he still resisted them they became more shameless. They kicked their heels high like dancers in an American musical. They even bared the first few inches of their thighs and reminded him that there was much more to see farther up in the shadows under their skirt. Or if he did not fancy them, they said, would he prefer some of the legs he would see during mass? The church would be full of legs. He would only have to drop his missal on the floor and bend his head down to retrieve it and there, under the seat in front of him, would be calves and ankles of all shapes to feast on.

Adrian never surrendered to the legs. Instead he made a pact with them. He promised that on that very Sunday night he would meet them in America and do whatever they asked of him. In return they were to leave him in peace until he had been to communion. The legs were always as good as their word. As soon as the pact was made they stopped bothering him and stroked and preened themselves discreetly out of his view.

During mass Adrian relaxed for the first time in days. He went to communion with his head high. On the bus trip home the legs caused no trouble. He found he could last for several minutes without looking at them. But before he left the bus he always nodded casually to them as a sign that he would observe the pact.

Only once had Adrian tried to break the terms of his agreement. He had made an unusually devout communion and on the bus after mass he was thinking what a pity it

35

was that his soul would be soiled again so soon. He began to pray for the strength to resist the legs in future.

Across the narrow aisle of the bus the legs drew themselves up into a fighting posture. They warned him they would come to his bed that night and tempt him as he had never been tempted before. They would strip themselves and perform such tricks in front of his eyes that he would never sleep again until he had yielded to them.

Adrian knew they could do it. Already their anger had made them more attractive than ever. He apologised to them and hoped he hadn't made too big a fool of himself in front of them.

Whenever Adrian's friends started talking about sex, he had to use his wits to keep them from guessing his most embarrassing secret. This secret bothered him every day of his life. He was sure no other young man in Melbourne had such an absurd thing to hide.

Adrian didn't like to put his secret into simple words—it humiliated him so much. But it was simple nevertheless: he had never seen the external genital apparatus of a human female.

When Adrian was nine years old and a pupil of St Margaret Mary's School in a western suburb of Melbourne, some of the boys in his grade formed a secret society. They met among the oleanders in a little park near the school. Their aim was to persuade girls to visit the park and pull down their pants in full view of the society.

Adrian applied many times to join this society and was eventually admitted on probation. On the afternoon of his first meeting, the society was expecting six or seven girls but only two turned up. One of them refused even to lift her skirt—even after the boys of the society had all offered to take out their cocks and give her a good look. The other girl (Dorothy McEncroe—Adrian would always remember her, although she was a scrawny little thing) tucked her school tunic under her chin and lowered her pants for perhaps five seconds.

As a probationary member of the society Adrian had been forced to stand at the back of the little group of boys. At the very moment, when McEncroe's pants were sliding down the last few inches of her belly, the boys in front of Adrian began to jostle each other for a better view. Adrian clawed at them like a madman. He was small and light for his age and he could not shift them. He got down on his hands and knees and wriggled between their legs. He pushed his head into the inner circle just as the dark-blue pleats of the uniform of St Margaret Mary's School fell back into place over Dorothy McEncroe's thighs.

Adrian never had a second chance to inspect Dorothy McEncroe or any other girl at that school. A few days after the meeting, the parish priest visited all the upper grades to warn them against loitering in the park after school. The secret society was disbanded and Dorothy McEncroe walked home every night with a group of girls and pulled faces at any boy who tried to talk to her.

As he grew older, Adrian tried other ways of learning about women and girls.

One wet afternoon at St Margaret Mary's the children in Grade Seven were allowed to do free reading from the library—a glass-fronted cupboard in the corner. Adrian took down a volume of the encyclopedia from the top shelf. The book seemed mostly about art and sculpture, and many of the pictures and statues were naked. Adrian turned the pages rapidly. There were cocks and balls and breasts everywhere. He was sure he would find what he wanted among all that bare skin. His knees began to tremble. It was the afternoon under the oleanders again. But this time there was no one to block his view, and the woman he was about to see would have no pants or tunic within reach.

The girl behind him (Clare Buckley—he had cursed her a thousand times since) jumped to her feet.

'Please, Sister. Adrian Sherd's trying to read that book you told us not to borrow from the top shelf.'

The room was suddenly silent. Adrian heard the whistling of the nun's robes. She was beside him before he could even close the book. But she spared him.

'There is nothing either good or bad in art,' she said to the class. 'Adrian must have been away when I told you all not to bother yourselves about this book. We'll put it away for safekeeping just the same.'

She carried the book back to her own desk. Adrian never saw it again in the library.

In later years Adrian sometimes came across other books about art with pictures of naked men and women. But whereas the men had neat little balls and stubby uncircumcised cocks resting comfortably and unashamed between their legs, the women had nothing but smooth skin or marble fading away into the shadows where their thighs met. Adrian suspected a conspiracy among artists and sculptors to preserve the secrets of women from boys like himself.

He thought how unfair it was that girls could learn all about men from pictures and statues while boys could search for years in libraries or art galleries and still be ignorant about women. He almost wept for the injustice of it.

In his first months at St Carthage's College, Adrian learned a little more from an unexpected source. Every Wednesday the boys went for sport to some playing fields near the East Swindon tram terminus. Under the changing rooms was a lavatory with its walls covered in scribble. Some of the messages and stories were illustrated. Even here, most of the pictures were of men's and boys' organs, but Adrian sometimes found a sketch of a naked female.

From these crude drawings he pieced together an image of something that was oval in shape and bisected by a vertical line. He practised drawing this shape until it came easily to him, but he found it impossible to imagine such an odd thing between two smooth graceful thighs.

When Adrian first joined the little group around Cornthwaite, Seskis and O'Mullane, he listened to the names they used for the thing he was looking for. Cunt, twat, hole, ring, snatch, crack—when he heard these words he nodded or smiled like someone who had used them familiarly all his life. But long afterwards he brooded over them, hoping they might yield a clear image of the thing they named.

Adrian's friends knew there were certain magazines full of information and pictures about sex. They knew the names of some of them—*Man, Man Junior, Men Only, Lilliput* and *Health and Sunshine*. They believed that non-Catholic newsagents kept the magazines hidden under their counters or in back rooms.

Cornthwaite often boasted that he could get any of the filthy magazines. All he had to do was ask a big bastard in his parish tennis club to walk into his local newsagent and ask for one. Adrian begged him to buy a *Health and Sunshine*. He had heard this was the one with the most daring pictures. They were rumoured to show everything. But Cornthwaite never remembered to get him one.

One afternoon in a barber's shop in Swindon Road, Adrian found a *Man Junior* among the magazines lying about for customers to read. He was desperate to see inside it, but he was wearing his school uniform and he couldn't bring St Carthage's into disrepute by reading a smutty magazine in public.

He kept his eyes on the barber and his assistant and moved along the seat until he was sitting on the *Man Junior*. Then he bent forward and slipped the magazine down behind his legs and into his Gladstone bag. It was the first time he had ever stolen something of value, but he was sure the magazine was worth less than the amount necessary to make the theft a mortal sin.

Adrian looked through his *Man Junior* in one of the cubicles in the toilet on Swindon railway station. He saw plenty of naked women, but every one of them had something (a beach ball, a bucket and spade, a fluffy dog, a trailing vine, a leopard's skin or simply her own upraised leg) concealing the place he had waited so long to see. It all looked so casual—as though the big ball had just bounced past, or the dog had happened to stroll up and greet the woman an instant before the camera clicked. But Adrian was sure it was done deliberately. The smiles of the women angered him. They pretended to be brazen temptresses, but at the last moment they draped fronds of greenery across themselves or hid behind their pet dogs.

It was not safe to take the whole magazine home.

Adrian tore out the three most attractive pictures and hid them in the lining of his bag. That evening he searched through his brother's *Boys' Wonder Book*. He had remembered an article entitled 'An Easy-to-make Periscope'. He found the article and made a note of the materials needed for the periscope.

Next day at school he talked to a boy who was crazy about science. Adrian said he had just thought up a brilliant idea to help the Americans spy on the Russians but he wanted to be sure it would work. The idea was to take pictures of the walls around the Kremlin or any other place the Americans wanted to see into. Then American scientists could aim powerful periscopes at the photographs to see what was behind the walls.

The boy told Adrian it was the stupidest idea he had ever heard. He started to explain something about light rays but Adrian told him not to bother. Adrian was glad he hadn't hinted at what he really wanted to do with a periscope.

Adrian gave his three *Man Junior* pictures to Ullathorne, who collected bare-breasted women. He handed over the pictures in a back lane in Swindon, well away from St Carthage's. It was well known that a boy had been expelled from the college after a brother had found dirty magazines in his bag.

One Friday, a few weeks later, Cornthwaite told Adrian that if he liked to turn up at Caulfield Racecourse on the following Sunday, he might meet a certain fellow from Cornthwaite's parish who often sold second-hand copies of his big brother's dirty magazines.

Adrian said he would only come if the fellow was likely to have some copies of *Health and Sunshine*. It was too far to ride his bike five miles to Caulfield just to buy *Man* or *Man Junior.*

Cornthwaite said the fellow could sell you any magazine you liked to name.

Sunday afternoon was cold and windy but Adrian didn't want to miss the chance to get *Health and Sunshine.* He had the wind in his face all the way to Caulfield, and the trip took longer than he had expected.

The racecourse was a favourite meeting place for the boys from Cornthwaite's suburb. Adrian found Cornthwaite and a few others racing on their bikes in and out among the bookmakers' stands in the deserted betting ring. Cornthwaite said the fellow with the magazines had sold out and gone home long before. He offered Adrian a few pages torn from a magazine and said, 'I bought a *Health and Sunshine* myself. But then Laurie D'Arcy turned up and I sold it to him for a profit. But I saved you the best picture from it.'

Adrian took the ragged pages and offered to pay Cornthwaite for all his trouble. Cornthwaite said he wouldn't take any money but he hoped Adrian would stop bothering him about pictures for the rest of his life.

Adrian took his picture to a seat in the grandstand and sat down to examine it. It was a black-and-white photograph of a naked woman walking towards him under an archway of trees. And this time there was nothing between him and the thing that his parents and teachers, the men who painted the Old Masters, the women who posed for *Man Junior,* and even Dorothy McEncroe at St Margaret Mary's School years before had kept hidden from him.

The woman in *Health and Sunshine* strode boldly forward. Her hands swung by her sides. As calmly as he could, Adrian looked into the hollow between her thighs.

His first thought was that *Health and Sunshine* was a fraud like *Man Junior*. The place was full of shadow. The woman had somehow managed to shield her secrets from the light. Even without a beach ball or a leopard's skin she had still foiled him.

But then he realised it was an accident. The shadows came from the branch of a tree above the woman. The whole scene was mottled with shadows from the trees overhead. And there *was* something visible in the shadows between her legs. In the dull light under the roof of the grandstand he could not make it out clearly, but he was not beaten yet.

He took the picture out into the daylight and looked closely at it. He was even more convinced that a shape of some kind was concealed among the shadows, although it would take much longer to make out its finer details.

Adrian put the picture inside his shirt and stepped onto his bike. All the way home he was frightened of having an accident. He saw a crowd of doctors and nurses undoing his shirt on the operating table and discovering a page from *Health and Sunshine* over his heart. If they knew he was a Catholic they might tell the hospital chaplain, who would discuss the whole matter with his parents around his bedside after he regained consciousness.

He arrived home safely and smuggled the picture into the bottom of his schoolbag. Next morning he took the last six shillings from his tin of pocket money. On the way to school he bought a reading glass in a newsagent's shop in Swindon Road. He told the man that he wanted the most powerful glass he could get for his money because he had to inspect some rare postage stamps.

The picture was still hidden in his bag. After school that day he hurried to the toilet cubicle on the Swindon station. He held the reading glass in every possible position over the picture. He moved his head slowly up and down and cocked it at different angles. The trouble was that the glass magnified all the tiny dots in the picture. He was still sure there was something between the woman's legs but the glass only made it more mysterious.

He remembered the story a brother had told about the scientists who searched for the indivisible particle that all matter in the universe was made of. The harder they searched for it, the more it seemed to be made up of smaller particles that danced in front of their eyes.

Adrian put the reading glass in his bag and crumpled up his pattern of dancing dots and left it behind in the toilet.

The next time he went to the barber he read an article in *Pix* magazine about the trade in negro slaves that still flourished in certain Arab countries. There was a market in the Yemen where young black women were being sold openly for forty pounds each at the present day. The girls were paraded before intending buyers like so many cattle, and when a likely purchaser showed some interest, the vendor would fling back the gaudy robe from a girl's dusky limbs and display every one of her assets for close inspection.

Adrian knew exactly what this last sentence meant. The Yemen was not too far from Australia. When he left school and started work he would soon save up forty pounds plus his fares. As soon as he turned twenty-one he would travel to the Yemen and visit the slave market and buy one of the young women.

Or he need not even buy one. He could simply rattle some money in his pocket to look like a customer, and wait until a gaudy robe was flung back. And if one of the girl's thighs blocked his view or a shadow fell across her, he would pretend to be a very cautious customer who insisted on seeing every detail of the goods he was interested in.

One morning Brother Cyprian spent some of the Christian Doctrine period talking about dreams. The boys were unusually attentive. They could see he was nervous and embarrassed. While he talked he adjusted the pile of books on his desk, trying to make it symmetrical.

Brother Cyprian said: 'At this time of your lives you might find yourself feeling a little sad and strange because you seem to be leaving behind a part of your life that was happy and simple. The reason for this is that you're all growing from boys into young men. There are new mysteries to puzzle and bother you—things you never thought about a few years ago. And many of you no doubt are worried by the strange new dreams you might be having.'

Adrian Sherd recalled the strangest dream he had had lately. It had come to him after he had worn himself out with three consecutive nights in America. On the third of those nights he had gone with Rhonda and Doris and Debbie to the Badlands of South Dakota. The women were jaded and bored. To liven them up he got them to play the most depraved party games he could think of. The games turned into an orgy, with naked bodies rolling in the purple sage. Afterwards Adrian had fallen asleep exhausted and wondering what more America could possibly offer him.

Brother Cyprian was saying, 'Chemicals and substances

are being made inside your bodies ready for the day when you enter the adult world. These strange new substances help to put into your minds the images that might shock you while you're asleep. Sometimes in your sleep you seem to be a different person doing things you'd never think of while you're awake.'

The dream had come to Adrian on the same night after he had fallen asleep in South Dakota. He saw a dark-brown misty land on the horizon. It was England—a country he had never wanted to visit. (English film stars were too reserved and aloof. And except for Diana Dors they never appeared in bathing suits.) Something compelled him to cross damp treeless wolds towards a manor house or castle of grey stone. As he travelled he looked for places where a man might take his lady friends for a picnic. But all he saw were a few copses or spinneys so small or so close to roads and lanes that the picnickers could never have run naked or cried out obscene words without being seen or overheard.

If he had been awake he would have despised this landscape. But in his dream he longed to know it better. It seemed to promise a pleasure more satisfying than anything he had known in America.

The stone house was on a hill. He stood outside it searching for a door or a low window to look through. Behind him, he knew, was a view of miles of green fields dotted with darker-green trees and intersected by white lanes. If he could find a beautiful young woman, even an English woman, he would enjoy to the full whatever rare pleasures the landscape concealed.

Brother Cyprian said, 'The important thing to remember is this. We can't help what happens to us while we're asleep.

We're fully responsible for what we do in the daytime, but in sleep there are chemicals and forces at work that we haven't the slightest control over.'

Somewhere inside the house was a woman or a girl of his own age with a face so full of expression that a man could stare at it for hours. She was wearing a turtle-necked Fair Isle sweater (so bulky that he saw no sign of her breasts), a skirt of Harris tweed and sensible shoes. As soon as Adrian found a window into her room they would exchange glances full of meaning. Hers would tell him she was willing to agree to whatever he asked. And his would tell her he wanted no more than to walk beside her all afternoon through the English landscape. And even if they found themselves alone in some green field screened on all sides by tall hedgerows, he would ask no more than to clasp her fingertips or lightly touch her wrist where it gleamed like the finest English porcelain.

Brother Cyprian said, 'So you see, we can't commit a sin in our sleep. No matter what strange things we dream about, there's no chance of us sinning.'

Adrian groped through thickets of ivy. Even the walls of the place were becoming harder to find. Inside somewhere, the woman was operating her expensive film projector. She was showing an audience of hundreds of well-dressed English gentlemen coloured films of all the landscapes she longed to wander through, and hinting to them what they must do to earn the right to escort her on summer afternoons.

Adrian stood on the beach below a towering cliff on the Atlantic coast of Cornwall. High above, on the Sussex Downs, a young couple promenaded on the smooth sward.

He heard the intimate murmur of their voices but before he could make out their words he had to escape from the incoming tide. When he saw the vast green bulk of the whole Atlantic coming at him he woke in his sleepout at Accrington.

Brother Cyprian was near the end of his talk. 'One of the most alarming things that might happen to us is to wake up in the middle of some strange dream. You might find your whole body disturbed and restless and all sorts of odd things happening. The only thing to do is to say a short prayer to Our Lady and ask her for the blessing of a dreamless sleep. Then close your eyes again and let things take their course.'

Adrian had been desperate to get back to sleep and try again to enjoy the pleasures of England. But of course had never seen anything like an English landscape again.

In the schoolyard at morning recess Cornthwaite said, 'Did you get what Cyprian was raving about this morning—all that about naughty dreams?'

O'Mullane and Seskis and Sherd were not sure.

Cornthwaite said, 'Wet dreams. That's what it was. You bastards have never had that sort of dream because you've flogged yourselves silly every night of your lives since you were in short pants. If you go without it for a couple of weeks, one night you'll dream the filthiest dream you've ever dreamed of. You'll even shoot your bolt in your sleep if you don't wake up in the middle of it.'

Adrian tried not to look surprised. It was the first time anyone had explained wet dreams to him. He had never had one—perhaps for the reason that Cornthwaite had suggested. He realised why the brother had been so embarrassed talking about dreams.

For nearly a week Adrian kept away from America. He was waiting for a filthy dream. If the dream was as good as Cornthwaite had claimed, Adrian might have to make an important decision. He would carefully compare the dream and the best of his American adventures. If the dream turned out to be more realistic and lifelike than his American journey, he might decide to get all his sexual pleasure in future from dreams.

But whenever he remembered the young woman and the innocent landscapes of England he wished for dreams that would never be contaminated by lust. He decided to resume his American journey. If he wore himself out in America night after night, there was always the chance that he might experience again the pure joy of a dream of England.

Some nights when Adrian was tired of visiting America he thought about the history of mankind.

While he lived in the Garden of Eden, Adam enjoyed perfect human happiness. If it occurred to him to look at a naked woman, he simply told Eve to stand still for a moment. And he never once suffered the misery of having an erection that he could not satisfy. Eve knew it was her duty to give in to him whenever he asked.

After he was driven out into the world, Adam still tried to live as he had in Eden. But now he suffered the trials of a human being. Eve wore clothes all day long and only let him near her when she wanted a child. Every day he had erections that came to nothing. Many a time he looked out across the plains of Mesopotamia and wished there was some other woman he could think about. But the world was still empty of people apart from himself and his family. Even in the vast continent of North America there was no human footprint from the green islands of Maine to the red-gold sandbanks of the Rio Grande.

But at least Adam could remember his pleasant life in Eden. His sons had no such consolation. They grew up in a world where the only females were their sisters and their mother—and *they* always kept their bodies carefully covered.

When the eldest son reached Adrian's age he still hadn't seen a naked female body. One hot afternoon he could stand it no longer. He hid among the bullrushes while Eve and her daughters went swimming in the Tigris. He only glanced at Eve—her breasts were long and flabby and her legs had varicose veins. But he looked hard at his sisters, even the young ones with no breasts.

When he was alone again, he formed his hand into the shape of the thing he had seen between their legs and became the first in human history to commit the solitary sin.

Although it was not recorded in the Bible, that was a black day for mankind. On that day God thought seriously of wiping out the little tribe of Man. Even in His infinite wisdom He hadn't foreseen that a human would learn such an unnatural trick—enjoying by himself, when he was hardly more than a child, the pleasure that was intended for married men only.

The angels in heaven were revolted too. Lucifer's sin of pride seemed clean and brave compared with the sight of the shuddering boy squirting his precious stuff into the limpid Tigris. Lucifer himself was delighted that Man had invented a new kind of sin—and one that was so easy to commit.

Luckily for mankind it was the first of many occasions when God's mercy overcame His righteous anger. The son of Adam never knew how close he had come to being struck dead on the spot.

Perhaps God relented because He saw how little joy the poor fellow got out of it. There were no newspapers or magazines to excite his imagination. All he could think of was one of the same girls he saw every day in his ordinary household in dreary Mesopotamia.

Eventually the sons of Adam married their sisters, and their descendants spread through the Middle East and became the ancient Sumerians and Egyptians.

By now the young men were much better off than the sons of Adam. Few of them had to commit sins of impurity alone. People matured so early in the hot climate that a young fellow of Adrian's age would be already married to a shapely brown-skinned wife.

If a young man couldn't wait, even for the brief time between puberty and marriage, he still didn't have to touch himself. There were slave girls in every city. If a young man fancied a certain slave girl he could ask his father to buy her and employ her in the house. If the young fellow was daring enough he would have her assigned to bathroom duties. She would fill his tub and fetch his towels on bath nights. Then he could arrange for the room to become so hot that the girl had to strip to the waist while she worked.

When the Jews settled in the Promised Land they were no less lustful than other peoples. Time after time God had to send a prophet to persuade them to repent. Even when the Bible did not name the sins of the Jews, it was easy to guess what they were. The weather in Palestine was always hot and the people often slept on top of their houses. The excitement of lying on the roof with hardly any clothes on, and hearing your neighbour's wife just across the way tossing about under her sheet, would have kept a Jewish man awake half the night thinking of sex.

In Old Testament times the only young men who kept up the solitary habit were poor shepherd boys far from the cities and the slave girls. When fire and brimstone rained on Sodom and Gomorrah, there were lonely herd-keepers who watched from the stony hills around and didn't know whether to be glad, because all the spoilt young bastards were being roasted alive with their wives and slave girls, or sorry, because they could never again peer down on the cities at dusk to watch the sexy games on the rooftops and catch a glimpse of some young woman they could remember afterwards in the desert.

By the time of Jesus, the Jews had become very reticent about sex. It was hard to judge how common or rare the solitary sin might have been in New Testament days. Jesus Himself never referred to it, but Adrian always hoped an Apocryphal Gospel or a Dead Sea Scroll would be found one day with the story of the Boy Taken in Self-Abuse.

The Scribes and Pharisees dragged him to Jesus and announced that they were going to stone him. Jesus invited the one without sin to cast the first stone. Then He started writing in the sand. One by one the old men looked down and read the dates and places of their boyhood sins and the names of the women they had used for inspiration. The boy read them too. And for years afterwards, instead of hanging his head in shame because the whole town knew about his secret sin, he remembered the pious old men who had tried it themselves in their youth and he looked the whole world in the face.

Adrian hummed or whistled his favourite hit tunes whenever he was alone, and especially at night when his parents had gone to bed with their library books and his young brothers were asleep. Sometimes he got up from his homework at the kitchen table and went into his room without turning on the light. He stared out of his window, trying to imagine the shape of the North American continent beyond the darkness that had settled over the south-eastern suburbs of Melbourne. He tried not to notice the lighted window in the house across the back fence where Mr and Mrs Lombard were still doing their tea dishes because it took them hours to scrub all their kids and put them to bed. He sang his favourite tunes softly until America appeared under its brilliant sunshine on the far side of the world.

The square-dancing craze was over. The women of America had stopped wearing shapeless checked blouses and cowboy hats that dangled behind their heads. They were crowded together on a riverbank listening to Johnny Ray sing 'The Little White Cloud that Cried'. Johnny threw back his head in agony and gasped out the last long syllable of his smash hit. The women threw their arms round each other and sobbed. They would have done anything to make Johnny happy, but he only stood with his eyes closed and thought of the waters of the Potomac or the Shenandoah rushing past on their way to the sea, and of how lonely the American countryside seemed to someone with no sweetheart.

The women followed the river to the sea. By sundown they were all strolling along the boardwalk of a great city, dressed in off-the-shoulder evening frocks and white elbow-length gloves. From the farthest horizon, rosy with sunset, the sound of the fishing fleet, returning to port at last, reached the throng of women. Jo Stafford's rendition of 'Shrimp Boats' came from loudspeakers all along the beach. When they knew their menfolk were coming, the women rushed into the lobby of the biggest luxury hotel in town. They pushed through the fronds of potted palms and crowded round the startled desk clerks and sang into their faces, 'There's dancing tonight.'

Rosemary Clooney grabbed the nearest bellhop boy and waltzed round the room with him while she sang 'Tell Us Where the Good Times Are'. Each time she shouted the chorus she held him so close to her plunging neckline that her big bouncing breasts almost rubbed against his nose. The shy young man didn't know where to look, and the crowd went wild.

By now the men had arrived and changed into their tuxedos. The happy couples crowded into an upstairs ballroom. Dean Martin sang 'Kiss of Fire' and everyone started to tango. When the song reached its climax, some of the more red-blooded men even tried to kiss their partners. But the women turned their heads aside because they knew what a kiss could do.

The crowd round the stage drew back and made way for Patti Page the Singing Rage with her version of 'Doggie in the Window'. As she moved among the dancers, the mystery of who made the dog noises was solved at last. It was Patti herself, and she looked so fetching when she yelped that some of the men tried to fondle her like a cuddlesome puppy.

The Weavers burst into the room singing 'The Gandy Dancers' Ball'. Everyone started dancing like miners or lumberjacks in an old Western saloon. But some of the women looked nervous. They knew what wild things the gandy dancers did when they were excited by dancing and pretty faces.

When the dust had settled after the dance, Frankie Laine sang 'Wild Goose'. A hush came over the room. Someone pulled back the velvet drapes to reveal a view of brightly lit skyscrapers. High up in the night sky, a flock of wild geese was passing over the city on their way to the Gulf of Mexico. The people listening to Frankie remembered the wide open spaces of America, far from the world of Show Business with its low-cut gowns and easy divorces. Between the big cities were rural landscapes where people were all in bed listening to the innocent music of wild geese honking in the night sky. When Frankie was finished, a few of the dancers were so moved that they walked out of their girlfriends' lives and went back to the dear hearts and gentle people in their home towns.

Jo Stafford grabbed the mike again and sang the first bars of 'Jumbalaya'. The dancers leaped to their feet. The words were puzzling, but everyone knew the song was something about Louisiana and the steamy tropical swamps where people wore shorts or bathers all day. To set the right mood for the song, Jo Stafford was wearing a grass skirt and a floral brassiere.

The tropical rhythm affected everyone. The dancing grew furious. At the end of each chorus, some of the men sang words that were rather risqué. Instead of the correct words 'big fun', they sang 'big bums'. And a few of the more shameless women giggled behind their hands and waggled their own bottoms.

As the song neared its end, more people behaved suggestively or sniggered over double entendres. They forgot about the rest of America in the darkness all round them. They couldn't have cared less about the thousands of Catholic parents trying to shield their children from the dangers of blue songs and films. They forgot everything except the sight of Jo Stafford swishing her grass skirt higher and higher in time with the wild pagan music and the off-colour words.

But nothing really evil happened. After a few minutes the song that had seemed to promise a lustful orgy came suddenly to an end.

Someone pulled back the drapes again. The cold grey light of dawn was spreading over the sky. The couples clasped hands and gathered at the windows while Eddie Fisher sang 'Turn Back the Hands of Time'.

The men were all vaguely dissatisfied (like Adrian Sherd after he had listened to three *Hit Parades* on Sunday evening). All night they had heard about kisses that thrilled, kisses of fire, lips of wine, and charms they would die for. But now it was time to go home and they had done no more than dance the night away.

While the men were stealing a goodnight kiss from their girlfriends in the lobbies of their apartment buildings or on the porches of their frame houses, some of them might have found themselves humming a different kind of music.

It was not really hit music, although it often made the *Hit Parade* for a few weeks. When Adrian Sherd heard it he remembered that not everyone spent their evenings dancing in nightclubs or folding charms in their arms. It was sad, lonely music—the theme from *Moulin Rouge*, or *The Story of Three Loves* or *Limelight*—and it seemed to come from countries very different from America.

When the people going home in America heard this music they wondered if there was some other kind of happiness that they had never found—and would never find as long as they spent their nights holding their loved ones dangerously near and tasting their lips.

One Monday morning Adrian's friends asked him what he had done over the weekend. All he could tell them was that he had listened to the *Hit Parades* on the wireless. Seskis and Cornthwaite laughed and said they were always too busy to sit and listen to music.

But O'Mullane said, 'The *Hit Parade* came in handy for me one night. I was lying out in my bungalow trying to think of an excuse to do it to myself and I heard this colossal song with Perry Como and a chorus of young tarts in the background. They were singing, "Play me a hurtin' tune" over and over again. I beat time to the music while I did it. The last few lines nearly made my head drop off. I'm going to buy the record and use it again some day.'

Every few months, on a Sunday afternoon, Mrs Sherd took her three sons to visit her sister, Miss Kathleen Bracken.

Adrian knew his Aunt Kath would have entered a convent when she was young if one of her legs had not been shorter than the other. Adrian's mother called her a living saint because she went to daily mass in all weathers with her big boot clumping along the footpath.

Miss Bracken lived alone in a little single-fronted weatherboard house in Hawthorn. While his brothers ate green loquats or figs from the two trees in the backyard, Adrian admired his aunt's front room.

Inside the door, near the light switch, was a holy-water stoup in the shape of an angel holding a bowl against its breast. Whenever Aunt Kath walked past it she dipped her finger in the bowl and blessed herself. Adrian did the same.

There were three altars in the room: one each for the Sacred Heart, Our Lady of Perpetual Succour and St Joseph. Each altar had a statue of coloured plaster with a fairy light burning in front of it (red for the Sacred Heart, blue for Our Lady and orange for St Joseph) and a vase of flowers. On certain feast days Aunt Kath burned a candle in front of the appropriate altar—a blessed candle obtained from the church on the feast of the Purification of Our Lady.

On a cabinet beneath a picture of Our Lady appearing to St Bernadette Soubirous was a flask of Lourdes water. Aunt Kath sprinkled a few drops on her wrists and temples when she felt off-colour. One day when Adrian's youngest brother ran a long splinter under his fingernail, she dipped the finger in the flask before she poked at it with a needle.

Adrian liked to ask his aunt about little-known religious orders or puzzling rituals and ceremonies or obscure points of Catholic doctrine. It was his aunt who told him always to burn old broken rosary beads rather than throw them away (so they wouldn't end up lying next to some dirty piece of garbage or be picked up by non-Catholics who would only make a mockery of them). She showed him leaflets about an order of nuns who dedicated their lives to converting the Jews, and another order who worked exclusively with African lepers. She knew all about the ceremony of Tenebrae, in which the lights in the church were put out one by one. And one Sunday afternoon she took Adrian and his mother to a churching for a woman who had recently had a baby.

Whenever his aunt was talking, Adrian thought of her mind as a huge volume, like the book that the priest used at mass, with ornate red binding and pages edged with thick gilt. Silk ribbons hung out of the pages to mark the important places.

'Why aren't Catholics allowed to be cremated?' he asked her.

She took hold of the dangling violet (or scarlet or green) ribbon and parted the gilt edging at the section containing the answer.

'At one time, certain heretics or atheists used to have themselves cremated to show that their bodies couldn't be resurrected after death. So the Holy Father issued a decree so that no Catholic would appear to be siding with the heretics.'

In a drawer in the front room Aunt Kath had a collection of relics of saints, each in a silk-lined box labelled CYMA or ROLEX or OMEGA. The relics were tiny chips of bone or fragments of cloth housed behind glass in silver or gilt lockets.

When Adrian had been younger he used to enjoy visiting his aunt. But after he had begun his visits to America he felt he was polluting her house, and especially the front room. He still read her magazines (*The Messenger of Our Lady*, *The Annals of The Sacred Heart*, *The Monstrance*, *The Far East*) but he kept away from her altars and relics. He was frightened of committing a sacrilege by touching them with his hands—the same hands that only a few hours before had been dabbling in filth.

One day when he had at least a dozen sins on his soul, his aunt showed him a new relic she had just received from Italy. She unpacked it from a box stuffed with tissue paper.

'Actually there are two of them,' she said. 'And I want you to have one.'

Adrian knew she prayed every morning that he would become a priest. Fortunately God saw to it that no prayers ever went to waste. His aunt's prayers would probably be used to lead some other more worthy boy to the priesthood.

She lifted out two tiny envelopes and held one up to the light. Adrian saw a dark patch in one corner.

His aunt said, 'They're only third-class relics—I've told you about the different classes of relics—but they were jolly hard to come by.'

She put one envelope in Adrian's hand. 'It's from his tomb,' she said. 'Dust from the tomb of St Gabriel of the Sorrowing Virgin. St Gabriel had an extraordinary love for Holy Purity. He's the ideal patron for young people to pray to today when there's so much temptation about.'

Adrian tried to look as though it had never occurred to him to pray to any saint for purity because it came naturally to him.

All the way home with the relic in his pocket, Adrian wondered how much the saints in heaven knew about the sins of people on earth. Did God in his mercy keep all the holy virgins and the innocent saints like St Gabriel from knowing about the foul sins of impurity committed every day? Or was the news of each sin broadcast all over heaven as soon as it was committed? ('News Flash: Adrian Sherd,

Catholic boy of Accrington, Melbourne, Australia, abused himself at 10.55 this evening.') There were people already in heaven who knew him. ('Yes, he was my grandson, I'm sorry to say,' says old Mr Bracken.) If Adrian managed to break the habit at last and get to heaven in the end, he would have to hide from his relatives.

But then there was the General Judgement. Even if no one in heaven had heard of his sins before then, every person who had lived on earth since Adam would learn about them on Judgement Day.

Adrian Sherd walked up to the platform between two stern angels. The crowd of spectators reached beyond the horizon in every direction. But even the farthest soul in the crowd heard his name when it was broadcast over the loudspeakers.

Towering above the platform was a huge indicator like the scoreboard at the Melbourne Cricket Ground. Beside each of the Ten Commandments was an instrument like the speedo in a car. The crowd gasped when the digits started tumbling over to show Sherd's score for the Sixth Commandment. The blurred numerals whirled into the hundreds. Somewhere in the crowd his Aunt Kathleen shrieked with horror. This was the boy she had wanted to be a priest, the boy she had once enrolled in the Archconfraternity of the Divine Child, the hypocrite whose filthy hands had touched the sacred dust from St Gabriel's tomb.

Brother Methodius told the Latin class one morning that the Romans in the great days of the Republic reached the highest level of culture and virtue that a pagan civilisation could possibly attain. Many of their greatest and wisest citizens were hardly distinguishable from Christian gentlemen.

Adrian Sherd did not believe the brother. He knew that one people did not conquer another just to give them paved roads or a new legal system. Adrian knew what power was for. If the citizens of Melbourne had made him their dictator he would have gone straight to a mannequins' school and ordered all the women to undress.

The Romans were no different from himself. Among the back pages of his Latin textbook was a story entitled 'The Rape of the Sabine Women'. (Adrian had waited all year for his Latin class to reach this story. But they progressed so slowly through the textbook that he suspected Brother Methodius of deliberately holding them back to avoid the embarrassing story.) Adrian often studied the illustration above the story and even tried to translate the Latin text on his own. Of course it was all watered down to make it suitable for schoolboys. The Roman soldiers only led the women away by their wrists. And even the Latin word *rapio* was translated in the vocabulary at the back of the book as 'seize, snatch up, carry away'. But Adrian was not deceived.

Whenever he read the story of a battle, Adrian barracked for the enemies of Rome. He had no sympathy for Roman boys of his own age. As soon as they started wearing the toga of manhood they could do whatever they liked with their father's slaves. But the young men of Capua or Tarentum or Veii had troubles like his. When they crept out as scouts towards the suburbs of Rome they saw young Publius or Flaccus enjoying himself in his orchard or court-yard with some young woman captured from a tribe like their own. But of course their own people were not strong enough to capture slaves.

But when the Roman legions finally invested their city, the young fellows saw every night, from the tops of their threatened walls, the goings-on in the Romans' comfortable camp. How many of them must have abused themselves for the last time when they lay down briefly between turns on watch and then fallen in battle next morning—killed by the very fellows whose pleasures they had envied so often.

As city after city was conquered in Italy and Gaul and Germany, everyone had the chance to own slaves. The only people who still kept up the habit of solitary sin were the slaves themselves. Some of them did it thinking of the flaxen-haired maidens they had once known on the banks of the Rhine and would never see again. Others did it peeping around the marble columns at the bare-armed Roman matrons teaching their daughters to spin and weave.

And then came Adrian's hero, a man sworn to destroy Rome and avenge the raped slave girls and wretched self-abusers.

Hannibal himself came from a lustful land. (It was later to be the home of the Great St Augustine, a sex maniac in his youth, but destined to be the holy Bishop of Hippo and a worthy patron saint for boys struggling to break the habit of impurity.) But as a young man, the Carthaginian had turned his back on all the pagan delights of North Africa. He spent the rest of his life wandering round the countryside of Italy, far from the luxuries of the cities.

It was probably a blessing that he was one-eyed. When he led his army to the gates of Rome he would have seen only dimly from his siege-towers the beauty of the women inside the walls that he would never breach. Not that anything would have tempted him to give up his ascetic way of life. It was clear from his superhuman courage and endurance that he was the absolute master of his passions.

After the defeat of Hannibal, the Romans did what they liked all over the civilised world. The only citizens who refused to join in the orgies were the early Christians, huddled by candlelight in their catacombs deep under Rome. Sometimes they could hardly hear the priest's words during mass for the squeals and grunts coming from overhead as a burly patrician subdued a slave girl in his *triclinium*, or chased her naked into the pool in his *atrium*. It was no wonder the Christians preached against slavery.

Outside the Pax Romana were the primitive tribes on the Baltic coast or in the darkest Balkans who could only afford one wife each. When Latin writers described these people as barbarians or hinted at their savage practices, they were probably referring to the habit of self-abuse, which the Romans themselves would have all but forgotten.

But the barbarians had their day at last. When the Goths and Vandals sacked Rome, the lucky ones who got there first leaped on the stately Roman matrons and even the trembling Christian virgins with all the ferocity of men who had been shut out for centuries from the delights of the Empire. Those who were still hurrying towards Rome saw the flames rising over the Seven Hills and sinned by themselves one last time at the thought of what must have been happening in the Eternal City (and what they would soon be enjoying themselves).

During the Dark Ages, bestial tribesmen from Central Asia roamed around Italy, grabbing the ex-slave girls and orphaned patrician girls who were still wandering bewildered beneath the cypresses on the grass-grown Appian

Way. Those who missed out on the women abused themselves in front of the shameless murals and mosaics in the crumbling villas or, if they could read, over the scandalous novels and poems of the corrupt last days of the Empire.

But as time passed, some people were sickened by the sexual excesses. Pious men and women went into the desert and lonely places to found monasteries and convents. The Christian way of life was gradually established in the lands once ruled by the Romans. And the sex maniacs, like the wolves and bears and wild boars of Europe, had to flee into the swamps of Lithuania and the glens of Albania and go back to their furtive habits of old.

Once a month the College Chaplain, Father Lacey, strolled down from the local presbytery to talk to Adrian's class.

The chaplain was a tired man with white hair. The only time Adrian had gone to him in confession, Father Lacey had said sadly, 'For the love of God, can't you use some self-control, son?' and then announced the penance and rested his head in his hands and closed his eyes.

One day Father Lacey said to the class, 'The other day I happened to read an Australian Catholic Truth Society pamphlet. It was written by a famous American Jesuit for young people in America, and I couldn't help thinking how much better off we are in Australia than the Americans—morally, I mean. No doubt there are many fine Catholics in America. There are wonderful men among the American clergy. Monsignor Fulton Sheen, Cardinal Cushing, Father Peyton the Rosary Priest—they're not afraid to denounce immorality or Communism. But decent Americans must be nearly swamped sometimes with temptations against purity.

'One of the things the pamphlet was discussing was what the Americans call petting. Now, this word "petting" was something I'd never come across before. I still think it sounds more like something you do to your dog or cat. Anyway, from what this priest was saying it seems that one of the gravest problems in America today is the petting that goes on amongst young people.

'It's hard to believe, but apparently American fathers and mothers allow their children to stay out half the night in cars and parks and on street corners. And these young flappers and hobbledehoys (because that's all they are at their age—they're still wet behind the ears, so to speak), well, naturally they face enormous temptations when they're alone in these places together. And boys, it's all so wrong. You know as well as I do that these things are for married people exclusively.

'Go back for a moment to the Middle Ages, to the great days of the church. In those days the whole of the civilised world observed the commandments of God and his church. There were no problems of courtship and company-keeping then. This petting that's worrying the people of America hadn't been heard of. Of course the young people of both sexes had the chance to meet each other and look each other over before marriage. They had their dances and balls in those days too. But it was all good wholesome fun. The young ladies were all chaperoned and watched over by their God-fearing parents. And the parents in their wisdom saw to it that no two young people had the opportunity to be alone together where they might face temptations that were too strong for them.

'Those were the days when knights sang about pure

love. And it *was* pure. If a young man fell in love with a young woman he might wear her colours into battle or write a poem to her, but he certainly didn't hang around with her in dark doorways on the way home from the pictures.

'Young fellows of your age would probably be off to fight the Turks under the banner of Our Lady. That's who your lady would be. It was the Age of Our Blessed Lady. It's no coincidence that the period of history when men were bravest and most chivalrous and most honourable in the way they behaved towards the fair sex—that age was also the greatest age in history for devotion to Our Lady.

'But to get back to America again. There's another expression I've heard and I suppose some of you must have too. It's a cheap, vulgar expression if ever there was one—sex appeal. The way some Americans behave, you'd think it was all that mattered when a man was thinking of marriage. As long as the woman has sex appeal, she's sure to make a good wife.

'Well, we can see the result of all this in the divorce courts. I suppose even at your age you've read about some of these Hollywood stars getting married—he for the fifth time and she for the third. Think of it. America has gone mad over this thing called sex appeal. But I shouldn't say that. We know there are thousands of good Catholics in America—people in the fine old Catholic cities like Boston and Chicago struggling to bring up their children away from all the madness in the pagan parts of the country. And I'm happy to say there are even a few good Catholics in Hollywood itself.

'I was reading the other day in a Catholic magazine about the film star Maureen O'Sullivan. You've probably watched her if you go to the pictures occasionally. Well, in the midst of all the temptations of Hollywood, that woman is still an outstanding Catholic mother. She's been married all her life to a good Catholic man and they've brought up six or seven fine young children. So it can be done. And don't forget Bing Crosby either—a decent Catholic father who's never had his head turned by Hollywood. But how rare these people are.

'Boys, whenever I think about Hollywood and what it's doing to the world I'm glad I'm an old man. I honestly don't know how I'd save my soul if I had to grow up with all the temptations facing you young fellows today. In my time we had nothing like the films and books and even the newspapers that you fellows have to fight against. Today I suppose there's not one of you who doesn't go to the pictures now and then and give the paganism of Hollywood a chance to infect you.

'"Ah, but I only watch harmless films for general exhibition," you're saying to yourselves. Well, I sometimes wonder if there's any such thing as a harmless film. Did you ever stop to think what sort of lives these actors and actresses lead outside their films? Did you know for instance that nearly every young woman film star has to surrender her body to the director or the producer or whoever he is before she gets the part of the leading lady? And these are the sort of people that the young men and women of today are supposed to have for their heroes and heroines.'

While the chaplain went on to talk about Our Lady again, Adrian thought hard about the film stars he met on his American journeys. If Father Lacey was right about Hollywood, some of these women might have been through unspeakable agonies when they were younger. For all Adrian knew, Jayne with her innocent smile or Marilyn with her serene gaze might have spent her younger days with her eyes shut tight and her mouth clamped to stop herself from screaming while some pot-bellied Cecil B. DeMille ran his sweaty hands over her naked skin.

The women had never mentioned those things to Adrian for fear of spoiling the fun of their outings together. They were generous courageous creatures. He should have spent more time getting to know their life stories instead of treating them as beautiful playthings. In future he would encourage them to share their old painful secrets with him. They would soon realise that nothing they could tell him about Hollywood would shock him.

Adrian's teachers often said that the name 'Dark Ages' was misleading and unjust. Protestant historians used the name to imply that the centuries when the church was at the height of its influence were a time of ignorance and misery. In fact, as all fair-minded historians agreed, Europe in the so-called Dark Ages was more peaceful and contented than it had ever been since. And the countryside was dotted with monasteries that were centres of learning. Catholics should get into the habit of using the term 'Middle Ages' to cover the whole period from the end of the Roman Empire to the Renaissance and the Protestant Revolt (or Reformation, as it was sometimes called).

Adrian was certain he would never have become a slave to sins of impurity if he had lived in the Middle Ages. A boy in those days grew up in a simple two-roomed cottage and slept in the same room as his parents and brothers and sisters. He fell asleep hearing the calm breathing of his family round him and the comfortable noises of the cows and horses in the byre through the wall. If his parents wanted to have another baby they waited until their children were all sound asleep before they did anything about it. In a home like this there was no opportunity for a boy to sin in his bed without being discovered.

The luckiest boys went off to monasteries as soon as they reached puberty. In a monastery a boy had so many beautiful things to inspire him that he soon forgot about women. Every day as he walked in procession along the cloisters, he glimpsed through the narrow gothic windows the rolling hillsides covered with fruitful vines or grazing cattle. Every morning he saw the ordained monks each bent over his private altar in the shadowy nooks behind the high altar of the monastery chapel. When the sunlight flashed from the bulky silver of the chalices, and the folds of the elaborate vestments hissed against each other, he knew he would never wish for a greater pleasure than to say mass alone like that each day.

If a boy stayed at home he still had fewer temptations than a modern boy, because he was hardly ever alone. The whole village worked together all day in the fields. And the itinerant Franciscan and Dominican friars wandering up and down the roads of Europe kept a sharp lookout for young fellows mooning around in copses or thickets.

For centuries, Europe was hardly troubled by sex. Her most imaginative young men devoted all their energy to making gold and silver ornaments or stained-glass windows or religious paintings or illuminated parchments.

Historians were right when they said the Modern Age

began with the Renaissance. Nude paintings and statues began to appear, even in the most fervently Catholic countries. And many of the female nudes were almost as attractive as twentieth-century film stars.

A young man of the Renaissance would have had many of the sexual problems that bothered Adrian Sherd. Even in those days, artists and sculptors had discovered the tricks that were used by photographers for *Health and Sunshine* magazine. The female statues had smooth marble between their legs and the women in the paintings stood in tantalising poses that did not quite reveal all.

The generation that grew up during the sexual excitement of the Renaissance became more and more resentful of the church's strict attitude to impurity. These were the people responsible for the Protestant Revolt.

The most important changes made by the Protestants were to remove two institutions which had been a nuisance to the sexually lax. They abolished the celibacy of the clergy and the sacrament of confession.

Martin Luther himself was a priest. Why was he so anxious to do away with the vow of celibacy? Because he himself wanted to marry. And why was he in such a hurry to get married? Adrian had heard many times from priests and brothers that Luther was an unhappy tormented man who should never have become a priest in the first place. It was common knowledge that he was a glutton and used foul language. It wasn't hard to imagine such a man having terrible battles against impure temptations. The woman he eventually married was an ex-nun. What if he had known her, or at least caught sight of her, while he was still a Catholic priest? Was it possible that all his troubles with the church first started when he realised he couldn't stop thinking about a certain pretty woman?

Adrian had arrived at an explanation for the Protestant Revolt. He believed it was quite likely that the whole thing had been started by a priest who was tempted beyond his endurance to commit a sin of impurity by himself. Adrian found it almost too shocking to think about. He would never have repeated it to anyone, not even a Protestant, because it reflected on the sacred office of the priesthood.

It was a fateful day in the history of impurity when the Protestant leaders decided that it was no longer necessary to go to confession to have your sins forgiven. In drab cities all over northern Germany young men suddenly realised that what they thought about in bed at night need never be revealed to another living soul. They could do what they liked all week and still stand up on Sunday and sing hymns at the tops of their voices and look the minister in the eye.

The doctrine of predestination was all that a young man could wish for. Once he knew he was one of the elect, he could sin every night of his life and still be saved. If Adrian Sherd could have been born in Geneva in the great days of Calvinism he would have found religion a pleasure instead of the worry it was to him in twentieth-century Australia.

In the Protestant half of Europe, the Middle Ages were swept away forever. In Italy, Spain, Poland and the other Catholic countries, things were much the same as before except that many a young man must have wanted to migrate to a Protestant land.

When the Catholics and Protestants reached the New World, it was easy to see which religion was easier to live under.

At the beginning of the Modern Age, a young Spaniard no older than Adrian stood beside the Rio Grande and looked north-east across unexplored territory. The plains before him stretched away through Texas and Kansas and on to Nebraska and far Iowa. It should have been a stirring sight, but the young Spaniard was deeply troubled. He foresaw all the afternoons when he would stand alone by clear streams among miles of waving grasses and remember girls and women he had seen in old Castile and feel the overpowering urge to commit a sin of impurity. By the time he had explored the American prairies he might have had a hundred sins on his soul. When he got back to a Spanish city he would have to go to confession. It was a terrifying prospect.

At the same time, a young English gentleman looked westwards from a hilltop in Virginia. He was eager to explore all he could of the great continent before him. He would be a long time alone in the forests and prairies, but he knew a trick to cheer himself up at night. While he did it he would remember the pretty young ladies he used to admire each Sunday in his little parish church in Devon. Or he could look forward to the day when he arrived back in England and shook hands with the minister and sat down in his old family pew and looked round to choose one of the young ladies for his wife.

Late one Sunday afternoon Adrian was lying on his bed in his room at the back of the house. The sky outside his window was full of high grey clouds. A strong wind thumped the outside of the house and rattled a piece of timber somewhere in the wall. Adrian's mother and his youngest brother were away visiting one of his aunts. His father was dragging a plank backwards and forwards across the backyard trying to level the sandy soil before he sowed it with lawn seed. Adrian's younger brother was on the path at the side of the house, bouncing a tennis ball against the chimney.

Next door, Andy Horvath and his wife and two or three other couples were having some kind of party in the bungalow behind the Horvaths' half-built house. At about three o'clock they had started singing foreign songs and they were still going strong. There was one song they kept coming back to. Adrian had heard it three or four times already. The way they sang the chorus made the hair prickle on the back of his neck. It was sad and savage and hopeless.

Adrian thought of all the quiet backyards stretching away for miles in every direction. Then he thought of America.

He went outside to the shed and sent his passenger train around the track. It stopped in the Catskill Mountains. He went back inside to his bed and pulled a rug over himself and thought about the green mountains of New York state.

Sherd grabbed Gene and Ann and Kim firmly by their wrists and bundled them into his car. He told them they were going to the Catskills just for the hell of it. Soon they were among steep hillsides where shady forests alternated with lush green meadows. Sherd stopped the car beside a lofty waterfall that hung like a veil of silver over a secluded glade.

He didn't waste time with idle chatter or a picnic lunch. As soon as they reached the little glade he told the women to get undressed. For some reason Gene and Ann and Kim wanted to tease him. They ran a little way into the trees and stood laughing at him.

But Sherd had come to the Catskills to save himself from being bored to death. He was in no mood to be trifled with. He ran after them. As they ran and stumbled ahead of him he had glimpses of their pink thighs and white undies that made him crazy with desire.

He caught the three of them in a meadow where the grass was waist-high and thick with wildflowers. He behaved like the strong silent type. He stripped all three of them. Then he flung himself on the woman of his choice and took his pleasure roughly and without a word of thanks. Afterwards he lay where he was and watched the meadows in the Catskills turning slowly from green to grey.

Mr Sherd came in from the backyard and said he'd call it a day because the sand was blowing all over him. Then Adrian's brother came inside and asked Adrian to play miniature cricket on the path and guess which way his spinners would turn. Adrian agreed to play for ten minutes and no more.

He stood at one end of the path while his brother bowled underarm spinners with a tennis ball. When his ten minutes of cricket were over he sat down and listened.

The Hungarians were still singing in their bungalow. They were starting again on their favourite song. Adrian guessed it was about far-off mountains and forests. He tried to memorise the tune. They started off shouting it, but something stopped them when they reached the chorus. Adrian ran over and pressed his ear against a hole in the fence. He could hear the separate voices of each man and woman trying to pick up the song again. They were making noises like sobs, as though they couldn't sing for crying.

At school next morning O'Mullane could hardly wait to tell his friends about his adventure on the Sunday afternoon. He said, 'I was watching the tennis on the courts near the racecourse and having dog fights on my bike with Laurie D'Arcy when I saw one of the strappers from Neville Byrne's stables—the one they call Macka—standing behind the pine trees smoushing this tart. She had red hair. I kept my eye on them and I saw Macka trying to get her into one of those old sheds behind the six-furlongs barrier. Well, he got her there at last and I said to D'Arcy we'd better be in this.

'So we sneaked up and peeped into the shed. Macka had her in a corner leaning back over a rail. He was still smoushing her and getting a handful at the same time under her jumper.'

Adrian said, 'Was she putting up a fight against him?'

O'Mullane said, 'Search me. Old Macka put a half nelson on her. He's a tough little bastard. She could have stopped him easily enough if she'd really tried, I suppose. She kept saying, "Not here, Bernie! Not here, Bernie!" Anyway, she got away from him in the end and ran down a little hill into that long grass near the big iron fence. But Macka caught up with her and pushed her over or she dragged him down or they both fell over but anyway they ended up on top of each other and the last thing we saw was old Macka going for all he was worth.'

Adrian said, 'You mean he was doing her? Out there in the grass beside the racecourse?'

O'Mullane said, 'What do you reckon? But listen to the end of the story. I was sure I'd seen the tart somewhere before and Laurie D'Arcy said the same. After tea that night D'Arcy came round to my place and said he could show her to me right then. So he took me over to the Yarram Road shops and there she was serving in the milk bar with an apron on over the same clothes she was wearing with Macka. She said, "Yes, boys. What'll you have?" I said half out loud, "The same as Macka got," and I reckon she almost heard me.'

For the rest of the day Adrian felt sorry for himself for having to spend his Sunday lying on his bed dreaming of the Catskills while O'Mullane was having a real adventure at Caulfield Racecourse.

That afternoon he left his train at Caulfield and walked across the racecourse to the paddock that O'Mullane had described. He walked quickly across it, looking for a place where the grass was flattened, but there was nothing to tell him where the strapper and the girl had been. He stood where the grass was tallest and looked all round. The place was really only a large yard. It was not even private—a footpath ran close by, and one end of the yard was the wire fence of the public tennis courts.

Adrian hurried out of the racecourse and down to the little shopping centre in Yarram Road. He went into the milk bar. A young woman with red hair came out through the curtained doorway and said, 'Yes, please?' He looked down to avoid her eyes and asked for two packets of PK chewing gum. He stared at her furtively while she served him. She was nothing like a film star but she was pretty in her own way. What surprised him most was how ordinary she looked for a girl in a story. He could see the pores in her cheeks and the freckles on the backs of her hands. And when she handed him his change and he stared at her apron, he saw the vague shape of her breasts rise and fall as she breathed.

He got out of the shop as fast as he could. The story of

Macka and the girl was preposterous. He could not believe that on an ordinary dull Sunday afternoon, while he was lying on his bed listening to the wind and the rowdy New Australians next door, a girl with freckles on her wrists and no make-up on her face walked out of her sleepy milk bar and rolled round in the grass on Caulfield Racecourse with some strapper.

O'Mullane must have made up the whole story—perhaps because he was bored too. And it was a pretty poor story compared with what happened in the Catskills.

When he was younger, Adrian Sherd used to wish he had been born the eldest son of an English country gentleman in the eighteenth or nineteenth century and gone to one of the great public schools.

At school he would have read the classics in his private study and played cricket or rugger every afternoon. In his holidays he would have ridden across the broad acres he was going to inherit from his father. The tenants would have tipped their caps to the young master and told him where to find birds' nests and badgers' setts.

But after he had gone to St Carthage's College and learned from Cornthwaite and his friends what women were for, he realised there was something missing from the life of the young English gentleman.

When the son of the manor visited his neighbours, he could never meet the daughter of the house alone. Her nanny or governess or music teacher was always with her. The young fellow stood beside the harpsichord and turned the pages of her music, but the neck of her dress was too high for him to see anything.

Sometimes in his own house he followed the maid into the pantry to look up under her dress when she climbed to the highest shelf. But he always heard a discreet cough behind him and turned round to see the butler looking at him severely.

On his rides across his father's estates he saw plenty of girls—the daughters of yeomen and labourers and game-keepers. But the English climate was so bad that they were always rugged up in spencers and mufflers. He wasted a lot of time dreaming of the warm weather when he might surprise a young woman bathing in a stream after a hard day's work in the harvest. And he realised why so many English poets praised the springtime.

At school it was painful to read stories of the pagan Greeks and Romans and their sunny Mediterranean lands while snow covered the quadrangle, and the only female in the building was the elderly Matron with her mustard plasters and camphorated oil. He was reduced to dreaming of a day when one of his chums would receive a party of visitors. The chum might invite him to take his sister's arm and do a turn of the garden path.

In the nineteenth century, when things were worst for young Englishmen (the women with iron hoops in their clothes and long leather boots and collars up to their chins), they heard about a land where people dressed less formally because it was summer for six months of the year. It was no wonder that so many of them flocked to Australia.

But if the young Englishman had a hard time, it was harder still for the poor Irish lad. Adrian Sherd had no doubt that in all the history of the world the worst possible place for a young man was Ireland after St Patrick had converted it to the Catholic faith.

To begin with, the country was overcrowded. Watchful old men sat outside every cottage door and pious old women in black shawls passed to and fro along every country lane. A young man trying to spy on a girl or catch her alone in a quiet place was nearly always reported to the parish priest.

Even the landscape was against the young Irishman. There were no dells or dingles or forests or prairies in Ireland. The country was mostly bare stony fields and peat bogs. When a young fellow finally grew so desperate that he had to do it to himself, the only place he could go was behind the largest stone on some hillside. Many a time the stone was not even big enough to hide him properly and he had to lie with his legs drawn up or crouch like a hare against the grass while he relieved himself as best he could. If he forgot himself in his excitement and let his twitching legs protrude from behind the stone, he was sure to be observed by some gossiping jarvey on the nearest road.

It was almost certainly this problem that drove the early Irish explorers out into the Atlantic. They were looking for the Western Isles or O Brasil, Isle of the Blest—some uninhabited place where a young man and his girlfriend or a man and his wife or just a young man by himself could get away on their own whenever he felt like it. If the Irish had reached America, as Adrian Sherd's father claimed they had, it would have been the perfect land for them. They certainly deserved it, after all the misery they had put up with at home.

But there was one thing that helped the young Irishman in his trouble. The women of Ireland practised the virtues of modesty and chastity like no other women in history.

Thousands of them spent their formative years as Children of Mary. They imitated Our Lady so faithfully that they ended up looking like Madonnas with their white complexions and their dark eyes demurely downcast. Thanks to the exemplary virtues of Irish womanhood, the young Irishman was never tormented by the sight of bare legs or daring swimsuits. In fact, Adrian suspected that with priests and parents watching them closely, and the women of Ireland so careful not to tempt them, many young Irishmen might have avoided sins of impurity altogether.

When Adrian was still at primary school he used to go every year to the St Patrick's Night concert in his local town hall. One of the items was always 'Eileen Aroon' sung by a choir of girls from Star of the Sea Convent, North Essendon. When the girls came to the words 'Truth is a fixed star', Adrian was always so inspired by the unearthly beauty of the melody and the innocent upturned faces with their rounded pink lips where no foul young man had ever planted an impure kiss, that he looked up past the blazing chandeliers of the town hall, out over the north-western suburbs of Melbourne and across the thistles and basalt rocks of the plains beyond, towards the dark sky over Ireland. There were fixed stars shining over Ireland—the stars in the dark-blue mantle of Our Lady, who was still guarding the daughters of that holy country as she had for centuries past.

The last time Adrian had seen the concert (in the year before he began at St Carthage's) he was so moved that he made a vow never to think an impure thought about any girl with an Irish-looking face or an Irish-sounding name.

Adrian had kept his vow faithfully. None of the hundreds of females he had used for his pleasure had been

Irish types. But he often wondered how he would have survived in the Ireland of his ancestors, where the only girls he ever saw would have been Irish colleens. Probably he would have emigrated as his ancestors had done. He hoped he would have had the sense to head for America instead of Australia.

On some afternoons Adrian Sherd caught a tram instead of walking down Swindon Road from St Carthage's to the Swindon railway station. The tram was always crowded with boys from Eastern Hill Grammar School and Canterbury Ladies' College. Adrian knew that these schools were two of the oldest and wealthiest in Melbourne. He felt very ignorant not even knowing where they were among the miles of garden suburbs beyond Swindon.

Whenever he looked at the Eastern Hill boys Adrian felt awkward and grubby. He held his Gladstone bag in front of his knees to hide the shiny domes in his trouser legs. He remembered all the brothers' talk about St Carthage's being a fine old school with a reputation for turning out Catholic doctors and barristers and professional men. It was bullshit. The Eastern Hill boys never saw Adrian, even when he was crowded so close that his sweaty maroon cap was only inches from their faces. When the tram lurched and he fell among them, the superb voices kept up their banter while one of the fellows brushed Adrian away like some kind of insect.

After a few weeks on the trams Adrian learned to stand unobtrusively near these young gentlemen, keeping his back to them but listening carefully.

One Eastern Hill fellow went to a party every Saturday

night. The parties were in strange places that Adrian had never heard of—Blairgowrie, Portsea, Mt Eliza. At Blairgowrie the fellow had met a girl called Sandy and taken her home and crashed on with her. He said he was going to ring her up and ask her out to a party at Judy's place in Beaumaris. Judy's parents were to be in Sydney for the weekend. The party would be a riot.

The fellow went on talking, but Adrian couldn't take any more. He wanted to sit down in a quiet place and try to comprehend the incredible story he had just heard. But then the fellow told his friends he must move along the tram and win Lois. Adrian had to watch.

The fellow walked purposefully up the tram and leaned over a group of Canterbury girls. A girl with shapely legs and large innocent eyes gazed up into his face. They talked. She nodded and smiled. The fellow said something funny. He let it slide out of the corner of his mouth. The girl leaned back and showed the full length of her white throat and laughed. The fellow stood back and admired his work. Then he said goodbye and walked back to his friends.

They took the whole thing quite calmly. One of them said, 'Are you going to ask her out?'

The party-goer said, 'I don't really know. She's a nice kid. She'd be lots of fun. I think her parents make her study most weekends. I might wait and take her out to some quiet party not too far from her home.' The others were gentlemen enough to drop the subject.

It was some weeks before Adrian dared to stand near the Canterbury girls. He didn't want to offend them with the sight of his pimply face and crumpled suit and the Catholic emblems on his pocket and cap.

There were four Canterbury girls who were always huddled at one end of the tram. Whenever Adrian sneaked a look at them they were chattering or smiling with their gloved hands pressed daintily to their lips. They spoke so confidentially to each other that he guessed they were talking about boys. Each day for a week he stood a little nearer to their seats, always keeping his back to the girls. He hoped to learn something that even the Eastern Hill boys didn't know.

When he finally stood within earshot of them he was shocked to hear them talking the whole time about clothes— the ones they wore last weekend, the shops where they bought them, the alterations they had to make before they could wear them, the way they creased or crumpled after wearing and what they were going to wear next weekend.

Adrian was disappointed at first, but he worked out later that the girls only worried about clothes because they wanted to look beautiful when they went to parties with the Eastern Hill fellows.

As Adrian got to know the Eastern Hill men better, he discovered that some of them weren't perfect. There was one chap who was on the training list for the first eighteen in the public-schools football competition. One day on the tram he was limping. He told his friends the story of the torn ligaments in his knee. Each time he said the word 'torn' he winced ever so faintly. It was the first time that Adrian had caught an Eastern Hill fellow doing what the boys at St Carthage's did so often. It was called putting on an act.

But when an Eastern Hill man put on an act it really worked. The fellow with the injured knee limped up to a group of Canterbury girls and told his story again. Each time he winced, the concern in the girls' faces made Adrian almost wince himself.

Sometimes a Canterbury girl put on an act too. One day Adrian heard some girls talking about a debate. They thought their own side should have won. The topic of the debate had been 'That the introduction of television will do more harm than good'. At St Carthage's any boy who tried to talk about schoolwork outside the classroom would have been howled down, but the girls in the tram chattered eagerly about the effect of television on family life and reading and juvenile delinquency.

Then a girl who was angry that her side had lost the debate said, 'Illogical. The opposition's case was utterly illogical.' The big words embarrassed Adrian. The girl was putting on an act.

Some Eastern Hill boys joined the girls. A tall fellow with a voice like a radio announcer's said, 'What are you so excited about, Carolyn?'

Adrian listened hard. The Eastern Hill boys never discussed schoolwork on the tram. What would the fellow say when he realised the girls were only talking about a debate?

Carolyn explained exactly why the opposition's case had been weak. When she was finished, the tall fellow said, 'I quite agree with you,' and looked genuinely troubled. Carolyn smiled. She was very grateful for the fellow's sympathy.

Late in the year the elms around the tram stop at the Swindon town hall were thick with green leaves. When Adrian boarded the tram after school the sun was still high in the sky. In the non-smoking compartment the wooden shutters covered the windows, and the Canterbury girls sat in a rich summery twilight. After Adrian left the tram it turned sharply in the direction of St Kilda and the sea. He always watched the tram out of sight and wondered whether the young men and women still on board could smell salt in the evening breeze.

The Eastern Hill fellows had begun to talk about the holidays. They were all going away somewhere. Some of them said they would try to catch up with each other on New Year's Eve, but God knew what they might be up to that night. The way they chuckled about New Year's Eve was not quite gentlemanly.

The girls were going away too. They were talking about beachwear and party frocks. Adrian wished he could warn them to be careful of their friends from Eastern Hill on New Year's Eve.

It was the athletics season at St Carthage's. On House Sports day the weather was as hot as summer. Adrian noticed a strange girl watching the races with O'Mullane and Cornthwaite. Nobody introduced her properly but Adrian worked out that she was O'Mullane's sister Monica from St Brigid's College, the girls' school along the street from St Carthage's.

The boys from St Carthage's rarely saw the girls from St Brigid's. But on St Carthage's sports day any St Brigid's girl with a brother at St Carthage's was allowed to miss the last period and visit the sports. (The girls had their own sports afternoon on the lawn behind their tall timber fence. Boys walking past heard them cheering politely but saw nothing.)

Adrian wasn't brave enough to talk to O'Mullane's sister but he wanted to impress her. He developed a limp. He explained to O'Mullane that his ligaments were probably torn somewhere. He sat down and ran his fingers along his calf and thigh muscles. The girl took no notice, but O'Mullane glared at him when his fingers moved above his knee.

Adrian tried to amuse the girl. He called out, 'Come on, Tubby,' to a plump boy struggling in a race. He told O'Mullane he would love to see some events at the sports set aside for the brothers—speed strapping contests, or sprint races with all competitors wearing soutanes. Monica O'Mullane looked at him but didn't smile.

Cornthwaite went onto the arena and left his tracksuit behind. Adrian tied the legs of the tracksuit together. When Cornthwaite came back and tried to pull the suit on he fell with all his weight against Adrian. Adrian lost his balance and knocked O'Mullane against his sister. The girl dropped her gloves and program and had to pick them up herself.

No one laughed. Cornthwaite said loudly, 'You pathetic idiot, Sherd.'

After the sports Adrian walked alone to the tram stop. He caught a tram much later than usual. He saw none of the young men and women he knew, but in one corner a strange fellow from Eastern Hill was chatting with a Canterbury girl as though they had been friends since childhood. Adrian heard part of a story the fellow was telling—something about him and his friends greasing the horizontal bar in the gym just before someone called Mr Fancy Pants started his workout. The girl thought it was the funniest story she had ever heard. As she laughed she almost leaned her head on the fellow's shoulder.

Adrian Sherd knew very little about Australia. This might have been because he never saw any Australian films. As a child he had seen *The Overlanders,* but all he remembered about it was how strange the characters' accents sounded.

Australian history was much less colourful than British or European or Bible history. The only part of it that interested Adrian was the period before Australia was properly explored.

In those days there was no reason for a man to go on being bored or unhappy in a city. Just across the Great Dividing Range were thousands of miles of temperate grasslands and open forest country where he could live as he pleased out of reach of curious neighbours and disapproving relatives.

Adrian had an old school atlas with a page of maps showing how Australia had been explored. In one of the first maps, the continent was coloured black except for a few yellow indentations on the eastern coast where the first settlements were. Adrian drew a much larger map with the same colour scheme, except that the dark inland was broken by tracts of a sensuous orange colour. They looked small on the map, but some of them were fifty miles across. They were the lost kingdoms of Australia, established in the early days by men after his own heart.

One fellow had chosen the lush plains of the Mitchell River near the Gulf of Carpentaria. On a low hill he had built a replica of the Temple of Solomon. The walls were hung with purple tapestries and the servants beat the time of day on copper gongs. The women went bare-breasted because the weather was always pleasantly warm.

Another man had chosen the park-like forests of the Victorian Wimmera. On the shores of Lake Albacutya he had set up a township copied from Baghdad in the days of Haroun Al Rashid. Each house had a fountain and a pool in a walled courtyard where the women were free to remove their veils.

In a valley of the Otway Ranges one man had a palace in which the walls were covered with copies of every obscene picture ever painted. A large tract in the Ord River district of Western Australia had been turned into Peru, with its own Inca and Brides of the Sun. Somewhere in Bass Strait was an island exactly like Tahiti before the Europeans found it.

Adrian had never seen any of the places in Australia where these palaces and cities might have been built. He had only been outside Melbourne two or three times. Those were the few brief holidays he had spent on his uncle's farm at Orford, near Colac, in the Western District of Victoria.

The landscape at Orford was all low green hills. Every few hundred yards along the roads was a farmhouse of white weatherboards with a red roof. Near every farm-house was a dairy and milking shed of creamy-grey stone, a stack of baled hay and a windbreak of huge old cypresses.

Adrian's uncle and aunt had seven children. They played Ludo and Happy Families and Cap the Dunce for hours on the back veranda. Sometimes they read *Captain Marvel* and *Cat-Man* and *Doll-Man* comics in the lowest branches of the cypresses or tried to act stories from their comics around the woodheap and the haystack. Adrian asked them whether any parts of their district were still unexplored. They said they weren't sure, but they climbed onto the cowyard fence with him to point out that their own farm was nothing but grass and barbed-wire fences.

Adrian stood on the highest rung of the fence and

looked all round him. The only hopeful sign was the roof of a strange building behind a line of trees on a distant hill. The heat off the paddocks made ridges and shapes like battlements in the roof. If the right sort of men had been the first to find their way to the lonely parts of Australia, the building might have been a temple of the Sun God or a palace of pleasure.

But on the following Sunday Adrian went with all his uncle's family to mass and found that the building on the hill was St Finbar's church.

Not just the things that might have happened, but many important events that actually happened were missing from Australian history books. Adrian often thought about the early settlers. What did a man think when he sat down at night and realised he was the only human being for fifty miles around? If he was an Irishman he probably remembered that God and his guardian angel were watching over him. But what if he was a convict shepherd who had never been to church, or an English farmer who didn't take his religion seriously?

Somewhere in Australia, in a warm sheltered valley overhung with wattles or in tall grass in the lee of an outcrop of boulders, there should have been a granite obelisk or a cairn of stones with an inscription such as:

NEAR THIS SPOT ON THE EVENING OF
27 DECEMBER 1791
ALFRED HENRY WAINWRIGHT AGED 19 YEARS
BECAME THE FIRST EUROPEAN
TO COMMIT AN ACT OF SELF-ABUSE
ON AUSTRALIAN SOIL

Of course the Aborigines had been in Australia for centuries before the white men, but no one would ever know their history. They had lived a carefree bestial existence. Some of them, like King Parajoulta of Blue Mud Bay with his eight wives, showed signs of imagination. But without books or films they had no inspiration to do unusual deeds.

Adrian knew he was right to complain about the dullness of Australian history when he found a certain illustrated article in *People* magazine. Far out beyond the prairies of America, in a place called Short Creek, Arizona, a reporter had discovered families of Mormons still practising polygamy. It seemed that when polygamy had been outlawed many years before, a few men who wanted to keep up the custom had found their way to a remote district and gone on living the life they wanted.

It was one more proof that Americans were more imaginative and adventurous than Australians. There were plains and mountain ranges in Australia where whole tribes of polygamists could have settled. But now there were churches like St Finbar's, Orford, on the hilltops and people like Adrian's cousins staring out across the plains.

Adrian studied the photos in *People*. The families of Short Creek were disappointing to look at. The women had plain, pinched faces with the rimless spectacles that so many Americans wore, and barefooted children hanging onto their cotton dresses. But behind the town of Short Creek, rising abruptly from where the dusty main street petered out, was an enormous mountain range—the sort of place where a tribe of pagans or a palace with a harem of a hundred rooms might be safe from discovery for many years yet.

●

One morning Father Lacey spoke to Adrian's class about the Catholic Press.

He said, 'I don't have to remind you that here in Melbourne we have two excellent weekly papers, the *Tribune* and the *Advocate*, to give us the Catholic interpretation of the news. One of these papers should be in every Catholic home every week of the year to give you the sort of news you won't read in the secular press. I know of several good Catholic families who read their *Advocate* or *Tribune* from cover to cover each week and don't buy any of the secular newspapers. I'm happy to say those families are better informed about current affairs and the moral issues of modern life than most people who can't do without their *Sun* and *Herald* and *Sporting Globe*.

'You boys are perhaps too young to realise it, but I'm simply amazed sometimes at the stories and pictures they print in the daily newspapers. In my day it was unheard of, but nowadays you can visit nearly any Catholic home and see papers lying around in full view of the children with stories of hideous crimes and lurid pictures staring up at you. It's one more sign that we're slowly turning into a pagan society. And far too many Catholics take this sort of thing lying down.

'There's one Melbourne newspaper in particular that regularly prints suggestive pictures which are quite unnecessary and don't have anything to do with the news of the day. I won't name the paper, but some of you have probably noticed what I'm talking about. I hope your parents have, anyway.

'This very morning for example I happened to notice a picture on one of their inside front pages. It was what they call a sweater girl. That's something else by the way that's crept into our modern pagan attitudes. I'm talking about the emphasis that some people nowadays put on the female bosom.

'Now, we all know the human body is one of the most marvellous things that God created. And great artists for centuries have praised its beauty by painting it and making statues of it. But a true artist will tell you that you can't make a great work of art if you emphasise one part of your subject matter out of all proportion to its importance. Any artist worth his salt knows that true beauty consists of fitting all the elements of a design into a harmonious whole.

'I'll speak quite frankly now. There are many famous and wonderful pictures of the naked female body with the bosom exposed—some of them are priceless treasures in the Vatican itself. But you'll never find one of these master-pieces drawing attention to the bosom or making it appear larger than it really is.

'But to get back to these newspaper pictures. I must say, I find it very sad to see a young woman being persuaded to stand up and pose in an awkward way to draw attention to the bosom that Almighty God gave her for a holy purpose—and all for the amusement of a few perverted men.

'Now, this particular newspaper has been doing this sort of thing so often that we can safely say it's all part of a deliberate plan to appeal to the lowest elements among its readers. The men who issue the instructions for these sort of pictures to be printed are sitting back smugly, imagining that all these sweater girls and bathing beauties are going to sell thousands of extra copies of their paper.

'But that's just where they're wrong. Boys, I'll let you

into a little secret. There are large numbers of decent Catholic men right now who are working to make this paper clean up its pictures or else they'll put it out of business.

'Yes. That's what I said. There are some of them who've formed a little group in this very parish of Swindon. This is real Catholic Action at work. No doubt some of your fathers are forming groups in your own parishes. The way these men are working is to bring these pictures of bosoms and underdressed women to the notice of their workmates and fellow parishioners and friends and point out how unnecessary they are in a daily newspaper. There's no doubt that every decent person, whether they're Catholics or non-Catholics, will object to these pictures leaping out at them over the breakfast table or on the tram to the office. And if every one of those people stops buying the paper concerned and writes a letter of complaint to the management we'll soon get results.

'Our men have a few other tricks up their sleeves too, only I'm not free to tell you about them at the moment. Let's just say I think you'll find these bare limbs and exaggerated bosoms will soon be disappearing from our streets and homes. And when they do we'll have the Catholic men of Melbourne to thank for it.'

Adrian Sherd was almost certain that the priest was talking about the *Argus*, which was delivered to the Sherds' house every morning because Mr Sherd said it was the best paper for racing and football. Most of the women that Adrian took with him on his American journeys had first appeared to him in the pages of the *Argus*. The poses they struck to excite him (leaning back against a rock with hands on hips and legs wide apart, or bending forward to expose the deep cleavage at the top of their bathers) came straight from the films section of the Saturday *Argus*.

If the Catholic men persuaded Mr Sherd to stop buying the *Argus*, Adrian would have no chance to meet new women. It was different for Cornthwaite and his friends, who were allowed out to films any night of the week. They had all the beautiful women in the world to choose from. But Adrian depended on the *Argus* to introduce him to new faces and breasts and legs. Without it he would have to live on his memories. Or he might even end up like those old perverts who got arrested for drilling holes in bathroom walls or women's changing sheds at the beach.

Adrian talked to his friends afterwards. Stan Seskis said, 'It's the *Argus* all right, and my old man's one of those that are going to clean it up. He buys it every day and draws big circles in red ink round all the pictures of the tarts. Then he cuts them all out and pastes them in a scrapbook and takes them to a meeting every week at Mr Moroney's house.

'And it's not just pictures he collects. Sometimes he cuts out a story about some court case. He puts a red line under certain words that shouldn't be seen in a family newspaper. I'll bet none of you bastards know what a criminal assault really means.'

No one knew. Seskis told them. 'It's the same thing as rape. And if you read the *Argus* carefully every day, in the end you'll find a story about a criminal assault. And if you use your imagination you can work out just how the bastard raped the tart.'

Adrian decided to prepare for the day when the *Argus*

had to stop printing the pictures he needed. Every morning in the train between Accrington and Swindon he looked around for young women who could eventually take over from his film stars and beauty queens. It was nearly a week before he found a face and figure to compare with the *Argus* women. He picked out a young married woman so carefully groomed that she must have worked in a chemist's shop or a hairdresser's salon. He studied her closely without anyone noticing him. That night he invited her to join him and two friends on a trip through the piney woods of Georgia. She came along cheerfully but Adrian soon wished she had stayed at home.

Adrian could not relax with her. Whenever he met her eyes he remembered he would have to face her on the train next morning. She would be dressed in her ordinary clothes again (in Georgia she wore candy-striped shorts and a polka-dot blouse) and he would be wearing the grey suit and maroon cap of St Carthage's College. It would be hard pretending that nothing had happened between them on the previous night.

There was another difficulty. Jayne and Marilyn and Susan and their many friends always had the same look about them—a wide-eyed half-smile with lips slightly parted. The new woman had an irritating way of changing her expression. She seemed to be thinking too much.

Worse still, Adrian realised when he saw her in Georgia that her breasts had no fixed shape. Each of the other women had a pair as firm and inflexible as a statue's. But the new girl's lolled and bounced on her chest so that he could never be sure what size and shape they were.

When the afternoon reached its climax Adrian gave up

trying to fit the new girl into Georgia and deserted her for his old favourites.

Next morning the young woman was in her usual place in the train. Her face was stern and haughty and her breasts had almost disappeared under the folds of her cardigan. When the train crossed the high viaducts approaching Swindon, the morning sunlight came through the windows. The carriage was suddenly bright and warm like a clearing in the piney woods. Adrian looked down from where he was standing and saw a picture in someone's *Argus*. It's title was 'Why Wait Till Summer?' and it showed a girl in twopiece bathers on the deck of a yacht. She had a smile that showed she was eager to please, and her breasts were a shape that could be memorised at a glance.

Adrian looked from the picture to the girl in the corner. Her seat was still in shadow. She looked grey and insubstantial.

In school that morning Adrian thought of writing an anonymous letter to the editor of the *Argus* praising pictures like 'Why Wait Till Summer?' and wondered if it would help to save the pictures from the Catholic men.

One very hot Saturday morning Adrian Sherd was staring at a picture of the Pacific coast near Big Sur. He hadn't been to America for several days, and he was planning a sensational extravaganza for that very night with four or perhaps even five women against a backdrop of mighty cliffs and redwood forests.

His mother came into the room and said she had been down to the phone box talking to his Aunt Francie and now Adrian and his brothers and mother and Aunt Francie and her four kids were going on the bus to Mordialloc beach for a picnic.

The Sherds went to the beach only once or twice a year. Adrian had never learned to swim properly. He usually sat in the shallows and let the waves knock him around, or dug moats and canals at the water's edge while the sun burned his pale skin crimson. At mealtime he sat at a grimy picnic bench with a damp shirt sticking to his skin and his bathers full of grit. His young brothers and cousins jostled him to get at the food, and he shrank back from the tomato seeds dribbling down their chins or the orange pips they spat carelessly around them.

On the long bus trip to Mordialloc, Adrian decided to make the day pass more quickly by observing women on the beach. He might see something (a shoulder strap slipping, or a roll of flesh escaping from a tight bathing suit just below the buttocks) that could be fitted into his adventures at Big Sur to make them more realistic.

The two families reached Mordialloc in the hottest part of the afternoon. They were going to stay at the beach until dark. The women and the oldest children carried baskets and string bags packed with cold corned beef, lettuce leaves, tomatoes, hard-boiled eggs, jars of fruit salad, and slices of bread and butter, all wrapped in damp tea towels.

Adrian put on his bathers in the changing shed. He looked into the toilet cubicles and shower room to read the writing on the walls. Most of it had been whitewashed only recently. The boldest inscription was in a toilet cubicle. It read simply: MISS KATHLEEN MAHONEY YOU BEAUT. There was no illustration.

Adrian pitied the young man who had written those

words. He was some larrikin who knew nothing about life in America. All he could use to excite himself was some girl he had lusted after in his own suburb. And Kathleen Mahoney was a good Catholic name. The girl had probably never looked twice at the uncouth bastard who scrawled her name in toilets.

If Adrian had had the time, he would have scratched out the inscription. But just then he found something much more important to worry about.

Even though the day was hot, his cock had shrivelled up to the size of a boy's while he was undressing. It was too small to dangle properly. When he pulled on his bathers it made a tiny pathetic lump that was clearly visible in the cloth between his legs. He walked out of the changing shed with small careful steps so his miserable button wouldn't be too obvious.

He got back to his mother and aunt and saw a strange woman in onepiece tartan bathers standing between them. When she turned round it was only his cousin Bernadette, who was no older than he was. He had taken no notice of her in her ordinary clothes. Her face was nothing much to look at and she always had her young sisters hanging round her. Now he saw that her thighs were as big and heavy as her mother's, and her breasts were a much more interesting shape.

Mrs Sherd and her sister Francie told all their children to swim in the shallow water until they were sent for. Francie said, 'We're going to sit down and have a good rest and we don't want any kids hanging round us.'

Adrian walked down into the sea and sat down. He kept his bathers underwater to hide the stub between his legs and looked around for his cousin Bernadette. She was nowhere in the water, or on the sand. He looked back at the pavilion. She was sitting in her tartan bathers beside the two women. She must have decided she wasn't one of the children any more.

Adrian was angry. He had to splash around in the shallows with his brothers and young cousins while Bernadette sat gossiping with the women. Yet he had romped with film stars on scenic beaches in America while Bernadette looked as though she had never even had a boyfriend.

He spent his time in the water making elaborate plans for his trip to the coast of northern California that evening. Bernadette would have looked at him differently if she could have known his true strength—in a few hours he was going to wear out three film stars one after the other.

At teatime Bernadette made a point of helping the women serve the food. Adrian stayed where his mother had told him to wait with the other children. When Bernadette came near him he pulled his shoulders back and drew himself up to his full height. He wanted her to realise he was taller and more powerfully built than she was. But she kept her eyes lowered and he had to sit down and cross his legs in case she noticed the insignificant wrinkle in the front of his bathing trunks.

While his cousin served the food she had to stand very close to Adrian. Two or three times she leaned across him so that her breasts were almost under his nose. Adrian thought he might as well glance at her body. Perhaps some detail of it would come in handy in America when he couldn't visualise one of his film stars as accurately as he needed.

Adrian pretended to be busy with his bread and butter

and hard-boiled egg while he inspected Bernadette at close range. It was the nearest he had ever been to a full-grown Australian female body in a bathing suit, but he was far from impressed.

The skin between her throat and breasts had been burnt a little by the sun. It was a raw flesh-pink colour instead of the uniform golden-cream he preferred in a beautiful woman. There was even a small brown mole on the very slope where one of her breasts began, which automatically disqualified her from perfection.

Whenever she walked, her thighs and calves turned out to be full of muscles. Even the slightest movement made one or other of the muscles tense or slacken. It was impossible for Adrian to tell whether the legs were shapely because she never once kept them in an artistic pose.

He risked a quick glance between her legs and saw something that shocked him. When she passed close by him again he looked a second time. He was not mistaken. High up inside her leg where the white of her thigh met the tartan fabric of her bathers, a single dark-brown hair, perhaps an inch long, lay curled against her skin.

He could not tell whether the hair had sprouted from the thigh itself or whether he was looking at the end of it only, and its roots were somewhere in the mysterious territory beneath her bathers. But it didn't really matter. Either way, the coarse coiled hair made nonsense of any claim she had to beauty. He could call to mind a whole gallery of beautiful legs. They were all motionless and symmetrical and as smooth as the finest marble.

After tea Adrian had to go back to the changing shed to put his clothes on. On the way to the shed he tried to remind himself of the trip to Big Sur that would make up for his miserable day at Mordialloc. But all his staring at his cousin had made him restless and tense. He thought he would probably never make it to California.

In the changing shed he gave in quickly. He locked himself in one of the toilet cubicles and set to work. He did not even close his eyes—he was in Mordialloc, beside Port Phillip Bay, Victoria, Australia, all the while. But he resisted with all his strength the images of blemished skin and bunched calf muscles and hairy thighs that urged themselves on him. He would not betray all the beauty of America for the sake of his lumpish cousin.

He looked all round him, staring at the walls in the twilight. Something white caught his eye. Of all the women he knew, in America and Australia, only Miss Kathleen Mahoney was with him at the end. He leaned his head against the soothing shapes of the letters of her name.

One morning late in the year Brother Cyprian announced to the class, 'After your exams we'll be having a Father Dreyfus at the school one night to show a film and give a talk and answer any of your questions on the subject of sex education.'

The brother read from a paper on his desk: 'The film has been shown to Catholic boys in secondary forms all over Australia. It shows in a perfectly clear and simple fashion all those matters which boys are often anxious to know but unfortunately are sometimes unwilling to find out from parents and teachers.

'The film offers the whole wonderful story of human reproduction from the moment of fertilisation to the hour of birth and illustrates clearly the workings of the human body both male and female.'

Brother Cyprian looked over the boys' heads at the back wall and said, 'All boys are urged to come to this film but of course there's no compulsion. Father Dreyfus is a man worth coming miles to hear on any subject. He's led an extraordinary life. He was in a Nazi concentration camp during the war. He rides a motorbike. He's what you might call a man's man.'

Adrian Sherd thought this was the best news he had heard all year. He tried to catch the eye of Cornthwaite or Seskis or O'Mullane to share his excitement. But they were all staring ahead as though there was nothing they needed to learn from any travelling priest and his famous film.

Adrian remembered the brother's words, 'from the moment of fertilisation'. He was going to see the most daring film ever made. At the very least he expected a statue or a painting of a man and woman doing it—a famous work of art that had been kept out of sight for centuries in some gallery in Europe. Yet if such a statue or painting existed it would have been the work of a pagan artist, and this was to be a Catholic film.

Perhaps he would see a married couple making a lump under the blankets of their bed. But Brother Cyprian had said, 'a perfectly clear and simple fashion'. The blankets would have to be thrown back to show the organs at work. The couple, of course, would be hooded or masked to protect them from embarrassment.

But surely this was too much to hope for. No film in all history had ever shown the act itself. Anyone, even a priest, would be arrested just for having it in his possession, let alone showing it to an audience. Adrian could only wait and count the days until he actually saw the film.

On the night of the film every boy in the class turned up. When Brother Cyprian blew his whistle to call them inside, they loitered and went on talking as though they weren't at all anxious to see whatever the priest had to show.

Father Dreyfus had a thick black beard—an unheard-of thing for a priest. He was sitting on top of the front desk with his hands in his pockets and his legs crossed. On all the other desks there were pencils and pieces of paper. The priest invited the boys to write down any questions they had about sex and marriage and said he would try to answer them before he showed his film.

Not many boys wrote down questions. Adrian tried to think of something to oblige the priest but he heard a familiar cough from the back of the room and remembered that Brother Cyprian was somewhere behind him in the shadows fiddling with the projector. If the brother saw him writing out a question he might think Adrian was preoccupied with sexual matters.

The priest read out the questions from the slips of paper and answered each one briefly. Most of the questions seemed childish to Adrian. He could have answered them himself with all the information he had got from Cornthwaite and his friends during the past two years.

There was only one really interesting question. Someone had asked what advice he ought to give to his best friend who hadn't been to confession for nearly a year because he was too scared to confess all the sins of impurity he committed by himself.

This was the first time that Adrian had ever heard the sin of self-abuse discussed in public. Priests and brothers often made vague references to it, but no one had ever mentioned it so boldly as the anonymous author of the question.

Adrian didn't hear the first part of the priest's answer. He was too busy trying to work out who had asked the question. The story about the best friend sounded unlikely. The questioner himself was the fellow who had a year's worth of sins on his soul.

All over the room, other boys were puzzling over the same matter. Adrian studied the faint turnings of heads and the surreptitious glances. Suspicion seemed to fall on Noonan, a big dull fellow. Adrian remembered Noonan getting up from his seat outside the confessional one First Thursday and leaving the church as though he wanted to be sick. It was a good trick. He could have practised it month after month while his total of sins mounted up.

After answering Noonan's question the priest said, 'Only the other day I was reading an American book on psychology. Young people and their problems. That sort of thing. I was very surprised to see some figures relating to the sin we're talking about. According to the book, over ninety per cent of boys have experimented with masturbation before they're eighteen years old. Of course these figures wouldn't apply to Catholic boys but it certainly makes you stop and think.'

After he had got over the shock of hearing the word 'masturbation' spoken by a priest (and in his own classroom), Adrian wondered what the figures implied. Perhaps he and Cornthwaite and the others wouldn't have felt so unusual if they had been lucky enough to grow up in America. Ninety per cent seemed a high figure at first, but of course American boys were subject to much fiercer temptations than Australians. Many of them had probably seen in the flesh the women that Adrian only saw in pictures.

When the priest had answered all their questions he told a boy to turn out the lights. Then he said to Brother Cyprian, 'Let her roll,' and the projector started.

It was an old, worn film. The sound crackled and boomed, and every few minutes a cloud of grey blobs and streaks fell across the screen like a sudden squall of rain. An overgrown child with long trousers and a bowtie was asking his parents how he had come into the world. The people were all Americans. It was obvious from the way they smiled and patted each other and held themselves stiffly that they weren't even proper actors. They belonged to the mysterious multitude that Adrian had never seen in films—the Catholic American families who lived in a pagan land but still kept up the struggle to save their souls.

A few more diagrams appeared. It rained hard all over the screen again. Adrian prayed for the rain to clear before the female organs and the moment of fertilisation came on the screen.

The rain died down, and she stood before them at last. Only it wasn't really a she. Adrian almost groaned aloud. The swindlers had made a sort of dressmaker's dummy and sliced it off just above the navel. The thing swung round noiselessly on a swivel to show its genital organs. Adrian half-expected it to topple forward like the corpses in films that were propped up in chairs until someone turned them round to see why they wouldn't talk.

The female thing stayed on the screen for perhaps ten seconds. Even while he was straining to fix it in his mind forever, Adrian was aware that all of the fifty and more heads around him were suddenly motionless—all except one. Just behind Adrian, at the back of the room, Brother Cyprian jerked his head around and stared into a dark corner when the thighs and belly started turning towards him. Adrian understood—the brother was under a vow of chastity, and for him the thing on the screen was an occasion of sin.

Between its legs the creature had a low bald mound with a suggestion of a cleft or fissure along its middle. Adrian cursed the people who made the dummy or statue or whatever it was for putting the mound or whatever it was so far down between the legs that its finer details were hidden. He was trying to imagine how the legs and the object between them would look walking towards him or stepping out of a bathing suit or lying down in an attitude of surrender, when they faded from the screen.

A huge diagram appeared. Adrian knew it like the back of his hand. It was the female reproductive system. He hardly bothered to listen while the commentator's voice explained what happened in the ovaries and oviducts and Fallopian tubes. Over the years he had found many sketches and diagrams and charts and sectional reliefs of the inside of a female body—but not one lifelike illustration of the outside.

He was trying to imagine the whole diagram enclosed in skin and packed away between two thighs, when he noticed something odd in the lowest part of the screen. A swarm of bees or a flight of tiny arrows was drifting through the lowest tube. It could even have been the grey rain in the film suddenly reversing and going back up the screen. But then the commentator announced what was really happening.

They were watching the moment of fertilisation. This was what Adrian and all his class had come from miles around to see. But it was nothing like real life. An army of little sperm-men was invading the diagram. The commentator got excited. He thought there was nothing so marvellous as the long journey of these tiny creatures. Adrian didn't care what happened to the little bastards now that the film had turned out to be a fraud.

The sperm cells were thinning out and growing weaker. The boys of Form Four at St Carthage's were still staring at the screen. They didn't seem to realise they had been cheated. Adrian stretched himself in his seat and wondered how the scene had been filmed.

Was it just an animated diagram like a cartoon? Or did the filmmakers pay some lunatic to shoot his stuff into a hollow tube inside the dressmaker's dummy? Or did they put a tiny camera inside a female organ so that Adrian and his class and even Father Dreyfus and Brother Cyprian were all sitting in the dark inside a woman's body while some huge fellow outside was doing her for all he was worth but none of them knew what was going on?

One day in December Stan Seskis told his friends he had read somewhere that a normal man should be able to have relations with a woman once every twenty-four hours unless he was ill or abnormal or something. Seskis said he had proved the truth of this by doing it to himself for ten nights on end and he was glad to know he was as good as any normal man.

Adrian Sherd had always been content to visit America three or four times a week. When he had tried it more frequently, his female companions always seemed listless and uncooperative and even the landscape was uninspiring. But he had to see whether Seskis was talking sense.

He reached a score of five consecutive nights. On the sixth night it was like torture. He arrived at a desert playground in Arizona. He was so jaded that he had brought two carloads of women with him instead of his usual two or three favourites. Jayne, Marilyn, Kim, Susan, Debbi, Zsa-Zsa—anyone who might come in useful was there.

He had to order them around like an army sergeant. He told one squad to strip off at once. A second squad had to take their clothes off slowly, dawdling over each item. Another group had to hide among the rocks and be ready to give in to him if he stumbled on them during the afternoon.

The fun and games dragged on for hours. The women began to complain. Sherd tried to think of some mad perversion that would bring everything to an end. The thing that finally did the trick was so absurd that he almost apologised to the women when it was over. He told them he didn't want to see any of them for at least a week. Then he flung himself down in the shade of a giant cactus and fell asleep.

The next day was Sunday. Adrian rode his bike to seven o'clock mass instead of going with his family on the nine o'clock mass bus. He told his parents he preferred the early mass because it left him the rest of the day for mucking around. But in fact he was tired of staying in his seat while his parents and brothers looked curiously at him as they climbed past his knees on their way to communion. He thought his father would surely guess soon which sin it was that kept him away from communion for weeks on end.

It was the Third Sunday of Advent, the last Sunday before school broke up for the long summer holidays. Inside the church, Adrian joined his hands and bowed his head slightly and looked at the people around him. He knew it was no use trying to pray unless he had some intention of giving up his sin in future.

The sermon was about repentance in preparation for the great feast of Christmas. The priest said, 'This is the season when we ought to remember all the ways we've offended Our Blessed Saviour during the past year.'

Some of the people near Adrian lowered their eyes and tried to look sorry for their sins. Adrian wished he could shout, 'Hypocrites!' in their faces. What did they know about sins? God saw into their hearts. He knew the year's total of mortal sins for everyone in the church. According to the records kept in heaven, the worst sinner, by a margin of at least a hundred, was a young man in the back row. He was pale and weary, as well he might be. Young and slightly built though he was, he had outscored people twice his age. More remarkable still, he had restricted himself to breaking one commandment, whereas they had the whole ten to choose from.

At communion time Adrian sat up to let the sinless ones past. A young woman's stocking brushed against his knee. The taut golden fabric shrank back from the drab grey of his school trousers. Adrian kept his eyes down. The champion sinner of Our Lady of Good Counsel's parish for

1953 was not worthy to set eyes on a pure young woman approaching the communion rail.

While the long queues of communicants moved slowly towards the altar, Adrian opened his missal at the page headed 'Making a Spiritual Communion' and tried to look as if he was making one. If a person was not in a state of sin, but could not go to communion because he had eaten a meal or drunk a glass of water that morning, that person could unite himself in spirit with Our Lord in the Blessed Sacrament. If the owner of the golden stockings noticed Adrian when she returned to her seat, she would probably see the heading on the page of his missal and think he hadn't gone to communion because of a mouthful of water he swallowed while he was cleaning his teeth that morning.

The owner of the stockings turned out to be a girl in a school uniform. The skirt and tunic were a rich beige colour. On the tunic pocket was a snow-covered mountain peak against a bright blue sky. A circle of gold stars and a gold motto hung in the sky. It was the uniform of the Academy of Mount Carmel, in the suburb of Richmond. The girl seemed no older than Adrian, although he knew already that her legs were heavy and rounded like a woman's.

Coming back from communion, the girl kept her eyes lowered. Her lashes were long and dark. She must have felt Adrian staring at her as she settled herself in her seat. She looked at him for less than a second. Then she knelt down and covered her face with her hands like all good Catholics after communion.

Adrian thought about the glance she had given him. She was utterly indifferent to him. If he had somehow reminded her that a few minutes earlier their legs had brushed together, she would have slapped his face. And if she could have seen the filthy state of his soul she would have got up and moved to another seat.

Adrian looked at the girl again. Her face was angelic. She had the kind of beauty that could inspire a man to do the impossible. He turned towards the altar and put his head in his hands. Slowly and dramatically he whispered a vow that would change his life: 'For her sake I will leave America forever.'

Adrian had often knelt outside a confessional and prayed the words from the Act of Contrition, 'And I firmly resolve, by the help of Thy grace, never to offend Thee again.' He had always known (and God had known too) that before a week was over he would be back in America again with his film stars. But in the back seat of his parish church, within a few feet of the girl in the severely beautiful uniform of the Academy of Mount Carmel, he felt strong enough to keep his promise.

He conducted an experiment to prove it. He looked the girl over, from her ankles to her bowed head. Then he closed his eyes and summoned Jayne and Marilyn. He ordered them to dance naked in front of him and to shake their hips as suggestively as they knew how.

The experiment was a complete success. With his beige-clad angel beside him, the naked film stars looked obscene and revolting. Their hold over him was broken at last.

He tried one more experiment. It was an unpleasant one, but he had to do it—the fate of his soul for all eternity might depend on it. He stared at the girl's jacket and tried to imagine himself taking it off. It would not budge. He looked at her skirt and thought of the white underwear just beneath it. His arms and hands were suddenly paralysed. The lust that had ruled over him night and day for more than a year, his mighty lust, had met its match.

Riding home on his bike after mass, Adrian sang a current hit song. It was called 'Earth Angel'. He sang the words slowly and mournfully like a man pleading with a woman to end his long years of misery.

He made his plans for the future. That very night, and every night after that, he would fall asleep thinking of a girl in a beige school uniform with a pale haughty face and dark eyelashes. He would shelter in the aura of purity that surrounded her like an enormous halo. In that zone of sanctity no thought of sin would trouble him.

On the following Saturday he would go to confession and rid himself for the last time of the sin that had threatened to enslave him. Every afternoon until school broke up, he would catch a different train from Swindon to Accrington and try to meet up with his Earth Angel on her way home. When school started again in February he would catch her train and see her every day.

On the last Monday morning of the school year, the boys in Adrian's form were all talking about the holidays. Stan Seskis explained to his friends a competition he had worked out in case they got bored in the long weeks away from school. All of them, Seskis, Cornthwaite, O'Mullane and Sherd, would keep a careful count of how many times they did it. They would be on their honour not to cheat, since they all lived in different suburbs and had no way of checking on each other. When they came back to school in February they would compare totals.

No one could think of a suitable prize for the winner, but they agreed the competition was a good idea. Adrian said nothing. Seskis asked him to rule up cards for them to mark their scores on.

Adrian had no intention of telling the others how his life had changed. He ruled up the scorecards during a free period in school. There were fifty blank squares on his own scorecard. When he returned to school there would still be no mark on them. He was sure of this. The women who had tempted him to sin in the past were only images in photographs. The woman who was going to save him now was a real flesh-and-blood creature. She lived in his own suburb. He had sat only a few feet from her in his parish church.

For too long he had been led astray by dreams of America. He was about to begin a new life in the real world of Australia.

PART TWO

Every afternoon in the last weeks of 1953, Adrian Sherd caught a different train home. At each station between Swindon and Accrington he changed from one carriage to another. He looked in every compartment for the girl in the Mount Carmel uniform but he could not find her.

Adrian realised he had to endure the seven weeks of the summer holidays with only the memory of their one meeting in Our Lady of Good Counsel's Church to sustain him. But he swore to look for her each Sunday at mass and to go on searching the trains in 1954.

He spent the first day of the holidays tearing all the unused pages out of his school exercise books. He planned to use them for working out statistics of Sheffield Shield cricket matches and drawing maps of foreign countries or sketches of model-railway layouts or pedigrees of the white mice that his young brother was breeding in the old meat safe in the shed. It would all help to bring February closer.

Adrian's soul was in the state of grace and he meant to keep it that way. He was ready for his passions if they tried to regain their old power over him. He was sitting alone in the shed with a pencil and paper in front of him when he found himself drawing the torso of a naked woman. As soon as he saw his danger he whispered the words 'Earth Angel'. Then he calmly turned the breasts of his sketch into eyes and the whole torso into a funny face, and crumpled the paper.

In bed that night he joined his hands on his chest and thought of himself kneeling in church beside the girl he loved, and fell asleep with his hands still clasped together.

On the second day of the holidays, Adrian's mother announced that none of the family would be going to her brother-in-law's farm at Orford in January because her sister had just brought home a new baby and the Sherd kids would only be in the way.

Adrian's brothers rolled around on the kitchen lino, howling and complaining, but Adrian took the news calmly. All year he had been looking forward to the bare paddocks and enormous sky of the Western District. But now he was secretly pleased to be spending January in the suburb where his Earth Angel lived.

That night Adrian thought of himself sitting beside the girl and listening to a sermon on purity. He felt so strong and pure himself that he let his hands rest far down in the bed, knowing they would not get into trouble.

He looked for his Earth Angel every Sunday at mass and rode his bike for hours around unfamiliar streets hoping to meet her. After Christmas when he still hadn't seen her, he decided she had gone away for the holidays. He wondered where a respectable Catholic family would take their daughter for the summer.

The wealthier boys at St Carthage's went to the Mornington Peninsula. Adrian had never been there, but every day in summer the *Argus* had pictures of holiday-makers at Rye or Rosebud or Sorrento. Mothers cooked dinner outside their tents and young women splashed water at the photographer and showed off their low necklines. Adrian began to worry about the dangers his Earth Angel would meet on the Peninsula. He hoped she didn't care for swimming and spent her days reading in the cool of her tent. But if she did go swimming he hoped the changing sheds were solid brick and not weatherboard. He lay awake for hours one night thinking of all the rotted nail holes in wooden changing sheds where lustful teenage boys could peer through at her while she undressed.

All round her in the shed the non-Catholic girls were putting on their twopiece costumes. But what did she wear? Adrian couldn't go to sleep until he had reassured himself that she chose her beachwear from the range of styles approved by the National Catholic Girls' Movement. (Sometimes the *Advocate*, the Catholic paper, showed pictures of NCGM girls modelling evening wear suitable for Catholic girls. The necklines showed only an inch or so of bare skin below the throat. There were never any pictures of bathers suitable for Catholics but girls were advised to inspect the approved range at NCGM headquarters.)

One morning the front-page headline in the *Argus* was HEAT WAVE. In the middle of the page was a picture of a young woman on a boat at Safety Beach. Her breasts were so close to the camera that Adrian could have counted the beads of water clinging to the places she had rubbed with suntan oil. All that afternoon he lay on the lino in the bathroom trying to keep cool and hoping his Earth Angel kept out of the way of men with cameras. He thought of some prowling photographer catching her as she stepped from the water with a strap of her bathers slipping down over her shoulder.

At night he had so many worries that he never thought of his old sin. On New Year's Eve he remembered the boys of Eastern Hill Grammar School. That was the night when they all went to parties in their fathers' cars and looked for girls to take home afterwards. One of the Eastern Hill fellows might have seen Adrian's Earth Angel on the beach and tried to persuade her to go with him to a wild party. Adrian tried to remember some incident from the lives of saints when God had blinded a lustful fellow to the beauty of an innocent young woman to protect her virtue.

One day in January Adrian went to a barber's shop in Accrington. One of the magazines lying around for customers to read was a copy of *Man*. Adrian studied the pictures quite calmly. The naked women were trying to look attractive, but their faces were strained and hard and their breasts were flabby from being handled by all the photographers who worked for *Man*—and probably all the cartoonists and short-short story writers and the editor as well. One glimpse of his Earth Angel's hands and wrists stripped of the beige Mount Carmel gloves had more power over him than the sight of all the nude women in magazines.

Late in January Adrian felt strong enough to take out his model railway. He sent passenger trains round and round the main line and the loop, but he was careful to snatch up the engine each time it slowed down. He still remembered clearly all the landscapes around the track where the train used to stop in the old days. So long as the train ran express through the scenes of his impure adventures he felt no urge to enjoy America again.

But one hot afternoon he was staring through the shed door at the listless branches of the wattle scrub over the side fence when he realised the train had stopped. He stood very still. The only sounds around him were the clicking of insects and the crackling of seed pods on the vacant block next door. He was almost afraid to turn and see what part of America he had come to.

He was far out on the plains of Nebraska. The long hot summer had ripened the miles of wheat and corn. For just one moment Adrian thought of grabbing the first American woman he could find and wandering off with her into the hazy distance to find some shady cottonwood tree beside a quiet stream.

The thought that saved him was a simple one, although it had never occurred to him in all the weeks since his Earth Angel had changed his life. It was this: the temptation that came to him on the prairies of Nebraska proved he could never do without romantic adventures in picturesque land-scapes. The way to keep his adventures pure and sinless was to take his Earth Angel with him.

That night Adrian proposed marriage to the beautiful young woman who had been educated at the Academy of Mount Carmel. After they had set a date for the wedding they sat down over a huge map of Australia to decide which scenic spots they would visit on their honeymoon.

On the hottest night of January, Adrian lay in bed with only his pyjama trousers on. He fell asleep thinking of the cool valleys of Tasmania where he and his wife would probably spend the first weeks of their marriage.

Later that night he was struggling through a crowd of men and women. In the middle of the crowd someone was gloating over an indecent magazine. Somewhere else in the crowd the girl from Mount Carmel was pushing her way towards the magazine. Adrian had to get to it before she did. If she saw the filthy pictures he would die of shame. People started wrestling with Adrian. Their damp bathing costumes rubbed against his belly. The girl from Mount Carmel was laughing softly, but Adrian couldn't see why. Everyone suddenly knelt down because a priest was saying mass nearby. Adrian was the only one who couldn't kneel. He was flapping like a fish in the aisle of a church while the girl he loved was tearing pictures out of her *Argus* and wafting them towards him. They were pictures of naked boys lying on their backs rubbing suntan oil all over their bellies. The girl put up her hand to tell the priest what Adrian had done on the floor of the church.

Adrian woke up and lay very still. It was daylight outside—a cloudless Sunday morning. He remembered vague bits of advice that Brother Cyprian had given the boys of Form Four, and something that Cornthwaite had once said about wet dreams. In those days he had been so busy doing the real thing that he never once had an impure dream. He mopped up the mess inside his pyjamas. He was ashamed to realise he hadn't experienced all the facts of life in Form Four after all. But he went back to sleep pleased that nothing he had thought or done that night was sinful.

That same Sunday morning Adrian went to seven o'clock

mass and walked boldly up to communion. He hoped his Earth Angel was somewhere in the church watching him. At the altar rails he knelt between two men—married men with their wives at their elbows. Adrian was proud to be with them. He belonged among them. He was a man at the peak of his sexual power whose seed burst out of him at night but whose soul was sinless because he was true to the woman he loved.

For days before he went back to school, Adrian wondered what he could say to his friends when they asked him his score in their competition. He couldn't simply hand in a blank scorecard. The others would never believe he had gone for seven weeks without doing it. They would pester him all day to tell them his true score. Even if he made up a low score they would still be suspicious and ask him what went wrong.

Adrian's worst fear was that Cornthwaite or O'Mullane or Seskis would guess he had met a girl and fallen in love. They would think it a great joke to blackmail him. Either he paid some preposterous penalty or they would find out the girl's name and address and send her a list of all the film stars he had had affairs with.

In the end he decided to fill in his card as though he had taken the competition seriously and tried his best to win. He marked crosses in the blank squares for all the days he might have sinned if he had never met his Earth Angel. He was scrupulously honest. He left blank spaces around Christmas Day, when he would have been to confession. But he added extra crosses for the days of the heat wave, when he would have found it hard to get to sleep at night.

123

On the first morning of the new school year the cards were handed round. The scores were O'Mullane, 53; Seskis, 50; Cornthwaite, 48; Sherd, 37.

The others all wanted to know what had happened to Adrian to make him score so poorly. He made up a weak story about getting sunburnt and not being able to lie properly in bed for a fortnight. He promised himself he would find some new friends. But he could not do it too suddenly. He was still frightened of blackmail.

That night Adrian went on searching through the Coroke trains for his Earth Angel. Two nights later he walked into a second-class non-smoking compartment of the 4.22 p.m. from Swindon and saw her. The face he had worshipped for nearly two months was half-hidden under a dome-shaped beige hat—his Earth Angel was absorbed in a book. If she loved literature they had something in common already. And it fitted in perfectly with the plan he had worked out for making himself known to her.

He stood a few feet from her. (Luckily there were no empty seats in the compartment.) Then he took out of his bag an anthology called *The Poet's Highway*. He had bought it only that morning. It was the set text for his English Literature course that year and it contained the most beautiful poem he had ever read—'La Belle Dame Sans Merci', by John Keats.

When the train swung round a bend Adrian pretended to overbalance. With one hand on the luggage rack, he leaned over until the page with the poem was no more than a foot from his Earth Angel's face. He saw her look up as he swung towards her. He couldn't bring himself to meet her eyes, but he hoped she read the title of the poem.

For the next few minutes he stared at the poem and moved his lips to show that he was learning it by heart. Each time he practised reciting a stanza he stared out of the window, past the backyards and clothes lines, as though he really could see a lake where no birds sang. Out of the corner of his eye he saw her watching him with some interest.

At the last station before Accrington he put his anthology away. He knew it was unusual for a boy to like poetry and he dreaded her thinking he was queer or unmanly. He pulled the *Sporting Globe* out of his bag and studied the tables of averages for the visiting South African cricketers. He twisted himself around and leaned back a little so she could see what he was reading and know he was well balanced.

For two weeks Adrian travelled in the girl's compartment. Every night he feasted his eyes on her. Sometimes she caught him at it, but usually he looked away just in time. His worst moment each night came when he opened the train door and looked for her in her usual corner. If she wasn't there it would have meant she had rejected his advances and moved to another compartment.

Some nights he was so frightened of not finding her that his bowels filled up with air. Then he had to stand in the open doorway for a few miles and break wind into the train's slipstream. His Earth Angel might have thought he was showing off—so many schoolboys hung out of doorways on moving trains to impress their girlfriends. But it was better than fouling the air that she breathed. In any case, she was still in the same compartment after two weeks, and he decided she must have been interested in him.

A wonderful change came over Adrian's life. For years he had searched for some great project or scheme to beat the boredom that he felt all day at school. In Form Four his journeys across America had helped a little. But it hadn't always been easy to keep the map of America in front of him—sometimes he had traced it with a wet finger on his desktop or kept a small sketch of it hidden under his text-book. In Form Five his Earth Angel promised to do away with boredom forever. All day at school she watched him. Her pale, serene face stared down at him from a point two or three feet above his right shoulder.

With her watching him, everything he did at school became important. When he answered a question in class, she waited anxiously to see if he was correct. If he cracked a joke in the corridor and made some fellow laugh, she smiled too and admired his sense of humour. When he rearranged the pens and pencils on his desktop or looked closely at his fingernails or the texture of his shirtsleeves, she studied every move he made and tried to guess its significance. Even when he sat motionless in his seat she tried to decide whether he was tired or puzzled or just saving his energy for a burst of hard work.

She was learning a thousand little things about him—how his moods changed subtly from minute to minute, odd little habits he indulged in, the postures and gestures he preferred. For her benefit he deliberated over everything he did. Even in the playground he moved gravely and with dignity.

Of course she couldn't watch him every single moment of the day. Whenever he approached the toilet block she discreetly withdrew. He wasn't embarrassed himself—he felt he knew her well enough to have her a few feet behind him while he stood up manfully to the urinal wall. But she was much too shy herself, especially when she saw the crowd of strange boys heading for the toilet block with their hands at their flies.

It was hardly ever possible for her to watch Adrian in his own home. She hovered above him on his walk home from Accrington station and saw that he lived in a nearly new cream-and-green weatherboard in a swampy street. (She was intrigued to see him choose a different path each night through the lakes and islands in his street—it was one of those teasing little habits that made his personality so fascinating.) But when he stepped over his front gate she melted away so she wouldn't have to see the dreary life he led with his family.

He was glad she would never see his bedroom furniture—the wobbly bed he had slept in since he was three years old, the mirror that had once been part of his grandparents' marble-topped washstand, and the cupboard that came originally from his parents' room and was always known as the glory box. He would have been ashamed to let her see the patched short trousers and the pair of his father's sandals that he wore around the house to save his school trousers and his only pair of shoes.

After tea when his mother made him wash the dishes, he was relieved to think his Earth Angel was safe in her carpeted lounge room on the other side of Accrington, listening to her radiogram while he was up to his elbows in grey dishwater with yellow fatty bubbles clinging to the hairs on his wrists.

Later at night when he was in trouble with his parents, and his father said that when he had been a warder he used to charge prisoners with an offence called dumb insolence for much less than Adrian was doing, he decided he would never even try to describe to his Earth Angel, even years later, how miserable he had been as a boy. And just before bed, when he stared into the bathroom mirror and pressed a hot washer against his face to ripen his pimples or held a mirror between his legs and tried to calculate how big his sexual organs would be when they were fully grown, he knew there were moments in a man's life that a woman could never share.

As soon as he was in bed he was reunited with her—not the girl who watched him all day at St Carthage's but the twenty-year-old woman who was already his fiancée. He spent a long time each night telling her his life story. She loved to hear about the year when they met on the Coroke train and he was so infatuated that he used to imagine her watching him all day at school.

While they were still only engaged, he didn't like to tell her he had thought of her in bed too. But she would hear even that story eventually.

Just out of Swindon, the Coroke train travelled along a viaduct between plantations of elms. On summer after-noons when the carriage doors were open, shreds of grass and leaves blew against the passengers, and the screech of cicadas drowned out their voices. The dust and noise made Adrian think of journeys across landscapes that were vast and inspiring but definitely not sensual.

Every day in February his Earth Angel was in the same corner seat. Sometimes she glanced up at him when he stepped into her carriage. When this happened he always looked politely away. He was going to introduce himself to her at the right time, but until then he had no right to force his attentions on her.

One afternoon on the Swindon station Adrian saw two fellows from his own class watching him from behind the men's toilet. He suspected they were spies sent by Cornthwaite and the others to find out who the girl was who had turned Sherd away from film stars.

Adrian edged along the platform before his Earth Angel's train pulled in. That night he got into a carriage well away from her own. He did the same for the next two nights, just to be safe. During his three days away from her he kept humming the song 'If You Missed Me Half as Much as I Miss You'.

When he went back to her compartment again he thought she glanced at him a little more expressively than before. He decided to prove that he really was seriously interested in her and not just trifling with her affections.

He waited for a night when all the seats in the compartment were filled, and he had to stand. He walked over and stood above her seat. He took out an exercise book and pretended to read from it. He held it so that the front cover was almost in front of her eyes. The writing on the cover was large and bold. He had spent half an hour in school that day going over and over the letters. It read:

Adrian Maurice Sherd (Age 16)
Form V
St Carthage's College, Swindon.

She looked at the book almost at once, but then she lowered her eyes. Adrian wanted her to stare at it and learn all she could about him. But he realised her natural feminine modesty would prevent her from seeming too eager to respond to his advances.

During the next few minutes she glanced at his writing twice more. He was still wondering how much she had read, when he saw her opening her own school case. She took out an exercise book. She pretended to read a few lines from it. Then she held it in front of her with her own name facing him.

Adrian heard the blood roaring in his ears and wished he could kiss the gloved finger that held the name out naked and exposed for him to stare at. He read the delicate hand-writing:

Denise McNamara
Form IV
Academy of Mount Carmel, Richmond.

When the train reached Accrington Adrian pretended to be in a hurry and dashed off into the crowd ahead of Denise. He did not want to look at her again until he had thought of a way to express the immense love and gratitude he felt for her.

That night in bed he turned to her and said her name softly.

'Denise.'

'Yes, Adrian?'

'Do you remember the afternoon in the Coroke train when you unfastened your case and took out an exercise book and held it in your dainty gloved hands so I could stare at your name?'

•

Adrian got used to calling her Denise instead of Earth Angel. Knowing her name made it much easier to talk to her in bed at night, although he still hadn't spoken to her on the train.

Each afternoon he stood or sat in her compartment and practised under his breath some of the ways he might start a conversation when the right time came.

'Excuse me, Denise. I hope you don't mind me presuming to talk to you like this.'

'Allow me to introduce myself. My name is Adrian Sherd, and yours, I believe, is Denise McNamara.'

Whenever he glanced at Denise, she was grave and patient and understanding—just as she was at night when he talked to her for hours about his hopes and plans and dreams. She wasn't anxious for him to babble some polite introduction. The bond between them did not depend on mere words.

Their affair was not all peaceful. One night a girl from Canterbury Ladies' College stood near Adrian on the Swindon station. She was one of the girls he used to see chatting to Eastern Hill boys on the trams. (Adrian wondered why she was waiting for a train to the outer suburbs when she should have lived deep in the shrubbery of a garden suburb.) If she got into his compartment and saw him looking at Denise and guessed that the girl from Mount Carmel was his girlfriend, the Canterbury girls and Eastern Hill boys would laugh for weeks over the story of the Catholic boy and girl who travelled home together but never spoke.

Adrian was ready to walk up to Denise and say the first thing that came into his head. But the Canterbury girl got into a first-class compartment, and he was free to go on courting Denise without being judged by non-Catholics who didn't understand.

Every day Adrian wrote the initials D. McN. on scraps of paper—and then scribbled them out so no one would know his girlfriend's name. It bothered him that he couldn't write her address or telephone number and enjoy the sight of them in private places like the back covers of his exercise books.

One night he stood in a public telephone box and searched through the directory for a McNamara who lived in Accrington. There were two—I. A. and K. J. Adrian knew how to tell Catholic names from non-Catholic. He guessed the K. J. stood for Kevin John and decided that was Denise's father. Kevin's address was 24 Cumberland Road.

Adrian found Cumberland Road in a street directory in a newsagent's shop and memorised its location. Every night, walking down the ramp from the Accrington station a few paces behind Denise, he looked across the railway line in the direction of Cumberland Road. There was nothing to see except rows of white or cream weatherboard houses, but just knowing that her own house was somewhere among them made his stomach tighten.

He longed for just one glimpse of her home, and envied the people who could stroll freely past it every day while he had to keep well away. If Denise saw him in her street she would think he was much too forward in his wooing. The only way to see her house was to sneak down Cumberland Road late at night, perhaps in some sort of disguise.

On Saturday nights Adrian worried about Denise's safety. He hoped her parents kept her inside the house, out of sight of the gangs of young fellows wandering the streets all over Melbourne. The newspapers called the young fellows bodgies, and every Monday the *Argus* had a story about a bodgie gang causing trouble. Bodgies didn't often rape (most gangs had girl members known as widgies) but Adrian knew a bodgie wouldn't be able to control himself if he met Denise alone on her way to buy the Saturday night newspaper for her father.

Adrian looked through the racks of pamphlets in the Swindon parish church. He bought one called *So Your Daughter Is a Lady Now?* The picture on the cover showed a husband and wife with arms linked watching a young man with a bowtie draping a stole over their daughter's shoulders. They were all Americans, and the girl was obviously going on a date. Denise hadn't been on a date of course (Adrian himself would be the first and only man to date her) but she was old enough to attract the attention of undesirables.

Adrian intended to warn her parents of their responsibilities. He sealed the pamphlet in an envelope addressed to Mr K. J. McNamara, 24 Cumberland Road, Accrington. He kept the envelope hidden in his schoolbag overnight. Next morning he could hardly believe he had planned to post it to Denise's father. He saw Mr McNamara opening the envelope and holding up the pamphlet and saying to his daughter, 'Got any idea who'd do an idiotic thing like this? Any young fellows been making calf's eyes at you lately?'

Denise looked at the young man in the bowtie and thought at once of Adrian Sherd who stood devotedly beside her seat in the train each afternoon. She was so embarrassed that she decided to travel in another carriage for a few weeks until Sherd's ardour had cooled a little.

133

Adrian tore up the pamphlet and burned the pieces. On the back of the envelope he rearranged the letters D-E-N-I-S-E M-C-N-A-M-A-R-A, hoping to find a secret message about his and Denise's future happiness. But all he could compose was nonsense:

SEND ME IN A CAR, MA
or SIN NEAR ME, ADAM C.
or AM I A CAD, MRS NENE?

He counted the letters in her name and took fourteen as his special number. Every morning at school he hung his cap and coat on the fourteenth peg from the end. Every Sunday in church he walked down the aisle counting the seats and sat in the fourteenth. He looked up the fourteenth verse of the fourteenth chapter of the fourteenth book of the Bible. It described Judah and the Israelites taking rich booty from captured cities. Adrian interpreted the text metaphorically. It meant that God was on his side and he would prosper in his courtship of Denise.

One night he wrote the names of all the main towns in Tasmania on scraps of paper and shuffled them together. The fourteenth name he turned up was TRIABUNNA. The quiet little fishing port on the east coast was destined to be the place where he and his wife would consummate their marriage.

The Tasmanian countryside was at its most beautiful in early autumn. In the days when dead elm leaves blew against the windows of the Coroke train, Adrian thought of the first days of his marriage.

Sherd and his wife spent their wedding night on a ship crossing Bass Strait. The new Mrs Sherd was still shy in her husband's presence. She went on chattering about the day's events until nearly midnight. Sherd knew she was worried about undressing in front of him. When she couldn't put off going to bed any longer he decided to make things easier for her. He took out a book and buried his face in it. He looked up at his wife once or twice, but only when she couldn't see him.

Sherd undressed quickly while his wife was kneeling with her face in her hands and saying her night prayers. Then he made her sit beside him on the bed. He kissed her gently and told her to forget all she might have heard from radio programs and films about the wedding night. He said he had never forgotten the story in the Bible about Tobias or someone who told his wife on their wedding night that they were going to pray to God instead of gratifying their passions.

Sherd said, 'The whole story of how we first met in Our Lady of Good Counsel's Church and got to know each other on the Coroke train and then learned to love each other over the years is a wonderful example of how God arranges the destinies of those who serve Him.

'I know you're tired, darling, after all you've been through today, but I want you to kneel down beside the bed with me and say one decade of the Rosary just like Tobias and his bride on their wedding night.

'We're doing this for two reasons: first to thank God for bringing us together like this, and second'—Adrian hung his head and sighed, and hoped she realised he had been through a lot before he met her—'because I want to make reparation for some sins of mine long ago and prove to God and you that I married you for love and not lust.'

Sherd was surprised how easy it was to spend his wedding night like Tobias. While his wife dropped off to sleep beside him in her nightdress (should it have been a style recommended by the National Catholic Girls' Movement, or was it all right in the privacy of the marriage bed for a Catholic wife to dress a little like an American film star to help her overcome her nervousness?) he lay with his hands crossed on his chest and congratulated himself.

He remembered the year long before when his passions had been like wild beasts. Night after night he had grunted and slobbered over the suntanned bodies of American women. Nothing could stop him. Prayers, confession, the danger of hell, even the fear that he might ruin his health—they were all useless.

Then he had met Denise McNamara, and in all the seven years since then he had committed not one sin of impurity, even in thought. Of course, many times during those seven years he had looked forward to marrying Denise. But he had proved on his wedding night that his dreams of marriage were certainly not inspired by any carnal desire.

His only regret was that Denise herself would never know his story. He could hint to her that she had changed his life and saved him from misery. But in her innocence she could never imagine the filth she had rescued him from.

Sherd lay awake for a long time thinking over the wonderful story of his life. As the ship neared the pleasant island of Tasmania, his heart overflowed with happiness at the thought of the weeks ahead. His honeymoon was the last chapter of a strange story. And one day he would write that story in the form of an epic poem or a play in three acts or a novel. He would write it under a nom de plume so that he could tell the truth about himself without embarrassment. Even Denise would not know he was the author. But he would leave a copy in the house where she would see it and read it. She could not fail to be moved by it. They would sit down and discuss it together. And then the truth would slowly dawn on her.

At school Adrian kept away from Cornthwaite and his former friends. He thanked God that they all lived on the Frankston line and never came near his train at night. He could never have faced Denise again if she had seen him with them and imagined they were his friends. He saw them leering at her and heard O'Mullane scoffing at him (almost loud enough for Denise to hear), 'Christ on a crutch, Sherd, you mean you gave up your American tarts for her?'

Adrian's new friends were some of the boys whose names he had once marked with golden rays on a sketch of the classroom. They were obviously in the state of grace. All of them lived in garden suburbs and travelled home on trams. They talked a lot about the Junction. (Adrian eventually discovered that this was Camberwell Junction but he was not much wiser, since he had never been there.) Every night at the Junction, girls from Padua Convent crowded onto the boys' trams. At St Carthage's, Adrian's friends squealed or waved their arms or pushed each other hard on the chest or staggered and reeled and did strange little dances whenever someone mentioned the Padua girls.

At first Adrian wondered if he had stumbled onto something shocking—a pact of lust between these fresh-faced boys and the Padua girls. Groups of them were meeting in a park somewhere in tree-shaded Camberwell and behaving like young pagans together. But when he had listened closely to his friends for a few weeks and learned to ignore their animal noises and bird squawks, he realised the most they ever did was to talk to some of the Padua girls on the crowded trams (although some of the more daring fellows did play tennis with the girls on Saturday mornings).

It puzzled Adrian that their only aim seemed to be to know as many Padua girls as possible. Sometimes they held frantic conversations that meant almost nothing but gave them the opportunity to blurt out dozens of Padua names.

'Helen told me Deidre couldn't play on Saturday because Carmel and Felicity called round with Felicity's mother to take them out in the car.'

'Yes, but Deidre told me she was upset to miss the doubles comp and Barbara had to forfeit. She couldn't have Maureen or Clare for a partner.'

Adrian listened to them impatiently. He wished he could have told them he didn't have to babble to a tramload of giggling Padua girls because he had already chosen the pick of the Catholic girls on the Coroke line for his own.

Sometimes a fellow said, 'Tell us about your social life, Adrian.'

Adrian always parried the question. His friends would never have understood that he and Denise had no need for tennis and dances.

Sometimes Adrian's new friends seemed so innocent that he wondered if they had ever experienced an impure temptation. But one morning Barry Kellaway rolled his eyes and pretended to stagger and said, 'It's all right for you lazy baskets. You were snoring your heads off last night while Mother Nature was torturing me.'

Martin Dillon made eyes at Kellaway and sidled up to him and said, 'Did Mummy's little Barry mess his pyjamas in his sleep, eh?'

Damian Laity grabbed Kellaway from behind and twisted his arms and said, 'Tell us everything, Kaggs. Who were you holding in your arms when you woke up this morning?'

Adrian listened quietly. He knew Kellaway had had a wet dream. Over the next few weeks, every boy in the group had one and talked about it next day.

Their talk was very different from the stories that Cornthwaite and his friends used to bring to school. Adrian's former friends were reticent and modest about their adventures. Seskis would say simply, 'Rhonda Fleming nearly killed me last night.' Or O'Mullane would say, 'I saw a colossal tart on the train and when I got home I went into the woodshed and rubbed myself nearly raw.' The others would nod quietly as if to say, 'It could happen to anyone.'

Kellaway and Dillon and Laity were proud of their dreams and recounted them like adventure stories with themselves as heroes. It was all the more fun because nothing they did in dreams was sinful. (Adrian had his own wet dreams now, but he didn't enjoy them. They were confused struggles in landscapes suspiciously like America.)

Adrian's new friends looked forward to their dreams. Laity marked his in his pocket diary. He had calculated that he had a wet dream every twenty days or so. On the eighteenth or nineteenth day he would tell the others it was due any day. Kellaway and Dillon would say, 'Better not stand too close to Catherine or Beth in the tram this afternoon or you might end up married to them in bed tonight.'

Adrian thought of himself and Denise in the Coroke train and was disgusted by the loose talk about the Padua girls.

If a fellow described a dream that was too unseemly he usually apologised at the end of his story. Kellaway said one morning, 'The tram was somewhere in East Camberwell. I kept praying, "Please, God, make the Padua girls get off before it's too late." But they kept crowding round me. The conductor asked me what was the matter and I told him to stand between me and the girls to hide what I was going to do. But then it happened. Some of the girls screamed. The conductor started wrestling with me. And I know you'll never forgive me for this, Dillon, but I reached out and tried to grab you-know-who. Yes, it was your one and only Marlene with the adorable legs. I just couldn't help myself.'

Some of the stories were lost on Adrian because the people or the places in them were known only to the Camberwell boys. But one morning he heard a story as sensational as any that Cornthwaite or his dirty friends had told.

It was the time of the Royal Tour of Australia. Every morning the *Argus* had full-colour pictures of the Royal couple, showing Her Majesty's frocks and hats in all their gorgeous detail. One Saturday the Royal car was due to pass only a few miles from Swindon. St Carthage's and every other school for miles around had a space reserved along the route. Nearly every boy from St Carthage's turned up early and waited for hours in the sun for the Queen and the Duke to drive past.

On the following Monday, Damian Laity gathered his friends together and told them solemnly that his dream had come a few days early and it was nothing to laugh about this time.

He said, 'It must have been all those hours I sat in the sun. I must have gone mad with sunstroke. I couldn't eat anything for tea except half a family brick of ice cream just before bed. All I can remember after that is waiting and waiting for Her car. When I saw it coming I turned into a raving lunatic. I ran out onto the road with only my singlet on and jumped up to the running board of the car. The kids from the public schools were all roaring and screaming at me. I think the Padua girls saw me too. I couldn't stop myself. I jumped into the back seat beside Her. She was wearing that beautiful lime-green shantung frock and the hat with white feathers. I tried to put my arms around Her. As soon as I touched Her elbow-length gloves it ended. Thank God I didn't do anything worse to Her with all those people watching. I lay awake for hours after it was over. I kept seeing the headlines in all the papers on Monday: MONSTER FROM CATHOLIC COLLEGE DISGRACES AUSTRALIA.'

Mr and Mrs Adrian Sherd arrived at Triabunna in the early afternoon. They had been married exactly twenty-four hours. They unpacked their suitcases in a sunlit room on an upper floor of a hotel with every modern convenience. Then they strolled hand in hand along the beachfront.

The place was deserted. Sherd was glad there was no one around to overhear them when they stopped every few yards and he whispered, 'I love you, Denise,' and his wife answered, 'I love you too, Adrian.' He remembered a fellow at school named Cornthwaite who used to change his seat in a train to get a better view of a couple smoushing (as he called it) and to watch where the fellow put his hands.

On the way back to the hotel for tea, Sherd seriously considered waiting for another night to consummate the marriage. He could see his wife was in no hurry for it—she was quite content just to hold hands and hear her husband say he loved her.

Sherd felt the same way himself. He was experiencing the truth of something he had first discovered years before (when he lay awake at night thinking of a girl in a beige school uniform to save himself from a habit of sin)—that the joy of hearing a beautiful chaste woman say, 'I love you' was far more wonderful than rolling around naked with all the stars of Hollywood.

Later that night, when they were sitting together reading, Sherd reminded himself that his wife had grown up in the same pagan world as himself, that she must have learned from films and magazines what people expected newlyweds to get up to on their honeymoon, and that if he didn't introduce her to the physical side of marriage soon, she might start brooding over it or even suspect that he was not quite normal in mind or body.

When she was ready to undress for bed, he decided after all that now was the time to reveal the mysteries of the marriage bed. But he was determined that what he was about to do should be as different as possible from the purely animal things he had once dreamed of doing to American women. Denise must not have the least suspicion that he had ever been attracted to her purely for the physical gratification he might get from her.

He knelt down and closed his eyes to pray while she got into her nightdress. When she had said her own prayers and climbed into bed, he turned out the light and undressed himself. He did not want her to glimpse his organ before he had prepared her for it by a long speech.

Sherd lay down beside his wife and spoke. 'Denise, darling, no matter how carefully you were protected by your parents and the nuns at the academy, you probably still stumbled on some of the secrets of human reproduction.

'Perhaps you had to go into a public lavatory once, and your eyes strayed up to the wall and you saw a drawing of a huge, thick, hideous monster of a thing and lay awake for weeks afterwards wondering whether men really had organs like that on their bodies and whether, if ever you were married, your husband would threaten you with one on your wedding night.

'Perhaps you borrowed a novel from a non-Catholic library without realising what it was about, and read a few pages about some American gangster with the morals of an alley cat. You shut the book in disgust and returned it to the library, but you wondered for a long time afterwards how many men treated women as pretty playthings to be used for their pleasure.

'Perhaps you innocently looked into the practical notebook of a schoolfellow who was doing biology and saw her drawings of a dissected rabbit and noticed the little lump with the label ERECTILE PENIS AND SHEATH and went away alarmed to think that male rabbits and therefore men, and your own future husband too, had something on them that could actually stretch and grow bigger.

'Perhaps you once spent a holiday on a farm and your parents were careless enough to let you see the bull running like a madman to climb on top of a cow. Or perhaps you were just shopping in Accrington one Saturday morning and there, right in front of your eyes, were two dogs in the gutter and one of them suddenly poked this long red sticky thing at the other one and forced it to submit.'

Adrian paused and sighed. He hoped Denise realised it was not his fault that she had had these rude shocks. If only it had been possible, he would have shielded her from all sight of male animals and broad-minded books and films. Then she could have learned the whole story from her husband.

He waited for her to speak. He was anxious to find out just how much she knew. Then she answered him, and he treasured for the rest of his life the words she said.

'Adrian, I understand how concerned you are for me, and I don't blame you for imagining that some of those dreadful things might have happened to me. But you needn't have been all that anxious.

'Oh, of course I was puzzled sometimes about things I read in the papers or heard non-Catholics whispering about. But don't forget I was a Child of Mary. (Didn't you ever go to eight o'clock mass on the third Sunday of the month and see the rows and rows of Children of Mary in our blue-and-white regalia and hope that your future wife was somewhere among them?) And whenever I did wonder a little about those things, I told myself they were none of my business. I knew if I ever got married I could learn all I had to know from the Pre-Cana Conferences for engaged couples. And if my vocation was to remain single, it was better for me to know as little as possible about that side of life anyway.'

When Sherd heard this he was so overjoyed that he kissed his wife and told her again and again what a rare treasure she was. He would almost have been content to lie there looking at her lovely face until he fell asleep. But he owed it to his wife to finish what he had begun explaining to her.

He said, 'Denise, my innocent angel Denise, now that I know how carefully you've guarded yourself all these years, it makes my task tonight so much easier.

'If you had in fact seen a dog or a bull chasing the female, or a foul drawing on a toilet wall, you probably would have thought people were no different from animals when they mated. I'm sorry to say there are plenty of men who do treat the whole thing as a kind of game for their own pleasure. But thank God you'll never come into contact with them. God Himself saw to it that your beauty and virtue attracted the sort of Catholic husband who understands the true purpose of sexual relations in marriage.

'I won't beat about the bush, Denise darling. In one sense, what I'm going to do to you tonight may seem no different from what a bull does to his cows or a Hollywood film director does to one of his starlets.' (Denise looked startled and puzzled. He would have to explain this point to her later.) 'It's not a pretty thing to watch, I'm afraid, but it's the only way our poor fallen human natures can reproduce themselves. If it seems dirty or even ridiculous to you, I can only ask you to pray that you'll understand it better as time goes by.

'The trouble is that a man is cursed with a very powerful instinct to reproduce himself. One day when we've been married long enough to trust each other with our deepest secrets, I'll tell you a little about 1953. That was a year when I plumbed the depths of despair because'—Sherd chose his words carefully—'I could hardly find the strength to resist the male instinct to reproduce my species. And when you hear my story you'll realise what a mighty urge it is and why you'll have to excuse me for giving in to it about twice a week—at least until you find you're expecting a child.'

Sherd wanted to say much more, but he was anxious not to confuse his bride with too much information all at once. The moment he had waited for all his life had arrived.

He switched on the bedlamp, kissed his wife to calm her fears and rolled back the bedclothes. She was still in her nightdress, but fortunately she had closed her eyes and gone limp. He removed the nightdress as gently as he could and admired her nude body.

Her eyes were still closed. He wondered if she had swooned. But he said in any case the words he had memorised years before for just this occasion. (They came from a book that his mother had borrowed from the sixpenny lending library in Accrington. When his parents were out of the house he used to look through their library books. Most were respectable detective stories, but in one historical novel he had found a scene where a man surprised a young woman bathing nude in the village stream. Young Sherd had been so impressed by the man's words that he learned them to use on his honeymoon.)

Sherd said over his wife's body, 'Denise, it's almost a crime that such charms should ever be concealed beneath the garments that our society decrees as conventional. Let me feast on your treasures and praise them as they deserve.'

Before Sherd could praise his wife's charms separately, she opened her eyes briefly and looked shyly up at him and said, 'Please, darling, don't keep me in suspense too long.'

As gently and considerately as he could, Sherd lowered his body into position and engaged in sexual congress with her.

Afterwards he lay beside her with the blankets covering them both. He was ready to say, 'I'm sorry, Denise, but I did my best to warn you beforehand,' when she looked at him and said, 'Why, Adrian, I think it was somehow rather beautiful. Not that I don't appreciate all you said to prepare me for the worst, but really, I can't help being amazed at the wonderful way God designed our bodies so they complement each other in the act of generation.'

While she pulled on her nightdress in the darkness she said, 'And Adrian, if you feel a need for my body again in the next few days, please don't hesitate to ask me. After all, I did promise to honour and obey you. So if this act gives you all the pleasure I think it does, you're welcome to do it whenever you wish—within reason, of course.'

The Tasmanian honeymoon of Mr and Mrs Adrian Sherd lasted for twelve days of a year in the early 1960s, but the thought of it sustained Adrian Sherd all through the autumn months of 1954. In all that time he never once confessed a sin of impurity in thought or deed.

Sometimes, while he knelt outside the confessional, Adrian arranged a debate between two of the many voices that started arguing whenever he tried to hear what his conscience had to say.

> FIRST VOICE: Sherd is about to tell the priest that the worst sins he has committed in the past month are disobeying his parents and losing his temper with his young brothers. But in fact he lies awake every night dreaming of coition with a naked woman in a hotel room in Tasmania. I submit that these thoughts are mortal sins against the Ninth Commandment.

SECOND VOICE: In denying the claims of the previous speaker, I rest my case on three points.

1. When Sherd thinks about his marriage to Mrs Denise Sherd, née McNamara, he does not enjoy any sexual pleasure. True, he experiences a sort of exalted joy, but this is purely the result of his finding himself married at last to the young woman he has loved since his schooldays. We can see the truth of this, my first point, if we examine Sherd's penis while he contemplates the happiness of his honeymoon. At no time does it seem aware of what is going on in his mind.

2. When, some time ago now, Sherd was unfortunately in the habit of thinking at night about the American outdoors and of lewd orgies with film personalities, he was enjoying something he knew to be quite imaginary. On the other hand, his thoughts of his marriage to Miss McNamara are thoughts of a future that he has every intention of bringing to pass. Far from indulging in idle dreams, when he thinks of his honeymoon in Tasmania he is making a serious effort to plan his life for the good of his immortal soul.

3. It goes without saying that in all his visits to America, Sherd never once married or proposed marriage to the women he consorted with. Mrs Sherd, however, is his wife. All the endearments he offers her are proper expressions of his conjugal love and, as such, are perfectly lawful.

Adrian Sherd as adjudicator awarded the debate to the Second Voice and was sure that any reasonable theologian would have done the same.

•

148

So long as Adrian was in love with a Catholic girl and in the state of grace, he wasn't ashamed to visit his Aunt Kathleen and talk about Catholic devotions.

One day when she said she had enrolled him as a Spiritual Associate of the Sisters of the Most Precious Blood, he was genuinely interested to know what benefits this would bring him. In the days of his lust, the things his aunt did for him had been wasted, but now they earned valuable additions to his store of sanctifying grace.

Aunt Kathleen said, 'The names of all Associates are kept permanently in a casket beside the altar in the Mother House of the Sisters at Wollongong. Each day after their Divine Office, the Sisters recite a special prayer for all Associates. And best of all, they keep a lamp burning perpetually in their chapel for the intentions of you and me and all the other names in the casket.'

While his aunt was out of the room, Adrian leafed through her stacks of Catholic magazines, looking for other leagues or confraternities with special privileges for members. He puzzled over a magazine he had never seen before—*St Gerard's Monthly*, published by the Divine Zeal Fathers at their monastery in Bendigo.

The centre pages were full of photos with brief captions: *The Hosking Family of Birchip, Vic.*; *The McInerney Family of Elmore, Vic.*; *The Mullaly Family of Taree, NSW.* Each family consisted of husband and wife and at least four children. Four was the bare minimum. In some of the magazines Adrian found plenty of eights and nines and tens. The record seemed to belong to the Farrelly family of Texas, Queensland. There were sixteen people in the photo. Five or six were adults, but Adrian assumed that these were the oldest children. One of the women was holding a baby—she was probably the mother of the fourteen.

Adrian thought at first that the families were entrants in some kind of competition. But there was no mention of prizes. Apparently the only reward for a family was the pleasure of seeing themselves in the pages of *St Gerard's Monthly* and feeling superior to the Catholic families with less than four children.

The mothers were all what Adrian's father would have called well preserved. Some were even quite pretty. There were none with fat legs or large sagging breasts like Mrs De Kloover, who led nine children into mass every Sunday at Our Lady of Good Counsel's.

It was this that interested Adrian most. He was planning to become the father of a Catholic family himself, and there were still a few things he wasn't sure about. One thing that worried him was whether he would still be attracted to his wife after she had borne him several children. The pictures in *St Gerard's Monthly* reassured him. Men like Mr McInerney and Mr Farrelly were apparently drawn to their wives long after the romantic excitement of the honeymoon had died away.

It would be possible for Denise to have at least ten children and still keep her youthful figure and complexion. Over the years she would probably develop a Catholic mother's face like some of those in the photos. This was very different from the face of a non-Catholic mother of two or three children. The Catholic mother wore very little make-up— the non-Catholic plastered herself with powder and lipstick and sometimes even a little rouge. The Catholic's face was open, frank, quick to smile, but still as modest as a girl's in the presence of any man other than her husband. The non-Catholic's looked as though it concealed many a guilty secret.

The difference between the faces was probably the result of Catholic husbands' copulating with their wives quietly in the dark while their children were asleep in the surrounding rooms, whereas non-Catholics often did it in broad daylight in their lounge rooms while their children were packed off to their aunts or grandparents for the weekend. Also, the Catholic men would have done it fairly quickly and without any antics that might have overemphasised its place in the marriage, while the non-Catholics probably talked and joked about it and thought of ways to make it last longer.

As well as a Catholic face there was a Catholic figure—Catholic breasts with gentle curves and not enough prominence to attract unwanted admirers, and Catholic legs with ankles and calves neatly shaped to lead the eye away from the area above the knees. As the years brought her more children, Mrs Denise Sherd would develop these too.

It was only logical that there were also Catholic and non-Catholic *pudenda*. Although Adrian had got out of the habit of thinking of such things, he allowed himself to distinguish briefly between a modest shrinking Catholic kind and another kind that was somehow a little the worse for wear.

Each issue of *St Gerard's Monthly* had a column called 'The Hand that Rules the World' by someone called Monica. Adrian read one of these columns.

> Recently on our holidays in Melbourne I boarded a tram with six of my seven. (Son No. 1 was elsewhere with Proud Father.) Most of my readers will be familiar

151

with the cool stare of scrutiny which I had from Mrs Young Modern in the opposite seat with her pigeon pair.

Of course I returned her gaze. After all, I had far more right to be critical, with six bonny young Australians to my credit.

Well, it turned out that she was more interested in inspecting my children than their mother. Of course she was hoping to find a shoe unshined or a sock that needed darning. 'Sorry to disappoint you, Mrs Two Only,' I said under my breath, 'but while you were gossiping at your bridge party or out in your precious car, I wasn't wasting *my* time.'

I had the satisfaction of seeing her face fall when she realised my six were at least as beautifully turned out as her two. If we had got on speaking terms I'm sure I would have had to answer the old question for the hundredth time—Readers, are you tired of it, too?—'How on earth do you manage?'

There was much more, but Adrian paused to think. He wished Denise could have read 'The Hand that Rules the World'. As the mother of a large family she would have to be ready for all those stares and questions from non-Catholics. Monica's columns were full of arguments that Catholic mothers could turn to when they were tempted to feel discontented with their lot. For instance, she pointed out that bringing a new soul into the world was infinitely more worthwhile than acquiring a luxury such as a washing machine. (And anyway, as she reminded her readers, a thorough boiling in a good old-fashioned copper did a much better job than a few twirls in a slick-looking machine.)

Adrian decided that after his marriage he would send a subscription to the Divine Zeal Fathers so Denise would get her *St Gerard's Monthly* regularly.

When his aunt found him reading the magazine she took it politely from him and said, 'No harm done, young man, but *St Gerard's Monthly* is really more suitable for parents only.' Adrian was angry to think there might have been much more useful information in the magazine that he hadn't found. He resented his spinster aunt treating him like a child when he was seriously concerned about the problems of Catholic parenthood.

One night towards the end of their honeymoon, Sherd reminded his wife that the natural result of their love for each other might well be a large family. He was about to list some of the problems this might bring, when she interrupted him.

'Darling, you don't seem to realise. Ever since I can remember, my mother got *St Gerard's Monthly*. It taught me what to expect from marriage and to accept whatever family God might send. And you might think this was silly of me, but after I fell in love with you, one of my favourite daydreams was opening up the centre pages of the *Monthly* and seeing a picture of the Sherd family from wherever we came from.'

While Sherd and his wife were still honeymooning in Tasmania, Adrian spent ten minutes each morning in the Swindon parish church searching among the racks of Australian Catholic Truth Society pamphlets. He was looking for one simple piece of information. When he found it he would know all that was necessary for his role as a Catholic husband.

Each day he borrowed two or three pamphlets and read them under the desk in the Christian Doctrine period. Next morning he returned them to the racks in the church and went on with his search. He read page after page advising husbands and wives to be courteous and considerate, to set a good example to each other, and to co-operate unselfishly in the upbringing of the children that God sent them. But he did not find the information he needed.

What he wanted to know was how often he should have carnal relations with his wife to be sure of fertilising her as soon as possible after the wedding. He believed there was a certain time each month when it was easy for a woman to conceive. If he (or his wife) could discover when this was, he could arrange to copulate with her on the correct date each month and so make it easier for God to bless them with children.

But the problem was to find when this important date occurred. Anyone could tell when a female dog or cat was on heat from the odd way it behaved, but it was unthinkable that Denise should have to get into a state like that to let him know she was ready to be impregnated. If women were no different from dogs or cats in this respect, the odds were that somewhere, at some time, he would have seen a woman on heat. But in all the years he had been watching women and girls on trains and trams he had never seen one who looked as if she was even thinking of sexual matters.

Adrian searched the pamphlet racks for a week and then gave up. But without the information he could not think realistically about his future. He decided to invent a game that would make his marriage to Denise seem true to life.

Each night when he got home from school he took two dice from his brothers' Ludo box. He shook the first and rolled it. An even number meant that Sherd (the husband) felt in the mood to suggest intercourse to his wife that night.

Before throwing the second of the dice he saw himself saying casually to Denise (they were still on their honeymoon, so the conversation could take place as they strolled back from the beach to their hotel) that it might be nice to give themselves to each other that night in bed. Then he rolled the die.

If it showed an even number, Denise would answer something like, 'Yes, darling, I'd be more than happy if you used your marriage rights tonight.' If it showed an odd number she said, 'If you don't mind, I'm not feeling strong enough for it. Perhaps some other time.' And she smiled warmly to show that she loved him as much as ever.

On a night when both dice came up with even numbers, Adrian would rest now and then from his homework and enjoy the quiet contentment that a husband felt when he knew his wife would willingly submit to him a few hours later. But it was almost as pleasant on the other nights to look forward to a half-hour in bed together sharing their inmost thoughts and looking forward to years more of such happiness in the future.

But throwing the dice was only part of the game. Assuming that a woman could conceive on one day of each month, there was one chance in thirty that an act of intercourse would be successful. Adrian chalked a faint line around a section of thirty bricks on the outside of the lounge-room chimney. On one of the bricks near the centre of the marked area he put a faint X. Then he hid a tennis ball in a geranium bush near the chimney.

Each morning after a night when the two dice had showed evens (and Mrs Sherd had yielded to her husband) Adrian walked quietly to the lounge-room chimney on his way back from the lavatory. He found the tennis ball and wet it in the dew or under the garden tap. Then he took aim at the panel of bricks, closed his eyes tightly and tossed the ball.

He tossed it carelessly and with no deliberate effort to hit the brick marked X. When he heard the impact of the ball he opened his eyes and looked for the wet mark on the bricks. If this mark (or the greater part of it) lay within the perimeter of the brick marked X, then the conjugal act of the previous night between Mr and Mrs Sherd would have resulted in conception.

Adrian shook the dice each night until the honeymoon was over. On four of those nights a pair of even numbers came up, but in each case the mark of the tennis ball was well wide of the lucky brick.

At the end of this time he was satisfied with the way the dice and the ball were working, except that things weren't happening fast enough. He wanted to share with his wife as soon as possible the joys of Catholic parenthood, but at the rate he was going it might take years—so many years, perhaps, that it might be time to marry Denise before he had discovered what marriage was really like.

He decided to throw the dice seven times each night. This meant he would experience a week of marriage every day of his life in Accrington. At that rate a year of marriage would take less than two months of 1954. By the end of

Form Five he would have been married for nearly four years and fathered as many children. At that stage he would probably have to speed things up a little more. He would have to be careful not to get too close to the time (he could hardly bear to think about it) when Denise would begin to show signs of ageing. According to the pictures in *St Gerard's Monthly* she could produce at least a dozen children before this happened. But if he had a lucky run with the dice and ball they might have twelve children long before they were forty years old.

After the birth of each child beyond the fourth, he would have a special throw of three dice to decide his wife's health. If the number thirteen came up, she would be showing signs of varicose veins in her legs. He would send her to a Catholic doctor for a thorough check-up. If nothing could be done for her, he could alter the rules of the game so that he abstained unselfishly from time to time to give her a sporting chance.

Living through seven nights of marriage each night was not as interesting as he had expected. The high point of each week came each morning at the chimney. Sometimes he had to toss the ball three or four times for a week when Denise had been unusually compliant.

At last, after eighteen weeks of marriage (eighteen days of Accrington time) he opened his eyes one morning at the chimney and saw a broad wet blotch in the middle of the brick that stood for conception. He had always thought he would be able to take such a thing calmly, but he found himself wanting to run and tell the news to someone—even his parents or brothers. All that day at school he wished he had a friend to share his secret.

Adrian went on throwing the dice for a few more nights. His wife couldn't be sure she had conceived until she saw a doctor. They were entitled to perform the act a few more times until then. But as soon as the doctor had pronounced her pregnant, Adrian put away the dice and spent his nights at Accrington living through the weeks when he and his wife spent their time before sleep holding hands and talking about their first child.

Much as he loved Denise, he found he was bored. It wasn't that he needed sexual gratification. He had always said, and he still maintained, that the touch of Denise's hand or the sight of her bare white shoulders was enough to satisfy all his physical wants. And it wasn't that he was running out of things to talk about. There were still hundreds of stories he wanted to tell her about his early years. The trouble was that he couldn't endure the long months of her pregnancy without the fun of seeing the dice and ball do their work.

The next day was Saturday at Accrington. Adrian knew what he had to do to make his future more inviting. He took the dice out into the shed in his backyard. He had a sheaf of pages from an exercise book to use as a calendar. There was enough space for all the years he wanted. He threw a die once to decide the sex of their first child. It was a girl. They named it Maureen Denise.

In the first week after the mother and child came home from hospital, nothing happened. Then the dice started rolling again. Adrian threw them thirty times and scored five acts of sexual union. He went outside and tossed the tennis ball five times without success. Then he went back to his calendar in the shed and crossed a month off his married life and rolled the dice again.

Adrian worked all day with the dice and ball. (He told his brothers he was playing a game of Test cricket, with the dice to score runs and the ball to dismiss batsmen.) By evening he had been married nearly nine years and was the father of five daughters and one son.

As soon as he was home from mass on the Sunday morning, he went out to the shed again. He was looking forward to throwing the ball at the chimney again, but he couldn't face another day with the dice. He decided on an easy solution. He would simply toss the ball ten times for each month. It seemed silly after so many years of marriage to be always asking his wife's permission before the act. In future she would have to submit to it ten times a month whether she liked it or not.

By midday the best part of his life was over. He had been married fifteen years and fathered eleven children— eight daughters and three sons. Their names and birthdays were all entered in his calendar.

Now that he had worked out a future for himself he was exhausted and a little disappointed. He was almost sorry he had cheated by speeding up events instead of using the dice and ball patiently and enjoying each year as it came. He knew what people meant when they said their life was slipping away from them.

He sat beside the chimney wondering what he could think about in bed that night. A simple solution occurred to him. He multiplied fifteen by twelve to obtain the number of months of his active sexual life. Then he went back to the shed and cut up small squares of paper. He numbered them from one to one hundred and eighty and put them all into a tobacco tin. Each night he would shake the tin and draw out a number. He drew out a number for that very night. It was forty-three. From his calendar he learned that in month forty-three he was trying to father his fourth child.

That night (Accrington time) Adrian went to bed eager to meet the Denise who was already the mother of three young children. And the next day at school he wondered which of all the possible Denises would share his bed that night after he had consulted the numbers in the tobacco tin. She might have been a radiant young mother, fresh from breastfeeding her first child, or a mature woman like the mothers in *St Gerard's Monthly* with the curves of her body gently rounded by years of child-bearing and about her eyes the faintest shadows of weariness from caring for her eight or nine children all day.

On the last evening of their honeymoon, Sherd and his bride stood looking at the scene that had been called *Triabunna with Distant View of Maria Island* in the coloured booklet, *Tasmania: A Visitor's Guide*, on the bottom shelf of the bookcase in Sherd's boyhood home.

The newlyweds had to decide where to make their permanent home. Sherd wondered what was to stop them from settling among the low hills of Maria Island that were just then strangely bright in the last rays of the setting sun. If he could have been sure there was a Catholic church and school and a Catholic doctor on the island, he and his wife would have been happy for the rest of their lives on a small farm that looked across the water to Triabunna.

He only decided to return to Victoria for the sake of his wife. She was just a little homesick, and she said she preferred to live where she could visit her mother two or three times a year.

All that Adrian knew of Victoria was the western suburb of Melbourne where he had grown up and gone to primary school, Accrington and the few south-eastern suburbs that he crossed in the train to St Carthage's or explored on his bike at weekends, the landscape on either side of the railway line between Melbourne and Colac and a few miles of farmland around his uncle's property at Orford. None of these places seemed a fitting backdrop for the scenes of his married life—carrying a radiant Denise across the threshold of their first home, bringing her home from hospital with their first child and so on.

But Adrian knew of places in Victoria that were worthy settings for a great love story. They were landscapes so different from the suburbs of his childhood that even the trivial events of his married life would seem momentous, and Adrian, the husband, would forget all those Sundays when he had come home from mass with nothing to do but climb the solitary wattle tree in the backyard and look across rows of other backyards and wait for the six o'clock *Hit Parade* in the evening.

As a boy Adrian had travelled each January by train from Melbourne to his uncle's farm at Orford. On the morning of each journey he leaned against the dark-green leather backrest and studied the photographs in the corners of his compartment.

The titles of the photographs were brief and sometimes curiously imprecise—*Erskine Falls, Lorne*; *In the Strzelecki Ranges*; *Road to Marysville*; *Walwa*; *Camperdown with Mount Leura*; *Near Hepburn Springs*. In some of the pictures a solitary traveller, with arms folded, leaned against a tall treefern, or a motorcar empty of people stood motionless on an otherwise deserted gravel road leading towards a tiny archway where distant trees closed over against the daylight. Adrian knew from the waistcoats and moustaches of the travellers and the shapes of the cars and the brown hues of the sky and land that the photos had been taken years before. The bewhiskered men and the unseen people who had left their motorcars standing on dusty roads might have died long since. But Adrian was sure, from their grave gestures and solemn faces and the way they had stationed themselves at unlikely spots in the forest or by the roadside, that these travellers of olden times had discovered the true meaning of the Victorian countryside.

Leaning back in his window seat at Spencer Street station while drab red suburban trains dragged crowds of clerks and shop assistants into Melbourne to work, Adrian wanted to leave the city forever and journey to the landscapes of the dim photographs. Somewhere among forests of mountain ash or damp treeferns or beside a foaming creek, he would search for the secret that lay behind the most beautiful scenery in Victoria.

But the Port Fairy train followed the same route each year and Adrian had to get out at Colac and travel with his uncle to the same bare paddocks near Orford. Yet, as a married man at Triabunna, Tasmania, Adrian had still not forgotten the country of the photographs. He told his wife they would make their home in a valley beside a waterfall at Lorne, or on a hillside overlooking Camperdown with Mount Leura, or, best of all, in the trees above a bend in the road near Hepburn Springs.

He would need a suitable job or profession. Farming was too hard—it would leave him too little time with his new wife. But there were men who drove up sometimes to his uncle's farm and strolled around the paddocks without soiling their hands. He would be one of them—a veterinary surgeon or an expert from the Department of Agriculture. Looking back, he saw he had always been destined for this sort of life. As a boy in Form Four he had often relieved his boredom by staring at pages in his General Science textbook with diagrams of dissected rabbits or pictures of soil erosion labelled *Before* and *After*.

Sherd took his bride to their new home on a timbered hillside near Hepburn Springs and bought a savage Queensland heeler dog to protect her while he was away in the daytime. On the first night, after they had arranged their furniture and unpacked their wedding presents, he sat down with her in the spacious lounge room and looked thoughtful.

When she asked him what was the matter, he said, 'I was only thinking of the grave responsibility on my shoulders—to carry on where the nuns and priests left off and teach you the rest of the facts about marriage. Perhaps I should deal with one topic each night.

'Tonight I'll discuss a subject that probably made you shudder if ever you heard it mentioned when you were young and innocent—birth control. What I'm about to say is a summary of all I've read about birth control in Catholic pamphlets, and all I've been taught by priests and brothers.

'Any impartial observer would agree that the marriage act—that operation I've performed on you in the privacy of the marriage bed—must have a serious purpose quite apart from the fleeting pleasure associated with it. The purpose, as any rational person will agree, is the procreation of children. Now, this purpose is a part of what philosophers and theologians call the Natural Law. And the Natural Law was designed by Almighty God to make the world run smoothly. It must be obvious, then, that any tampering with the Natural Law is likely to have disastrous consequences. (Can you imagine the consequences if someone interfered with the way the planets revolve around the sun?)

'Well, birth control violates the Natural Law by removing the purpose from the marriage act. (You may be wondering how this is done. Without going into the sordid details, I can tell you there's a certain little piece of slimy rubber that non-Catholic chemists sell for profit. Armed with this disgusting weapon, a man can enjoy the pleasure without the purpose and defy the Natural Law.)

'You won't be surprised to learn that this grave sin has grave consequences. It's a known fact that artificial birth control causes profound physical and mental disturbances. I've heard from a priest who knows all about these matters that many non-Catholic couples are so afraid of the psychological effects of birth control that they just will not practise it. So you see the Natural Law is not just something the Catholic Church made up.'

While Sherd paced up and down the lounge-room carpet, his wife reclined on the sofa and drank in every word he said. Behind her the huge windows framed a vista of a twilit forested valley more satisfying than any of the scenes that the young Adrian used to stare at in railway carriages, wondering what was the secret behind their beauty.

When the Sherds had first moved into their home near

Hepburn Springs, they were so happy that they seemed to be enjoying a taste of heaven on earth. But looking through his lounge-room window after his discussion of birth control, Sherd realised that all they were enjoying was their rightful reward for following the Natural Law.

What he saw through his window was a valley where no sexual sin was ever committed. The Natural Law governed everything in sight. It caused the sky to glow and the tree-tops to tremble all over the forests near Hepburn Springs. It was at work too at Walwa, on the road to Marysville and in Camperdown with Mount Leura.

Sherd knew now what had drawn him to these scenes in the Port Fairy train years before. The mysterious secret beyond those lonely roads, the thing that travellers had abandoned their cars to search for, was the Natural Law.

He himself would never have to search for it again. He could see it in operation outside his lounge-room windows and even in the privacy of his own bedroom.

One night when the dice and the numbered tickets had transported Adrian to a night in the fourth month of his marriage when he would have liked to be intimate with his wife but she wasn't feeling up to it, he lay back with his hands behind his head and began to discuss with Denise the history of marriage down the ages.

He said, 'The union of Adam and Eve in the garden of Eden was not only the first marriage—it was the most perfect marriage in history, because it was God who intro-duced the young couple to each other and because the way they behaved in marriage was exactly as He had intended.

'You can imagine them meeting for the first time in

some leafy clearing far more pleasant than any place we know of near Hepburn Springs. They were both naked— yes, stark naked, because Adam's reason was in full control over his passions and there was no need for Eve to practise the virtue of modesty. With their perfect understanding of what God wanted them to do, they would have agreed to live together there and then—there was no long courtship such as we had to observe. No doubt they went through some simple wedding ceremony, and surely it was God who officiated. What a wonderful start to married life!

'They had no need to go away for a honeymoon. There were scenic spots and secluded walks all round them already. What happened next? Well, we can deduce that their acts of sexual communion would have been the most perfect ever performed. They would have looked into each other's eyes one afternoon and understood it was time to co-operate with God in creating a new human life. As they lay down together Adam's body would have shown none of those signs of uncontrollable passion that you might have glimpsed on me some nights in bed. Of course, at the last moment, when it was time to deposit his seed in the recep- tacle designed for the purpose, his organ must have behaved more or less like mine, but whereas I (with my fallen human nature) tend to lose control of myself for a few moments, he would have lain there quite calmly with his reason fully operative. He may well have chatted to Eve about some gorgeous butterfly flitting above them or pointed out some inspiring view through the trees around them.

'They lived in such close contact with God and obeyed His Will so completely that in all probability it was He who reminded them now and then that it was high time they mated again. The Bible tells us that God came and walked with them in the cool of the evening. You can imagine Him politely suggesting it to them as the sun sinks below the treetops of Eden. They smile and say what a good idea it is and then lie down on the nearest grassy bank and do it without any fuss.

'Of course they wouldn't have been the least ashamed to have God beside them while they did it. And He wouldn't have been embarrassed either—after all, it was He who invented the idea of human reproduction. I can see Him strolling a little way off to look at a bird's nest or let a squirrel run down his arm. Occasionally He glances back at the young couple and smiles wisely to Himself.

'Just to remind you of the vast difference between our First Parents in their perfect state and ourselves with our fallen natures, I'd like you to imagine how we would have managed if we'd tried to live like Adam and Eve.

'Think of me getting into your compartment on the Coroke train for the first time. I haven't got a stitch of clothing on and neither have you. (We'll have to suppose the other passengers are naked too.) I look at your face to try to assess your character, but I'm such a slave to my passions that I let my gaze fall on your other charms below. Meanwhile you notice the way I'm looking at you, and you can't decide whether I'm thinking of you as a possible mate for life or just the object of my momentary lust. So you don't know whether to sit still and meet my eyes or fold your arms in front of you and cross your legs tightly.

'And when I put my schoolbag on the rack above your head and I lean on tiptoes over your seat and the most private parts of me are only a foot or so from your face, what do you do? If your human nature was as perfect as Eve's in Paradise, you would look calmly at my organs to satisfy yourself that at least I was a fully developed man capable of fathering children. But because you have a fallen nature you're too frightened or horrified to look at them dangling in front of your eyes, so you go on reading your library book.

'This example might seem far-fetched, but believe me, it's the way God intended us to court each other. It was the sin of our First Parents that made us shy with each other. If we hadn't been born with Original Sin on our souls, our whole courtship would have been simple and beautiful. Instead of waiting all those months just to speak to you, I would have walked hand in hand with you to your parents' place on the first night I met you. (Your home would have been a mossy nook with walls of some vivid flowering vine—Accrington before the Fall would have had a subtropical climate and vegetation.)

'We find your parents sitting happily together coaxing a spotted fawn to eat from their hands. They come forward smiling to greet me—both naked, of course, but their bodies have no wrinkles or varicose veins or rolls of fat. I take no notice of your mother's body because I've seen thousands like it all over Melbourne. Your parents talk to me and soon understand what an ideal partner I'd be for their daughter. Next morning I come to take you away. There's no long-winded ceremony or speeches. They give us their blessing and we go off to find our own bower of blossoming foliage.

'It all seems so impossible and of course it is, because we live nowadays in a fallen world. And the worst result of our First Parents' sin is that a man can scarcely look at a woman now without his passions urging him to sin with her in thought or deed.

'I can see you're surprised to hear this, but you must remember that very few men have learned self-control the way I have. It's unpleasant to talk about, I know, but many men use their wives entirely for their own selfish pleasure.

'This sort of thing apparently began almost as soon as Adam and Eve's descendants started to populate the earth. The oldest cities in the world, Sumer and Akkad, had their walls covered with obscene drawings and carvings, so Brother Chrysostom told us once in his History class. The men of those cities must have had sexual thoughts all day long. The hot climate probably helped, but the main reason would have been that they had never heard of the Ten Commandments.

'You might have heard in your Christian Doctrine classes, Denise, that God gives every man a conscience, so that even a pagan in the days before Christ knew the difference between right and wrong. I'm afraid I find that hard to believe.

'One day I deliberately imagined myself growing up in Sumer or Akkad in those days. I discovered I would have had no conscience at all. I would have been a thorough pagan like all the others and enjoyed scribbling filth on the temple walls. (Don't be alarmed, darling. It's not the real me I'm talking about. The real Adrian Sherd is the one who's in bed beside you now.) I saw myself strolling along the terrace between the Hanging Gardens and the river. The sky was blue and cloudless. I was wearing sandals and a short tunic with nothing underneath. All the women walking past wore brief skirts and primitive brassieres.

'Well, as soon as a young woman took my fancy, a kind of raving madness came over me. (Remember, it's only an experiment I'm describing.) No thought of conscience or right and wrong entered my head. I was very different from the young Catholic gentleman who courted you so politely and patiently in the Coroke train. I was as bold as brass with the pagan girl—asked her name and address and arranged to meet her that evening at one of the lonely oases beyond the city walls.

'I didn't wait to see what happened after that, but it wasn't hard to guess from the storm of temptations rising up inside me. From that day on, I knew that if I hadn't been lucky enough to be born a Catholic and learn the proper purpose of my instincts, I would have been some kind of beast. No girl in Sumer or Akkad would have been safe from me.

'But it wasn't just the pagans who couldn't control themselves. If you read your Old Testament you'll realise how far some of the Patriarchs were from being good Catholic husbands. Solomon had hundreds of wives and treated them like playthings to minister to his lust, David coveted another man's wife, and Abraham had a bondwoman to amuse himself with when he tired of his lawful wife.

'I have to confess that when I was much younger I sometimes felt like complaining to God that I was born in New Testament times instead of the centuries BC. It didn't seem fair that those old fellows all pleased God and got to heaven after having all the women they wanted, while young Catholic chaps like me had to turn their eyes away from pictures of girls in bathers and only go to films for general exhibition.

'But after I met you and fell in love, I realised the men of the Old Testament were far worse off than me after all. They never knew the rare pleasures that I enjoyed in the years when I was wooing you. Solomon might have gazed all day at the hundreds of indecently clad wives sprawling on cushions in his luxurious palace, but he never knew the happiness of sitting in the Coroke train and waiting for one long soulful look from a girl who kept her beautiful body carefully concealed beneath a convent uniform. And no matter what pleasure he got from his women when he summoned them to his bedchamber, it could not have equalled my joy when I first kissed you on the day we became engaged and I knew I would one day possess a bride who had never even glanced immodestly at another man.'

A few weeks before the September holidays, Adrian's mother told him he deserved a rest from all his studies and homework. His uncle and aunt had agreed to have him at Orford for a week. If he behaved himself around the house he could go by himself on the train.

Adrian was anxious to let Denise know about his trip. When he went with his mother to book his seat at the Tourist Bureau he took away a coloured leaflet entitled *Spring Tours to the Grampians—Victoria's Garden of Wildflowers.* (The Grampians were a hundred miles from Orford, but there were no leaflets for any place nearer.) The following night on the Coroke train he stood near Denise and made sure she noticed him poring over the leaflet. She might have been surprised to think he was interested in wildflowers, but at least she would know what direction from Melbourne he was when she wanted to think of him during the holidays.

Adrian had a window seat in the 8.25 a.m. to Warrnambool and Port Fairy. He left a few inches between himself and the window for Denise. He and she were not long back from their honeymoon, and the trip to Orford was to show her off to his relatives and let her see something of the Western District.

The pictures in the carriage were *Treeferns, Tarra Valley* and *Bulga Park, Yarram*. Adrian whispered to Denise that a moist valley in Gippsland would be the perfect spot for a weekend trip. She snuggled closer to him and squeezed his fingers. She understood that he was thinking of the kisses he would give her under the shady treeferns.

They looked into all the slum backyards between South Kensington and Newport and told each other how lucky they were to be able to live in a modern home with the bush right up to their windows. After Newport, when miles of grazing land came up to the windows for their inspection, they passed the time by imagining how they would like to live in this or that farmhouse, and giving each place a points score out of ten.

Adrian's uncle, Mr McAloon, met them at Colac station. Adrian left a space for his young wife in the back seat of his uncle's car. He watched her face closely all the way and enjoyed the surprises she got. She had no idea that Colac was such a busy town. She had never seen such green paddocks and rich red soil as she found on the farms near Orford. And she thought the view of rolling plains from the McAloons' house was nearly as exciting as all the mountain scenery in Tasmania (and gave Adrian's hand a squeeze when she mentioned the place where they had spent their honeymoon).

172

Two of Adrian's cousins, a boy and a girl, sat in the back seat with him. They had pale faces with freckles of all shades from fawn to deep chocolate. Adrian always found it hard to talk to them. The girl went to the little brick Catholic school at Orford and the boy to the Christian Brothers in Colac. He travelled to and from Colac each day in a truck driven by a Catholic neighbour of the McAloons.

Mr McAloon said to Adrian, 'I suppose you've read in the papers all about the school-bus dispute.' (Adrian had never heard of it.) 'It's the same old story. Catholics have to pay taxes to support the secular education system, but when they ask for a few seats in the high-school bus to Colac, all the non-Catholic bigots and wowsers for miles around are up in arms and writing to the Chief Inspectors in the Education Department in Melbourne.

'Of course all the top inspectors and public servants are Masons, as you should know.' (He spoke as though Adrian and his parents should have done something about this years before.) 'Anyway, the result is that all the Catholics round here have banded together and organised a roster of cars and trucks to take the kids to secondary schools, and all the Catholic teachers in state schools have resigned from their union because of the anti-Catholic stand it took. We've got a long hard fight on our hands but we're not going to give up until we get elementary British justice for our children.'

After lunch Adrian showed his wife, Denise, around the farm. The freckle-faces weren't interested in going with him. They stayed on the back veranda and played Bobs and Disney Derby. Adrian pitied them. They mooned around the house all day and never knew what was missing from their lives. Two or three of them were old enough to have boyfriends or girlfriends. The miles of green dairy country should have inspired even the dullest freckle-face to fall in love with a face across the aisle in St Finbar's Church and then wait for months in suspense until the face turned round one day and showed by the faintest of smiles that there was some hope.

Adrian of course was much more advanced in his love affair than that, because he had so many proofs already that Denise returned his devotion. As he walked towards the farthest paddock he was already sharing with his wife the joy of looking back on the September holidays in 1954 when he walked alone across bare paddocks and wished his loved one had been with him.

That night Adrian found he had to share a bed with his oldest cousin, Gerard McAloon. Adrian kept his genitals carefully hidden while he undressed. Since meeting Denise he had rarely looked at them himself. They were no longer exclusively his, but the joint property of his wife and God and himself, to be used only in the marriage act on the nights when his wife agreed to it. He shuddered to think of the pale McAloon boy peering at things that were a secret between Denise and himself.

Next day Mr McAloon took Adrian and Gerard and two younger McAloon boys to visit a place called Mary's Mount. They drove to Colac and then south into the steep timbered hills of the Otway Ranges. Adrian's uncle talked all the way about the people of Mary's Mount.

'They're modern saints. Some of them are doctors and legal men and chaps with university degrees. They've given it all up to get back to the medieval idea of monasticism and living off the land. They bought nearly six hundred acres of bush with only two cleared paddocks and they're turning it into a farm to supply them with all their needs. Except for books and clothes they share almost everything in common. They built their cottages and chapel with their own two hands. In a few years they'll be weaving their own clothes and tanning their own leather for sandals or shoes. It's the only sensible way to live.'

Mr McAloon aimed his words at Adrian. 'I don't know how much your father has told you about the world yet, young fellow. But if you're going to grow up a responsible Catholic layman it's time you realised this country has never been in worse danger. I don't know how you city people survive with all those trashy books and films. And what about the spread of Communism?

'The only safe place to bring up a family nowadays is somewhere like Mary's Mount. You'll find in a few years there'll be thousands of Catholic families getting back to the land and cutting themselves off from the city altogether. If anything can save Australia, the move back to the land can do it. Closer settlement. We haven't got much time left. The experts reckon by 1970 at the latest the whole of Asia will have gone Communist. We need a population of at least thirty to forty million to defend ourselves. You can see what the Communists are doing right now in the jungles of Malaya. Well, people like the settlers at Mary's Mount are doing something about it.'

It was early afternoon, but the hills were so steep that the road between them was deep in shadow. Mr McAloon said, 'I think the time I admired them most was when the Bishop of Ballarat refused to give them one of his priests to live on the settlement as their chaplain. Well, some of the leading families fixed up some tarpaulins and made a sort of covered wagon and loaded some tents and blankets on pack horses and started off walking and riding from Mary's Mount to Ballarat.

'I forget how many days it took them, but they got there and drove their wagon up the driveway of the Bishop's Palace and squatted right there on the lawn. Now, don't get me wrong. They're fine folk. It's just that they're influenced by the customs of Catholic Europe. They don't seem to care what ordinary Australians think of them. Some of the men wear their hair down over their collars, and one fellow who used to belong to the university has a bushy black beard. And I heard they had some homemade wine in their wagon and they started drinking the stuff on the Bishop's lawn and handing round pieces of rather ripe cheese on the end of a knife. And Doctor Ray D'Astoli (he's a talented man, Ray—gave up a wealthy practice in Melbourne to go back to the land), Ray D'Astoli rang the bell and said, "The Catholic farmers of Mary's Mount within this diocese are come to wait upon the pleasure of His Grace, the Bishop, and crave audience with him."

'Those were the very words he used. He's a wonderfully clever man, Ray. And the young priest who opened the door got all hot and bothered and didn't know how to answer him. And they say the Bishop himself peeped through the curtains upstairs and thought a tribe of gypsies had descended on him. In fact the police in Colac went down to the camping ground when they were passing through because someone actually rang up and said the gypsies or some escaped lunatics had come to town.'

Adrian said, 'And did they get their priest?'

'Unfortunately, no. It's a long story and some of it's not for young ears.' (Mr McAloon glanced at his sons.) 'You'll see for yourself when we get to the Mount the single men and women have their own separate dormitories at least a hundred yards apart with all the married couples in between. But some people—even Catholics, I'm sorry to say—some people love to spread scandal and gossip whenever they see young men and women living up to ideals too high for themselves to match. More than that I'm not prepared to say. The Bishop didn't want one of his priests serving a community with even the faintest breath of scandal about it. And so Mary's Mount only has a mass in the chapel when a young priest comes down from Melbourne—he's a brother of one of the founders of the settlement.'

Mary's Mount was on the side of a hill so steep that the driveway for cars stopped halfway up. The McAloons and Adrian walked up a footpath with logs set into the slippery soil for steps. They passed small timber cottages that reminded Adrian of the illustrations in *Heidi*.

Mr McAloon stopped at a long building like a barn and asked a man was Brian O'Sullivan at home. The man led them inside. Mr McAloon whispered to Adrian, 'The single men's quarters—laid out like the dormitory of a Cistercian monastery—marvellous stuff.'

Ten little alcoves opened off a central passage. O'Sullivan came out of his alcove and took them inside. He and Mr McAloon sat on the bed—a camp stretcher covered with army blankets. Adrian and his cousins sat on stools cut from logs with globules of amber sap still stuck to their wounds.

O'Sullivan said, 'I spent the morning weeding potatoes, and now I've been reading St Thomas Aquinas.'

He held up a large volume entitled *Summa Theologica*. 'You know what we say up here at the Mount? "A man know's he's living well when he gets callouses of equal sizes on his knees and hands and backside." It means he's been kneeling in the chapel and working on the farm and reading in the library—all in equal proportions.' Mr McAloon laughed loudly.

When the men started talking about the potato crop, Adrian asked could he visit the chapel. The McAloon boys took him outside and further up the hillside. The chapel walls were of logs with the bark still on them. The seats inside were of unvarnished timber, but the altar and tabernacle were the real thing—polished wood draped with starched linen and coloured silk. And in the tiny sacristy Adrian opened the drawers of the cupboard and saw a coloured chasuble in each. While Adrian fingered the vestments, Gerard McAloon said he thought some clever women from the Mount had made them all with their own hands. There was supposed to be one lady who spent her whole time washing and ironing them and dusting the chapel and polishing the sacred vessels ready for the day when the community would have its own priest to say mass there every morning.

Adrian shut the drawers and stood still. Leaves were scraping against the chapel roof. A blue-green bull-ant wandered across the well-scrubbed floorboards. Specks of dust drifted in and out of a thin shaft of sunlight.

Denise was still beside him (although he had almost forgotten her in the excitement of visiting Mary's Mount).

He led her out of the chapel and pointed out to her the beauty of it all—the cottages half-hidden among the trees, the rows of green potato plants in the rich red soil, the little sawmill with its heaps of pale-yellow sawdust—and whispered to her, 'How could we think of bringing up our children near Hepburn Springs when we could have them all here protected from the world with our own chapel on the property?'

Back in the single men's quarters, Mr O'Sullivan said, 'I tried my hand at baking bread yesterday. It's not too bad.' He gave them each a piece spread with soft butter from a billy-can. Adrian's piece tasted like a salted scone, but he finished it out of politeness.

On the way home Adrian asked his uncle whether the McAloon family might settle at Mary's Mount one day.

Mr McAloon said, 'Don't think I haven't given it a lot of thought. The only thing that stops me is I'd like to wait a bit longer and see what sort of farmers they turn out to be. Last year they lost a lot of money on potatoes through planting them at the wrong time. And they can't sell any milk or cream because they won't make their dairy conform to health standards. They should manage to be self-supporting in a few years, but they'll always need some ready cash to pay for the little extras they can't make themselves—like trucks and generators and machinery and rainwater tanks and cement and stuff.'

Adrian said, 'And books?'

'Yes, books too. But just quietly I think some of those university chaps ought to spend a bit more time dirtying their white hands with work and a bit less time with their books.'

At the top of a low hill near Colac Adrian looked back towards the Otways. From that distance he could see only gentle grey-blue slopes rising up from the cleared country. He was relieved to think that none of the people in Warrnambool trains or the cars that passed along the Princes Highway would guess what was hidden beyond those timbered slopes. Even if the Malayan terrorists or the Chinese Communists invaded Victoria, the Catholic couples of Mary's Mount might still be safe and undiscovered in their shadowy gully.

Mr McAloon said, 'Now, don't get me wrong. Those people ought to put us to shame. One day the rest of Australia will copy their way of life. But there's always got to be humble soldiers like yours truly to go on fighting Communism in the outside world. I could tell you about the Communists we're up against in the Labor Party, but that's a story in itself. You just wouldn't believe the terrific battle that's going on all round us right now.'

They left Colac behind and headed north towards Orford between tranquil green paddocks and through the long afternoon shadows of huge motionless cypresses.

Sherd and his wife spent several weeks planning their move from near Hepburn Springs to a Catholic rural co-operative called Our Lady of the Ranges, deep in the Otways. Denise was taking just two dresses, two sweaters, two sets of underclothes and her bathers. Her husband was taking one suit, one old pair of trousers with an old shirt and jumper to match, a pair of overalls and his swimming trunks.

They filled a small crate with all the books they would ever need—a Bible, the Catholic Encyclopedia, a History of

180

the Church in twelve volumes, a bundle of Australian Catholic Truth Society pamphlets (mostly on purity and marriage to instruct their children in years to come) and some leaflets on farming published by the Department of Agriculture.

They were going to sell their house and furniture and pay the proceeds to the co-operative. They would draw a small living allowance if they needed it—Our Lady of the Ranges was a true community like a medieval monastery. (People often forgot that monks and nuns were practising the perfect form of Communism centuries before Karl Marx was ever heard of.)

One night just before they left for the Otways, Mrs Sherd asked her husband to continue the talks he had begun a little while before on marriage through the ages.

Sherd propped a pillow under his head, arranged the lacy collar of his wife's nightgown into a pretty frame for her chin, and said, 'Like everything else, marriage changed a great deal after Our Lord came down to earth to teach. We know that He made marriage one of the seven sacraments of His new Church, but we don't know exactly when He did it. Some theologians think He instituted the sacrament of matrimony while He was a guest at the wedding feast at Cana. If so, then the lucky couple of Cana were the first man and wife to be properly married in the Catholic Church.

'This doesn't mean, of course, that all the couples who married in Old Testament times were not properly married. If their intentions were good and they were following their consciences to the best of their ability, then their marriages were probably valid. (It's the same with well-meaning non-Catholics today—many of their marriages are quite valid.)

'Anyway, the important thing is that Our Lord did make marriage a sacrament. And He taught his disciples quite a bit about it too. He said, "What God has joined together let no man put asunder," which of course makes all divorce impossible. And He said those beautiful words about the physical side of marriage. (I used to feel embarrassed whenever the priest read them out in the Sunday Gospel, but I suppose they were over your innocent head.) You know—the bit about a man leaving his father and mother and cleaving to his wife so they become one flesh.

'But the words I can never forget, the saddest words, I think, in the whole New Testament, are the ones He said when the Scribes and Pharisees told Him about the woman who had seven husbands on earth and asked Him which one would have her for his wife in heaven. And He told them there was no marrying or giving in marriage in heaven.

'They say everyone finds some stumbling block in the Gospels—some teaching of Christ that doesn't make sense and has to be accepted on faith alone. Well, those words about marriage are my stumbling block. I think they're cruel and unreasonable, I wish they weren't true, but because Christ Himself said them I believe in them.

'Bearing in mind what Our Lord Himself has said, let's be coldly realistic about the life we'll lead in heaven. After the end of the world and the Resurrection of the Dead and the General Judgement we'll all be given back our bodies. They'll be glorified bodies of course. So, beautiful and flawless as your body is now'—Sherd gently stroked the whiteness of his wife's throat—'it will be a thousand times more perfect in those days. And let's be quite frank about it—none of us will be wearing clothes. Theologians believe we'll lose all our blemishes and moles and scars. I think myself we'll probably also be without the ugly hair under our arms and elsewhere on our bodies.

'There'll be millions of people around heaven, but eternity is a long, long time and sooner or later you and I will meet up with each other again. Our glorified bodies will be based on those we had as young adults. So there we are, just as we were in the early years of our married life, meeting in some place even more beautiful than Tasmania. How will we feel towards each other?

'Well, because I'm in heaven and my soul is saved, it would be absurd to think of me having an impure temptation when I see you, even though you're stark naked and more beautiful than ever you were on earth. Besides, I would have got used to seeing beautiful young women naked all over the lawns every day in heaven (including, I suppose, a few film stars who repented on their deathbeds). In fact, if Our Lord was right about heaven (and He should have known, because all the time He was on earth His Divine Nature was enjoying Itself in Heaven, and as God the Son He helped to create the place anyway), you and I won't feel any more affection towards each other than we feel towards any of the millions of other men and women of all colours in heaven—because otherwise we'd start to fall in love again and want to get married.

'But the unfortunate thing is, we can't help remembering all our lives together on earth. So when I look at your perfect body and all its most striking features I actually recall how excited they used to make me, although I don't feel the slightest excitement any more.

'When I look at your firm young breasts I probably

183

admire them for the part they played in God's plan for us by catching my eye some nights as you slipped into your nightgown and prompting me to ask you to yield to me in bed. Or else I simply praise them for the wonderful job they did each time you brought another child into the world—swelling to a prodigious size before the great day and then pouring out gallons of nourishing milk through the conspicuous nipples during the weeks when your infant pressed its hungry mouth against them.

'And when I happen to glance at your supple white thighs and my eye quite naturally travels up them and rests for a moment on the intimate place enclosed between them, I suppose all I do is praise God for designing your body so that a part of it could accommodate my seed and afterwards perform its noble task of propelling another new creature into the world.

'And that, I'm afraid, is all that will happen between us in heaven. I still think we'll be allowed to stroll now and then through pleasant groves that remind us of Tasmania or Hepburn Springs or the Otways. And because those places once meant so much to us, we surely wouldn't be breaking the laws of heaven if we held hands now and then or even exchanged an innocent friendly kiss.

'If we feel like it we can both dive into a crystal-clear stream and swim around naked. You can even lie floating on your back all afternoon if you like and I won't be the least bit interested. I won't even have to be on guard against strangers finding our secluded spot. If a whole tribe of men and women saints suddenly appears beside our stream and stands looking down on us, we'll just wave to them and go on swimming.

'In fact our little outing will probably end with some handsome young man wading out to you and looking down on you with nothing but friendship in his eyes and telling you the story of how he was martyred fighting the Saracens in the siege of Acre. You and he will stroll off hand in hand, with you looking up into his eyes and telling him how you were married to a chap in the twentieth century and all about your children. I'll watch you go, knowing I mightn't run into you again for years, but I won't be at all concerned.

'Well, that's what the Gospel teaches us, anyway. I still think it's hard that couples like us who love each other so passionately must be no more than good friends in heaven. Perhaps the trouble is that my love for you is far greater than God expects of a husband. After all, He only requires people to be attracted to each other so they'll marry and ensure a constant supply of new souls to do His Will on earth and glorify Him in heaven. If you and I have the largest possible number of children and turn them out good Catholics, that should be a sufficient reward in itself. We've got no right to expect that we'll enjoy for all eternity the emotional and physical pleasures of being in love.

'If you look at the history of the church you won't find any saints who got to heaven simply because of their love for a wife or husband. The people honoured by the church as saints are those who never yielded to their emotions or passions. And I don't mean just priests and brothers and nuns. Only today I was looking through my Daily Missal at the notes on some of the saints who were ordinary lay people like you and me.'

Sherd picked up the missal from beside his bed and read from it.

St Praxedes consecrated her virginity to God and distributed all her wealth to the poor.

St Susanne, a holy virgin of high lineage, refused to marry the son of Diocletian and was beheaded after grievous torments.

St Frances of Rome was the type of a perfect spouse and, after her husband's death, of a perfect religious in the house of Oblates which she founded.

St Cecilia, of an illustrious Roman family, converted her husband Valerianus and her brother-in-law Tiburtius, preserved her virginity and was beheaded.

St Henry, Duke of Bavaria and Emperor of Germany, used his power to extend the kingdom of God. By agreement with his wife he preserved virginity in marriage.

'These are the people we're supposed to model ourselves on. There's no record of any man who was canonised because he had an extraordinary love for his wife and gave up every other happiness to serve her as I've done for you.

'When the saints I've mentioned got to heaven you can be sure they didn't moon around looking for their lost loved ones. St Henry would have smiled politely whenever he passed his wife on some heavenly avenue. He might not have seen her for months, but he didn't miss her because he had learned on earth that there are things more important than conjugal love.

'I've never mentioned this to you before, and I hope it doesn't dismay you, but I think I envy the people who haven't been baptised. At least they have a chance of meeting their wives or husbands again in limbo and continuing their great love affairs. Limbo, as you know, is a place of perfect natural happiness. It seems reasonable to suppose that the greatest natural happiness of all will be permitted there. In fact, when all bodies have been resurrected after the General Judgement, there might be nothing to prevent a man and his wife in limbo from enjoying also some of the purely physical pleasures they once enjoyed in this life.'

Early in the third term Adrian's class went on a retreat at the monastery of the Pauline Fathers. For three days and nights the boys lived at the monastery and observed some of its rules. They kept the Great Silence from evening prayers until after mass next morning; they ate their meals in the refectory while a lay brother read aloud the life stories of great saints; and they walked in the garden for a half-hour of meditation after breakfast.

The monastery was in a garden suburb a few miles from Swindon. Adrian arrived in a bus after dark. Next morning he stood at his upstairs window and looked across the huge lawns to the tall front fence and couldn't work out the direction of Swindon or Accrington. He knew the name of the street and the suburb where he was. But it was a part of Melbourne he had never visited before. He might have walked for miles from the front gate of the monastery before he came to some tramline or railway station that could give him his bearings.

All the time Adrian was at the monastery he enjoyed feeling cut off from the world. He was hidden for a few days in one of the best suburbs of Melbourne for the purpose of looking into his soul and making sure he was on the right path.

Before the retreat, the brother in charge of Adrian's class had suggested that each boy should take some spiritual reading. He said there would be free periods during the retreat when the best thing a boy could do was to read and chew over the sort of things he didn't usually have time to read because of the pressure of his studies.

Adrian arrived at the monastery with three Australian Catholic Truth Society pamphlets and a *Reader's Digest* in the bottom of his bag. The pamphlets were called *Purity: The Difficult Virtue*, *Now You're Engaged* and *Marriage Is Not Easy*. The *Reader's Digest* had an article entitled 'Physical Pleasure—What Should a Wife Expect?' Whenever the retreat program allowed free time, he went to his room and read.

On the last evening of the retreat, the priest in charge called the boys into the monastery parlour and invited them to start a discussion on some problem facing a Catholic young man in the modern world. The priest said he would act as chairman and perhaps give a short summing-up at the end.

The boys seemed embarrassed about talking in front of a strange priest, but at last John Cody stood up and said they ought to discuss the moral problems of boys and girls mixing together. The priest said it was an excellent topic and told Cody to start the ball rolling.

Adrian was glad he had taken a seat on the very edge of the boys and almost out of sight of the priest. He was angry with the priest for letting the boys choose such a frivolous topic.

The boys in his class talked for hours at school about girls they met on trams or at dances. They said such and such a girl was adorable or gorgeous or luscious or cute, but no boy ever dared to claim one of them was his girlfriend. Adrian knew that all these fellows dreamed of was to walk some girl home from tennis on Saturday or fetch her a paper cup of lemonade at the learn-to-dance class and stand beside her while she sipped it.

Adrian was sure none of his classmates ever lay awake for hours at night planning seriously his whole future with the young woman he loved. They wasted their time on tennis and dances and parties, and yet they were ready to discuss in all seriousness (in a retreat house, too) the moral problems of their childish games.

Adrian was spared all the petty troubles of teenagers because he had found quite early in life a young woman worthy to be his wife. At the first sign of any temptation against purity with any female he happened to see in the street, he only had to think of Denise McNamara and the danger was over. But his danger was far less than other fellows' anyway—knowing that Denise returned his affection, he didn't have to worry about dances and parties and company-keeping and goodnight kisses and all the rigmarole of modern courtship.

He looked out of the window into the dusk. The fence around the monastery was hidden in shadow. From where he sat he could see no sign of any street or even a neighbouring rooftop. If he could have kept his eyes on the dark shapes of trees and shrubbery and shut out the affected voices of his classmates as they stood up by turns and had their say and sneaked a look at the priest to see if they were saying anything heretical, he could have imagined himself in a forested landscape—the sort of place he preferred when he wanted to talk seriously to Denise.

A boy was saying, 'Although we're all students, and the main duties of our station in life are to obey our teachers and pass our exams, just the same we have to live in the world outside. You know what I mean—we go to dances and mix with the opposite sex. Some of us might even attend parties where the girls' parents don't come to collect them afterwards. So we're expected to walk the girls home to their front doors. Now, the problem I'd like to hear discussed is this business of the goodnight kiss. You take this girl home and get to the front door and she says, "Thanks for everything." And then what do you do? I mean, do you kiss her or just leave her standing there? I'd like to hear some other fellows' opinions on this.'

Adrian was very anxious to be alone with Denise. Only a few hours before, in the recreation period after lunch, he had found information in his pamphlets and his *Reader's Digest* that he had to share with her.

There was no time to fuss over which month or year of their marriage they were meeting in. He led her straight out through the french windows onto the deserted veranda. She sat on the stone parapet and leaned back prettily against the ivy-covered pillar. They both stared into the sombre forest.

Sherd said, 'I know the *Reader's Digest* is a non-Catholic magazine, but a lot of the things it says are quite useful if you're careful to see that they're not about faith or morals and they don't contradict the church's teachings.

'Only today I found something in a *Digest* article that you ought to think about carefully. It seems that one of the causes of so much boredom in marriages these days is the wife always waiting till her husband asks her whether they can be intimate. This might shock you (I was a little surprised myself when I read it) but there's no reason why the woman shouldn't ask the husband sometimes whether he feels inclined to perform the act.

'From my own point of view, I wouldn't think any less of you if you whispered to me in bed now and then that you wouldn't say no if I asked you.

'And just to prove that all this isn't just some idea dreamed up by sensual Americans—I've read in an ACTS pamphlet that each partner in a marriage founded on Christian charity learns to anticipate the moods and inclinations of the other. Which means for our purposes that you could make an effort sometimes to watch my moods and learn to tell when I'm likely to approach you. Then you can take some of the responsibility off my shoulders by asking me before I have to ask you.'

This was one of the most difficult conversations that Sherd had ever had with Denise, and he thought it best to leave her alone for a few minutes while the full meaning of it sank in. He turned back to the parlour of the retreat house.

Barry Kellaway stood up and said, 'Wait a minute. Doesn't it make all the difference whether the girl's a Catholic or not? I mean, if she's a good Catholic she'll naturally be very careful what happens when she's alone with a chap outside her front door.

'If she thinks it's the time and the place for a quick little goodnight kiss, the chap can do it quickly and she'll make sure none of them puts themselves in any moral danger. And if she's not a Catholic, then the chap ought to examine his conscience because he could easily be going into an occasion of sin whenever he takes her home on her own.'

Kellaway sat down and looked at the priest in the corner.

The priest said, 'For argument's sake we'll assume we're talking about Catholic young people. It's hard enough to make rules for ourselves without trying to sort out non-Catholics' consciences for them. But I do agree that there's no reason whatsoever for boys of your age to be hanging around front doorsteps with non-Catholic girls.'

Adrian went back to Denise and took her hand. He was a little afraid he might have spoken too frankly to her or given her too much new information at once. But her smile told him she was grateful for all the trouble he was taking to explain the whole range of Catholic teaching on marriage and the latest findings from America.

He said to her, 'It's interesting to note that both the ACTS pamphlets and the *Reader's Digest* think it's most important for each partner to make the act of love enjoyable for the other.

'The pamphlets don't use those words exactly, but they do point out that either partner would commit a mortal sin if he or she executed the sexual act for no other reason than his or her selfish enjoyment.

'I think we both ought to examine our consciences to see if we're doing all we can for each other in this matter. And perhaps in future you'll do your best to make the act more enjoyable for me, while I make sure you're perfectly comfortable with a nice soft pillow under your head and treat you gently and not get carried away with selfish lust.'

Denise stared into the twilight. All the talk about intimacy had put Sherd in the mood for it, and he hoped Denise would soon notice he was a little more agitated than usual and guess the reason for it.

Just then Alan McDowell stood up behind him and said, 'No matter whether the girl's a Catholic or not, she must have seen some modern films and realised it's the custom nowadays for young people to have a quick good-night kiss at the front door after a night together. If you don't do it you could be making a fool of yourself and next time you see her she won't be so easy to get on with.'

McDowell kept his eyes away from the priest, but several boys looked round as though they expected the priest to break in and explain how wrong McDowell was. The priest only pressed his lips tightly together and made notes on a slip of paper.

McDowell kept talking: 'I reckon it all depends what sort of kiss you give her and how long it takes.' (The room was suddenly very quiet.) 'If it's just a quick little one where you just brush your faces together it's probably no worse than a venial sin. But if it's one of those other sorts you sometimes see in films where they take a long time to finish'—someone blew his nose with a peculiar sound that might have disguised a snigger—'well, I think they're probably dangerous and they ought to be forbidden for Catholics.'

Adrian didn't bother to listen any more. It digusted him to think of big, lumpish Alan McDowell trying out different sorts of kisses on girls he had no intention of proposing marriage to.

Sherd put his hand gently on Denise's knee and said, 'I found something else very interesting in the *Reader's Digest*. You know, for many years people have thought it was only the man who was supposed to get some pleasure from the marriage act. The woman was expected to be a good wife and put up with whatever her husband did to her and get her happiness from the romantic love they shared.

'Well, just lately these scientists and doctors in America have discovered that if a woman tries hard enough and learns not to be frightened, and the man doesn't hurry too much, she might be able to get a sort of pleasure almost equal to her husband's.'

On the veranda it was almost too dark to see what Denise thought of this. Sherd wondered whether she would say she didn't need any more pleasure than she already got from seeing him happy and rested after the act, or whether she would smile shyly and say she would try to be more relaxed next time and see if the *Reader's Digest* was right.

But before Denise could speak, Bernard Negri said, 'It's all right for Alan to concentrate on what sort of goodnight kiss you're going to give a girl, but I think the most important thing for a Catholic boy to worry about is where the kiss takes place. I mean, we've been taught all our lives not to go into an occasion of sin. I think I heard once that if you deliberately go into an occasion of sin that you know full well will probably cause you to sin, you've already committed a mortal sin as serious as the one you thought you were probably going to commit anyway.

'Well, as I was saying, it depends where you are when the kiss takes place. If you're standing on her front veranda with the front light on and you know her parents are sitting up inside waiting for her, there's probably no danger in it. But if you're at one of these parties where the parents go away and leave the young people on their own and somebody turns the lights off, isn't there a grave danger that you'll be tempted to do something worse than kissing?'

Adrian congratulated himself for having avoided all the tangled moral problems of company-keeping. He kissed Denise tenderly on the forehead and said, 'So much for the pleasures of marriage. To speak of more serious matters—

even many good Catholics are not aware of all the graces and spiritual benefits they're entitled to get from marriage. Luckily for us, I've always read everything I could find on the subject. And buried away in an ACTS pamphlet today I found a wonderful bit of news.

'The author (a priest, of course) says marriage is a sacrament that goes on providing grace for the marriage partners all their lives. Year after year they can draw on this bottomless reservoir of grace to increase their own sanctity and earn for themselves a higher place in heaven. How? Well, believe it or not, every act of sexual intimacy between the partners (provided it's performed with the right motives and isn't sinful for some other reason) actually earns them an extra amount of grace.

'That's something to think about some night when you're just about to say you're too tired for it. If you can make a special effort to oblige me, you'll enjoy a spiritual reward.'

It was now completely dark on the veranda. Sherd couldn't see his wife's face, but she squeezed his fingers to show she was quietly thrilled by what he had told her.

Inside, the boys had finished their discussion and the priest was walking out from his corner into the middle of the room to sum up.

The priest said, 'You'll notice I kept right out of the discussion, boys. It's very important in a job like mine to hear the views of people like yourselves who have to live in the world, and let you explain your attitudes without any fear of having your heads bitten off by a priest for contradicting the church's teachings.

'By and large, most of you seem to have a fairly sound

idea of where a young Catholic man stands when he's dealing with the opposite sex. But I think the whole discussion went wrong somehow when you got onto this business of the goodnight kiss.' (He looked at the notes in his hand.) 'Now, I don't want to single out any one boy for what he said, but one of you seemed to think that just because "it's the custom nowadays" or "everybody's doing it" or "you see it in all the latest films", then a Catholic has to be in it and go along with the mob for fear they'll laugh at him or think he's old-fashioned.

'If any boy still thinks after all his years at a Catholic secondary school that he's going to decide what to do in life by what the rest of the world is doing, he'd better use the time remaining in this retreat to sit down and ask himself some very serious questions. Or, better still, he'd better make an appointment to see me or one of the other priests for a man-to-man chat.'

The priest paused and looked at his notes. The boys all knew it was childish and unfair to look at Alan McDowell just then, but most of them sneaked a look, even so. McDowell was pale and still, but otherwise he was taking it fairly well.

The priest said, 'Perhaps this is the time to go over very briefly the few facts a Catholic has to know about this whole matter of mixed company-keeping.'

While he talked, the priest looked hard at one boy after another. Adrian was sure the priest was annoyed with the boys. He hoped the priest had noticed how he himself kept aloof from the childish discussion. Perhaps the priest would even realise from the look on Adrian's face that he was far beyond the stage of kissing on doorsteps and already deep into the church's teachings on married life.

The priest was saying, 'It's quite simple, really. The basic rules cover all possible situations that you're likely to come up against. To commit a mortal sin you have to fulfil three simple conditions. There must be grave matter, full knowledge and full consent.

'Now, there's no need to explain about knowledge and consent. All of you are sane, rational creatures and you all possess free will. You know what it means to know fully what you're doing. And you know what it means to consent to something fully with your will. These things are clear-cut. The third condition—grave matter—might not be so clear in your minds, but the church's rules are very simple.

'The pleasures of the body are for married people alone. At your age anything you do with a girl that gives rise to physical pleasure is sufficient material for a mortal sin. With regard to the bosom, the breasts of a girl—those are grave matter at all times. And you shouldn't have to be told that her private places are absolutely out of bounds.

'But of course you can commit a mortal sin with any part of a girl's body. I can readily imagine the circumstances when a young fellow would sin over a girl's hands or arms, the exposed skin around her neck, even her feet or her bare toes.

'It's no use saying afterwards, "But I only intended to give her an innocent kiss." The church is older and wiser than any of you. Listen to her advice.'

While the boys followed the priest into the chapel for evening prayers, Adrian looked at their solemn faces and pitied them. They could do no more than look at the faces and forearms, and perhaps the ankles and calves, of all the girls they met until they finally married. How could they face such a bleak future without the thought of someone like Denise to inspire and console them?

Sherd's daily life at Our Lady of the Ranges left him plenty of time for thinking. Thrusting his potato fork into the clotted red soil and lifting out the ponderous tubers, swollen with nourishment, or perched on a handmade stool in the milking-shed, resting his head against the glossy flank of a Jersey cow and squirting her warm creamy milk so that it rang against the silvery metal of the bucket or lost itself with a rich satisfying sound in the fatty bubbles all over the surface, he looked back on his youth or pondered over the problems of the modern world.

He often remembered the year before he met Denise— the year when he became a slave of lust and couldn't sleep at night until he had seduced some film star. When he looked back on that year from the peace of the Otways (where he and his wife went to mass and communion every morning and confession every fortnight—although they had only a few petty faults to confess) he squirmed with shame. It was the episode in his life that still disturbed him.

Sometimes, to make himself more humble and less self-satisfied, he deliberately paused just before making love to his wife and thought, 'If I were to do to this angelic creature beneath me what I once did to those bold-faced film stars; if I grabbed those parts of her that I used to handle and slobber over on their bodies; if I did everything slowly to prolong the act and tire her as I tired them; or if I lost control of myself at the last moment and said to her the crazy things I used to blurt out to them—' But he could never imagine what she would do—the very idea was preposterous.

He often tried to work out why he had turned, in that year, from a normal Catholic boy in a decent household to a sex-crazed satyr rampaging across America. Thinking it over in the quiet valleys of the Otways, he was inclined to blame American films.

Not that he had ever seen his favourite film stars on the screen. It was not as simple as that. Adrian Sherd the schoolboy never saw more than five or six films a year. Half of those were Walt Disney films and the rest were chosen by his mother because they were classified 'For General Exhibition' and recommended for children.

Adrian's mother used to say before he went to one of these films, 'There's bound to be a bit of love and romance and that sort of rot. But just put up with it and wait for the adventure parts.'

From the distance of the Otways, Sherd suspected that these supposedly harmless films might have started him on his year-long orgy of lust. Meditating on a leafy hillside, he watched them again and blended their complex plots into one.

An American man arrives in a strange town near a jungle or a desert or an enemy country that he must soon venture into. He looks across a hotel lobby crowded with foreign faces and finds himself staring into the eyes of a beautiful American woman aged about twenty-five. He falls in love with her at once, but he knows from the cold way she meets his eyes that others before him have fallen for her and been repulsed.

The man goes to hire the native porters for his expedition or to rendezvous with an army officer or a master spy who will give him his final instructions. When he returns to the hotel, he finds the woman sitting alone at a table in the dining room. Because he is leaving next day on a mission that may well cost him his life, the man is keyed up to an extraordinary pitch of bravery. He sits down at the table without being asked, and even starts a conversation with the woman.

He soon learns that she is single. (If she had been married, the romantic interest of the plot would have ended there and then—the man would have apologised for bothering her and left the table.) She has never allowed a man to do anything more than hold her hand or give her a friendly goodnight kiss. (This becomes apparent when the man's eyes glance downwards at the inch or so of cleavage above the neckline of her evening frock. She catches him at it and gives him a long severe look that makes him glance away and fiddle with his glass from embarrassment.) She is visiting remote parts of the world to recover from a broken heart. (She is understandably vague when she talks about her past, but the most likely interpretation of her pauses and broken sentences is that she fell in love with a man in her home town in America but found her love was not returned.) Finally, she has no steady boyfriend just at present. (She says quite explicitly, 'There's been no one else since—I don't think there ever can be.' The man at the table understands from this that he is free to become her suitor.)

The man and woman dance together in the hotel ballroom, then walk out to the marble balcony. He tells her a little about the journey that he must begin next morning. A stranger leaps out of the shadows and throws a knife at the man. The man dodges the knife and shields the woman with his body. He is so anxious to protect her that the

200

mysterious stranger escapes. However, the man is well rewarded when the woman leans on him and clutches the lapels of his coat. He does not hide his pleasure at having her so close to him. And it makes it clear to her that she has awakened his strongest instinct—the urge to protect a beautiful helpless woman at a moment of danger.

Because she is now frightened of the foreigners in the hotel, the woman asks the man to her room for a drink. While he fills her glass and hands it to her, he looks her over. Her hair is so neatly done and her lipstick and make-up are so carefully applied that she would obviously not welcome any man who tried to kiss or embrace her and disturb it. Her dress is securely fastened across her breasts. (It has not slipped a fraction of an inch during the whole time that Adrian has been watching it.) The dress is such a tight fit that no man could hope to loosen it even a little without her noticing what he was trying to do. Below her breasts the cloth is as taut and forbidding as a suit of armour—and there are no fastenings visible on it that a man could try to interfere with. Even the furniture in the room is designed to keep a man at a distance. She sits with her arm outflung along the back of a thickly padded couch that makes her look as regal and unapproachable as a queen.

Nevertheless, the man does dare to kiss her once before he says goodbye and leaves her room for the night. He does it in a restrained polite way, pressing his lips against hers for no more than half a minute and holding her so that no other parts of their bodies come into contact.

The man starts on his journey next day. He has many worries on his mind, but when he looks back for the last time at the town where the young woman is waiting, he is obviously hoping she will be true to him until he returns to continue his wooing.

Soon afterwards, the woman learns how perilous the man's journey is and prepares to set out after him. When she explains this to a girlfriend, the girlfriend teases her and accuses her of getting too serious about a man who is only an adventurer. The young woman denies this, but with a dreamy look in her eyes that suggests she really is falling in love. She appears to have known from the way the man kissed her that he was in love with her, and now her own heart is beginning to melt.

For a long time after this the film shows only the troubles of the man on his journey. The woman is captured on her way to join him. It seems as though they will never meet again and have the chance to declare their love for each other. But in the end, the man (helped by loyal natives or friendly foreigners) outwits his enemies and approaches the place where the woman has been kept captive.

The very last scene between the couple has to be watched closely to reveal its full meaning. First, the man notices that the top buttons of the woman's blouse have come undone during her struggles with her captors. She is still tied to a post with her hands behind her back. She is at his mercy. If he were only interested in her body he could lean forward for a moment and peep down the front of her gaping blouse or even slip his hand inside it or do much worse to her. But he does not even pause to consider these possibilities. He rips away the ropes that bind her and takes her tenderly in his arms.

This time she lets him kiss her more than once. She knows from the gentlemanly way he has rescued her that he really is in love with her. And in the excitement of being rescued she sees no harm in allowing him a few extra kisses, especially since the leader of the native porters or the foreign peasants is standing only a few yards off and grinning at them.

The film ends before the man actually proposes marriage. But anyone can see from the more relaxed way they behave towards each other that the man is only waiting for the right moment to ask her and that he knows already what her answer will be. And the woman seems to know what is in his mind and to be only waiting for the chance to say yes.

Looking back at such films from the pure air of the Otways, Sherd understood how they had contributed to his year of sin. The films had introduced him to a kind of woman he never came across in Australia—the attractive young woman in her twenties who had no boyfriend but travelled around waiting for the right man to fall in love with her and begin courting her. Because her heart had been broken in the past, she was fairly reserved with a new suitor. She only let him kiss her after he had given some proof of his devotion, and she would have slapped his face if he had tried to touch her improperly.

Adrian had never seen one woman of this kind in Accrington or anywhere in Melbourne. Yet he learned from films that thousands of them sat waiting at hotel tables from Maine to California—and even in foreign cities. If Adrian had had a girlfriend of his own at the time, he could have rejoiced to see films showing other people achieving the same kind of happiness that he himself enjoyed. But those were the days before he had met Denise. When the films were over he went home to his lonely bed and envied the men who met these young women on their travels.

What happened next was only too familiar to the man Sherd. He remembered it and did penance for it every day. In the heat of his lust he had invented a sequence of events that was a travesty of the films that inspired them. Like the male stars of the films, he had met eligible young women. But instead of courting them patiently and waiting for some sign of encouragement before he kept exclusive company with them or ventured to kiss them, he had undressed them and defiled them only hours after their first meeting. It was all so absurd compared with what really happened in films.

After years in the peaceful Catholic community of Our Lady of the Ranges, Sherd could see clearly all the faults of modern life in Australia. He knew there was something very wrong with a society that made it so hard for young men to meet young women with a view to marriage.

A young man growing up at Our Lady of the Ranges was free to choose a girlfriend from one of the families he mixed with every day. Their affection for each other grew steadily over the years. A smile from her at morning mass or a few words as they met on a rustic pathway would inspire him to work like a Trojan all morning in the potato paddocks or bend over his books of theology and church history all afternoon in the library. The years passed quickly until the fellow was old enough to call on her parents and ask for the young woman's hand. From then until the day of the wedding, the young couple would sit together by the riverbank on Sunday afternoons, within sight of their elders but far enough away to talk privately together.

As more and more people left the cities and settled in co-operative rural communities, there would be fewer young women in any country who had to spend hours doing their hair and putting make-up on their faces and then sitting alone at hotel tables waiting for the right man to turn up. And of course there would be fewer single men walking past those tables and noticing the women sitting there. But best of all there would be fewer young men who had to spend years of their lives as solitary sex maniacs because they could only watch those single men and women meeting in films and never get the chance to do the same thing in real life.

During a House football match one Wednesday, it rained so hard that the brother who was umpire sent the boys to shelter under trees. Adrian Sherd and his teammates crouched under the dripping branches and looked for a break in the weather. The sky was unnaturally dark. Someone started talking about the end of the world.

The boys of Adrian's class often discussed this topic when no brother was around. One or two of them had tried to bring up the subject in Christian Doctrine periods, but their teacher had always ended the discussion before it got interesting. The brother would agree that the world was going to end some day, but he insisted that no one—not even the most learned theologian or the holiest saint—knew whether it would happen tomorrow or a thousand years from now. The brother would allow that parts of the *Apocalypse* described the last days of the world and the signs of the coming end, but he said it was a risky business trying to look for these signs in the present day. All a

Catholic boy had to do was to live each day of his life as though it was *his* last day on earth, and leave it to God to work out His plans for bringing the world to an end.

A boy looked out at the sodden football ground and said, 'We know He won't destroy the world again by water or send a terrible deluge again because in the Old Testament He showed Noah the sign of the rainbow when the flood had gone down.'

Another boy said, 'It can't happen yet because the prophet Elias hasn't come back to earth. And there was someone else in the Old Testament who didn't die properly either. Elias went up body and soul in a fiery chariot, and the church teaches that he has to come back to earth again and die properly. I've heard he'll come back when the church is really in trouble and lead us in battle against our enemies.'

All the boys around Adrian joined in the discussion.

'The Antichrist is going to be the church's worst enemy. But he hasn't come yet, and the world can't end until he does.'

'Will Elias know he's Elias when he comes back? Or will he grow up thinking he's just an ordinary Catholic schoolboy? He could even be one of us now.'

'He'd have to be a Hebrew, though, wouldn't he?'

'Wouldn't he more likely come back the way he went up? I don't mean in a fiery chariot, but roughly the same age.'

'His body is somewhere in heaven right now. Seems creepy to think about it.'

'That's nothing. Our Lady's body is there too according to the dogma of the Assumption.'

'But what about the Antichrist? He won't call himself that, will he?'

'I used to think Stalin was him, the way he persecuted Catholics. But he's dead now and the church is still going strong. Anyway, isn't the church supposed to be defeated or nearly die out just before the end of the world? That's not happening now, is it?'

'There are four hundred million Catholics all over the world.'

'Our Lord said, "Behold I am with you all days even to the consummation of the world." The church can never be defeated.'

Stan Seskis joined in and said, 'Listen. My old man's a nong most of the time. But he's right when he talks about Communism. You droobs don't realise what the Communists are doing in Australia right now. When my father heard the Russians were coming into our country during the war he packed everything into a little leather bag and my mother carried me and my little brother in her arms and we got for our lives. After the war we sneaked across the border of Germany into the West. We had to cross a ploughed paddock and I was bawling the whole time because my shoe fell off and I couldn't go back to get it. That's all I can remember—I lost my shoe. I wonder what the Reds did with it if they ever found it. But my father knows what Communism means because he's lived with it.'

Seskis kept talking. No one wanted to interrupt him. 'And you know all this Petrov business and all the facts about Russian spies in Australia? Well, my old man's known all about it for years. He knows the names of dozens of Communist spies in all the unions and the Labor Party and if it hadn't been for him and his anti-Communist mates, the Commoes would have taken over Australia already. When I was a kid and we had all those strikes in Australia and grass was growing on all the train tracks and tramlines for months, well, my father came home one night and told us the Communists were just about ready to overthrow the government. He said it could happen any day, only this time they weren't going to drive him out of his homeland a second time—he was going to stay and fight. And if you saw the list of Communists in his secret notebook (they're all written in code) you'd be amazed how many enemies we've got all round us.'

Another fellow said, 'That Bishop from China who spoke to all the senior forms that day—the one with the white beard who wrote Chinese words on the blackboard and showed us his chopsticks—didn't he say the Chinese Communists had a plan to come down through the islands to Australia? That's why these terrorists are fighting in Malaya right now.'

Someone else said, 'But the Bishop told us there were millions of secret Catholics all over China—all the people the Columban Fathers had converted for fifty years. And if they get the chance they'll rebel against the government and kick the Communists back where they came from.'

Adrian Sherd said, 'I was reading in a *Reader's Digest* the other day how the greatest allies the West has are the millions of Russians and Poles and Czechs and so on who hate Communism. They're waiting for the chance to rise up if only we could encourage them.'

'Well, why doesn't America just send an army in? The Russian people wouldn't fight for Communism, would they?'

'But the Russians have got the hydrogen bomb. There was a story in the *Argus* one day about a foreign power dropping a hydrogen bomb on Melbourne. (They meant the Russians, of course.) Well, this old bushman from the Dargo High Plains rode his horse down to Gippsland once a year and caught the train to Melbourne. Only this year he wondered why everything was so quiet and the trees all looked as though a bushfire had passed through. And about fifty miles from Melbourne he started to notice all these dead bodies. Well, he headed back to the bush, but the whole of Melbourne was wiped out.'

'But why would the Russians pick on Melbourne anyway? Wouldn't they bomb New York or Washington first?'

'You know Therese Neumann. She's a living saint in Germany. She's still alive today in a village called Konnersreuth. For thirty years now she's never eaten any food or drunk any water. The only thing that keeps her alive is her holy communion every morning. And every Thursday night she starts to suffer all the wounds and pains that Our Lord suffered in His Passion. And by Friday afternoon her face is covered with blood as if she had a crown of thorns pressing into her forehead, and all the marks of the stigmata appear on her hands and feet. The cleverest Protestant doctors in Europe have studied her for years and no one can explain how it happens. My mother wrote away to Germany once and got back a bundle of holy cards from Therese Neumann's own village. All the prayers were in German but my cousin translated some of them. And there was this little leaflet with the whole story of the Miraculous Stigmata of Therese Neumann.

'Anyway, Therese Neumann has made some prophecies,

and the worst one I can remember is that priests will be hanging from lamp posts in Melbourne in 1970.'

No one spoke for a while. All round the tree where they crouched, the raindrops made little holes like bomb craters in the mud. On the far side of the deserted football field, a ragged file of boys stumbled and ran towards the pavilion. Further still, on the other side of the creek, was a long grey paling fence that marked the end of all the backyards in some street of a suburb that Adrian Sherd had never entered. (He guessed it was Woodstock or Luton or even the edge of Camberwell.) The back porches were swept by rain and the doors and windows were all shut.

A boy said, 'What's the percentage of Catholics in Australia, anyway?'

Adrian answered, 'Only about twenty-five per cent,' and looked at the rows of locked non-Catholic houses on the hills around them.

A man came towards them with a black oilskin cape hiding his face. It was a brother to tell them the football matches had all been abandoned and they'd better get for their lives back to the pavilion.

The football pavilion had timber nailed over the windows where the glass should have been. The sky was so dark that the boys inside could barely recognise each other. Some of them went on talking about prophecies while they changed into their school uniforms.

A boy said, 'There was an old Irish monk centuries ago. His name was Malachy, I think. He made all these prophecies about the popes who were going to come after his lifetime. He said a few words about each pope like "Great Builder" or "Defender of the Faith" or "Destroyer of Heresies", and so far they've all turned out true. He called Pius the Twelfth "Very Saintly Shepherd" or something, and it's true he's one of the holiest of all the popes.

'Well, the scariest thing is—there's only five or six popes left on Malachy's list. So if he's right, the end of the world could happen before the year 2000. Because the Catholic Church has to last until the end of time, and if there's no more popes that's the end of everything.'

A fellow said, 'But the Antichrist still has to appear. He's probably alive now—a young man growing up in Russia or China and planning to destroy the church.'

They all joined in again.

'Antichrist will have to beat Elias first.'

'Who wins in the end, anyway? Does the *Apocalypse* say whether the Catholics or Communists win the last battle?'

'Our Lady told the children at Fatima that if enough people all over the world offered up prayers and penance, she would make sure Russia was converted and there'd be no Third World War after all.'

Adrian Sherd said, 'We won't have to fight the Russians on our own. I read a *Reader's Digest* article about Turkey, and the Turks have always hated the Russians, even before they turned Communist. And they're ready to fight them again if the Russians start anything. The end of the article was this big Turkish soldier looking across the frontier and saying, "One Turk has always been as good as three Russians in battle."'

'What about the secret message that Our Lady of Fatima gave to the children in a sealed envelope and told them not to open it for twenty years? And didn't Francesca give it to the Pope and when he opened the first part of it a few years ago he fainted? And Francesca is a nun now, and her hair's turned white because she knows the first part of the message too. When are they going to open the second and third parts?'

'I'm not sure, but the nuns told us at primary school that when the Pope was seriously ill a few years ago he had a vision of Our Lord that he wouldn't tell anyone about. But people in the Vatican think Our Lord must have told him something about the future and what will happen to the church and he's hardly ever smiled or laughed since.'

'If only Our Lord or Our Lady would appear to the Russians and show them a cross in the sky to frighten them or convert them or make them leave us alone.'

'Even if they appeared in Australia to tell us how many years we've got before the end of the world! If it's only going to be a few years we all ought to study for the priesthood instead of going to work or getting married.'

'Did anyone read in the paper last year about that woman who drowned her two little kids in the bath and tried to gas herself because she didn't want to be alive when the Communists took over the world? They put her in the loony bin but one of my mother's friends knew her well and she said she could understand how any woman with young kids would do a thing like that nowadays.'

Adrian and the little group around him were the last to leave the pavilion. They walked across the playing fields in pouring rain to the East Swindon tram terminus. No one talked any more about the end of the world.

In the tram back to Swindon, Adrian stood near the door because his clothes were too wet to sit in. He stared at the enormous houses along the tramline and wondered, as he always did, who else beside doctors and dentists and solicitors could be wealthy enough to live in such places. In all his life he had never been inside the front gate of any house like them. But instead of envying the people inside (as he usually did), he almost pitied them.

While hundreds of millions of Chinese and Russians were preparing for a Third World War, the people of Melbourne's garden suburbs were going about their business as though there was nothing to worry about. They were thinking of wall-to-wall carpets and radiograms and washing machines while saints and prophets and the *Reader's Digest* foresaw at least a terrible war and perhaps the last days of the world.

Even if they went to church, the garden suburbs people only sang Protestant hymns or listened to long sermons about Hospital Sunday or gambling or being converted in your heart. Their sons went to Eastern Hill Grammar and enjoyed themselves at parties or looked forward to years at the university and careers in the professions, while Adrian prayed to God every night to put off the end for a little longer so he could enjoy a few years of happiness as the husband of Denise McNamara.

But it wasn't unfair that thoughtful Catholics had such worries while non-Catholics enjoyed themselves in their spacious homes. It was far better to look at the future realistically than to live for the pleasure of the moment. Adrian and his classmates had been brought up to think deeply about the things that really mattered. Their Catholic education had trained them to use their reason—to probe beneath the shallow surface that Protestants and atheists never questioned. And if the price that Catholic intellectuals

had to pay was to worry about the terrible times ahead—
well, at least they would have the last laugh one day when
the Communists took over the garden suburbs or the armies
of Elias and Antichrist drew up for battle on the outskirts
of Melbourne.

Adrian hoped that all these prosperous doctors and
solicitors and their spoilt sons and daughters would have
time before the end to apologise to the Catholics and admit
they were right after all. Of course the fools would spend
all eternity blaming themselves for their folly anyway, but
it would be very satisfying to have some big golden-haired
Eastern Hill fellow come up to the boy he hadn't even
noticed on the trams years before and say, 'For God's sake,
why didn't you Catholics tell us what was coming?'

The answer to the fellow's question, of course, was
that he wouldn't have listened anyway. All over Australia,
Catholics like Stan Seskis's father were trying to warn
people about Communists in the unions, but how many
listened to them? Only forty years before, Our Lady of
Fatima had worked one of the most spectacular miracles
of all time—the sun had danced and spun around and
floated down towards the earth in front of sixty thousand
witnesses—but how many people were doing what Our
Lady had asked, and praying and offering up penance so
that Russia would be converted?

Even while the non-Catholics of Melbourne were sitting
in front of their electric fires and their wives were fiddling
with their expensive pressure cookers, a holy woman in
Germany was still alive after fasting for twenty-five years—
but who listened to her prophecies or took notice of her
visions?

The tram climbed the last hill towards the Swindon town hall. Adrian looked back at the miles of dark-red roofs and grey-green treetops and the mass of rain clouds above them. He knew it was wrong to gloat over the fate of thousands of people who had never deliberately done him harm. But he whispered into the breeze blowing past the tram that they were all doomed. And he saw the end of the world like grey rain bearing down on suburb after suburb—Oglethorpe by its winding creek, Glen Iris on its far hills, yes, and even Camberwell, the leafiest of them all—and the people in their last agony crying out that if only they could have had a Catholic secondary education they might have seen it coming.

Early in the third term, the boys of St Carthage's started practising for the House Sports Meeting. Adrian Sherd decided to train for the B-Grade 880 yards. Three nights each week he got out of Denise's compartment at Caulfield and went to the racecourse to run. On those nights he always let his bag dangle open in the train so Denise would see his sandshoes and running singlet and realise he wasn't deserting her for some frivolous reason.

He thought of her all the time he trained. In his last year at St Carthage's, after he had started to talk to her on the train, she would tell a white lie to her teachers and turn up at the Swindon Cricket Ground to see him run in the A-Grade 880. Meanwhile he improved his stamina by hissing her name under his breath as he ran.

One night three other boys agreed to run a trial 880 yards with him at the racecourse. Adrian dropped out well behind them in the early part of the race. His breath came easily and he barely whispered Denise's name. With about three hundred yards to go, he began his run. The effort to reach the others made him puff. He hissed the beloved name fiercely and didn't care who heard him.

The other runners were stronger than Adrian had expected. In a last desperate effort to catch them he fixed her face, pale and anxious, a little to one side of the winning-post and punished his weary body savagely for her sake. A few yards short of the finish he caught and passed one of his rivals, but the other two were already crossing the line.

When the runners all stopped and looked at each other, Adrian suddenly heard the strange noise he had been making. It was always hard to fit the word 'Denise' into the rhythm of his breathing, and in the strain of the last hundred yards it had changed to a meaningless gasp, 'Nees-A! Nees-A,' that was no help at all to him.

That night, for the first time since he had met Denise, he wondered if her influence over him might be weakening.

A few nights later Sherd and his wife were climbing down towards a lonely riverbank in the Otways. It was Sunday afternoon and they wanted to be alone for a few hours, away from the people of Our Lady of the Ranges. They were surprised to hear squeals coming from the river. They got to the little beach in time to see a naked man and two naked women dash out of the water and sprint towards a big beach umbrella and a heap of towels and clothes.

One of the women was a tall leggy brunette, and the other was a blonde with ample curves. Each of them kept an arm across her breasts and a hand between her thighs as she ran, so that Adrian was not forced to shield his eyes from them. But he flung himself in front of his wife to save her

216

from seeing the man's big hairy organ flopping up and down.

Sherd took his wife to the far end of the beach, but he kept thinking of the man and the two women. More than once he was tempted to stroll over and start a friendly conversation with them. He tried to convince himself there would be no harm in it, since the women would almost certainly be fully dressed. But when he remembered he was a married man with a beautiful young wife beside him, he came to his senses and admitted he was experiencing an impure temptation.

The boy Adrian Sherd was as shocked as the man when he realised how close he had come to turning his back on his wife and going into an occasion of sin. A few months before, the thrill of chatting to his wife in her bathers would have been so powerful that he could have kept his back turned all day on a beach full of naked film stars.

He realised that the married life of the Sherds was becoming too remote from the daily life of the young Adrian Sherd. Mrs Denise Sherd was a wonderful wife, but perhaps a boy in Form Five needed someone nearer his own age.

Adrian decided to act. On the very next night, he lay down in bed as usual, but instead of reaching out a hand to stroke the long black hair and the pale shoulder of his wife, he leaned across the compartment in the Coroke train and said to Denise McNamara, 'Excuse me, but I've been meaning to speak to you for some time.'

He wasn't brave enough to look her in the eyes as he spoke. He watched her hands and was encouraged to see her fiddling with her gloves and exposing the creamy-white skin of her wrists. When she answered him, her voice was just as gentle and sincere as he used to dream it might be when he sat opposite her in the train and waited for them both to grow older so he could talk to her and begin his long patient wooing.

They called each other 'Denise' and 'Adrian' without formally introducing themselves—although they were both too shy to mention the day when they showed each other their names on exercise books. There was so much to talk about—the subjects they studied at school, the sports they played, the radio programs they listened to at night, the things they did at weekends. When Denise said she liked going to the pictures when she got the chance, Adrian knew she was inviting him to ask her to the pictures in Accrington some day when they knew each other better.

Adrian got more pleasure from hearing the schoolgirl Denise talk about her likes and dislikes and hobbies than he had once got from imagining her as his wife. He chatted to her every night for nearly two months. The only bother he had was that sometimes when he stood near her in the train of an afternoon, he almost forgot himself and blurted out the story he was saving for their conversation that night.

When it was almost December, Adrian decided to speed up events so he would be deeply involved with her before they had to part for the long summer holidays. One night in bed he asked her quietly would she care to go to the pictures with him on the following Saturday night. It was much easier than he had expected. She even blushed a little as she answered, proving that this was the first time any young man had asked her out. She told him she would ask her parents, and the next day it was all arranged.

On the Saturday night Adrian and Denise sat together in one of the special buses that took crowds of young couples from outlying suburbs into Accrington to the Plaza or the Lyric.

During the first picture Adrian leaned his upper arm against Denise's shoulder and was pleased to see she did not draw away from him. At interval he gently grasped her elbow when she was jostled by the crowds around the ice-cream counter.

The main picture had a lot of kissing and romance. Adrian was not interested in the plot. He was planning for the moment when he would reach out boldly and take Denise's hand. It was lying naked and limp and easily within his reach, just above her knee. He couldn't approach it where it was—Denise might see his hand coming and think for an instant he was going to touch her on the thigh. But at last she lifted it onto the armrest between them, which he had left unoccupied for that very purpose. He still had to wait until there was no kissing on the screen. (He reasoned that if he reached for her hand at a moment when a man and woman were pressed together in the film, Denise might think he was planning to court her with kisses and hugs like a man from Hollywood.)

At last, when a band was playing a song with only a suggestion of romance in its words, he rested his hand on hers. The white hand did not move. He lifted it up with all the tenderness that his five fingers could express and laid it between his palms (keeping it as far away as possible from his own thighs and lap). Still it did not even twitch or tauten. He saw from the corner of his eye that Denise was watching the film as if nothing had happened to her hand.

He knew it was only modesty that made her hand so

limp. She must have suspected he was deeply in love with her, but she would have to be absolutely certain of it before she could yield any part of her body to him. He kept her hand in his and tried to convince himself that his dream really had come true at last, that he was actually sitting beside Denise McNamara and caressing her hand. And then he had a powerful erection.

It was the biggest and strongest that he had ever had in a public place—almost certainly more fierce than the monster that had appeared for no reason one morning in Form Three and lasted all through a Latin period. It made a conspicuous mound in his trousers as it tried to stand upright and flex itself.

Adrian's first thought was that he must keep the thing hidden from Denise. He lifted her hand back onto the armrest, gave it a farewell pat, and left it there. Then he slid his left hand (the hand farther from Denise) into his trousers pocket and slowly eased the huge thing until it lay pointing along the inside edge of his thigh. It was uncomfortable and restless in its new position, but at least it no longer made a threatening lump in his trousers. He thanked God that Denise kept her eyes on the screen while all this was going on.

Adrian gave up trying to follow the film and prepared for the moment when the lights came on and he had to stand up and walk outside with Denise beside him. He concentrated on the most frightening thoughts—losing his trousers on the way back from the communion rails at mass; letting off a thunderous fart as he walked past the microphone to receive his prize on the stage of Swindon town hall at St Carthage's Speech Night; vomiting all over his examination answers just before the supervisor came to collect them in the crowded Exhibition Building. But he could not make his erection go down.

When the film finally ended Adrian kept his left hand in his pocket to hold the thing down. He had to walk very slowly, but he pretended to yawn a lot so Denise would think he was tired. In the bus he had some trouble getting Denise to sit on his right side, away from the battle going on in his trousers.

Denise invited him to her house for a cup of tea. Adrian limped towards her front gate, trying to look down at himself in the light from a street lamp to see how much was visible.

He prayed that her parents would be in bed, but they were in the lounge room listening to *Geoff Carmichael's Supper Club* on the radio. Of course Adrian had to take his hand out of his pocket to be introduced to them. He was sure Mrs McNamara didn't notice anything unusual. (She looked to be in her forties, so she probably hadn't seen anything like it for years.) But Denise's father looked him up and down quickly before shaking hands. Adrian was sure the father of a girl as beautiful and innocent as Denise would be always alert for signs that her purity was threatened. If Mr McNamara had noticed the least sign of movement in Adrian's trousers he would be too polite to say anything about it with his wife and daughter in the room, but he would tell his daughter afterwards that she was forbidden to associate with that young Sherd fellow any more.

The parents soon left the young people alone in the dining room. Denise leaned forward across the table to talk to Adrian about the film. He said to himself (slowly and distinctly, so the message would travel down his nerves into his groin) that he was looking into the eyes of the most chaste and modest and beautiful girl in the world. But instead of dying of shame, the thing in his trousers reared up as if he had promised it some filthy pleasure.

For the rest of his time in the dining room, Adrian let his erection do what it liked out of sight under the table while he took a pure delight in looking at Denise's pink earlobes, the white hollow at the base of her throat, and the faultless symmetry of her face.

When it was time to go, he walked behind her to the front door. Then he dodged quickly past her and said goodnight over his shoulder. He had never intended to kiss her after their first outing together. He wanted to emphasise that it was not physical gratification he was looking for when he went out with her. It was just as well—he shuddered to think what might have happened if he had stood with his body close to hers and no free hand to keep in his pocket.

By the time he had closed the McNamaras' front gate his erection had shrivelled up and promised to cause no more trouble that night. But Adrian was already planning how to outwit it when he next went out with Denise.

After school a few days later, Adrian took a tram from Swindon into the city and went to a shop he had learned about from advertisements in the *Sporting Globe*. In the window he saw wheelchairs, artificial legs, bedpans, braces for injured backs, strange thick stockings and things he supposed were trusses. He asked the man at the counter for an athletic support and hoped he looked like a footballer or bike rider who needed one for a genuine reason. The man

222

came towards him with a tape measure. Adrian shrank back. He couldn't believe he had to take out his privates in the shop and have them measured. But the man only pulled the tape measure around Adrian's waist and went to some drawers behind the counter. Adrian would have asked for a size smaller than his fitting but he was afraid the man would think he was some kind of pervert who tortured his organ before he masturbated.

That night Adrian wore the jockstrap to bed under his pyjamas. Before he lay down, he pressed his penis flat against his testicles and pulled the belt of the jockstrap as high as it would reach around his waist. Purely as a part of his experiment, he teased his organ by poking it with his fingers. It swelled a little, but the elastic easily held it down. Adrian was satisfied it would give him no trouble that night, no matter how long he held Denise's hand, or even if she responded by squeezing his.

A little later he was chatting to her again in the Saturday night picture bus to Accrington. Everything was peaceful between his legs because he knew he wouldn't be reaching for her hand until they had settled down in the theatre and the lights had gone out. Suddenly the young woman in the seat in front of them leaned her head on the shoulder of the young man beside her and shifted her body until it pressed against his. Adrian shifted an inch or so away from Denise to show her he didn't approve of couples making an exhibition of themselves in public. Denise sat very still. He supposed she was as irritated as he was by the couple. But then she placed her hand calmly and deliberately on the seat between them, with the fingers neatly arranged as though she meant him to place his own hand over them.

Before he had time to consider whether Denise was actually inviting him to hold her hand and whether he ought to take it so early in the evening, there was trouble in his jockstrap. His member was straining against its bonds and arching itself into a shape like a banana. He clasped Denise's hand quickly to distract her attention.

He held Denise's hand all through both films. He avoided giving it any unusual signs of affection such as squeezing it or stroking it, and he was glad to find that it lay quietly under his the whole time. Some time after interval his penis seemed to concede defeat and lay down peacefully.

As the film ended Adrian was looking forward to talking with Denise on the bus and in her dining room. He was halfway to the bus stop before he realised he had underestimated the enemy in his jockstrap. While he had been watching the second film it had eased itself into a new position. (He might even have helped it unwittingly when he shifted his legs around.) Now it was pointing ever so slightly upwards and stretching just enough to keep itself there. Whenever it chose—in the bus, or in McNamaras' lounge room in front of Denise's parents, or more likely on the front veranda when he tried to kiss her goodnight, it could draw itself up to its full height and stand out like a broomstick against the front of his trousers and make a mockery of his courtship.

Adrian stood for a minute in the middle of his darkened bedroom. He took a few steps forward and then reached down once more to check what was happening beneath his pyjamas. His enemy had consolidated its position still further.

Adrian realised he could never escape from the danger of mortal sin. He would always be at the mercy of his own penis. He took off his jockstrap and hid it in his wardrobe. Then he put on his pyjamas and climbed into bed.

There was just one more thing to do before he went to sleep. He walked up the path to McNamaras' house and knocked on the front door. Denise herself opened it. She was not his wife or his fiancée or even the young woman he had twice taken to the pictures. She was a sixteen-year-old schoolgirl in the tunic and blouse and jacket of the Academy of Mount Carmel.

She hesitated to ask him inside because her parents were both out and she was alone in the house. He stepped past her and strode into the lounge room. She closed the front door and stood in front of him. She had never looked more beautiful and pathetic. She said something like, 'I always thought it would end like this,' or 'It was impossible from the start.' But he was not really listening.

He gripped both her wrists with one hand. With his free hand he tore at her clothing. Something, perhaps the memory of all she had once meant to him, made him hesitate to undress her completely. He simply exposed the charms that he would never enjoy and stared at them for a long, solemn moment. Then he released her.

She stumbled backwards and fell among the cushions on the couch. She lay there, fumbling with her clothes to cover herself. The last thing Adrian saw before he turned and walked out of the house forever was the emblem on the pocket of her jacket, the snowcapped holy mountain of Carmel with a circle of stars above it, falling back into place over her naked left breast.

After his jockstrap had let him down, Adrian still caught his usual Coroke train, but he got into the rear carriage, well away from the Mount Carmel girl's carriage, and he only travelled as far as Caulfield. He was training every night at the racecourse for the House Sports. He wore his new jockstrap whenever he trained, and found it improved his running.

One morning instead of the usual Christian Doctrine period, Adrian's class had a priest to speak to them.

The priest was a stranger. He put his hands in his pockets, leaned back against the brother's desk and said, 'My name is Father Kevin Parris and my job is to visit secondary schools to give advice to any young chaps like yourselves who want to find out about the work of the secular priest.

'You all know the difference of course between a secular priest like myself and a religious priest—a member of a religious order—who takes a vow of obedience to the head of his order. I think it's fair to say that the secular priests are the backbone of the church. Not even the most ancient of the religious orders can trace its history back as far as we can. The first priests that Christ ordained were secular priests. I'm talking of course about the Apostles—the very first Catholic clergy. And the work that Christ sent them out to do is the same work that the secular priests of the Melbourne Archdiocese are doing today.

'You boys know without being told what that work is. Maybe a few of you live in parishes that have been entrusted to some order or other, but the great majority of you were baptised by a secular priest, you made your first confession to a secular priest, and you received your first communion from a secular priest. Those of you who marry in later life will probably receive that sacrament in the presence of a secular priest. And when you come to die, please God you'll receive the last sacrament from one of us too.

'Of course there's a thousand and one other tasks we perform as well. You might compare us to the rucks and rovers in a football team. We have a roving commission to go wherever we're needed and do the heavy work. And boys, just like any other football team, the priests of your archdiocese need a steady stream of recruits.

'You might be interested in a few facts and figures about vocations to the priesthood here in Melbourne. I was ordained myself in 1944—that's ten years ago now. At the ceremony in St Pat's Cathedral there were seventeen of us ordained for this archdiocese. Now, in those days, seventeen new priests were barely enough to meet the demands of the archdiocese. I remember the Archbishop telling us all that we were only going to fill the gaps left by deaths and serious illness among the priests of Melbourne.

'Well, that was 1944. Now, I don't have to tell you how Melbourne has grown in the last few years. Think of all the new suburbs stretching for miles out towards Frankston and Coroke and Dandenong where there were only farms and market gardens a few years back. And all those suburbs need Catholic churches and schools for the families growing up there. Then think of the thousands of New Australians who've come to this country since the war—most of them from Catholic countries. All these people need priests to serve them.

'And what do we find? This year, 1954, we had twenty-three ordinations. That's just six more than in 1944. You can see we're not really keeping up with the demand for priests. It's been calculated that we need a minimum of fifty to sixty ordinations each year until 1960 just to properly staff the parishes we've already got and keep some of our overworked priests from cracking up under the strain. Our team is up against it. We've got our nineteenth and twentieth men on the field and we're fighting overwhelming odds. The coach is crying out for new recruits. And this brings me to the point of my little talk to you.

'Theologians tell us that God always provides enough vocations for the needs of His church in every age. In others words, this year all over Melbourne God has planted the seeds of a vocation in the hearts of enough young men to meet the needs of our archdiocese. But God only calls— He never compels. So if we find next year an insufficient number of candidates entering our seminary, we can only conclude that a great many young men have deliberately turned their backs on a call from God.

'And now I'm going to speak bluntly. Bearing in mind the needs of our archdiocese at present, I would say that each of the major Catholic colleges (and this includes St Carthage's of course), that each of them should have at least ten boys in the matriculation class this year who've been called by God to be priests in the Archdiocese of Melbourne. Next year most of you chaps will be in matric and the same will apply to you. Which means there could well be ten of you listening to me now who've already been called, or will soon be called by God, to serve Him as priests.

'To have a vocation to the priesthood, a boy needs three things—good health, the right level of intelligence and the right intention. Good health means an average constitution strong enough to stand up to a lifetime of hard work—you all look to me as if you've got that. As for intelligence, any boy who can pass the matric exam (including a pass in Latin) will have the intelligence to cope with the studies for the priesthood. Health and intelligence are fairly easy to judge. The third sign of a vocation is the one you have to be really sure of.

'A boy who has a right intention will first of all be of good moral character. Now, this doesn't mean he has to be a saint or a goody-goody. He'll be a good average Catholic boy who's keen on football and sport and works hard at his studies and doesn't join in smutty conversations. Of course he'll have temptations like we all do. But he'll have learnt how to beat them with the help of prayer and the sacraments. And as for the right intention, well, it could be the desire to win souls for God—to give up your whole life to do His work.

'An example of a wrong intention would be, for instance, to want to be a priest as a way of advancing yourself in the eyes of the world. But thank God in these days it's very rare for anyone to offer himself for the priesthood for reasons like that.

'And that's really all there is to it. If you have good health, the right level of intelligence and a right intention, you've almost certainly got a vocation to the priesthood. The trouble is, too many young fellows think they have to get a special sign from heaven. They expect an angel to tap them on the shoulder and say, "Come on, son, God wants you for a priest!" Or perhaps they think they'll have a vision some morning after mass, and see Our Lord or

Our Lady herself beckoning to them. Nonsense! All the priests I know have been thoroughly normal young chaps like yourselves who realised one day that they had all the signs of a vocation. Then they prayed and thought about it and talked it over with a priest and that was that.

'Sometimes a fellow can realise he's got a vocation in funny ways. One of our outstanding young priests always maintains he got his vocation at a dance. It seems he was standing in a corner watching all the happy young people enjoying themselves around him when he suddenly realised that all this was not for him. God was calling him all right, and compared with the life of a priest, all the pleasures of the world seemed worthless.

'Some men say they knew from the time they were small boys that they had a vocation. Others never realise it until they're grown men—sometimes years after they've left school. The idea that God is calling you can grow on you slowly or it can hit you like a flash of lightning. There may be someone in this room right now who has never before asked himself this simple question, "Is God calling me to be a priest in the Archdiocese of Melbourne?" If any one of you is in this position, it might be a good time now, when you're approaching your last year of school and wondering what you're going to do with your life—it's a good time to ask yourself seriously and honestly, "Is God calling me?"

'Boys, would you each take a pencil and a piece of paper and write down something for me. For the sake of privacy I must ask you all to write something. If you can say in all honesty that you definitely don't have a vocation to the priesthood, just write "God bless you, Father" or something like that on your paper and don't put your name.

230

If you're at all interested in the priesthood, just sign your name and write the word "Interested".

'Those who are interested can have a chat with me in the brothers' front parlour some time today. I'm not a salesman, remember. No priest would ever dare to put pressure on a boy in such a serious business as this. If you care to have a chat with me I'll arrange to send you some literature and leave you my phone number if you want any further advice from time to time.

'Now, would every boy write on his paper and fold it up small and pass it to the front, please.'

Adrian wrote, 'Definitely interested—Adrian Sherd.' He folded his paper and passed it forward. Then he sat back and told himself he had just taken the most dramatic step of his life. But then he remembered you couldn't make a decision as important as this without a lot of prayer and thought. Yet the young man at the dance had decided in a flash that he would give it all up. (Some of the girls in their ballerina frocks would have been almost as beautiful as Denise McNamara.) And now that man was an outstanding young priest and the girls were all happily married to other chaps.

Soon after lunch a message came for a certain boy to see Father Parris in the brothers' parlour. The whole class watched him get up from his seat and go. They were not surprised—he was quiet and solemn and he objected to hearing dirty jokes.

Adrian waited for his turn to visit the priest. He was worried about Seskis and Cornthwaite and O'Mullane seeing him leave the class. He saw them putting up their hands and saying, 'Please, Brother, Sherd can't talk to the

231

vocations priest—last year in Form Four he committed nearly two hundred mortal sins.'

Father Sherd stepped up to the pulpit to begin his first sermon in his new parish. He saw the three of them grinning up at him from the back seats. They were ready to heckle him with shouts of 'What about Jayne and Marilyn?' They had already sent an anonymous letter about him to the Archbishop.

But God would keep their lips sealed. He would never allow one of His own priests to be reproached in public for sins that had been forgiven years before. And how could Seskis and the others speak out without revealing their own guilty secrets?

When it was Adrian's turn to leave the classroom, he stood up boldly and strode to the door and silently offered up his embarrassment as an act of reparation to God for the sins of his past life.

Adrian said to the priest, 'My story is probably unusual, Father. When I was at primary school I served as an altar boy for years and developed a great love for the mass and the sacraments and often wondered whether I might have a vocation to the priesthood. But I'm sorry to say a few years ago I fell among bad companions and had a bit of trouble with sins of impurity—not with girls, fortunately, but on my own—mostly thoughts, but sometimes, I'm sorry to say, impure actions.

'Luckily I never gave up trying to fight against these sins and I'm happy to say that now for a long time I've led a normal life in the state of grace. I've thought a lot lately about the life of a priest, and I'll certainly be praying about it before it's time to make up my mind next year about entering the seminary. But I sometimes wonder if my past sins would mean that I couldn't possibly have a vocation.'

Adrian was surprised at how calmly the priest heard him out. Father Parris said, 'Take my advice and forget all about whatever you might have done years ago. You know your sins have all been forgiven in the sacrament of penance. What counts now is the sort of fellow you are now. Keep on praying to God and Our Lady and you'll soon find out what's expected of you.

'Now, let's have your name and address and I'll send you a booklet about the life our young fellows lead in the diocesan seminary. Have a good look at it and just go on quietly with your studies and have a chat to your parish priest from time to time. And next year, if you're still interested, we can talk about your applying to enter the seminary.'

The priest looked at his watch and consulted a list of names in front of him. He said, 'Now, would you ask John Toohey to see me when you get back to your room?'

When Adrian left school that afternoon he knew he could catch Denise McNamara's train if he strolled down Swindon Road to the station. But he walked into the Swindon church and knelt in one of the back seats.

He saw how the last few troubled years of his life were really part of a wonderful pattern that could only have been worked out by God Himself.

First came the year of his American nonsense—it revolted him now, but its purpose had been to show him that sinners were never happy. Then came Denise's year. God had arranged for him to meet Denise because at that time the influence of a pure young woman was the only thing that could have rescued him. Now, Denise had served her purpose. The terrible scene in her lounge room only a few nights before had proved that she no longer had the power to keep his lust in check. It was God's way of warning him not to rely on a mere woman to save his soul.

Now, after a year without sin, Adrian was the equal of those average Catholic boys of good moral character that the priest had talked about. The next part of the pattern was becoming clear. He was almost certain he had a vocation to the priesthood. Like the young man on the dance floor he had sampled the joys of mixing with the opposite sex and found them shallow and unsatisfying.

He still had a year to wait before he could enter the seminary. He would devise a scheme of meditations on his future as a priest to sustain him through his year of waiting.

Adrian knelt and prayed until he knew he had missed Denise's train. Then he left the church and hurried to the station. He decided to visit the church each afternoon until the end of the year to spare himself and Denise the embarrassment of meeting again after it was all over between them. She would be puzzled for a while, but a girl so beautiful would soon attract other admirers. And one day, eight years later, she would open the *Advocate* and see pages of pictures of the newly ordained priests and realise what had been on his mind when he stopped seeing her on the Coroke train years before, and forgive him.

In the last weeks of the school year, Adrian had to spend most of his time preparing for his Leaving Certificate exams. But every night before he began his studies he allowed himself to consider his future as a priest.

He lifted the well-polished bronze knocker and rapped at the door of a comfortable double-fronted solid-brick house in a peaceful valley of a suburb beyond Camberwell. The middle-aged woman who answered the door was a stranger to him, but when she saw his Roman collar she said, 'Come in, Father.'

Reverend Father Sherd remembered that a priest should never give occasion for scandal. He asked the woman, 'Are you alone in the house, madam?' When she said yes he began talking to her on the doorstep, where the neighbours could see them if they were peeping from behind their front curtains.

The woman and her husband were lapsed Catholics. She admitted to Father Sherd that they played golf on Sundays instead of going to mass. Father Sherd chatted amicably to her for a few minutes to show her he was human. Then, when he saw that she was off guard, he gave her three minutes of his best preaching.

He used all his most powerful arguments—the infinite mercy of God; the joy of the angels in heaven when a sinner repented; the sufferings endured by Christ to redeem every member of the human race; and many more. When he had finished, the woman bowed her head. He allowed himself to touch her gently on the arm as he said kindly, 'Tell your husband I'll be expecting you both at mass next Sunday.'

As he walked down the path between the neat beds of standard roses, he reminded himself that his success with the woman was not due to any ability he might have possessed but to the grace of God working through him.

A booklet with the title *The Priest* came in the post to Adrian from Father Parris. It was made up of articles written by young priests of the Melbourne Archdiocese. Adrian was especially interested in the articles describing life at the seminary where the young priests had trained. This was the life he himself would lead for seven years after he had left school.

The seminary was surrounded by quiet farmland a few miles past the western suburbs of Melbourne. The students were safe from all the distractions of the city. Instead of reading about the Cold War and the bodgie gangs in the *Argus*, they got up before six each morning and went to mass. They had hours of lectures each day. They called their teachers 'professors'. The place was like a university except that the seminary courses were longer and harder. And instead of the merely descriptive sciences such as physics and chemistry, the seminarians studied the Queen of Sciences—theology. Adrian wondered how he could wait a whole year before he threw himself into the life of the seminary.

Several articles in the booklet were written by young priests to describe their experiences in their first parishes. They could hardly express in words the joy and excitement of their first masses and the satisfaction that they got from administering the sacraments to people.

Father Sherd settled himself in the dark confessional. He adjusted the violet-coloured stole around his shoulders and pulled back the wooden screen near his head. A young man began his confession. Father Sherd kept his eyes closed to avoid embarrassing the penitent.

The fellow confessed impure thoughts about the young woman who worked beside him and occasional impure actions by himself. Father Sherd advised him to keep his eyes on his own desk at work and to take up a hobby to occupy himself in his spare time at home.

The fellow said 'What hobby did you take up to cure yourself, Sherd?' It was O'Mullane grinning through the grille of the confessional.

What could the young priest do? Force O'Mullane to confess the additional sin of sacrilege for having shown disrespect to one of God's anointed priests? Tell him the true story of how a good Catholic girl had saved him, Sherd, from a life of sin and then bind O'Mullane under pain of mortal sin never to repeat the story outside the confessional? Ask the Archbishop for a transfer to a quiet rural parish where O'Mullane and the others would never find him? But the list of priests' transfers was always published in the *Advocate*. O'Mullane or Cornthwaite or Seskis would read about his transfer and drive to his parish to torment him. If ever they were short of money, they could try to blackmail him—five pounds each week from the collection plate or else they would print the story of his past life on a duplicator and leave sheets on all the seats in the church before his Sunday mass.

Adrian worried whether he was truly suitable for the priesthood. He knew that Canon Law would not allow a man to be ordained if his appearance was likely to cause amusement. (This law was hard on devout young men with St Vitus dance or huge warts on their faces. But its purpose was to preserve the dignity of the priesthood.) If the enemies of the church got to hear about the pranks being played on young Father Sherd, other clergy might be subjected to disrespect.

Adrian visited his Aunt Kathleen. He remembered the

many occasions when he would sit in her front room among her altars and flickering fairy lights, asking her about indulgences and reliquaries and other esoteric Catholic subject matter while inwardly he was like the Pharisees in the Gospels—a mass of corruption. Now, at last, he could look her in the eye with nothing to conceal from her.

He said, 'I've been wondering lately whether I might have a vocation to the priesthood, but whenever I think of the daily life of a priest in his parish it doesn't attract me. I mean, being for years in some suburb like Accrington and trying to preach to people and save their souls but they remember me when I was a schoolboy in short pants.'

His aunt did not answer at first. She bowed her head and moved her lips. She walked to her statue of Our Lady and murmured something. Then she sat down beside Adrian and said, 'No one can ever say I've tried to influence any of my nephews or talk them into vocations. All these years, I've deliberately said nothing to put the thought into your mind. But now I can tell you my great secret. Every day since you were born, I've prayed that you or one of your brothers would be called by God. And now that my prayer has been answered, I'll see that nothing stands in your way.'

She looked hard at him. 'Now, who's been talking to you about the life of a secular priest? They've sent their vocations salesman around the schools, have they? And I suppose he told you the secular clergy have got first claim on you, and the religious orders shouldn't come poaching on the seculars' territory.'

She got up and walked to a corner of her bookshelf. 'I've left these here for ages, hoping you'd take an interest in them, but you were always more interested in my magazines whenever you visited me. The poor old Orders never get a chance to reach you young chaps in secondary schools.'

She was holding a stack of booklets and pamphlets. She dealt them like cards all over her coffee table and said, 'Last year, when they held that big Catholic Life Exhibition in the Exhibition Buildings, I went to every one of the stalls run by religious orders of priests and collected their vocations literature. Young fellows just don't realise what a wonderful life they could have in a religious order instead of being stuck for year after year in a dreary parish.'

Adrian and his aunt spent all afternoon comparing the different orders that he could join. Mostly, he leafed through the pamphlets and booklets while his aunt talked. It was like learning about the histories and traditions and club colours and mottoes and past champions of the various clubs in some glorious football league, and savouring the pleasure of deciding which club to give your allegiance to.

Some orders had special devotions or aims. The Blessed Sacrament Fathers dedicated themselves to the perpetual adoration of Our Lord in the Blessed Sacrament—at every hour of the day or night, a member of the order watched and prayed before Our Lord exposed on the altar in the chapel of the monastery. The Carmelites spread devotion to Our Lady under her title of Our Lady of Mount Carmel and promoted the wearing of the miraculous scapulars (brown, red, white, blue and green) that she had given to St Simon Stock when she appeared to him in a vision. The Columban Fathers worked all their lives as missionaries with the aim of winning over the whole of Asia to the church. The Dominicans were the intellectuals of the church and were often to be found in the great Catholic universities of Europe. The Redemptorists were famous as orators. They travelled from parish to parish conducting missions. Some of their sermons about the punishments of hell had converted lifelong sinners. The Passionists had a special devotion to the Passion of Our Lord—his sufferings during his last days. Each Passionist, in addition to the usual vows of poverty, chastity and obedience, took a vow to spread this devotion worldwide.

Some orders had attractive habits or emblems. Adrian admired the sweeping white robes and black capes of the Dominicans. The brown of the Franciscans was quietly distinctive. The Redemptorists wore peculiar collars that looked as if they were missing a button. The Passionists caught Adrian's eye in their black robes with a striking white badge over their hearts.

When Adrian had made himself familiar with the uniforms and special devotions of the different orders, he spent a pleasant hour with an atlas of Australia, studying the location of their provincial houses, monasteries, seminaries, retreat houses and priories. He was especially curious about the places where the students and novices spent their years of training. He was delighted to see that most orders kept their students well away from the capital cities, in converted mansions or huge brick buildings with cloisters and a private chapel and rows of windows overlooking a formal garden and views of farmland or distant mountains.

Adrian's favourite picture in all his aunt's collection showed a group of young men with a billy can and a sugar bag of provisions setting out for a picnic. The men were in the driveway of a massive stone building with a tower that seemed to Adrian to belong in the Balkans. Behind the building was a broad vista of farmland and beyond it a blur of rooftops in the outlying streets of a fair-sized country town. Visible in the background of this picture was a path bordered with flowering cannas. A student might have walked up and down that path, reciting the Divine Office or praying or meditating, with nothing to distract him but the sound of bees in the shoulder-high canna blossoms. Each time the student reached the end of the path and turned to stride back, he glimpsed the vista of paddocks and the distant roofs. Men were at work in the town. Women were shopping. Children were swinging their legs under their desks in school. All of them—men, women and children—had forgotten the real purpose of life. The student in the grounds of his hilltop monastery, with the Blessed Sacrament in the chapel under the Balkan tower and a library of theology books somewhere on the second storey and the rules of his order regulating every hour of his day and bringing him gradually nearer to perfection—the student would offer up a pious ejaculation on behalf of the people in the far town and would turn back to his meditation between the stately cannas.

The caption beneath the picture read: *Lads off for a day's hike at the Charleroi Fathers' junior seminary near Blenheim, NSW.* But who were the Charleroi Fathers, and what was a junior seminary?

Adrian's aunt explained that some religious orders allowed boys of secondary school age to test their vocations in junior seminaries—places just like boarding schools except that students followed a modified version of the rule of the order concerned. Junior seminaries were common in the Catholic countries of Europe, according to Aunt Kathleen. She thoroughly approved of them. It was tragic how many young chaps felt they had vocations at the age of thirteen or fourteen but later got distracted by the temptations of the world.

As for the Charleroi Fathers, their real name was the Congregation of Christ the King, which was too much of a mouthful for most people. They had been founded at Charleroi in Belgium in the early eighteenth century by St Henry de Cisy. He was a young nobleman who wanted to serve as a soldier in the cause of the Catholics against the Protestants. But as a young man he had a vision of Christ wearing a golden crown and enthroned as the King of the World. Christ asked Henry why he chose to serve an earthly ruler when he could serve a heavenly king, and Henry was a changed man from that moment. He studied for the priest-hood and later founded the Congregation of Christ the King. The special aim of the order was to turn the whole world into the kingdom of Christ. Their mother-house was in Belgium, and they had numerous houses in Europe, but they were a comparatively small order in Australia, and Aunt Kathleen didn't really know much about them.

When Adrian heard about the junior seminary in the remote countryside of New South Wales, he knew that he had found his order. If his parents agreed, he could join the Charleroi Fathers as a junior seminarian as soon as the Christmas holidays were over.

Before he finally committed himself, there were a few more things he had to find out. What sort of robes did the Charleroi Fathers wear? The pictures of priests showed them in black cassocks, but some sort of emblem could be seen near the collar. Adrian's aunt believed it was a cross surmounted by a crown. Adrian hardly cared what the design was, so long as it was embroidered in a rich colour. His aunt seemed to recall that it was red or blue.

Where exactly was Blenheim, and where would a Charleroi student study for the priesthood after he had left the junior seminary? Adrian and his aunt consulted the leaflet. Blenheim was about a hundred and twenty miles south of Sydney on the main railway line to Melbourne. After the junior seminary came the novitiate year in the hills near Adelaide and then three years of philosophy at a modern brick monastery in Canberra followed by three years of theology in the headquarters of the Australian and New Zealand Province of the order—a spacious building of two storeys in a northern suburb of Sydney.

Adrian would do none of his training in Victoria. By the time he was ready to be ordained, the boys of St Carthage's, and even Denise McNamara, would have forgotten him.

Last, what sort of work did the Charleroi Fathers do? Did they manage any parishes in Victoria, for instance? As far as Aunt Kathleen knew, the order mostly conducted missions in parishes all over Australia and gave retreats for priests and nuns, although they were not often seen in Victoria. Reverend Father Sherd CCR (the letters stood for the Latin *Congregatio Christi Regis*) would spend most of his time far from the dreary suburbs of Melbourne, the site of his shameful sins and romantic daydreams.

Mission priests worked in pairs. During the fortnight of each mission, they preached in the parish church at night and visited Catholic homes by day, always with the aim of rekindling the faith in the lukewarm or the lapsed. In the late 1960s, Father Sherd began a mission in an outer south-eastern suburb of Melbourne. During his first sermon, he thought he recognised one of the several upturned faces in the congregation. He faltered for a moment but quickly recovered. From that moment on, he preached like a man inspired. Each time he paused for breath, he saw some tough old workingman drop his head into his hands or some hard-faced housewife press her hand to her mouth in shame.

Next day, in a quiet street, Father Sherd rang the door-bell of a neat cream-brick veneer. According to the parish records, it was the home of Mr and Mrs Gerard O'Connell and their five children. The young mother opened the door. It was Her!

They looked at each other for a few moments before either spoke. Motherhood had made her even more beautiful and rounded the curves of her still-youthful body. She would have seen lines in his face and hollows in his cheeks from the harsh life that he led as a religious priest, but his eyes burned with the zeal of a man who had given up everything for God. And in his gaze was no trace of the regard he had once had for her—respect, yes, but romantic affection, no!

They sat for five minutes in her lounge room. He addressed her as Mrs O'Connell, and she called him Father. Her younger children played around her while he asked her politely about the state of her soul. Of course, she was as pure and devout as ever. Her husband was at work. She said he was a God-fearing man who treated her well.

When Father Sherd was leaving, she asked him to bless her and the children. She knelt on the polished boards of the lounge-room floor and gathered her children around her.

He stood, tall and gaunt in his black cassock, above her. The afternoon sun streamed through the venetians and lit up the red or blue insignia below his collar. He uttered the Latin formula for the blessing with all the fervour that he could summon. Then he farewelled her and strode to the front gate without looking back.

The sermons given by Father Sherd on the following nights were so impassioned that word of his preaching spread to neighbouring parishes. A loose-living bachelor named Cornthwaite thought he would travel from one of those parishes to sit in a front seat and embarrass the acclaimed mission-priest. Cornthwaite rode over on his motorbike, but the church was empty. The fortnight of the mission had ended, and Reverend Father A. Sherd CCR was in a window seat of the *Spirit of Progress* express, travelling back towards New South Wales in the service of Christ the King.

PART THREE

It was hard for Adrian to convince his parents that he had to leave for the Charleroi Fathers' junior seminary in the new year. His mother asked why he hadn't mentioned his vocation in all his years at secondary school. His father said no boy could observe the rules of a religious order if he couldn't even obey a few simple rules in his own house. And he reminded Adrian of all the fights he had with his brothers and the smart answers he gave his parents.

Adrian worked on them for days. He had two main arguments. First he made them recall the Sunday afternoons when he was only seven or eight and they all lived in the western suburbs. As soon as the Sunday dinner was over he used to spread a tea towel over the dressing table in his bedroom and celebrate mass. He wore a towel for a chasuble. His chalice was a two-handled sugar basin half-full of cold tea. The hosts were Life Saver lollies. He read aloud the Latin prayers from his Sunday missal while his parents peeped around the door at him. Sometimes they knelt in front of him at communion time and received a

Life Saver each on their tongues and went away with their heads bowed.

While his parents were thinking this over, he made them read a paragraph he had found in a story about Blessed Peter Julian Eymard, the founder of the Blessed Sacrament Fathers.

'The man who was to give his life to spreading devotion to the Blessed Eucharist showed at a tender age unmistakable signs of his future vocation. As a small child he would dress himself like a priest and reverently imitate the ceremonies he had witnessed at mass, even piping the Latin in his boyish voice.'

Adrian's mother was impressed, but his father said if you took a monkey to mass often enough it would start to imitate the priest when you put it back in its cage.

Adrian's second argument was to remind them of the quiet thoughtful life he had led for the past few years. While other boys of his age were at the pictures or at dances, he was always reading in his room or meditating in the back shed. He knew he was deceiving them. Most of his time alone he had been thinking of journeys across America or his marriage to Denise. But the circumstances of his vocation were so unusual that no one would have believed the true story.

Once again his mother became thoughtful. But his father said that was just the point, that Adrian had led a sheltered life and some priest had got at him and persuaded him to leave the world before he even knew what he was giving up.

Adrian was ready for this objection. He took the vocations pamphlet of the Charleroi Fathers out of his pocket and read a paragraph aloud.

Satan's trump card, if you let him play it, is that you should first have a taste of life. 'How do you know you can give up the pleasures of life, until you try them?' How many a splendid vocation has been destroyed through a taste of life! Because the real intention of the devil is to lead you to have, not a taste of life but a taste of sin. Do you go into the infectious disease block to see if your health can fight off the germs? If you want to have first a taste of life you have nothing to gain, but a divine vocation to lose forever.

That stopped Mr Sherd for a while. But Adrian wished he could have assured his father that he knew exactly what he was giving up. Adrian had tasted all that life could offer—first, unbridled sensuality and then the joys of a Catholic marriage. And he had given it all up one morning without a second thought.

In the end it was his Aunt Kathleen who won his parents over. She had found from the telephone directory that the Charleroi Fathers had a small house in Melbourne, a stopping place for priests conducting missions in Victoria. She telephoned the place and a priest explained that Adrian would study the New South Wales Leaving Honours course at the junior seminary. At the end of his year there, he could return home if he found he wasn't suited to the Charleroi life. Then, if he wanted to go to Melbourne University, his New South Wales certificate would be as good as a Victorian matriculation pass.

Adrian was never sure, but he believed his aunt had promised to pay for all his expenses at the junior seminary. One of Mr Sherd's first objections, when Adrian had told him about his vocation, was that his family couldn't afford to pay for his upkeep at a seminary year after year.

Aunt Kathleen took Adrian and his parents to visit the Charleroi house one Saturday afternoon. The priest who met them answered all the parents' questions patiently. Adrian saw that the device near his collar was embroidered in crimson. The priest explained that it was a crown over the Greek and Latin letters XR for Christus Rex. Adrian would wear it after his year at Blenheim, when he entered the novitiate and assumed the Holy Habit.

Adrian took away some forms to be filled in by his parish priest, his school principal and his doctor and sent to the Father Provincial of the Congregation of Christ the King in Sydney. When his parish priest saw the form he wanted to know what had attracted Adrian to such an obscure order and why he hadn't come and talked over the life of a secular priest when he first thought he had a vocation. But the priest said he would give Adrian a good reference because he had seen him at the sacraments regularly.

The Principal of St Carthage's College looked at the Charleroi device at the top of the form and said, 'You've chosen a hard, strict order, son. But I think you've got what it takes.'

Adrian took his medical form to the local clinic. A young doctor he had never seen before said, 'What the blazes is this?'

Adrian realised this was his first taste of the ignorance and incomprehension he would meet all his life from non-Catholics. He explained that he was applying to enter the junior seminary of a religious order, and the medical examination was to see whether he could stand up to the hard life of the priesthood.

The doctor was not contemptuous, only very curious. He said, 'How old are you?'

Adrian said, 'Almost seventeen.'

'And you've decided you're going to sign up with these monks, these'—he looked at the form—'these Christ the King chappies? Do they keep you for life?'

'I don't have to take my solemn vows until I'm quite sure I'm suited to the life. That won't be for three or four years.'

'Solemn vows, eh? So you won't be getting married or anything like that?' He sat back in his chair and looked at Adrian.

'There are three vows—poverty, chastity and obedience. Their purpose is to perfect a man spiritually.' Adrian was embarrassed, but he offered up his discomfort to God and told himself he was acquiring the virtue of humility.

The doctor said, 'Poverty and obedience too? They drive a hard bargain, don't they?'

Adrian began another explanation, but the doctor jumped to his feet and began his examination. He filled in the form as he worked, and said he would post it next morning to the Chief Monk.

In the last few weeks at school Adrian quietly told a few friends about his future. Cornthwaite and his little group soon knew about it, but none of them tried to make a joke of it. Adrian wondered whether it was because they had given up their habits of sin or because he already had the air of a priest and they were treating him with the respect due to the clergy.

On the very last afternoon he found himself with

Cornthwaite, Seskis and O'Mullane on the Swindon station. No one mentioned his vocation. A Coroke train pulled in and Adrian boarded it. The others stayed on the platform to wait for their Frankston train. Adrian stood in the doorway and waved to them as his train moved off. He knew he might never see them again on earth, and he wanted them to know that he bore them no grudge.

O'Mullane and Seskis waved awkwardly until Cornthwaite nudged them in the way that had always meant he was going to tell them a really foul joke. While they watched him he made an odd, exaggerated gesture with his right arm. No stranger watching would have understood it, but Seskis and O'Mullane did, and laughed.

Adrian was speeding away from them, but he understood the gesture. Cornthwaite was aping the movements of a fellow committing a sin of impurity by himself. Adrian sat down and resolved to include his former friends in the list of people he would pray for every day for the rest of his life.

On the first day of the summer holidays Adrian worked out a Divine Office to say each day until he left for New South Wales. Eight times a day at regular intervals he paced up and down the path from the back door to the shed, reciting prayers from his missal. He knew his parents thought he was taking things too far, but they no longer criticised him or tried to tease him. He guessed his Aunt Kathleen had warned them what a grave sin it was for a parent to oppose a child who was following a divine call.

After Christmas his mother told him he could spend a week with her relations at Orford. She said it would give her a last chance to get used to being without her eldest son. Adrian saw she was trying to tell him how much she would miss him when he was in New South Wales. But he said nothing. He had already shown her the paragraph in the Charleroi Fathers' pamphlet telling parents what a joy it was to give a son to God.

At Orford his aunt and uncle treated him as if he was already ordained. They gave him a bed to himself and asked him to lead them in a decade of their family rosary each night. After Sunday mass they took him to the sacristy to shake hands with the parish priest, who said he had once visited the Charleroi house in Rome.

That afternoon Adrian's aunt took him to the local convent. When they were leaving, some of the nuns asked him to pray for them. He held up his hand solemnly like a priest about to give a blessing.

Adrian would have liked to visit the settlement at Mary's Mount, but his uncle didn't seem anxious to go. He told Adrian that some of the settlers had gone back to Melbourne and the others were having a hard struggle to make ends meet.

One hot afternoon Mr McAloon drove Adrian and some of his cousins to a beach a few miles past Cape Otway. They climbed down a flight of narrow stairs cut in the cliff face. The little bay was deserted. Mr McAloon said that very few people knew about the place, but it was safe for swimming if you didn't go out too far. The two McAloon girls went to the far end of the bay and disappeared behind a tall rock to get changed.

Adrian stayed in the shallow water. He had to be careful not to risk his life before he was ordained. (It would be a tragedy if he died before experiencing the fullness of the priesthood.) And he had to cope with a strange idea that had just occurred to him.

He realised he was standing at last on the sort of deserted beach he had dreamed of visiting in Tasmania or America. At Triabunna or on the coast of California the sight of a lonely beach had made him want to do something sublime or queer or wicked. Now at Cape Otway he had the chance to identify the mysterious influence that worked on him in solitary places.

The McAloon boys were watching him. They probably thought he was teaching himself to meditate like a priest. The thought of meditation gave him his answer. For centuries, priests and monks had gone off to meditate in lonely places. They knew they were close to God in caves and secluded valleys. The agitation that troubled Adrian in scenic spots was only his awareness that God was near.

At the far end of the beach the two girls, his cousins, were going behind the rock. They had scrawny arms and legs, and freckles all over their faces, but he had noticed the shapes of breasts in the older girl's bathers. In the warm sunny corner, beside a limpid rock pool, the girl was peeling the damp cloth down from her shoulders. There were goosepimples on her white, freckled skin. She stretched her legs apart and rubbed with the towel to get the sand from the insides of her thighs.

Adrian threw himself into the water. The splash startled the McAloon boys. He wondered had they heard of the holy hermit who used to roll naked in snowdrifts and thorn bushes to drive away temptations of the flesh.

When he returned home to Melbourne Adrian found a letter with the Charleroi insignia on the envelope. It told him he had been accepted as a candidate in the junior seminary of the Congregation of Christ the King. He was expected to present himself in the first week of February.

Adrian showed the letter to his parents and asked his mother to book his ticket on the *Spirit of Progress* and to make sure the train stopped at Blenheim. Then he visited his Aunt Kathleen to say goodbye and thank her for all she had done for him.

He had never seen his aunt so excited. She said she had a thousand things to tell him before he left. First of all he must always wear the brown scapular of Our Lady. Aunt Kath gave him a new one in case his old one was worn or grubby. (He hadn't worn a scapular since his first one had fallen to pieces in primary school.)

She told him the story of a young Australian soldier in New Guinea during the war. The soldier's mother had asked him before he went away never to be without his scapular. One day he was on patrol in the jungle near the Japanese lines. He was about to walk into a clearing when he felt something holding him back. He kept trying to move forward but this thing kept stopping him. Suddenly there was a noise of firing in the clearing. A Japanese sniper was shooting at the Australian patrol. If the young soldier had gone ahead he probably would have been killed. Then he found out what had held him back. His scapular had caught on a branch. Our Lady's brown scapular had saved his life.

Aunt Kathleen urged Adrian to take as his chief patron St Gabriel of the Sorrowing Virgin, who had been proclaimed by one of the popes as a model for young people in the modern world. St Joseph of Cupertino would help him to pass his exams. St Joseph had desperately wanted to be a Franciscan priest, but he just couldn't learn his Latin. When the time came for his final exams, the only Latin he knew was a certain paragraph he had learned by heart. He prayed all the night before, and sure enough the Bishop examining him asked him to repeat that very paragraph. So he became a priest and worked many remarkable miracles.

St Anthony of Padua would always find lost objects for anyone who prayed to him. St John Chrysostom would help Adrian become a great preacher. (Chrysostom was Greek for Golden-Tongued.) And the Curé of Ars, St John Vianney, would make him a successful confessor. People used to travel from all over Europe just to go to confession to St John Vianney. One day a man finished his confession and the saint said, 'But you've left out your worst sin.' And it was true. The man had been too frightened to confess it, but St John Vianney could see into people's hearts in the confessional.

Above all, Adrian's aunt urged him to have a special devotion to Our Lady. He should choose one of her many titles (Aunt Kath's favourite was Our Lady of the Seven Dolours) and consecrate his whole life to her. Adrian said he had holy cards of Our Lady under some of her titles, but he would love to go through his aunt's book, *The World's Great Madonnas*, and take his time over the great works of art in it.

His aunt got the book from her shelf and said it could be a going-away present for him. He was so grateful that he told her it would always be with him in his cell—on a little shelf among his spiritual reading.

When he was leaving she reminded him of all the sodalities and confraternities and societies she had enrolled him in since he was a small boy. Adrian thought of the lamp in the convent in Wollongong that had been burning night and day for his intentions, and wished the nuns could know that their prayers had worked after all, and he was going to be a priest.

On a table in the hallway his aunt kept a Jacky Mite Box—a little moneybox of red and yellow cardboard with pictures of Chinese boys in coolie hats and wide sleeves. Visitors were supposed to feed Jacky Mite Box with pennies for the Missions in the Far East. Just before he said goodbye, Adrian fed Jacky a two-shilling piece to make up for all the times he had let him go hungry in the years when he was neglecting his religion and disappointing his aunt.

That night Adrian organised a sacred beauty contest. He tried not to think of it as a beauty contest—he knew that Catholics were advised not to take part in such things. And he had never forgotten that a bishop in America once excommunicated a young woman for appearing in the Miss Nude Universe Contest.

Adrian's competition was not judged according to physical beauty, although the winner would have to be graceful and pretty. He intended to find among all his pictures of Our Lady the one that would most arouse his devotion. After he had decided on the winning picture, he would take it to Blenheim and paste it inside the door of his room. Each time he left the room he would glance up at the picture and carry away the beautiful image of Our Lady in his mind. She would inspire him in his work and study just as the image of Denise McNamara had inspired him in the old days at St Carthage's. And each night when he lay waiting for sleep, the face of the purest woman who ever lived would watch over him.

Adrian spread out all his holy cards of Our Lady. He wanted to choose two finalists from the cards and two from *The World's Great Madonnas*, and then wait a few days before the Grand Final.

Since his first years in primary school, Adrian had heard Our Lady praised as gentle, loving, kind, pure, modest, meek, patient and spotlessly chaste. He had always been sure that such a woman would have a perfect face and body to match her virtues. But he had never heard any priest or brother or nun mention her physical beauty.

Sometimes he did hear bits of information that agreed with his own ideas about her beauty. A priest would say, 'When God was looking for a human being to be the mother of His own beloved Son, he had to choose the most perfect human nature that the world has ever seen.'

Once, a brother had told Adrian's class, 'The great theologians think that God would never have asked Our Lady to endure the sufferings and discomforts of giving birth as we know it. When the time came for Our Lord to be born, it seems almost certain that the Divine Child simply appeared miraculously in her arms.'

And then there was the doctrine of the Assumption and the story of how the Apostles found Our Lady's body gone from its grave and a mass of white lilies growing where it had rested. Our Lady had been assumed body and soul into heaven because it was not fitting that the flesh from which Our Lord's body had been formed should be corrupted in the grave. Her body, still youthful and perfect, was some-where in heaven even in the twentieth century while Adrian was looking for a worthy picture of it.

As he judged the pictures, Adrian looked only at the faces.

Some of the holy cards showed full-length views of Our Lady but she always wore long loose robes that reached to her wrists and ankles. He had once seen in a book of old masterpieces a Madonna with the Child on her knees and two naked breasts poking out of her dress. If that picture had been entered in his contest he would have disqualified it—it was not a genuine portrait of Our Lady. The idea of her breastfeeding the Child Jesus in public was preposterous. If some sort of feeding bottle had been invented in those days she would surely have used it. Or God could even have nourished the Child miraculously, just as He had caused him to be born in a supernatural way.

Some of the contestants were quickly eliminated. Our Lady of Perpetual Succour had sharp, foreign-looking features and a stern expression. Her lips were pale and thin like a nun's. She was not nearly feminine enough.

Others were ruled out because their faces were spoilt by grief. They had dark circles under their eyes or tears rolling down their faces. Our Lady of the Seven Dolours had a fiery glow where her chest should have been, and her heart was exposed to view with seven little swords stuck into it.

The two finalists from the holy cards were Our Lady of Fatima and a young modern Italian Madonna.

Our Lady of Fatima wore a long cream-coloured robe braided with tiny gold stars and falling away to reveal a pure-white ankle-length tunic underneath. Our Lady was barefooted, and the skin of her feet was the same flawless golden pink as her facial complexion. Her hair was hidden beneath her mantle, but her colouring suggested she was an ash-blonde.

The Italian Madonna wore the traditional blue with a

mantle of white. The mantle was draped a little carelessly over her head, exposing a few tresses of a bright auburn shade. Her complexion was breathtaking—Adrian had only seen its equal on two or three film stars. But of course the film stars would have used layers of expensive cosmetics, whereas the Madonna's skin had the radiance of natural good health.

Her delicate eyelids drooped as she clasped the infant Jesus in her arms. The mother and child were in a glade of roses, and the subtle tints of the blooms echoed the glory of the Madonna's face. Behind them a pastel-hued dawn was breaking over the roof of a noble building of white marble. They were in some corner of the classical world that had never been defiled by the sensual Romans.

There were nearly a hundred entrants from the pages of *The World's Great Madonnas*. The first to be eliminated were all the Asian and African and Red Indian and Eskimo Virgins, grotesque and impossible to venerate. Adrian would have described them as ugly if it hadn't seemed vaguely disrespectful to the Mother of God.

The two finalists from the book were *Mater Purissima* from England, painted by Frederick Goodall RA, and the Mother from *The Holy Family* by C. Bosseron Chambers, one of America's greatest contemporary artists.

Mater Purissima was a queenly figure with two turtle-doves pressed to her breast. Her eyes were downcast and her expression was as innocent as any that Adrian had seen beneath the convent hat of a Catholic schoolgirl. The American Mother was a little older than the other three finalists—a beauty matured by her experience of the world.

One of the four finalists was to be Adrian's Patroness for life. He would serve her as a knight in the olden days served his lady. Adrian got scissors and paste and mounted the four Madonnas on strong card. Out of fairness to the contestants he made the four pictures exactly equal in size. He had to mutilate the two pages of *The World's Great Madonnas*, but it was in a worthy cause.

A few days later he sat in the stalls of a city theatre waiting to see *Anna*, starring Silvano Mangano. He had overheard Cornthwaite talking about this film during the last term at St Carthage's. Adrian knew it was pretty hot, but not bad enough to be condemned by the church. He would not commit a mortal sin by watching it, but it might put a few mild temptations in his way.

Before going into the theatre he had calculated how long the film would last and divided this time into four equal parts. As the film started, he took out of his pocket the first of the four finalists in his contest. He held the picture in his cupped hands to hide it from the people around him while he stared at it for a minute or so. Then he put it safely back in his pocket.

During the first quarter of the film there were several scenes (shots of deep necklines, close-ups of women with lips ajar and nostrils quivering, long passionate kisses) that started the alarm bells ringing in his conscience. Each time this happened, Adrian closed his eyes and called on Our Lady of Fatima to protect him. He took careful note of everything that happened in his mind during the few seconds that followed. Usually it was like a scene from a film all his own. The pale dignified figure of Our Lady of Fatima floated slowly into centre screen. The scantily clad, sultry Italian woman who had tempted him took one look at the cream-gowned Lady hovering above her and fled from the screen, with one hand covering her face for shame and the other trying to rearrange her scandalous neckline.

During each quarter of the film Adrian used a different one of his four finalists to guard his purity. On the train home to Accrington he compared the results and prepared to announce the winner of the contest.

He had been rather alarmed to find that none of the contestants was totally effective on every occasion when he had called on her. There had been two or three nasty moments when a nearly naked film star had planted her hands firmly on her hips and stared at the Patroness of Purity and tried to brazen it out. Once, the temptress had looked meaningfully at Adrian and edged towards him as if to say that she had first claim on his loyalty because he had loved film stars long before he loved Our Lady.

However, all four finalists had managed one way or another to keep him from the brink of mortal sin. As the train neared Accrington he began the speech leading up to the announcement of the winner.

Our Lady of Fatima, he was sorry to say, was just a little too dim and ethereal under her pale voluminous mantle. He meant no offence, but she was after all an apparition designed to appeal to Portuguese peasant children forty years before. In the turmoil of modern life in the 1950s she did not seem quite corporeal enough to be the Patroness of a young man who had once been excessively hot-blooded.

(Before dismissing each of the unsuccessful finalists Adrian promised he would pray to her from time to time with minor requests that she would easily be able to grant him.)

Mater Purissima was very beautiful indeed. Her only fault was that in the stress and panic of temptation he had tended to confuse her with memories he had of senior Catholic schoolgirls sitting with downcast eyes in Melbourne trams and trains. He had never been able to imagine himself talking familiarly with those virtuous aloof creatures. And unfortunately for Mater Purissima he found her, too, just a little beyond his reach.

The Mother from Chambers' Holy Family was a real flesh-and-blood woman. He could readily see himself falling at her feet in time of trouble—even flinging his arms around her gowned ankles as he cried out to her to save him. But even she, he regretted to say, would have to forgo first prize. He hesitated to put his reservation into words for fear it might convey a hint of sacrilege. But he assured her he was only describing what had actually happened when he had thrown himself on her mercy.

In the most perilous moment of his worst temptation in the theatre, when he had stared intently at her face, there had been a horrible instant when she seemed to be not the Mother of God who would freeze with one glance the raging fires of his passions, but an ordinary human being—a smiling young married woman who thought he was looking to her for human affection. No doubt this was his fault and not hers, but the mere fact that it happened made it impossible for Chambers' Mother to be his Patroness.

It was clear by now that the winner of the grand final was the young Italian Madonna who had entered the contest without even a title. Before enthroning her as his Patroness and consecrating his life to her, Adrian wanted to confer a distinctive title on her.

He recalled the moments during the film when he had fled to her from the snares of women who were actually, he was sorry to say, her fellow Italians. She had saved him not by confronting the temptresses as the other Madonnas had done. She had not even deigned to look at the giddy misguided film stars. Instead she had signed to him to follow her through the dense rosebushes burdened with gold and vermilion blooms. Moments later, with her as his guide, he stood in a landscape where no temptation from the modern world could reach him. He breathed an air that no city had ever contaminated and looked up at a sky of other days. She had taken him back to the Great Age of Our Lady.

He would address her ever afterwards by the name of her lost kingdom. He tried to remember Golden Ages of the past. Into his mind came a name, a harmonious name that recalled a civilisation where she and he would have been at home among soft sea mists and monasteries full of illuminated parchments and the distant sound of hymns in Latin and Gaelic. He knelt before her and addressed her as Our Lady of Dalriada. He swore that from that day on, whenever danger threatened, he would spurn the allurements of the modern world and flee with her to the sanctuary of dim Dalriada.

In the last fortnight before he left for the junior seminary, Adrian Sherd thought about the duties and privileges of the priesthood.

A priest had to love the mass. Adrian would not find this difficult. He was looking forward already to the privilege of holding the chalice, which no lay person was allowed to touch. As a priest, he would know the feel of the gold-plated lining that actually came into contact with Our Lord's Precious Blood. He would lean forward over the altar so that the congregation saw only his hunched back, and hear from only a few inches away the awesome crackling noise as his anointed fingers gently fractured the Host.

His aunt had once told him a story that showed how deeply a priest ought to love his mass.

During the war an Australian priest was imprisoned by the Japs in a POW camp. The Japs knew he was a priest, and because they hated the Catholic religion they had threatened him with death if he tried to say mass. They had confiscated all his vestments and sacred vessels, and they searched his cell every day and even shone torches on him at night to make sure he was not trying to celebrate mass in secret.

Day after day the priest prayed to God for the means to offer just one mass. At last he thought of a desperate plan. He took a teaspoon and the back of a silver watchcase and blessed them and hid them in his mattress. He squeezed a few drops of juice from a grape into the teaspoon and left it for a few days until it fermented. Then he got a tiny morsel of bread and hid it with the other things.

The night after his grape juice had fermented, he pretended to be sleeping on his stomach in bed. While the Jap guard was walking up and down outside with his bayonet exposed, the priest began to whisper his mass. He used the teaspoon for a chalice and the watchcase for a paten. He knew the prayers of the mass by heart, so he didn't need a missal. He ran a terrible risk—if the guards had suddenly burst in and found his drops of wine and speck of bread they would have killed him on the spot.

Adrian understood how a priest could take such a risk for love of the mass. But he also understood the priest in a very different story that a brother had once told. One morning this priest found himself experiencing a terrible temptation during mass. At the moment of consecration he suddenly doubted that the bread and wine really did change into the Body and Blood of Our Lord. Like all Catholics, he knew the appearance of the bread and wine never changed—only their substance. This had never puzzled him before, but now that his faith had begun to waver he couldn't see how it was possible. Each day at mass his doubts grew worse. Fortunately he had the sense to pray about it. He asked God on his knees to give him back his faith in the Blessed Eucharist.

One morning just after the consecration he looked down and saw on the white altar cloth a little pool of scarlet blood. Drops of real blood were trickling from the consecrated Host. God had rewarded him with an unmistakeable proof that He really was present on the altar.

Adrian would never expect to be favoured like that with a sign from God. Luckily his own faith was strong. But he knew he must never take his faith for granted. The Catholic religion was full of mysteries that could only be accepted by a person with faith. And faith itself was a free gift from God. A person who had not been given this gift could not believe in the mysteries, even if he wanted to. Adrian had heard a story to illustrate this.

A famous and very clever non-Catholic was being shown around a religious house. When he came out of the chapel he asked why a little lamp was kept burning beside the altar. The priest who was with him explained that in every Catholic church where the Blessed Sacrament was reserved, a light burned night and day to remind people that Our Lord was really present.

Then the visitor said, 'But I didn't notice any of your priests in the chapel just now.'

The priest asked the visitor what he meant. A strange, sad look came into the non-Catholic's eyes and he said, 'You know, your doctrine of the Real Presence is the most wonderful thing I've ever heard of. If I could really believe it, I would spend my whole life kneeling in a Catholic church talking to God. You Catholics believe the doctrine and yet you leave your God alone in the church for most of the day.'

That was a man who would have made a wonderful Catholic, and yet for some mysterious reason God had not given him the gift of faith.

A priest was expected to protect the Blessed Sacrament against disrespect or sacrilege. The devil hated the Sacrament because of all the souls it brought closer to God. In times of war he inspired non-Catholic soldiers to break into Catholic churches and commit outrages against the Sacred Host. Adrian knew a shocking story from the Spanish Civil War. Some Communist soldiers rode their horses into a church during mass and shot the priest and anyone in the congregation who tried to escape. Then they snatched the chalice and ciborium and scattered the Sacred Hosts on the floor and rode around the sanctuary stabbing their bayonets into them.

Whenever a priest had warning of an outrage like that, he was supposed to consume the Sacred Species as quickly and reverently as possible. When the Communists were taking over China, a community of monks saw the Red Army coming in the distance. There was still time for the monks to escape. But they went solemnly into their chapel and consumed all trace of the Blessed Sacrament. The Communists arrived just as they were finishing. The monks were captured and put to death, but the Blessed Sacrament was saved.

As a priest, Adrian would hear confessions. He couldn't imagine himself being tempted to break the seal of confession—unless the Communists came to Australia and tortured him to reveal the sins of some leading Catholic layman. If this happened he could only pray for strength and remember the story of St John of Hungary.

John was confessor to the Queen of Hungary. The King wanted to know what sins his wife had been confessing. He tortured John for days to make him tell. In the end John died with the secrets of the confessional still safe in his heart. The King had his body thrown into the river. It floated there all night, beneath the walls of the royal castle, with a strange light shining from its tongue, and the King's subjects saw it and knew what their ruler had done.

The seal of the confessional required more of a priest than just refusing to talk about peoples' sins. A certain priest in a poor parish in Ireland found that money was disappearing from his room, even though he kept it in a secret place. One day his housekeeper told him in confession she had found where he hid his money and had been stealing from it ever since.

The obvious thing for the priest to do was to find a new hiding place for his money. But under the seal of confession he was not allowed to act on any information he had obtained in the confessional. He had to leave the money where it was and never mention the matter to his housekeeper.

Adrian read again a paragraph from the Charleroi Fathers' vocations pamphlet.

> Under the Ensign of the King, the Charleroi Fathers are striving to hurl back the satanic legions that menace the souls of men. Today the evil forces of Antichrist must be broken on an ever-widening battlefront. Boys and young men are wanted to take up their station beneath the Royal Standard of the Cross. Can there be any greater or more urgent duty? Can there be anything nobler?

Of course there was no career more wonderful than a priest's. His main task was to win souls for God. At the end of each day he could look back and judge his success by the number of immortal souls he had saved. But Adrian knew there would be days when the going was tough—when the devil's score of souls seemed to be more than his own. At such times the only thing to do was to pray harder and set a holier example to people. Otherwise he would be in danger of despairing and ending up like the few unfortunate priests he had heard about.

Yes, there were priests who neglected their duties or found the struggle too much for them. Only very few, perhaps one in ten thousand, but Adrian was realistic enough to face the facts about them.

Somewhere in Melbourne was a priest who owned racehorses. Adrian's father had heard about him. He had inherited a lot of money and (because he was a secular priest) he had been able to keep it for his own use. He wore sports clothes to the races and kept his real name out of the racebooks, but his horses all had names from the New

Testament. He owned a hurdler called Boanerges, a mare called Dorcas, and Philemon, a smart two-year-old. It was a great pity that he wasted his money when he could have used it to save souls. It would have built a new school in an outer suburb or paid off a parish debt.

Adrian's cousins at Orford had told him about a priest in a little parish out on the Western Plains who spent most of his time fishing and shooting. He kept curly coated retriever dogs in the spare rooms of his presbytery. He had started with only a pair of them but the dogs had gone on breeding until they were all over the house. His poor old housekeeper had left because of the mess, and the priest hadn't bothered to employ a new one. He just batched in a couple of rooms and let the dogs take over the rest of the presbytery.

Priests were only human, and now and then one went out of his mind under the strain of his grave responsibilities. A brother at St Carthage's recalled that when he was a boy in Melbourne, marching along Bourke Street in the St Patrick's Day Procession, someone in the crowd used to shout out a few lines from a Latin prayer as each Catholic school went past with its banner high. It was a poor old fellow who had gone mad years before and run away from the priesthood.

The brother had used this little story to illustrate something about the sacrament of Holy Orders that was remarkable, even miraculous. When a priest was ordained, his priestly powers were given to him for life. No matter what sins or heresies he was guilty of afterwards, he was still a priest with the power to consecrate bread and wine and to forgive sins and administer the other sacraments. But it was a fact that no priest (not even the blackest renegade who had ended up preaching and writing against the church) had ever used his priestly powers for evil.

What sort of evil could a renegade priest do? The brother had explained that an evil priest could walk into a bakery and whisper the words, 'This is My Body.' The brother had paused to let his Christian Doctrine class appreciate the full horror of it—a bakery stacked to the roof with the Body of Our Lord.

Or the lapsed priest could work the same mischief with all the vats of wine at a vineyard. But the brother had reminded his class of the point he was making. These things just did not happen, which surely proved there was something miraculous about the priesthood.

In all his life Adrian had heard of only two priests who had broken their vows. One morning he had read in the *Argus* that a young priest was missing from a Melbourne parish and fears were held for his safety. For the next few days all the Melbourne papers had reports near their front pages telling how the priest had still not been located. Adrian's teacher had asked his class to say a little prayer that the priest would be found alive and well and that there would be no scandal for the enemies of the church to seize on.

About a week later a few lines in an obscure corner of the *Argus* announced that the priest had come forward in New Zealand and that a spokesman for the Melbourne Archdiocese had said the matter was closed. Adrian's teacher told the class it was none of their business now. The priest should be left to sort things out between himself and God and his Archbishop. The brother said it was remark-able how anti-Catholic journalists and historians always concentrated on one priest who couldn't live up to his vows and conveniently ignored all the other faithful priests and the good work they did.

Adrian never discovered why the priest had run away to New Zealand. But there was one case, the saddest of all, where he knew the whole story.

He heard it from Damian Laity, who had heard it from his father. Laity said that one of the teachers at the Oglethorpe High School, a man named Quinlivan, was really a priest from Queensland who had run away from his parish and eloped with a young woman and married her in a registry office. The Quinlivans lived in a weatherboard house just like any ordinary couple and had two children at the state school. Every morning Quinlivan caught a bus to the Oglethorpe High School to teach Latin and History.

Mr Laity had known about the apostate priest for years. When the fellow had first run away with the woman, little groups of responsible Catholic laymen in all the big cities started to look out for him. They had reason to believe he might do something that would bring the church into disrepute. At first they thought he would change his name and disguise himself and try to get a job as a lay teacher in a Catholic college. But he may have known they were watching for him, because he joined the Education Department under his own name. The Catholic laymen had watched him for some time, but so far he had kept fairly quiet.

From all reports, Quinlivan was a most unhappy man, tortured by his conscience. Laity had heard that sometimes at the High School when Quinlivan had to utter a Latin word that was in the prayers of the mass, his face twitched or he dropped his head in his hands for a moment. He often paced up and down like a priest saying his office and stared into the distance, remembering the glory he had run away from.

The suburb of Oglethorpe was on the far side of the great valley that fell away to the east of Swindon. From the upper-storey windows of St Carthage's, Adrian had sometimes looked at the hazy hillside suburb and thought of Quinlivan, the renegade and black sheep, looking west-wards to the faint lump of St Carthage's College on the horizon and remembering the days when he had been a Catholic secondary student who dreamed of a life in the priesthood.

After Adrian himself had decided to become a priest, he had looked more often towards Oglethorpe and told himself he was much more fortunate than Quinlivan had ever been, because he, Adrian, knew a story to prove what a grave step he was taking and what a fate was in store for him if he proved unworthy of the priesthood.

In his last year at St Carthage's, Adrian won the prize for Latin in Form Five. On a Saturday morning in December, he and the other prize winners in his class met their teacher in Cheshire's Bookshop to choose their prizes. Adrian felt obliged to choose a book for his spiritual reading in the junior seminary. While he was standing in front of the shelves marked RELIGION, the brother came up and handed him a book called *Elected Silence*, by Thomas Merton, and said, 'One of the great books of the twentieth century.'

Adrian chose the book as his prize because he didn't like to offend the brother and because it seemed from the dust jacket to be about a man like himself who had sampled all that the world had to offer and then turned his back on it to become a priest.

He didn't begin reading *Elected Silence* until he was packing his suitcase in the last week of the holidays. But then he couldn't put the book down. He sat all day in the shed in the backyard to finish it. Afterwards he put it carefully in his case beside his daily missal and the notebook entitled *Resolutions for the Future*, and walked up and down the back path meditating on the story of Thomas Merton.

The brother had been right about the book. By every test that Adrian knew, *Elected Silence* was the greatest book he had ever read. There were passages in it that had brought goosepimples to his arms and legs and made the hair stiffen on the back of his neck. Many a time he had closed his eyes and turned a paragraph from the book into a scene in a film, with a mighty orchestra playing the climax of a gem from the classics, such as *Overture 1812* or *Capriccio Italien*.

Often he had wanted to rush to the drawer in the kitchen and grab the writing pad and dash off a letter to congratulate the author because his book described exactly what a young man in far-off Australia had felt at important moments in his own life. This was the most remarkable thing about *Elected Silence*—that the story of Thomas Merton, the young man who had never known true happiness until he entered a Cistercian monastery in America, was so like the story of Adrian Sherd.

Of course there were some details in Merton's life that didn't match Adrian's—Merton began life as a Protestant and attended several famous universities and travelled in many countries and had once joined the Communist Party—but Adrian was struck by the remarkable similarities.

Merton had grown thoroughly sick of the pagan materialism of the modern world. Once, when he was coming back from a visit to a remote monastery, he looked up at the bright lights of a city and saw a sign, CLOWN CIGARETTES, and felt disgusted. This was exactly how Adrian felt when he remembered the view from St Carthage's of miles of garden suburbs full of people who practised artificial birth control so they could afford cars and radiograms.

Merton had had trouble with impurity in his younger days, just as Adrian had. The passage that revealed this was very brief—only a few lines buried in the great bulk of the book—but Adrian had not missed it. The passage was not very explicit either. But Adrian had once acquired the skill of skimming though pages of adult books for their few risqué lines and thinking over them for hours afterwards to get their full meaning.

So when Merton mentioned briefly that he had no wish to wake the dirty ghosts of his past, it told Adrian all he needed to know. The man had fallen in his youth, just as Adrian had, and perhaps as often. Merton was man enough to admit it. And some day when Adrian wrote his own autobiography he would mention his American year in a frank paragraph or two.

Merton described a summer holiday somewhere in the Appalachians when he sat outside his cabin every evening and read the *Book of Job* while his mates went down into the village chasing girls. Merton called them 'mousey little girls'.

Adrian saw the lean ascetic figure looking up calmly from the pages of the Old Testament, staring for a few

277

moments into the peaceful leafy woods high above the pleasure-crazed cities of north-eastern America and pitying his weak sensual friends in the hot noisy cinemas in the valley below.

Adrian had had to fall in love with Denise McNamara to learn that the joys of human love could never satisfy him. Merton had learned this lesson without the help of any girlfriend. Not that he scorned women. He had chatted freely with them at the university and at parties, but always about intellectual matters.

There was another amazing parallel in the way that Merton and Sherd had discovered their true vocations. When Merton first decided to be a priest, he applied to join the Franciscans. Before he actually joined them, he went to make a retreat at the Cistercian monastery in Kentucky.

He travelled by train from New York to Kentucky, through some of the splendid American landscapes that Adrian had once dreamed about. It was late at night when he reached the monastery. A lay brother opened the great door and led him into the silent building. The brother asked him if he had come to join the Cistercian order. Merton said he hadn't, and began to explain that he was committed to joining the Franciscans. The brother said simply, 'I was a Franciscan once.'

Although Merton hadn't dwelt on it, that was for Adrian the most stirring moment in the book. As the brother's words echoed among the austere walls of the monastery, a mighty chord resounded. As Merton followed the brother down the shadowy corridor another chord rang out, and another. Then all the orchestras that Adrian had ever heard on the soundtracks of American films combined together in a heroic tune while the monastery faded and scenes from Merton's early life surged up from the past.

Only a few days before he was to leave for the junior seminary, Adrian was lying on his bed thinking of *Elected Silence*, and enjoying a profound spiritual peace. Suddenly, without any warning, he experienced a powerful attraction to the Cistercian order. He leaped up and paced the backyard and tried to think of harmless thoughts. But his mind was filled with vivid pictures, rich in details that excited his imagination—long rows of white-robed monks chanting in choir or walking in silence to their day's work through fields of golden wheat or hacking and hewing at logs of wood while their cowls flapped about their faces and muttering, 'All for Jesus! All for Jesus!' as Merton had described them doing.

Adrian was alarmed. The Charleroi vocation he had nurtured for weeks was threatened by a crazy temptation. If it had been an ordinary impure thought he could have called on Our Lady of Dalriada for help. But it was hardly fair to ask Our Lady to banish the Cistercians from his mind—they were one of her favourite orders. Merton had explained how the monks named all their monasteries after her. The Charlerois loved her too, but she couldn't be expected to show a preference for one or the other order.

His urge to join the Cistercians would not go away. He told himself that his parents would never allow him to join an order that lived all their lives enclosed in a monastery and talked only in sign language. And he asked himself how he could afford the fares from Melbourne to Kentucky.

But he seemed to remember reading in the *Advocate* about some Irish Cistercians founding a small monastery in

Australia. He walked to the phone box three streets away and spoke to his Aunt Kath.

She said, 'Yes, some Cistercians from the famous Irish monastery of Mount Melleray have established themselves up in the hills past Yarra Glen, about forty miles from Melbourne. Whatever made you ask?'

She was suspicious. He said, 'A friend from school asked me. He thinks he might have a vocation to the Cistercian life.'

'Tell him to pray about it. And don't you trouble yourself about them just when we've got you all packed up and ready to join the Charlerois. Read that pamphlet I gave you. Your own order leads a much fuller life than the Cistercians.'

Adrian went home thinking his aunt was prejudiced against the Cistericans. But he read his pamphlet again and noted all the references to a monastic way of life among the Charlerois. As he peered at the photographs of Charleroi houses with their extensive grounds and distant views, his temptation slowly faded. It was hard to imagine an inspiring landscape only forty miles from Melbourne, where the Cistercians had their monastery. And if he decided to join them he would have to go back to St Carthage's for his matriculation year. His friends would be puzzled. Cornthwaite and the others would think he had fallen into his old habit over the long holidays.

In the end it was the thought of the journey to Blenheim that brought back his old feelings for the Charleroi Fathers and finished off the Cistercians. The trip to the Cistercian monastery would take him thirty miles by train and then ten in a bus. He would never be able to reflect on Merton's great journey to Kentucky while he was looking out of an electric train at the eastern suburbs of Melbourne.

He would still take Merton's book with him to Blenheim. He could read the best parts of it whenever his life with the Charlerois seemed dull or tedious. He could even follow some of the Cistercians' rules and customs in private if the Charleroi life didn't challenge him sufficiently. And the mere sight of *Elected Silence* among his spiritual reading would remind him to prepare for that great day years later when he was a priest of the Congregation of Christ the King and he welcomed into his monastery some worried young fellow seeking advice about his vocation and asked him, 'Have you come to join the Charlerois?'

The young fellow would say, 'No. I think I want to become a secular priest.'

Then Father Sherd CCR would say, his voice charged with emotion, 'I was nearly a secular priest once.'

Adrian had to catch the late-afternoon train for Sydney. On his last day at home, three telegrams arrived for him.

FATHER CAMILLUS TO MEET YOU AT BLENHEIM
STATION BLESSINGS—CASIMIR CCR RECTOR

ALL PRAYERS AND BEST WISHES AS YOU BEGIN
GREAT CAREER—KATHLEEN

ALL BEHIND YOU IN YOUR NEW STEP
—MCALOON FAMILY

In the afternoon his parents and young brothers went with him to Spencer Street station. A priest from the Charleroi house in Melbourne met them on the platform.

Adrian's mother had been crying quietly to herself for hours. The priest said to her, 'It always seems a little hard when you're saying goodbye, Mrs Sherd. But believe me, you never lose a child who goes into the religious life. Young Adrian might be hundreds of miles away, but he'll be closer than ever to you in spirit.'

Adrian was annoyed with her for not cheering up after the priest's kind words.

When the warning bell rang on the platform, Adrian shook hands with his father and brothers and let his mother kiss him and told them all he would pray for them. Last of all he shook hands with the priest and said he hoped the next time they met he would be wearing the Charleroi habit.

It was a hot, bright summer afternoon. The train would be almost to New South Wales before night fell. Adrian leaned back in his window seat. All the scenery was new to him. He was impatient to be out of the suburbs of Melbourne and into the great swathe of country opening up ahead of him.

Workers were going home from factories in the suburbs. They waited respectfully at railway crossings for the Sydney train to pass. Adrian saw their faces staring up at him. They were tired and worn. In a few years he would be able to forgive their sins and ease their burdens a little—although they were probably too attached to material goods to experience the true peace he could offer them.

In the grazing country north-east of Melbourne, Adrian chose the kind of small town where he would preach one of his best missions. There was one place where the little Catholic church had a proper stained-glass window, and the presbytery (where he would be a guest for the fortnight of the mission) was a spacious two-storey bluestone house.

The town itself was drab, but in the countryside around it Adrian noticed several huge homesteads sprawled among trees on low hilltops. During his mission he would call at the Catholic properties and sip cold drinks on their wide shady verandas. Each night of the mission, the little church would be crowded. The families from the grazing properties would be there, as well as the poorer people from the township. Father Sherd would remind them that Christ had said it was easier for a camel to pass through a needle's eye than for a rich man to enter heaven. The graziers would squirm in their seats and resolve to be more generous in future, while their well-dressed wives and daughters would wonder at the courage of the young mission priest, who was obviously not impressed by their wealth.

After sundown it was harder to see the towns and farms and people in the land that was waiting to be conquered for Christ the King. Adrian sat back in his seat and thought of the long history of the priesthood.

All primitive peoples had an instinctive urge to offer sacrifices. This urge had been implanted in man by God Himself. All over the ancient world, people slew beasts or poured wine onto the ground or set fire to altars in an effort to appease the gods. Unfortunately most of these sacrifices were wasted because they were offered to idols of brass or stone or nature spirits or even demons.

The only ancient people who pleased God with their offerings were the Jews, because they acknowledged Him as the one true God. The Jewish prophets and holy men were inspired by God to make elaborate laws about their sacrifices. God was using the Jews to prepare the world for the arrival of His Son, who would establish the One True Church and the most perfect sacrifice of all.

So, by the time of Christ, people were used to the idea of having a special priesthood who wore elaborate vestments and offered sacrifices in a building set apart for the purpose.

The first Catholic priest was Christ Himself. At the Last Supper He celebrated the first mass in history. From then on, people had no further need to slaughter bullocks or burn corn. The mass was the most perfect sacrifice that man could offer to God.

The Last Supper was also the world's first ordination ceremony. Christ turned His disciples into priests and told them to offer the mass in future just as He had done. Ever since, Catholic priests had followed His instructions, so that you could walk into a Catholic church anywhere in the world on any day of the year and see a faithful re-enactment of the Last Supper.

Priests had a hard life in the early days of the church. If Adrian had lived in those days he might not have had a vocation. There were so many persecutions and so many pagan countries to be converted, and few of the compensations that a modern priest enjoyed—such as quiet presbyteries with shelves of theology books and flowerbeds outside to walk among. Worse still, some of the early priests had wives and families to look after.

No doubt many of these married priests worked hard, but the church soon learned that the best priests were those like St Paul, who never married, or St Peter, who left his wife as soon as he was called by Christ.

There were several good reasons why the church, quite

early in its history, insisted on the celibacy of the clergy. (In the dusk near Violet Town Adrian checked them off. Some hostile non-Catholic would be sure to start an argument about celibacy with him one day.)

First, a celibate priest is able to serve his flock twenty-four hours a day, whereas a married priest would have to give some time to his wife and family. Adrian imagined the embarrassment of refusing an invitation to an important meeting of priests because your wife was expecting a baby.

A celibate priest was somehow more dignified and commanded more respect than a married one. It would be hard, for example, to preach an exalted sermon to people who had seen you the night before with an apron over your clerical suit washing the dishes for your wife.

Most important of all, many people would be reluctant to confess their sins and talk over their troubles with a man who lived in close contact with a woman. Even the best of wives would ask you every night about your day's work. One night you would let slip some item you had heard in confession, and next day it would be all over the district.

Anyway, Christ had said somewhere in the Gospels that a man who wanted to be perfect should cut himself off from all family ties. Our Lord knew it was almost impossible to perfect yourself with a wife and children distracting you all the time.

Even before the celibacy of the clergy had been made binding, there were many priests who sought to be perfect themselves by abstaining from marriage and practising extreme poverty and mortification. These were the early hermits and Desert Fathers, the forerunners of the monks.

There were famous hermits who walled themselves up

in caves or hid themselves in forests and never spoke to a living person for fifty years and more. The state of holiness that a man would reach after living alone with God in a cave for half a century was too much for Adrian to imagine. Yet he himself would probably not have been suited to the life of a hermit. After a few years of saying mass alone with a rock for an altar and only the birds and animals to watch him he would have longed for a gilt tabernacle and a silken chasuble to remind him of the dignity of his office.

As the centuries passed, there was an increasing range of choices for a young man wanting to be a priest. The great monastic orders—Benedictines, Carthusians, Cistercians—were founded. Their rapid spread all over the civilised world was proof (if any were needed) that their founders had been divinely inspired. The orders of friars—Franciscans, Dominicans and Augustines—provided for those who liked to travel and to preach against heresies in the marketplace.

It was significant that the Protestant leaders of the Reformation spoke out fiercely against the celibacy of the clergy. It may well have been the devil himself who inspired them. The devil knew that his worst enemies were the clergy, who won back thousands of souls from his clutches every year. It would have suited him very well to do away with celibacy and so distract priests and religious from their great work.

Of course his schemes had almost no effect on Catholics. But he easily persuaded the Protestants to allow their clergy to marry. The results were plain for anyone to see. The Protestant clergy were pitifully outnumbered by Catholic priests and brothers and nuns, despite the fact that the

Protestants were free to marry and satisfy all their fleshly urges. All over the world young Catholic men and women flocked in their thousands to seminaries and convents to embrace the challenging life of a celibate religious. Thomas Merton had written about the great monastic revival sweeping the United States. Young men all over the country were realising that a monastery was the only place where they could live a sane life.

The priesthood and the religious life had a long and glorious history. Past Wangaratta, when it was quite dark outside the train, Adrian put his face against the window and saw that history as a succession of pictures. The pictures hovered over the dark countryside just as the spiritual world of God and His angels and saints hovered over the Modern Age, although many people were unaware of it.

The pictures were line drawings from the pages of the *History Readers—Catholic Syllabus*, which had been Adrian's textbooks each year at primary school. To represent the early centuries under the Roman Empire, there was St Peter in chains with the angel about to rescue him. For the Middle Ages, the Great Age of Faith, there was St Cuthbert and the otters. The Renaissance was typified by the portrait of a great Pope who patronised many of the leading artists of those days. England after the Reformation was illustrated by Blessed Edmund Campion being led to the scaffold. St Francis Xavier, baptising a crowd of several thousand pagans in India, stood for the Discovery of the New World.

As yet, there was no picture for the Modern Age. No doubt in years to come the authors of Catholic history books would assess the true importance of the many great modern priests and religious. Adrian thought of several who could serve as illustrations in his series—St John Bosco, the modern Italian priest who converted boys by juggling or walking tightropes in the streets; St Bernadette, who was visited by the Apparition of Our Lady at Lourdes and ended her life as a nun; Monsignor Fulton Sheen of America, who had converted thousands with his radio and television programs.

At Albury the railway gauge changed and the passengers walked along the platform to another train. By midnight Adrian was deep into New South Wales. It was the first time he had ever been outside Victoria. He peered out to see how different the landscape was, but he saw nothing in the darkness. He prayed silently that Father Camillus would be at Blenheim to meet him. Then he stared at the jumble of reflections in the dark glass beside him and tried to think again about history.

He realised that non-Catholics had their own version of history. Once, at primary school, he had glanced at a history book belonging to a state-school boy in his street. The only illustrations he saw were shadowy portraits of Oliver Cromwell and William, Prince of Orange, and a picture of the Duke of Monmouth lying on the floor with his hands clasped around the knees of King Charles the Second. The state schools kept religion out of their history courses.

The bigotry of non-Catholic historians was most evident when they wrote about priests or religious. The Spanish missionaries in South America were supposed to have baptised Indian babies and then dashed their heads against trees to send their souls to heaven. The Jesuits in England were always plotting to overthrow 'Good' Queen Bess. Monks and friars were fat and jolly and fond of a good time, like Friar Tuck. The Pope was no different from a temporal ruler, and his cardinals dabbled in politics.

These opinions were not just the ravings of a few fanatical anti-Catholics. The daily press in Australia and the majority of people educated in state schools accepted them as true history.

The train entered a fair-sized town and stopped at a station. A voice through loudspeakers said, 'Cootamundra.' Adrian realised he was hundreds of miles from home. Around him were dark shapes vaguely lit by weak electric lamps, and all he had to go by was the name—Cootamundra.

He must never forget that Australia was a Protestant country with Catholics a barely tolerated minority. As he passed into the darkness on the other side of Cootamundra he remembered the day when he had first suffered for the Catholic faith.

His mother was in hospital and he was having some of his meals with the family next door. One night the woman said to her husband, 'Here, Dad, here's the Pope's nose, and I hope it does you good.'

The man took the piece of meat and ate it from his fingers and spat out the bones into his cupped hand. Adrian was disgusted. He had always been taught to call the tail of a fowl the parson's nose. But when he tried to correct the non-Catholics they only laughed at him.

Adrian's first week in the junior seminary at Blenheim was like a holiday. The Master of Students, Father Camillus, told the boys they would have a week to get to know the priests and their fellow students before the full seminary timetable began. In the meantime they were expected to attend mass each morning, join the priests and lay brothers at midday and evening prayers in the chapel, and spend their mornings working in the garden and their afternoons playing sport or hiking to the river.

There were fifteen students. When they sat in the refectory in order of seniority Adrian was seventh. The four oldest were grown men in their twenties—late vocations. If these fellows had joined almost any other order they would have gone straight into the novitiate year. They would have worn the habit of the order and followed its rule and undergone spiritual trials and hardships to test their vocations. But the Charleroi Fathers sent all their new entrants—no matter how old—to the junior seminary for a year. The Charleroi novitiate was considered too hard for a fellow who had come straight from the world.

During his first week Adrian tried to look like someone who had discovered at last the life he was destined for. When he was chipping weeds out of the gravel path and Father Camillus walked past, Adrian pretended to be so absorbed in his task that he hardly noticed the priest. When he was setting off for a hike he smiled at the trees and flowerbeds and parted his lips as though he saw all nature as a visible manifestation of God—and hoped one of the priests was watching him from a window.

At the end of the week the students were given copies of the timetable. Each day began at 5.40 a.m. ('Morning Bell— Rise, dress and wash') and ended at 10.00 p.m. ('Retire to bed—All lights out'). Adrian pinned his timetable to the door of his room and read it over and over, savouring its harshness. ('The Great Silence begins each evening immediately after Night Prayers and continues until after Mass on the following morning. During this period, students will observe silence in all parts of the building. At other times, students must also observe silence in corridors, study hall, washrooms and showers.')

Adrian counted the hours until the timetable came into force. He thought of it as a religious rule, and he knew that the rule of every religious order had been approved by the Pope as a valid means of attaining sanctity. This meant that anyone who faithfully followed such a rule would perfect himself as a human being and be sure of reaching heaven after death.

When the morning bell sounded next day at 5.40, Adrian stumbled out of bed before he was properly awake. He was following the example of the saint who once said that a religious should leap up at the morning bell as though the bedclothes were on fire. He put on shorts and a shirt and pulled his long black soutane over his head. He hurried to the washroom. The timetable allowed him five minutes to splash his face and brush his teeth before he was due in chapel for morning prayers. (The students showered in the afternoon, after sport.)

After mass Adrian flung his head into his hands to make a brief thanksgiving while the other students were walking upstairs to their rooms. A hand fastened on his shoulder and a voice said, 'Haven't you read your timetable? It's time to make your bed and tidy your room.' It was the Dean of Students, a boy no older than Adrian but one of those who had been at the seminary for several years.

Adrian obeyed the Dean, but wondered what right he had to interrupt the prayers of his fellow students. All morning Adrian tried to find a few moments for the thanksgiving that he was used to saying after mass. But whenever he thought he had a free minute, the bell sounded and he had to begin a new class or hurry to some other part of the building.

That night in his room he read his timetable again and counted more than twenty bells from morning to 'Lights Out'. While he was counting, the bell for 'Lights Out' sounded, but he left his light on for a moment. He took a pencil and the notebook he was going to fill with the fruits of his meditations and spiritual reading. The door of his room opened. The Dean put his head in and said, 'Turn off your light at once and go to bed!'

Next morning during the study period before breakfast, Adrian knocked on Father Camillus's door and told the priest he wanted to discuss a spiritual problem.

Adrian said, 'Father, I know the timetable here is a sort of preparation for the Charleroi rule that we'll follow next year in the novitiate. And I know we must follow the timetable without murmuring, and obey the Dean of Students because he represents the authority of the Rector. But twice yesterday the Dean interfered with my private devotions.' And he told the priest about the two incidents.

The Master of Students heard Adrian out, but he looked as though he listened to similar stories from new boys every year. He said, 'Our Founder, St Henry de Cisy, had a wonderful saying: "A holy religious has no time to be holy."

'St Henry meant of course that true holiness consists in doing the Will of God with all your strength all day long. God's Will for you right now is to follow the timetable. A great saint once wrote that the bell in a religious house is the voice of God Himself telling each member of the community what he should be doing at any particular moment.'

Whenever the priest dropped his eyes Adrian looked at the bed in the corner. Every Charleroi priest and lay brother slept on a thin mattress of straw with only planks beneath it. Adrian wished the students could have proper Charleroi beds to test themselves on.

Father Camillus smiled at Adrian. 'Believe me, we know what we're doing when we keep you running with those bells all day long. Out in the world last year you were always looking for a quiet place to pray and talk to God about your vocation. Well, now you can really test that vocation. Follow the timetable here for a year with all your heart and soul. By the end of the year you'll have found out some surprising things about yourself.

'Some people would say it's easy to obey a few bells and turn your light out when you're told to. But you're finding already it's quite a challenge. Are you equal to that challenge? Let's find out.'

Adrian went back to the morning study class and put his head down over his books because it was God's Will that he should do nothing but study at that time. At the first sound of the bell he slammed his book shut without finishing the sentence and was second into the refectory for breakfast—just behind the Dean of Students.

For the next few weeks Adrian followed the timetable exactly. In recreation periods he learned all he could about the Charleroi life from the students who had been at the seminary in previous years.

He heard about scruples—the worst of all ailments that could afflict a religious. Living in retirement in one of the back rooms of the seminary was an old priest, Father Fidelis, who suffered severely from scruples. He spent most of his time alone in his room with the door locked. He ate alone from a tray prepared by the lay brothers and said his morning mass in one of the private oratories in the priests' wing.

None of the students knew exactly what kind of scruples the old priest had. Whatever they were, they kept him from meeting any of the students. Sometimes when Adrian was walking along a corridor he saw the old priest come round a corner ahead of him, stop, and then scuttle back out of sight. Usually Father Fidelis made for the priests' wing, where the students were not permitted. But if he was cornered in a distant part of the building he was likely to hide anywhere—behind a staircase, in the toilets or in a broom cupboard. Once Adrian saw a fold of a black habit showing from behind a pillar in the cloisters. He had forced the poor old priest into dodging round the pillar to avoid him as he walked past.

A boy who had once served mass for Father Fidelis said the priest had taken nearly five minutes to say the prayers of consecration. He whispered '*Hoc est enim corpus meum*' over and over, as though he couldn't be sure they would work unless he concentrated on them with all his might.

Some of the younger students tried to sneak up behind Father Fidelis when they saw him in the distance. But Adrian and the more serious students considered his case a warning to them not to overdo their piety.

Adrian heard about Father Malouf. He was a secular priest from the Blenheim parish who spent a lot of time at the seminary. It was rumored that he was unhappy in his parish work and wondering if he ought to give it up and join an order like the Charlerois.

Father Malouf had scruples of a different kind from

Father Fidelis's. He couldn't sit still or kneel down. When he visited the seminary he walked for hours up and down the garden paths and round the cloisters. He would talk to a student, but you had to jog along beside him to keep up a conversation. When he stayed overnight at the seminary he came down to the chapel with the Charleroi priests for night prayers, but he paced up and down outside the chapel door and you heard his voice joining in the prayers from the hallway.

Whenever Father Malouf stayed overnight he said mass in an oratory the following morning. At the parts of the mass where he had to stand still, he lifted one foot after the other like a runner before a race. And he said mass probably faster than any priest in Australia. The students who served his masses always timed him behind his back. His record was nineteen minutes.

Adrian learned from the boys of the previous year that students were not allowed to form particular friendships. You were supposed to be equally friendly with every one of your fellow students. Otherwise, so the boys explained, you might be unhappy in later years if you were sent to South Australia, say, and your particular friend was in New South Wales.

Adrian was told why the priests and brothers (and those boys who knew) never passed a certain table in the front corridor without taking a plastic button from one of two bowls and dropping it in the other. Each button represented the soul of a dead Charleroi priest or brother from the Australian province. Each time you passed the bowls you picked up a button and offered a brief mental prayer for the repose of that soul. If the fellow was already in heaven, the merit earned by your prayer would of course be transferred to another button.

He heard about the discipline. The Charleroi Fathers were one of the few orders who still practised this extreme form of self-mortification. Each priest and brother kept in his room a leather whip with knotted thongs. (One of your first tasks in the novitiate would be to make a leather discipline for yourself in recreation periods.) Two or three times a week the priests and brothers disciplined themselves while they recited their office together.

The students who told Adrian about the discipline said if he didn't believe them he could look up the Constitution of the Order where it was all written in Latin. A fellow in the senior Latin class had translated it for all the students the year before. Every religious had to lift up the back of his habit with one hand and strike himself firmly across the buttocks with the discipline all through the prayer called Miserere.

A younger student asked what underclothes the Charlerois had to protect their buttocks. Two or three students answered at once—this was something they had learned long before. Every Charleroi wore a long flannel thing like a nightshirt and a pair of huge baggy underpants. The novices years ago had nicknamed the underpants 'grey horrors'. Any boy interested in them could duck around behind the building on a Monday morning. In a clearing among the fruit trees was a line where the religious laundry hung. On an average Monday morning you could see half a dozen grey horrors dangling in the breeze.

Every morning after breakfast the students were assigned to house duties for twenty minutes. Adrian's duty for the first week was to clean the priests' showers and toilets.

The priests' rooms and oratories were upstairs in one wing of the building. At each end of their corridor was a door with a sign, ENCLOSURE, on the outside. Adrian knew that anyone taking a female person past either of those doors was instantly excommunicated. He looked along the passage that no girl or woman had ever seen or, please God, would ever see. It was silent and peaceful. The doors of the priests' rooms were all closed. Adrian knew their windows looked out beyond the town of Blenheim to the timbered hills of the Southern Tablelands of New South Wales.

A man would climb the stairs from the chapel below, walk through the door marked ENCLOSURE and leave behind all the distractions, all the lust and avarice and ambition of the secular world. He could shut himself in his room and sit at his desk with a vast Australian landscape in front of him and prepare a sermon to persuade a whole parish to set up a door marked ENCLOSURE in their hearts, with a room beyond it where they could forget their senseless pursuit of pleasure and sit in silence with God.

Adrian wiped the priests' showers and poured disinfectant down their toilets and checked their supplies of toilet paper. Then he walked gingerly along the corridor to savour the religious atmosphere.

Behind one of the last doors someone switched on a radio. Adrian stopped to listen. It was the breakfast session from 2GL Goulburn. He read the sign on the door. The room belonged to Father Pascal, an old retired Charleroi who had a bad leg and spent most of the day in his room. Adrian left the priests' wing hoping that Father Pascal had only switched the radio on to hear the weather forecast. A man who had perfected himself by following the Charleroi rule for a lifetime would surely prefer the blessed silence of the priests' enclosure to the noise of a breakfast session on the radio.

Adrian's second house duty was to lay out the vestments and set up the sacred vessels for the mass of the following day. He had thought it would be years before he could handle holy things. But Father Camillus had told the students when they began their roster of duties, 'According to Canon Law you're all classified as postulants of a religious order and you're therefore permitted to handle things that ordinary lay people can't touch—the burse, the corporal, the purificator, the spoon and the pall. You may also touch the exterior metal of the chalice, the paten, the ciborium and the monstrance, but not, I repeat, not the inner gold-plated areas that come into contact with the Sacred Species.'

Each morning Adrian took a chalice from the safe in the sacristy and stood it on the priests' bench. He arranged all the other sacred vessels and cloths to make the neat parcel that the priest would carry to the altar next morning. Over them all he draped the chalice veil, which had to be the same colour as the vestments of the day.

Whenever he held the chalice or the paten in his hands he could not help thinking that those were the same hands that only sixteen months before had been polluted by an unnatural sin. Alone in the sacristy he endured the humiliation of remembering his past. But he hoped that before he was ordained he would learn to touch sacred vessels without thinking of the sins his hands had committed years ago. His mass each morning would be a burden to him if it only reminded him of self-abuse.

On certain days in the sacristy he had to stack sixty

small altar breads into a ciborium to be consecrated and given in communion to the students and lay brothers over the following few days. Adrian learned from the student who had done this duty before him how to rest a fountain pen inside the ciborium and stack the breads around it so the priest could lift them out easily for communion.

Each time Adrian rested the pen against the gold lining of the ciborium, he wondered why the plastic of the pen (which only a moment before had been in contact with his skin) could touch the sacred vessel while his own fingers could not. Sometimes he almost convinced himself it would be no more disrespectful to the Blessed Sacrament to touch the gold lightly with his fingertips than to rest a plastic pen against it. He brought his finger as near as a sixteenth of an inch from the sacred metal and held it there. No priest or brother or student would ever know he had closed the gap and made the faintest contact. But something always held his finger back.

In a cupboard in the sacristy Adrian found a tap and a tiny stainless-steel sink shaped like a spitoon with a drainpipe that disappeared through the floorboards. He learned that this was where the priest always rinsed the chalice and paten after mass. There was always a chance that a few minute fragments of the consecrated Species adhered to the sacred vessels after mass. It would have been a grave insult to the Body and Blood of Our Lord to wash these crumbs or drops down a common sink and force them to mix in the drains with all kinds of dirty substances. But the special drainpipe in the cupboard ran down into the natural soil under the building, where the Divine Body and Blood could decompose decently.

About a month after his first talk with the Master of Students, Adrian went back to the priest and said, 'Father, I think I can say I've followed the timetable exactly and never murmured against it. And I've learned all I could about the rules and customs of the seminary and the Charleroi order. But I still don't feel I'm becoming any holier—I still commit plenty of venial sins and my character is just as full of faults as it was when I came here. Are there any extra penances I could do to develop myself spiritually?'

Adrian had expected the priest to be at least a little surprised by his fervour. But Father Camillus only said, 'So you've proved you can observe the letter of the law, but you're looking for something more? Well, how about trying to observe the spirit of it? You know there are fourteen other students in this place. Do you behave towards all of them with perfect charity at all times? You say you follow the timetable perfectly. Are you proud of yourself because of it? The virtue of humility is one of the hardest of all to acquire.'

Adrian went away dissatisfied. But then he suspected that the priest was only testing his patience and humility. A truly humble religious accepted meekly every reproof from his superiors. Adrian told himself he deserved Father Camillus's censure. He even decided to follow the priest's advice for a trial period.

He seized every chance to observe the spirit of the rule. At recreation periods he deliberately picked out the two or three students he felt the least liking for and talked and played ping-pong with them as though he found them delightful companions.

On the weekly hike to the river he carried the haversack

full of bread and sausages for longer than he had to, and then pretended he hadn't noticed the time slipping away.

One afternoon when sport was over, Father Camillus sent two boys to the kitchen for a crate of soft drinks. When the students crowded around to get their drinks, Adrian hung back and offered up his thirst. But when he thought the priest was looking at him he pushed in among the others so he wouldn't appear to be making a show of his patience and self-denial.

One day when he was rostered to wash the dishes in the kitchen, he stood staring at a scrap of newspaper wrapped round a parcel. The Dean of Students snatched the parcel away and said, 'You know we don't read newspapers in the seminary.'

Adrian knew the rule about newspapers but he hadn't thought he was breaking it by glancing at the advertisements on an old torn page. If he had given way to his normal human feelings he would have argued with the Dean, but he bowed his head and said nothing.

One day at baseball when he stood under the ball ready to take the catch that would win the game for his team, he wondered whether he should deliberately spill the catch to forgo the pleasure of having his teammates crowding round and slapping his back. But then he realised that if he dropped the catch he would cause them to suffer considerable anguish. On the principle that charity towards others overrode all one's own interests, he caught the ball and held it firmly.

When he was with the others at mass or prayers in the chapel, he kept his hands loosely joined and his eyes wide open. He avoided any posture or gesture or facial expression that might have suggested he was unusually intense in his prayers.

On one of the weekly hikes along the riverbank, Adrian was sitting as usual with the least popular of the younger boys. He lay back with his head against a warm rock and prepared to enjoy the sight of the languid brown pool with its beach of pale pebbles, and the view beyond the river of grazing country with scattered trees. Since coming to the seminary he had learned to look at a peaceful landscape without any urge to make it the setting for a sin of impurity. The pleasure he got from staring at quiet pastures or deserted riverbanks was now quite innocent.

Or perhaps it wasn't. Adrian sat up suddenly and brought his reason to bear on a new problem.

If he were still a layman there would be nothing wrong with taking pleasure from the sight of a landscape. But he was now a religious who had given up the world. He was bound by a strict timetable and would soon follow the exacting rule of the Congregation of Christ the King.

By the standards of the religious life, the pleasures of the emotions were as reprehensible as unlawful sexual pleasures were in the world outside. It was no use mincing words—to lie on his back in the sunshine and feast his eyes on the countryside was a form of spiritual masturbation. In future he would resist any inclination to indulge in such pleasures. He would keep his eyes away from landscapes and works of art. Even his fondness for chalices and richly coloured vestments was no more than spiritual sensuality.

For the rest of that afternoon Adrian deliberately avoided looking at the long stretch of river or the miles of farmland around it. And all the way back to the seminary he walked with his eyes on the ground ahead of him. At the top of each hill he called on Our Lady of Dalriada to stand between him and the broad sunlit paddocks all around.

After two months at Blenheim Adrian was fairly satisfied with his progress towards perfection. By following the timetable exactly he was doing God's will at every moment of the day. Poverty, chastity and obedience didn't bother him. He wanted no material goods; he was relieved to be away from all sight of girls and women; and he delighted in obeying the Dean and the Master of Students for the practice it gave him in meekness and humility. He had proved he could cope with the religious life. His next step was to speed up his spiritual development.

The inner life, the life of prayer, attracted him. The great saints of the inner life had described years of painful struggle to reach even the lowest levels of the *via contemplativa*. They warned beginners that only one soul in a thousand ever travelled the long upward path to its end, which was nothing less than mystical union with God Himself.

Adrian calculated that if he had taken eight weeks to master the life of a religious, he could expect to be contemplating the Divine Essence within three or four years.

His first task was to stop thinking of prayer as the repetition of prescribed words and phrases—Our Fathers, Hail Marys and the like—and to begin composing his own spontaneous prayers to suit his different moods or the particular glory of God that he was contemplating. He considered the prayers of the mass. He had believed until then that the most meritorious way to pray at mass was to follow from his missal the exact words of the ceremony.

Since deciding to be a priest he had read those words in Latin and been pleased to find he could keep up the speed of the average priest and still understand a good half of them.

Now he wanted to understand the true meaning of the mass so he could look up from his missal and, with one piercing glance at the altar, pray a wordless contemplative prayer more appropriate than the long Latin formulae.

He struck trouble at once. All his life he had heard priests and brothers and nuns talking of the Holy Sacrifice of the Mass: of how it was the centre of Catholic devotion, a re-enactment of the sacrifice of Calvary and a means of earning incalculable graces and merit for those taking part in it. Now Adrian was surprised to find he did not know exactly how the sacrifice worked.

His first attempt to understand the mass he called the Theory of the Perfected Victim. Adrian worked out this theory during a morning study period. Whenever the Dean looked at him Adrian pretended to be translating his Livy. In some circumstances it could have been sinful to deceive the Dean and neglect one's studies, but Adrian had asked God for a dispensation from his studies until he had properly understood the true meaning of the mass.

THEORY OF THE PERFECTED VICTIM: The priest and the congregation offer to God the Father bread and wine representing a proportion of their worldly goods. They then persuade Him by means of their prayers to accept their sacrifice, humble though it is. Just when He is deciding how much spiritual merit to award them, the priest changes the offering into the body and blood of Jesus Christ. The priest says, in effect, to God the Father: 'You were gracious enough to accept our bread and wine. Now see what it really is that we offer You.' God then increases his generosity towards them in keeping with the increased value of what they have offered.

Objections: 1) How could the congregation claim that the bread and wine represented a sacrifice on their part? (Adrian understood that in the early days of the church the people brought their own loaves and wine to the altar. But no modern congregation would have been allowed to mill around the sanctuary, dropping breadcrumbs and spilling wine on the carpet.)

2) Why must God the Father be in any way pleased to be offered the body and blood of His Son under the appearance of bread and wine? Why must He reward those who offered Him such a sacrifice, if sacrifice it was?

Adrian had to wait until the evening recreation period to work out a better theory. At recreation the students were expected to mix widely with one another. No one was allowed to read or to sit apart from the others. Most played ping-pong or darts or gathered around the piano for a sing-song. Adrian usually played darts but he knew he couldn't concentrate on his theories while he aimed at the dartboard. Instead, he stood with the group at the piano. During the last verse of 'Drink to Me Only with Thine Eyes' his second theory occurred to him.

THEORY OF THE DISGUISED PRIEST: The death of Jesus Christ on Calvary was the most perfect sacrifice ever offered because Christ Himself was both priest and victim. He Himself offered his own body and blood to God the Father, who derived infinite satisfaction from it. Whenever a priest celebrates mass he says, in effect, to God the Father: 'Here is the very same Victim who pleased you so much when He was offered to you on Calvary. Moreover, I, the humble priest who offers Him to you'—and here the priest, metaphorically speaking, throws off his disguise—'I am really the same Priest who offered the sacrifice of Calvary, because His power is working through me.'

A few minutes later, during the 'Drinking Song' from *The Student Prince*, Adrian saw a fault in his latest theory.

Objection: When Christ first offered His body and blood to the Father, He earned for mankind an inexhaustible treasury of merit that could be drawn on in any age. How could it be necessary for us to re-enact the death of Christ whenever we wanted some of this merit? Surely God the Father did not have to be reminded every morning of His Son's death before he would deliver the spiritual goods that it purchased.

Despite their busy timetable and their long periods of enforced silence, the students found plenty of time to talk among themselves—at recreation, on their weekly hike to the river, during their hour of sport every weekday afternoon, and in the cloister between classes. Adrian was disappointed that they hardly ever talked about doctrine or theology. They sometimes commented on the different mannerisms they observed among their priest-teachers during mass or other ceremonies. Sometimes they compared the Charleroi way of life with those of other religious orders—usually to the advantage of the Charlerois—but Adrian missed the sort of discussion that might have helped him work out his deepest concerns.

Once, during the weeks when Adrian was working out his theories about the mass (as a preparation for a more intense life of prayer), he overheard two students commenting on the ugliness of the Roman chasuble and telling each other how pleased they were that the Charlerois wore only the more voluminous Gothic style. Adrian was ready to break in and say, 'It's all very well to compare styles of vestments, but have you ever tried to understand why the mass is a sacrifice?' But he checked himself. The two he had overheard were so-called late vocations—young men who had left school and tried other careers before deciding they were called to the priesthood. One of the two had played senior rugby in New Zealand. Adrian feared he might seem childish or a cissy if he tried to turn these men, as they seemed to him, from discussing vestments and to talk theology with them.

One Saturday afternoon, when the students were sitting in the cloister and polishing the brass candle holders from the chapel, Adrian singled out the most serious-seeming young man and asked him abruptly why the mass was a perfect sacrifice. Adrian hoped no priest would stroll past and overhear the conversation. He had learned that the priests seemed to discourage such discussions among the students and to prefer them to talk about their tasks at hand or to joke with one another. Adrian was reminded of the many days at St Carthage's when he had looked over his shoulder while he huddled with Seskis and O'Mullane and told dirty jokes or talked about sex.

As a result of his conversation in the cloister, Adrian postulated a third theory: THE SEPARATED SPECIES THEORY. The mass is basically the same kind of sacrifice as was offered by the Jews of the Old Testament. The congregation offer to God their most prized possession—not a calf or a lamb but the most outstanding member of their

307

own kind, Jesus Christ Himself. The Jews of old had killed and burned their victims. In the sacrifice of the mass, the death of the victim is merely symbolised by the fact that the Body and Blood are consecrated separately and remain separated on the altar.

Objection: When the Jews sacrificed beasts or crops they actually deprived themselves of valuable property. How could a Catholic at mass claim that the Divine Victim was his to offer?

Adrian could devise no better theories than these three. He set about deciding which of the three would best assist him in contemplative prayer. On each of three consecutive mornings he left his missal closed during mass and stared at the altar while he concentrated on one or another of his theories. None of them gave him the exalted feeling he had hoped for.

Next morning, something told him to look for guidance in the prayers of the mass for that day. In the Post-communion Prayer he found the words 'O Lord, by the working of this Mystery may our vices be purged away and our just desires fulfilled.'

Adrian had found his answer. He, a mere student in a junior seminary, had wasted days trying to understand the meaning of the mass while the learned theologians who composed the official prayers of the church were content to call the whole business a mystery and to humbly ask God to make it work.

He felt suddenly free to enjoy life again. He was still in the chapel and mass was still in progress. He looked up at the chalice. It was a pure silver-white in the morning sunlight. He savoured the deep, rich violet of the Lenten vestments. He derived an innocent pleasure from the winking of the sanctuary lamp behind its ruby-coloured glass. This was how the mass ought to be experienced! God the Father and His Son between them understood how the sacrifice worked and how it earned boundless merit for mankind. The people, and even the priest, had only to follow the ceremony with reverence and to wait for their souls to be showered with spiritual treasures.

To put an end the intellectual puzzle that had tormented him for days, Adrian arranged his newest insight in the form of a theory: THEORY OF THE CELEBRATION OF THE MYSTERY. This was so simple and satisfying that he felt a rare form of excitement. He would have called it an intellectual excitement except that it gave him his first erection since he had arrived at the seminary.

He tried not to panic, but he recalled at once an anecdote in a book of modern psychology that he had once found by chance in the State Library of Victoria. A young student of theology (he would surely have been a Protestant) became so tense whenever he was working on a difficult theological proposition that he was obliged to masturbate as soon as he had solved all his theoretical problems.

Adrian was determined not to allow theology to do that to him. To save himself, he turned away from theological theorising to the purely sensuous satisfactions of the mass. The door of the tabernacle was ajar. He stared at the frilled white satin exposed for a moment inside, and his erection quietly subsided.

Marco Zovic was in his early twenties. All that Adrian knew about him was that he came from Western Australia, where he had managed one of his father's shops selling jewellery and souvenirs and smokers' requisites.

On the second Thursday after classes began, Father Camillus told the students that Marco wouldn't be going with them on their hike to the river. Some of the previous year's students looked at each other, but no one else made any comment. Adrian supposed Marco was sick or staying back to receive an important visitor.

Later that afternoon Father Camillus met the boys at the chapel door before meditation. He said, 'I have a piece of sad news for you all. Marco has gone home to Western Australia.'

Adrian saw the same fellows look at each other again and nod. Others gasped or looked shocked. Someone asked the Master why Marco had gone, but the priest said, 'I'm sorry, but that's all I can tell you. Marco is no longer one of us.'

Adrian learned afterwards from the fellows who had nodded over Marco that this was always how a fellow left the seminary. Sometimes, they said, you could tell beforehand when a student was thinking of leaving. He would mope in a corner during recreation or daydream in study periods. He might have long talks in private with Father Master. Of course he might whisper to the others that he was thinking of going home, but this was strictly against the rules.

Once the fellow and Father Master had agreed that he ought to go home, he left the seminary by the first train to Sydney or Melbourne. This was because a student who knew he was going back to the world could have a damaging influence on the others. He couldn't see the sense of obeying the rules any more and he might even make fun of the hard life the students led. He always disappeared without saying goodbye to the others in case he made them homesick or tempted them to give up their vocations.

Adrian asked the fellows from the previous year what proportion of students went home each year. They reckoned that of the fourteen still left after Zovic, two or three would be sure to disappear during the year. They told Adrian that if ever a fellow was missing from his desk in the study room or absent from morning mass, you could bet Father Master would announce a little later that the fellow had gone home. And if you ever heard voices from the driveway in the early hours of the morning and car doors slamming, it would probably be a student taking a taxi to Blenheim station for the night train.

Adrian began to take a fresh interest in the other students. He wondered which were the two or three who were doomed to go back to the world, and when they would disappear in the night. At recreation periods and on hikes to the river he investigated them all in turn. He would tell a fellow a little about his own past and then wait for the fellow to open up about himself.

Bernard Cleary, the oldest student, was a qualified optometrist with his own business in Sydney. He had lived with his mother in one of the best suburbs on the North Shore. One night he had heard a lot of cars coming and going in his neighbour's yard. He found out next morning that his neighbour (a wealthy dentist and a good friend to Cleary and his mother) had shot himself and left a note saying he couldn't see any point in living.

Cleary had suddenly realised there was more to life than making money. He had always been an average sort of Catholic but now he started going to daily mass and wondering what else he ought to live for apart from money and possessions. A few months later he had contacted the Charleroi Fathers and now, here he was in the seminary to test his vocation.

Adrian said, 'It was lucky you weren't engaged or married.'

This started Cleary talking about his experiences with women. His mother had always been at him to take out this or that daughter of families she knew. He had taken out a few to please her, but no matter where they went there was always a floor show with a comedian telling double-meaning jokes. Cleary had got fed up with the embarrassment of it.

Adrian doubted whether Cleary had a true vocation. He was probably suited to a life of chastity, but the poverty of the religious life might be too much for a man with his wealthy background. When he was over the shock of the dentist blowing his brains out, he would probably be tempted to go back to his optometry business.

Daryl Drummond, the second-oldest student, was twenty-four. He had been a schoolteacher at Grafton in northern New South Wales. He told Adrian his story in strict confidence one day at the river, but Adrian often saw him talking quietly to other fellows and wondered how many had heard Drummond's history.

Drummond had been brought up a High Anglican. Every Sunday as a boy he had travelled ten miles by train to a church in Sydney where Anglican priests in proper vestments celebrated a kind of mass and believed they were actually consecrating the bread and wine like Catholic priests. It was always his ambition to become an Anglican priest and join the Community of the Resurrection—an order of Anglicans who lived a monastic life.

When he was eighteen Drummond had a spiritual crisis. It started with worries about the Apostolic Succession. He couldn't be certain that the Anglican priesthood could trace back their orders in an unbroken line beyond the English Reformation. (If they couldn't, they had no power to consecrate bread and wine, and their lives were dedicated to an illusion.)

He read articles and books by Anglo-Catholics who said they had preserved the succession, and Roman Catholics who refuted the Anglicans' claims. At first he used to spend a few weeks believing the Anglicans and then go over to Rome for a few weeks. Soon he was spending no more than a day in each camp, and the time came when he changed sides every few minutes.

He spent one whole Sunday afternoon casting lots from the Bible—saying a prayer for guidance, then opening a page at random and trying to find an answer in the Sacred Text. When this failed he made two little cardboard churches and labelled one CANTERBURY and the other ROME. He put them a few feet apart on the floor of his room and tied a blindfold over his eyes. He whirled round and round until he was giddy and then started crawling towards the churches with one hand groping in front of him. He blundered into a wall and found he couldn't move. His willpower or something was all gone. He stayed where he was until late at night, and decided he had to see a psychiatrist. He had been weeping for hours without noticing it. He went to the bathroom and stood on the scales and saw he had lost a stone since his first doubts about Anglican orders.

He chose a psychiatrist who was reputed to be an atheist—a Catholic or an Anglican might have been prejudiced. But the atheist was no use anyway. He made Drummond tell his whole life story and then insisted that his real troubles had nothing to do with religion. Drummond told the psychiatrist the main historical facts about the Reformation in England and asked him whether he thought Canterbury was a branch of the One True Church. The psychiatrist said a church was a group of people united by their beliefs and obviously no one church was exclusively true.

In the end Drummond had worked out for himself that he could be converted to Rome without having to decide whether Anglican orders were valid or not. If they weren't valid he would have made the right choice, and even if they *were* valid he would have lost nothing. The priest who received him into the Catholic Church had told him to wait for a couple of years before he applied to enter a seminary in case his old worries came back, but they never did.

Adrian asked Drummond what he thought about the validity of Anglican orders now that he was safe inside a Catholic seminary. Drummond turned his pale-blue eyes away and stared at something far off—perhaps the Community of the Resurrection, where a handful of lonely men tried to imitate the great Catholic monastic orders but never realised they were worshipping a piece of plain white bread. He said, 'That's the one question you must never expect me to answer.'

Adrian thought Drummond just then looked no different from any sanctimonious Protestant minister, and was sure the ex-Anglican would disappear from the seminary one night and sneak back to Canterbury.

314

Kevin Gilchrist was twenty-one. He had worked in a government office in New Zealand for four years. Adrian thought he was the most manly of all the seminarians because he used to own a share in a racing dog and enjoy a glass of beer after work. He and Adrian became friendly after Adrian had told him a little about the rough mates he used to knock around with at St Carthage's and how they were always trying to show him hot magazines.

Adrian asked him one day how he had discovered his vocation. Gilchrist said, 'You mightn't believe this, but one night my boozy cobber said he had important business to do and would I like to come along and help him. He took me down to the slum parts of Wellington to a shabby house. The front door was unlocked. Inside there was a queue of men in the hallway. My cobber took his place in the queue and whispered to me to have two pounds ready. I was so innocent it took me a long time to work out what was going on. A big ugly fellow and a middle-aged woman were sitting at the foot of the stairs keeping an eye on us. Every few minutes a man came down the stairs and said goodnight to the ugly fellow and went outside. Then the ugly chappie told the man at the head of the queue to go upstairs and which room to go to.

'When I was sure what the queue was for, I sneaked outside. My cobber was so drunk he hardly noticed me go. When I got outside I'd had such a shock I tramped three miles home to my boarding house to clear my head and think things over.

'I knew I was at a turning point in my life. I had sunk about as low as a man could. The next step was into the gutter. I still went to mass every Sunday and said a few daily prayers, but that was all the religion I had left. Still, I had no doubt what had saved me that night in the nick of time—it was the grace of God.

'All the way home I asked myself why God would make such a special effort to save me. Next Saturday I made a clean breast of everything in confession and started to lead a better life. The funny thing was, that didn't satisfy me either. It had to be all or nothing for me. I'd scraped the bottom of the barrel and now I wanted to reach for the stars. So I contacted a Charleroi priest and asked him was it possible I had a religious vocation. He told me to wait and pray for six months, and here I am.'

Adrian was confident that Gilchrist would go on to be a priest for the same reason that he was sure of his own vocation—each of them had tasted the pleasures of the world and found them not worth the price. Other students might be tempted to go back and try the pleasures they had never experienced, but Gilchrist and Sherd knew that sensuality led only to misery.

Cleary and Drummond and Gilchrist were the only students who could describe for Adrian an actual incident that had prompted them to think of a vocation to the priesthood. Most of the others were not so precise or so candid when they spoke of their past lives.

Terry McKillop was a twenty-year-old trainee accountant from Newcastle. Adrian had sometimes heard him saying he had left a girlfriend behind when he entered the seminary. One day on a hike Adrian got McKillop on his own and asked him what sort of girl she was.

McKillop said, 'She was a wonderful dancer. We had loads of fun together at dances and balls.' Adrian waited to hear more but McKillop had nothing to say.

Adrian said, 'I suppose you took her to other places as well as dances.'

McKillop said, 'Oh, yes. I met her parents. That was the trouble really. Her mother was so anxious to marry her off—always dropping hints about the future and asking me about my accountancy studies. Then I sat down one day and tried to imagine what it would be like married and I knew I was meant for something better.'

Adrian couldn't decide whether McKillop had a genuine vocation or not. He wondered what sort of fun McKillop had had with his girlfriend at dances. If they had gone to casual dances where the lights were dimmed and the couples shuffled round with their bodies pressed together, then McKillop would have known what he was giving up when he rejected marriage. In that case he was likely to end up a priest. But if he and his girlfriend had only gone to old-time dances where the girl's body was usually at a safe distance, then McKillop might decide one day to go back to the world and taste to the full the pleasures he had barely sampled as a young man.

John Medwin was only fifteen but he claimed he had read nearly half of St Thomas Aquinas's *Summa Theologica*. When he played ping-pong at recreation he chanted Gregorian antiphons under his breath. Each time he played a shot he stressed whichever syllable he happened to be up to. His opponent heard a loud *sanct-ISS-imus* or *OMN-ibus* just as he was trying to play his own shot, and sometimes told Medwin to shut up, which was against the spirit of charity that was supposed to pervade the recreation room.

Medwin sang Latin hymns to Our Lady under the shower and while he was sitting on the toilet seat. He was

317

the only boy who tried to talk about theology on hikes or at work in the garden. Some students believed he was a genius. Others nicknamed him the Boy Bishop and said he was a religious maniac. Most tried to avoid him, but Adrian often listened to him as a penance.

When Adrian questioned Medwin about his vocation, the Boy Bishop started talking about grace and free gifts of God and labourers in the harvest and those who cast out devils in My name. The only information he gave about his own case was that from his earliest years he had been blessed with vivid liturgical dreams in which he himself came to take a more central part as he grew older.

Adrian looked at Medwin's cheeks and top lip. The Boy Bishop had not yet begun to shave. Medwin had somehow been preserved from experiencing a normal puberty. If so, Adrian could not judge whether his vocation was genuine until Medwin had had some dreams about pagan orgies and film stars instead of the liturgy.

Philip Da Costa was the best all-round sportsman that Adrian had ever met. He was only seventeen but he had represented New South Wales in junior cricket and boxing. When the seminarians played cricket he hit twenty runs off the first over and then gave an easy catch to get himself out. At tennis he beat all the priests the first time he played them, but afterwards he used to return some of their serves into the net to give them a sporting chance.

Adrian was irritated by Da Costa's modesty. He could not believe it was genuine. When Da Costa hit up a dolly catch at cricket or pretended to be beaten by a ball from Drummond (who was hopeless at cricket) or jumped the net to congratulate a fellow he had allowed to beat him at tennis, Adrian remembered the boys from Eastern Hill Grammar, far away in the garden suburbs of Melbourne, who affected such gentlemanly manners but secretly lusted after the Canterbury girls. Adrian looked forward to the day when Da Costa showed his true self at last and swept every ball of an over from Drummond into the trees or served four straight aces to a priest and grinned at the spectators with not a trace of humility.

Paul Kupsch from South Australia was the youngest student. He was fourteen and suffered from homesickness and didn't care who knew it. Adrian was sure a fellow so young could have no real idea of what a vocation meant, and never bothered to find out why Kupsch had come to the seminary. The only time anyone took much notice of young Kupsch was at meals. Word had got round that Kupsch could eat as much as two or three grown men. When the servers carried round the second helpings, boys leaned forward to see Kupsch heap his plate. Every Saturday afternoon some of the students carried Kupsch into the kitchen and made him swing by his hands on the butcher's scales. He was said to be putting on three pounds in weight every week.

There were six other students including the Dean—all of them younger than Adrian. They were exactly what Adrian had imagined seminarians to be. They had been taught by the nuns at primary school and then by the brothers. They had been altar boys for years and had loved the mass all their lives. Their heroes were young priests who had stripped to their bathing trunks on altar boys' picnics and behaved like he-men and ducked the boys in deep water. Their devotion to Our Lady had kept them chaste during puberty. They had danced with girls at school socials but never allowed themselves to be alone with any one girl unless adults were present. Then, at fifteen or sixteen, they had entered the junior seminary to realise their lifelong dreams. They were such healthy well-balanced fellows; their lives had been so normal and predictable that Adrian found them dull by comparison with chaps like Gilchrist, who had knocked around in the world, and Drummond, who had been through a dark night of the soul.

Adrian was annoyed by the serene faces and uncomplicated motives of these ideal seminarians. He wished the Master of Students would impose some harsh burdens on everyone so the serene six would realise the seminary was not just a pious boarding school. He knew they would probably all reach ordination anyway, but he consoled himself by thinking what nasty shocks they would get when they started hearing confessions and learned what some young men got up to at an age when they (the serene ones) had been dreaming of celebrating their first masses.

But a time came when Adrian had to admit that some of these six fellows were heroes in their own way. One Saturday afternoon when the students were weeding the front garden, some of them swapped stories of how their parents had tried to keep them at home a few more years before they entered the seminary.

In each case there had been one parent who refused to let the boy leave home. Fortunately the boy had managed to win over the other parent, so that the prejudiced one gave way after a few months of quarrels and arguments. One fellow's mother had cried every night for weeks until she saw she couldn't make him give up his vocation that way. Another boy's father had taken him on a week's holiday in the middle of a school term and hired a fishing boat every day and talked for hours to persuade him that life in a seminary was unnatural for a boy of his age.

But the best story of all came from a quiet South Australian named Brophy who was only fifteen. When Brophy's parents were on their way to the station to farewell him, his mother had collapsed in the taxi. Brophy's father and sister revived the mother in the railway waiting room, but then she threw her arms around her son and swore she wouldn't let him go. The last thing he saw from the train window was the father holding her back from running after the train.

After that, Adrian had more respect for some of the younger fellows, especially Brophy. Even Gilchrist climbing up from the gutter was perhaps not so heroic as the boy from South Australia who had broken his mother's heart to follow his call from God.

At five each afternoon the students assembled in the chapel for fifteen minutes' meditation. When he had first seen MEDITATION on the timetable, Adrian thought they would simply kneel in silence for fifteen minutes while each boy meditated on the spiritual topic of his choice. It turned out that the Dean read aloud to the others from a book called *First Stages in Practical Meditation* by a famous German Charleroi. The book had detailed instructions for a hundred short meditations on texts and incidents from the Gospels. The Dean read the first step in a meditation and then paused. The students dropped their heads into their hands and meditated while the Dean kept an eye on his watch. After three minutes the Dean read the second step. The heads came up to listen. Then he paused again and the heads dropped for three minutes more.

Adrian was impatient with these simplified meditations. He longed for a half-hour at least of unbroken silence so he could begin an arduous course of contemplative prayer. Instead of following the Dean's childish instructions he used the fifteen minutes to think practical thoughts about his future.

The wonderful thing about being a Charleroi student was that his future was clearly set out. The future he had once planned with Denise McNamara had been based on his own hopes and conjectures. But his future as a Charleroi was guaranteed by God Himself.

At the end of the year he would pass his exams for New South Wales Leaving Honours. A week before Christmas the seminary would break up. Adrian would take the train back to Melbourne for a month's holiday. It would be the last holiday he would spend at home—once he had entered the novitiate even his holidays would be spent as his superiors ordered.

During his last weeks at home he would give away all his old toys and his model railway to his young brothers. He would do odd jobs around the house to compensate his parents for leaving them. (He need not do too much, because he would be saving them hundreds of pounds in board and lodging by leaving home.) Each Sunday at mass he would walk to the altar rails with the confident stride of an experienced seminarian. After mass he would stay in his seat making a long thanksgiving—not hiding his face in his hands like a meek layman but staring boldly up at the tabernacle to show he had a special relationship with God. He would not deliberately look for Denise McNamara, but if she happened to see him she would notice a difference in him and guess he had lived the past year under a strict religious rule.

Of course he would visit his Aunt Kathleen. She would question him for hours about life in the seminary and the ways of the Charlerois. He would be guarded in his answers. He didn't want to offend her—after all, it was she who first introduced him to his order—but things like the discipline and the straw mattresses were not fit topics for women's gossip. Even on the subject of his devotions he would not say too much to his aunt. Already, with his meditations and his efforts to perfect himself, he was outgrowing his aunt's kind of religion, which depended too much on holy pictures and relics and burning candles.

He would like to spend a week with the McAloons at Orford. Whenever he spoke at the tea table the whole McAloon family would stop to listen. His uncle might even ask his opinion on the spread of world Communism or some statement made by the Bishop of Ballarat in one of his pastoral letters.

Adrian would ask his uncle to drive him just once to some rocky beach near Cape Otway. He would not go into the water. It would detract from his dignity as a religious if the others saw his skinny white body in bathers. While his cousins were swimming he would walk alone past a headland or in among the huge rocks at the base of a cliff. He would stand silently and prove once and for all that the Australian outdoors had no power to make him sin. After his year in the seminary he would have such control over himself that he could ponder on some spiritual topic in the very places where, twelve months before, he had struggled with thoughts of girls peeling off their wet bathers.

In his last week at Accrington he would urge his parents to practise their religion more fervently after he had gone. As the parents of a priest they would have to set an example to their Catholic neighbours.

And this time, when he boarded the interstate train at Spencer Street station, his mother would surely not give way to human weakness and weep in public. She would have had a whole year to reconcile herself to losing him for good.

He would take the train all the way to Adelaide. The journey would be even longer and more stirring than his trip from Melbourne to Blenheim. The novitiate was in an outer suburb. He would feel strange and confused in an unfamiliar city, but they would surely send a priest to meet him.

Each novice would have to take a religious name at the start of the year. Adrian was already preparing at the junior seminary for this. Every afternoon he stayed only a minute under the shower. If he hurried back to his room he had at least five minutes of spare time before meditation in the chapel. His room was only a few yards from the students' library (a huge old-fashioned bookcase in a corner of the study hall). It was a rule that a student must ask Father Master's permission before taking a book from the library—not because there were any improper books on the shelves, but to remind the student that even his reading came under the jurisdiction of his superiors in religion. However, Adrian absolved himself from this rule on the grounds that Father Camillus would not understand the peculiarly personal reason that drove him to the library each afternoon.

Each day Adrian sneaked a volume of Butler's *Lives of the Saints* into his room and skimmed through a few of the thousands of entries. He was looking for a saint whose name could be his own name in religion. He required only two things of the saint—his name must be unusual and distinctive, and he must have been a notorious sinner in his youth. After going through nearly half the entries, Adrian had a short list of two names—Isidore and Hyacinth.

Blessed Isidore of Portugal was a thirteenth-century Dominican. As a young man he had given himself up to every vice and even practised sorcery. One night a fearful demon appeared to him and cried out, 'Amend thy ways!' Isidore made a pilgrimage to the shrine of St James at Compostela and began a life of exemplary piety and severe self-mortification. He was received into the Order of Preachers and died in the odour of sanctity.

According to Butler, there was some doubt as to whether Blessed Isidore had actually existed. One afternoon when Kevin Gilchrist lost his wristwatch in the long grass of the sports paddock and the students were all sent out to look for it, Adrian prayed silently to Blessed Isidore and asked him to prove he was a real person by finding Gilchrist's watch. Within a few minutes someone had picked up the watch, and Adrian quietly apologised to the saint for having doubted his existence.

St Hyacinth of Antioch was a holy hermit. In his youth he had been a pagan much given to luxury. His old school-master became a Christian and engaged in philosophical dispute with Hyacinth until the young man embraced the true faith. Thereafter he sought only to commune with God in solitude, and repaired to a savage place beyond the city. In later years the fame of his holiness and the miracles that he wrought attracted so many pilgrims to his hermitage that the saint had to withdraw several times to more remote refuges.

Adrian found St Hyacinth not as attractive as Blessed Isidore. First, there was the name itself. Adrian wrote faintly on scraps of paper: *Rev. Hyacinth Sherd CCR.* He was quite prepared to bear a name that ignorant people might smile at. (He had learned that the Greek root meant simply a colour.) But he thought his superiors might advise him to take a more masculine name that would give the enemies of the church no excuse to mock the priesthood.

Then there was Hyacinth's life story. It did not resemble Adrian's own life as closely as Blessed Isidore's did. Young Hyacinth had grown up in luxury, whereas the Sherds had no floor coverings in their house and Adrian had worn his school uniform to mass because he had no other good clothes. Hyacinth had been converted by his teacher, but Adrian would never have dared confide his troubles to the brothers at St Carthage's.

On the other hand, Adrian's gambolling with film stars in the green grass of the Catskills or the blue waters of Florida had been a sort of luxury. And St Hyacinth retreating further and further into the wilderness prefigured Adrian's wanting to live a devout life in the remotest parts of the Otways.

At the novitiate he would live the full Charleroi rule, which was famous for its severity. People who knew almost nothing else about the Charlerois could tell you they broke their sleep each night to chant the first part of their office. Some students had asked Father Camillus about this at Blenheim one day.

The priest had said, 'Of course you realise the Fathers here at Blenheim don't do it. Because of the smallness of the community and the demands made on us as teachers, we say most of our office privately each day. But just wait till you reach the novitiate. The bell goes at two every morning. You fall out of bed and pull on your sandals (you sleep in your habit, of course). Then you stagger down to the chapel. If it's winter your toes are freezing and your fingers are too stiff to turn the pages of your breviary.

'But seriously, it's a wonderful experience—especially on Sunday mornings. You think of all the other fellows your own age all over Australia coming home drunk after some party or taking girls home from dances and getting into all sorts of trouble—and there you are shivering in the chapel and chanting the beautiful words of the divine office and offering reparation to God for all the sins being committed all over Australia at that very moment.'

There were other hardships to look forward to in the novitiate. As a training in obedience, the novice had to ask the Novice Master's permission to do anything that was not covered by the Charleroi rule. If he wanted a drink of water while he was working in the garden he had to ask permission first. And to train himself in humility, he had to confess his faults each week to the whole community—priests, lay brothers and his fellow novices—and ask them to impose a suitable penance on him.

Novices had to observe a severe fast during Lent and on Ember Days and Fridays throughout the year. And of course in the novitiate you made yourself a leather discipline and gave yourself your first taste of it.

After the novitiate, Adrian would take a vow to remain

with the order for three years. He would spend those three years studying philosophy in the Charleroi house in Canberra. Then he would make his final profession—his vow to remain with the order for life—and do three years of theology before his ordination.

Adrian had no clear idea of what he would be studying in his six years of philosophy and theology. But he knew his philosophy would enable him to refute the arguments of any atheist or agnostic from a university. And his knowledge of theology would equip him to advise even Catholic surgeons and barristers in problems arising from their work.

Some of his courses would teach him things he would never have learned as a layman. For example, he would learn all the intricacies of the church's laws on marriage—the acts that were forbidden to married couples because they were unnatural; the valid reasons (if any) on account of which a couple might decide to have no more children, and the means they might use to that end; such matters as how often a man might exercise his rights in marriage before his wife could reasonably complain to her confessor about his excessive demands.

After his ordination he would be so well informed that he could visit any married couple and look them both in the eye because there was nothing they could do in private together and no moral problem they could face that he had not read all about in his studies.

It would be seven years altogether from the time Adrian entered the novitiate until he was ordained and ready for his life's work as a priest. Every day in the seminary at Blenheim he asked God to keep Australia safe for at least seven years. If a foreign power invaded the country or the

Communists took it over from within, his whole future would be ruined.

The students at Blenheim never saw a newspaper or heard a radio. In all his letters home Adrian asked for news of the Emergency in Malaya and the crisis in the Labor Party. His parents couldn't tell him much about Malaya, but his mother wrote in one letter:

> Your Auntie Margaret McAloon wrote to me about a nasty business on election day. Your Uncle Cyril was handing out how-to-vote cards for the Anti-Communist Labor Party outside the Orford State School. After a while the ALP chap started moving up close to him and getting in his road and stopping your uncle from giving out his tickets properly. Cyril could smell spirits on the chap's breath and he tried not to start trouble but then the fellow started mumbling foul language and calling Cyril a traitor. Well, Cyril touched his arm gently and asked him to move back a bit and then the fellow turned on him and swung a punch. Next minute there was a real donnybrook. Cyril tried to defend himself and he could have handled the ALP fellow all right only three or four criminal-looking types turned up from nowhere and said they saw Cyril start the fight and joined in on the ALP man's side. Lucky for Cyril some Catholic men from the parish came to his rescue and in the end everyone backed off. Cyril heard later from someone high up in the Anti-Commo party that these sort of things were happening all over Victoria on election day.

Some of the big Communist unions sent tough fellows with criminal records to all the polling booths to start fights and grab all our men's how-to-vote cards. It gave me a creepy feeling, especially when Margaret said the police were called to some booths but they wouldn't lift a finger to arrest the guilty ones.

Adrian could sense some kind of disaster ahead for Australia or even the world. His worst fears came to him on the very days when the seminary and the countryside around it seemed most peaceful.

One fine autumn afternoon he stared through the classroom window at the great mass of cannas beside the driveway outside. One of the last blossoms suddenly came adrift from its stem. It fell, not to the ground, but onto a bare spike among the tattered foliage. The crimson petals flapped like the folds of a brilliant flag shot down from a masthead.

Adrian looked out past the garden. In the autumn sunlight the empty paddocks and the distant roofs of Blenheim were strangely distinct. Even the farthest hills were clear of haze. It all seemed beautiful, but it could not last. The landscape was poised on the brink of something.

Out of the tall grass beside a hidden creek, on an afternoon just like this, would come the burst of machine-gun fire that ripped the cannas to shreds and shattered the seminary windows.

What would the Charlerois do when they heard the first shots? The best plan would be for old Father Fidelis to go to the chapel and consume the Sacred Species and then wrap the chalices and ciboria reverently in clean cloth and bury them in the garden. Anyone who chose martyrdom could stay behind with Father Fidelis and old, lame Father Pascal. Meanwhile the rest of the community would go to the laundry and grab a shirt and trousers each from the old working clothes in the cupboards there. They would discard their habits and soutanes and sneak out into the world disguised as ordinary working men. Before they scattered they would arrange to write to some secular address to keep in touch with each other.

In the western suburb of Melbourne where Adrian had spent his early childhood, there was a football oval set in a small park with elm trees and dusty oleanders and a sparse lawn. In a corner of the park was a small weatherboard grandstand. Under its wooden tiers was a dark room where the curator of the little park stored trestles and benches and odd lengths of timber. In the sixth grade at primary school Adrian and a few friends had discovered where the curator hid the key to this storeroom. Sometimes after school they unlocked the room and shared a packet of Maypole cigarettes in the dark among the cobwebs and timber.

While the Communists were desecrating the Charleroi monastery, Adrian was making his way overland across New South Wales. He slept in haystacks and washed in creeks and lived on vegetables and milk from farms. Weeks later he reached the outskirts of Melbourne. He hid until evening in long grass in Fawkner Cemetery. Then, after dark, he crept through side streets to his old suburb. Miraculously, the key to the room under the grandstand was in its old place. Adrian unlocked the door to the dusty room, put the key back in its hiding place, and went inside and slammed the door behind him.

Years passed. Adrian studied and prayed by day in

his hideout and visited loyal Catholic families and fellow religious by night. In a moving ceremony in a damp cellar he was ordained by a bishop disguised in overalls. His parents were present to receive his first blessing, but they had to leave soon afterwards because they were in a gang doing forced labour on a collective farm past Dandenong.

Alone under his grandstand each day, Sherd the priest (his religious name hardly mattered now) stared through a chink in the boards at the sunny park where he had played as a child. And he grieved continually over the sufferings of Australia.

The worst loss of all was the liturgy. No more could the faithful crowd their churches to watch their priests intercede for them with God in a cloud of incense at the high altar. There were boys growing up who would never see a priest, bowed down by a sumptuous cope and humeral veil, elevating a bulky gold monstrance in the sight of an adoring congregation. And Sherd, who would gladly have worn himself out in solemn processions or high masses that lasted for hours, was reduced to creeping into backyard sheds by night, dressed like a workman, and celebrating masses on tabletops for a few frightened onlookers.

He longed to live once more under a religious rule and to perfect himself by obeying its every detail. In a Charleroi monastery he would have had regular penances such as breaking his sleep each night for divine office and fasting every Friday. As a priest under Communism his life was disordered. He never knew what his hours of sleep would be or when he might have to leap up from his bed and flee for his life. And it was impossible to fast when he was half-starved for most of the time.

He would never know the joy of walking down a crowded street in a clerical suit and staring proudly back at the bigoted non-Catholics who looked at him curiously or even insolently. Now, if he made a show of his religion he might be shot on sight or arrested and tortured.

One of the advantages of dressing as a priest was the effect it had on women. Even the most attractive girl or young matron would have dropped her eyes modestly before Sherd in a clerical suit to acknowledge that he could not be affected by her charms. But under totalitarian rule he had no way of demonstrating his dedication to celibacy. The pretty women he met in the streets stared boldly into his face to see how he responded to their good looks.

In a religious house, with fellows like Medwin talking endlessly about the spiritual life or Drummond worrying aloud about the history of the Church of England, he could have earned merit by deliberately associating with the companions he liked least. As a priest in hiding he was often so lonely that he talked to people for no other reason than to enjoy their company.

He had once looked forward to the poverty of the Charleroi life—having to ask his superiors for train fares and the price of some devotional book that he needed. Under the grandstand he had no chance to practise the virtue of poverty—he had to spend hours each day devising schemes to feed and clothe himself.

When things got too bad for the priest under Communism he could always tell himself it was all a bad dream and melt back into the seminarian who was thinking of the future. But Adrian Sherd, looking across the paddocks in the mild autumn sunlight, could not be sure it was not real.

He wrote to his mother a few days later:

> Tell Uncle Cyril the priests and seminarians of Australia
> are all praying for him and his party. It's a pity there are
> so many lukewarm Catholics who can't be bothered
> fighting Communism with him. If only they would try
> to imagine what life would be like in Australia with all
> the monasteries closed and all their priests in hiding.
> That would bring them to their senses!

One morning Father Camillus told the students he had
arranged their first Whole Day for the year. They were
going by special bus to Sydney to spend four hours on the
harbour in a hired boat.

The younger students talked a lot about the trip but
Adrian tried not to look forward to it, because a good
religious lived only for the present and avoided vain specu-
lations about the future.

Fathers Camillus and Fabian and two lay brothers were
going with the students. Father Camillus warned the boys
not to be shouting out 'Father' and 'Brother' on crowded
beaches but to call him 'Cam' and the other priest 'Fabian'
and the brothers by their religious names, Sylvester and
Ambrose, so they wouldn't attract attention or give occasion for idle gossip among non-Catholics.

The bus left the seminary at seven on a fine morning.
The trip to Sydney was to take three hours. Adrian made
sure he was last into the bus so as to miss out on a window
seat (out of consideration for the others and to earn merit
by an act of self-denial).

Apart from the weekly hikes to lonely stretches of the

Blenheim river, it was Adrian's first trip into the world since entering the seminary. He had intended to guard his eyes carefully all day—only glancing at the more striking scenery, avoiding all sight of girls and women and offering up a silent aspiration when he saw someone who obviously needed his prayers. But so many things disturbed him in the first few miles that he ignored his resolutions and gaped around him like any undisciplined layman.

After only two months in the seminary he had forgotten what an irreligious place Australia was. In Mittagong the morning sun caught the cross above the Catholic church while the neat paths and dewy lawns below were still in shadow. People were leaving the church after morning mass. Adrian counted only four women and three school-girls. He wondered what the other hundreds of people in Mittagong had been doing while the sacrifice of Calvary was re-enacted in their main street. He saw women beating mops and dusters, schoolboys feeding pet dogs and men yawning and stretching after heavy breakfasts. All of them would have said they were much too busy to share in the spiritual treasure that was poured out on Mittagong every morning of the year.

In Picton the shops were opening for the day. A chemist stood in front of his newly polished window and threw back his head and laughed at something the barber next door was telling him. Adrian read the chemist's name: H. J. Carmichael. He was probably an Ulster Protestant. His laughter must have been forced—he had surely never known the true happiness that came from being in the state of grace. Adrian was in the state of grace, and he could have laughed a louder laugh than Carmichael if only he had understood why God allowed sinners to be just as happy as people who spent their lives obeying His will.

Adrian thought he might experience a few temptations during a day in the world. But the first one took him by surprise. Approaching Camden he saw an old brick house well back from the road and surrounded by a half-acre of lawns and trees. One of the front rooms had french windows.

Before he realised the danger he was in, Adrian had seen himself getting up from his desk and stepping through the french windows for an early morning stroll across the lawns. He was a lecturer in English at Melbourne University. After returning to Melbourne at the end of 1955 he had undertaken an honours degree in the School of English at Melbourne University. For four years he had done nothing but study. Poems, plays, novels—he interpreted and criticised them with the intellectual precision he had acquired in the seminary. His academic results were so outstanding that he reached the position of lecturer before the age of thirty. He lived alone in his rambling brick mansion, his only passion being his enormous library.

The trouble with this absurd reverie was that it presupposed Adrian would reject his vocation to the priesthood for the selfish pleasures of a life among books and gardens. As soon as he saw this, he drove the temptation from his mind.

The bus reached the outer suburbs of Sydney. The dense traffic, the acres of factories and the jumble of advertising signs made Adrian uneasy. Thousands of people were making goods in factories or carrying them in trucks or selling them in shops as if their lives depended on it. The people of Sydney had all the wrong priorities. In the calm of the seminary Adrian had seen the world as it really was.

Everything depended on prayer. On the Day of Judgement the world would be amazed to discover how often God had almost let it destroy itself but relented because of the prayers of a few faithful priests and religious.

The students and priests and brothers left the bus at a little wharf in a suburb of Sydney and boarded a boat for their trip round the harbour. The boat took them first into some of the bays and inlets upstream from the city. Adrian saw back gardens reaching down to rocky beaches with private boat ramps, and blocks of flats whose windows overlooked miles of blue water.

It was a block of flats that gave rise to his second temptation. The topmost flat was a kind of penthouse with trees in tubs and sun umbrellas in a walled roof garden. A. M. Sherd was a lecturer in philosophy at Sydney University. He had obtained his master's degree with a thesis that constructed an entire system of philosophy starting from basic questions about the nature of man and ending with the conclusion that the highest good a man could pursue was the enjoyment of intellectual and aesthetic pleasures. True to his philosophy, Sherd had purchased an apartment overlooking the harbour, where he sat each day admiring the beauty of the waves and jotting down corollaries to his conclusions.

Adrian fought this temptation by exposing it to ridicule—he could never end up like that because no honest philosophical investigation could explain away the Christian revelation and its message of self-denial in place of hedonism.

In mid-afternoon the boat stopped at a little bay somewhere east of the city. The New South Wales students looked awed and said the place was Frenchmans Cove, one of the toniest beaches in Sydney.

Adrian's party all went swimming. They were almost the only people in the water. The students ganged up on the priests and brothers and ducked them in the waves. They roared, 'What's the matter, Cam?' or 'Poor old Sylvester!' and enjoyed the chance to call the men by their religious names without the usual 'Father' or 'Brother'.

Adrian soon left the water and walked towards the dressing sheds. They were part of a new cream-brick building on a neat lawn above the sand. He walked with his head down. He was trying to overcome a temptation to be angry with his fellow students for romping and yelling like schoolboys on such an exclusive beach. One of his feet was planted firmly in the sand before he saw it was only inches from a deep-tufted dark-green beach towel.

He sprang sideways. A slight noise—something between a drowsy murmur and a snarl of resentment—told him there was a woman on the towel, but he dared not look at her. She would have seen the boatload of boys and men arriving at the jetty and heard their rowdy horseplay in the water. Now, one of the louts was sneaking up to spy on her while she sunbathed.

Adrian hurried away with his face averted so she wouldn't be able to describe him to her husband or boyfriend or recognise him in years to come if she saw him in the streets of Sydney in a clerical suit. And he wanted to be as quick as possible in the dressing sheds so the woman on the towel (and anyone else who had seen the incident) wouldn't think he had gone into a toilet cubicle to masturbate like a common pervert.

He put his foot so firmly on a royal-blue-and-yellow towel that he undermined the leg of a woman lying face downwards. The leg rolled slightly towards his own and a few square inches of lean brown calf muscle touched his pale hairy skin before he could pull away. A head tossed angrily under a huge sunhat and a face glared at him. It was framed by a white silk scarf. The lips were unnaturally pale.

All the way up the beach Adrian repeated under his breath the word 'sorry' in the idiotic voice that must have sounded to the woman like a child's. She herself was in her twenties—too old for him to court on a beach in real life, but the ideal age if he had been a schoolboy again and looking for companions for his American adventures.

In the dressing sheds he dragged the towel roughly across his skin. (It was a seminary towel—thin and faded and stiff from being boiled every week in the laundry copper.) When he lifted his right leg he saw a thin coating of sand grains on a part of his shin. He stopped and stared. Underneath these grains was a smear of oil from the calf of the leg of the golden-skinned woman in her twenties. She had rubbed the oil on with her fingers. The same fingers had rubbed other parts of her body. Wherever her suntan extended, the fingers had been—spreading the gentle oil with delicate strokes.

He stared at the patch of sand until he began to tremble. He would not touch it. He would pull on his trousers with the sand still clinging to his skin, and that night in his room he would anoint his own fingers with the last traces of the precious oil to see what images it might bring to his mind. On the contrary, he would put on his bathers again and run back down the beach into the cold water and stay close to the priests and brothers all afternoon. Better still, he would knock on Father Camillus's door that night and say that an extraordinary occurrence had made it necessary for him to go to confession at once, and when he had confessed his temptation or sin, whichever it was, he would ask for some crushing penance such as having to stay home when the students went on their next Whole Day's outing.

There were other possibilities. He could pull on his trousers and walk around naturally all day and wait to see whether the friction of the cloth rubbed off the oil anyway. If it had gone by night he could take it as a sign that Our Lady of Dalriada or Blessed Isidore of Portugal had come to his aid in a time of danger.

He could even take the most extreme course of all— give up his struggle against impure temptations and devote himself to a life of lust with glamorous suntanned women like those at Frenchmans Cove. It would be so easy. He saw clearly every step he would have to take—walk in to Father Camillus next morning and say he was going home because the Charleroi life was too hard; get a job in the Victorian public service and study for his matriculation at night; pass his matric and enrol at the university in the Arts Faculty, where female students outnumbered males; then, on the first warm day of the first term, stroll round the lawns looking boldly at the bare arms and legs until he found a girl who was in one of his lectures or tutorials and think up some excuse to start a conversation with her.

He noticed he was dressing himself even while he considered all these alternatives. And in the end the best course of action suggested itself. He dressed nonchalantly, as if there was nothing wrong with his right leg, then rolled

340

up his towel and bathers and decided to look for an omen in the first thing that met his eyes when he was outside again.

He strode across the sunlit courtyard of the dressing sheds and made for the exit. He noticed two men sitting astride a wooden bench in the courtyard. They were white-haired and stout but their skins were dark brown and leathery and they were both naked. They were playing cards quietly and solemnly. One old fellow put his cards down for the other to see. On the bench between his legs was a wrinkled bag. Adrian thought it was a pigskin purse for coins or poker chips. But when the man turned idly around to look at the staring boy the bag moved with him. It was the larger side of a huge old scrotum.

Adrian hurried outside away from the stern, creased face and the sun-blackened naked skin. He hoped the man hadn't thought he was a rare kind of homosexual who was attracted to older fellows.

He supposed they were wealthy retired businessmen. He wondered how they could sit so calmly in the nude while young women in twopiece bathers were sprawled on the sand only a hundred yards away. Their organs, lolling on the bench, were unnaturally torpid. If Adrian Sherd, a student for the priesthood, had sat there naked he couldn't have seen his cards for his towering erection.

Perhaps the men were so exhausted by years of lust that their bodies no longer responded even to the stimulation of a day at the beach. And perhaps this was the omen he was looking for.

The tired old weatherbeaten genitals had been shown to him as a sign. It was God's way of telling him, 'All right, walk down to the water's edge right now and call out, "Cam, I'm giving up my vocation here and now. The other boys can go back to Blenheim tonight. I'm going to spend the rest of my life taking pleasure from the bodies of young pagan women on beaches." Then do just that. Let your eyes roam freely over their golden-brown thighs and midriffs and cleavages. Then lock yourself in a cubicle in the dressing sheds and sin foully in thought and deed. Go back to Melbourne and follow your plan to live a life of lust at the university. Take your fill of carnal pleasures. I won't lift a finger to punish you. Your punishment will be the natural result of your excesses. One day you'll find yourself with white hair and a wrinkled belly playing cards in a sunny corner with some worn-out boon companion. The beach nearby is alive with suntanned women. But your once-proud organ lies slack and useless against your thigh. And when you lift it gently to gather up your cards it gives no sign of recognition—even to the man who served it so faithfully all his life.'

In the bus back to Blenheim Adrian worked out the implications of the day's events. He had experienced three serious temptations. The first had been to give up his vocation for the life of a lecturer in English. He had to convince himself once and for all that the attractions of literature were only an illusion compared with the real happiness that awaited him as a priest.

Adrian had always got high marks in English at St Carthage's because he wrote so enthusiastically about the set texts. *Kidnapped* by Robert Louis Stevenson, *Macbeth* and *Twelfth Night* by Shakespeare, *The Ballad of William Sycamore* by Stephen Vincent Benét, *Prester John* by John Buchan, *X=0* by John Drinkwater, *Captain Dobbin* by Kenneth Slessor, *Felix Randal* by Father Gerard Manley

Hopkins—it had been so easy to study them. The worlds they had opened up for him were almost as real as the Great Plains of America or the forest near Hepburn Springs. And there was almost nothing in those worlds that went against Catholic teaching. The authors were not all Catholics, but their ideas were sound. A brother had even said one day that scholars had listed hundreds of quotations to show that Shakespeare thought like a Catholic.

But in Form Five Adrian had realised there were mysterious areas of English literature where a Catholic went at the risk of his faith. The public examinations syllabus for that year allowed a choice between two novels—*The Mayor of Casterbridge* by Thomas Hardy and *Great Expectations* by Charles Dickens. The brother at St Carthage's told Adrian's class to cross Hardy off their book lists and buy only the Dickens title. There was just a hint of vehemence in the brother's voice when he dismissed Hardy from the course. Adrian noticed it at once and asked, 'Is there something wrong with Thomas Hardy, Brother?'

The brother said, 'Dickens had a healthy Christian attitude to man. Thomas Hardy was a pagan and an atheist. Most critics agree that his books are much too gloomy and pessimistic to be considered good literature. The man himself led a most unhappy life and died in a state of despair. There's an anti-religious clique at the university who take a delight in pushing this sort of book onto impressionable young people—especially Catholics. I can assure you a page of Dickens will interest you much more than a whole novel by poor old Hardy.'

Adrian went on earning high marks for English and passed comfortably in the public examinations at the end of the year. But he often thought of Thomas Hardy and visualised the landscape of the novels he had still not read.

It was only vaguely English. Adrian could not have enjoyed the real England. He remembered the wrongs that English Catholics had suffered since the days of Henry the Eighth and the plundering of the monasteries. But in Hardy's country he could almost forget he was a Catholic. It was a green place neither good nor evil. The scenery did not tempt a man to sensual sin as America's did. Instead it provoked a longing for refined emotional pleasures. And over it all hung the threat of despair—the danger that a traveller there might find himself lost, far away from both heaven and hell.

In the bus back from Sydney to Blenheim Adrian saw the meaning of his temptation in Camden that morning. It was his old feeling for Hardy's country—his dream of escaping into a landscape where he need not judge things according to strict Catholic values.

Safe among his fellow seminarians, and with Father Camillus in the seat behind him (he was 'Father' again now that they were nearly home), Adrian looked out at the lonely paddocks beside the highway. He was somewhere on the Southern Tablelands of New South Wales, about forty miles from Blenheim and four hundred miles from Melbourne. He wondered how he had ever thought of tramping the bleak moors and heaths in search of Casterbridge or the Wood-landers. And he thanked God that he was going back to the familiar life of the seminary, where heaven and hell were always within reach.

Then there was his temptation to give up his vocation for philosophy. He had never understood what philosophy was about until a brother had explained it all in a Christian Doctrine period in Form Five.

The brother drew two circles on the board—a large one enclosing a smaller one. He labelled the larger circle TRUTH and the smaller one REASON. He used the diagram to prove that human reason could discover only a small amount of all that was eternally true. The only Mind that could comprehend all truth was God's. Furthermore, because human reason was itself created by God, its proper function was to discover Divine Truth. Anyone who tried to use his reason for any other purpose was perverting a gift of God.

Proper philosophy, as it was taught in seminaries and great Catholic universities like Louvain, used human reason to uncover some of the noblest truths about God and man. (The brother tapped at the large circle on the board.) There was another kind of philosophy, however. This kind was taught in such places as the Philosophy Department at Melbourne University, which was a hotbed of atheists and agnostics. The half-baked university philosophers would tell a student to forget all he had ever been taught at school (yes, even his religion if he happened to be a Catholic) and start all over again using his reason to build up any sort of philosophy that took his fancy. It was not hard to imagine where this would lead. (The brother tapped various points on the board far outside the larger circle.)

In the bus among the Charlerois, Adrian closed his eyes and used pure reason to defeat his philosophical temptation at its own game.

Suppose he went back to Melbourne, passed his matriculation exam and enrolled for an honours degree in philosophy at the university. And suppose he did what the atheists told him and built up a system of philosophy based on his own reason. He was not a fool. He had been told by the brothers that he had a better than average mind. Sooner or later the iron laws of logic would compel him to admit the truth of the church's teachings.

It might not happen until the final year of his course, or even until he was a tutor or lecturer adding the finishing touches to his philosophical system. But one day he would have to be honest and step back inside the circle that the brother had drawn on the blackboard years before. And then there would be nothing left for him but to write humbly to the Charleroi Fathers and ask to be accepted as a late vocation. The atheists at the university would jeer at him, and it would serve him right.

The last of his three temptations had been his scheme for a life of debauchery beginning with his pursuit of female students at Melbourne University. The trouble had started on the beach when Adrian was doing his best to guard his eyes. (It was typical of the modern world that a celibate couldn't walk fifty yards staring at the ground without stumbling over near-naked female bodies.) If he couldn't avoid seeing such temptations, he must learn to stand up to them and fight them.

That night at the seminary Father Camillus told the boys they could have an extra hour's sleep in the morning in place of morning study. Adrian woke at the usual time. He dressed quietly and sneaked along the corridor to the library cupboard. He took down a book he had found by chance a few weeks before and smuggled it back to his room. It was a volume from an old encyclopedia called *Peoples of the*

World. He found three pages that suited his purpose and marked them with strips of paper. Then he closed the book with the three strips dangling from between the pages.

He sat on the bed with the book beside him and closed his eyes. He was about to perform a spiritual exercise. Its purpose was to strengthen him against the most common of all temptations. He would perform it regularly until he was completely indifferent to the sight of bare skin on a woman.

He was Rev. Isidore Sherd CCR and newly ordained. His superior had sent him to visit a Jesuit in the Catholic College of Melbourne University. He had taken a short cut through the university grounds. It was lunchtime on a warm day. Students of both sexes were sprawled on the grass in light summer clothing. As he walked along a path near the Old Arts building he noticed a suntanned girl in a low-necked frock almost beneath him on the grass.

Adrian opened the book at the first marker and stared at the full-page photograph with the caption: *A haughty Latuka maiden from the Anglo-Egyptian Sudan displays her finery.* The young Latuka woman was bare above the waist, with prominent black nipples.

Sherd the priest walked on. Near Wilson Hall he had to stop and tie a shoelace. He happened to glance up just as a young woman strolled along the elevated pavement. A light breeze lifted her frock a little.

Adrian opened the book at the second marker. The caption read: *These Nuba women believe their mutilations beautiful.* Adrian concentrated on the foreground of the photo, which showed a close-up view of a young woman's bare buttocks.

Reverend Father Sherd followed a path past the sports

oval. The shouts of girls made him look up. A women's hockey team was practising only a few yards away. They wore thin blouses and short skirts. As they ran and jostled and feinted, the muscles moved in their calves and thighs and their breasts leaped and bounced.

He opened the book at the last of the markers. The photograph was captioned: *A high-spirited dance in the French Cameroons celebrates a betrothal in the Tikar tribe.* Adrian stared at the flurry of bare limbs and especially at one young woman whose skirt had been partly raised by her primitive movements. He remained quite calm. Even the shadow under the skirt did not make him wish the sun had shone from a slightly different angle or the photographer had chosen his moment with more care.

He walked on—past the university library with its shelves of Thomas Hardy's novels and the Philosophy Department where the lecturers undermined the faith of students, and through a throng of young women who actually brushed their bare arms against his sleeves. He recalled a day long before, at Frenchmans Cove in Sydney, when he had been tempted to give up his vocation for these things. Then he laughed aloud and strode on to his meeting with the learned Jesuit.

It was the season of Lent. Each day the prayers of the mass spoke of penance and mortification. Adrian examined his conscience.

He was still thinking too much about the future— perhaps because the daily routine of the seminary wasn't providing enough stimulation for his imagination. Life in the seminary was still too easy.

He told the Master of Students he wanted some extra penances for Lent. The priest insisted that no penance was more suitable for a fellow in Adrian's position than the faithful observance of his daily routine. He gave Adrian a book for spiritual reading and said, 'Read that and you'll see what true penance is.'

Adrian took the book into the chapel for the fifteen minutes of spiritual reading before the midday meal. He studied the title—in bold crimson letters against a background of subdued gold. He repeated it under his breath: '*Suffering with Christ*.' He was cheered up already. He moved to the centre of a patch of warm sunlight and settled himself comfortably in his seat to read.

But he could not enjoy the book. Its message was no more than Father Camillus had told him. True suffering, according to the book, was not something you could choose for yourself. It came from submitting to God's Will and denying all your own inclinations and preferences. The model for anyone who wanted to suffer properly was Christ Himself, who spent every moment of His life in perfect obedience to the Will of His Father.

The author was a French Benedictine and a renowned authority on the interior life, but Adrian disagreed with him. If he, Adrian, were to give up looking for severe penances and do no more than follow the Will of God, instead of suffering properly he would only feel continually miserable.

There was another way to refute the Benedictine. If the most perfect form of suffering was to oppose all one's personal preferences and desires, then Adrian would have to oppose his greatest desire, which was to suffer. He ought to gorge himself at meals and heap his bed with extra pillows and make sure his showers were comfortably warm to avoid the sort of suffering he preferred. But this was absurd. Therefore the Benedictine's argument was illogical.

After this, Adrian could not endure to read *Suffering with Christ*. In spiritual reading periods he propped the book open in front of him and devised sufferings that would really satisfy him.

He made himself sit absolutely still in class and timed himself by his watch. One afternoon he sat for eighteen minutes without moving a muscle and only gave up because he thought the priest was looking curiously at him.

He remembered the story of St Benedict Joseph Labre, who was despised as a halfwit all his life but was really a great saint. He, Adrian, would suffer the humility of appearing a fool in the eyes of the world. When he combed his hair before mass each morning he deliberately did not touch the unruly tuft on the crown of his head, so that it stood up like the long spikes of hair on Dagwood Bumstead in the comic strip.

If he found a pimple on his face ready for squeezing, he left it with its white head plump and prominent for anyone to see and shudder at. Sometimes, if his skin was clear, he dipped his finger in black shoe polish or scraped it across the soap and put a little black or white smear on his face. One of the students usually told him about it on the way to breakfast so that he had to wipe it off, but at least he had looked ridiculous during morning prayers and mass.

He could not do these things too often in case one of the students realised they were penances and told the others about his extraordinary piety. The only penance he could use every day was a small, sharp pebble in his sock. He trod on his pebble as often as he could. He veered from side to side to add extra steps to his walks along the cloisters. And if someone called to him in the recreation room he walked to the fellow by the most circuitous route he could devise.

But even with the sharpest edge of his pebble pressing into his heel and his tuft of hair standing straight up on his head, he was not content. Arranging his own sufferings day after day was a hardship. It would have been much easier to live under a strict rule that provided easy opportunities for penance.

At Easter the mood of the liturgy changed from penance to rejoicing. On Easter Sunday the students were served three separate desserts with their midday meal and allowed the whole afternoon for recreation. Adrian sat in the sun and watched a game of quoits. He had eaten too much and his stomach was aching. He kept shifting in his seat to relieve his pain. He blamed it on the Charlerois and their absurd custom of forcing students to eat extra sweets on great feast days.

Near him a student named Cerini was talking about some monastery he had visited before he decided to join the Charlerois. Adrian suddenly realised the fellow was talking about the Cistercians. He questioned Cerini afterwards and learned his story.

Cerini came from Albury, New South Wales, where his father was a wealthy builder. At the age of fifteen he had read *Elected Silence* by Thomas Merton and longed to give up his comfortable life and join the Cistercians. He wrote to the abbot of the monastery at Yarra Glen near Melbourne and spent a week of his school holidays in the Cistercians' guest house. But his parents had persuaded him to join an order nearer to home. He told Adrian he would never forget the Cistercians and offered to answer any questions about their life.

That night Adrian knelt beside his bed for nearly an hour after 'Lights Out'. A layman or someone with little faith would have said it was only an amazing coincidence that he should have heard about the Cistercians again just when he was looking for a better way of life. But Adrian saw the Hand of God behind it. He could not have applied to join the Cistercians the previous year because he had been too young. So Divine Providence had led him to Blenheim to prove that he had a religious vocation. And now, when he realised he was called to a more demanding order than the Charlerois, God had put a fellow in his way who could answer the few questions he still needed to ask before he found his way to his true vocation.

Next morning Adrian stopped Cerini outside his room. He made sure the Dean was not about (because talking was forbidden in the corridors) and whispered to Cerini, 'What's it like in the monastery at Yarra Glen—the silence, I mean?'

Cerini said, 'It's wonderful. Pure silence. Nothing like what they call silence at this place.' And he and Adrian whispered together for a few minutes about the advantages of perpetual silence.

That afternoon Father Camillus asked the students to give up their sport and dig a drain in the seminary grounds. Adrian made sure he was put in the same gang as Cerini. He asked Cerini about the hard manual work of the Cistercians. He leaned on his shovel and listened to stories of monks ploughing and harrowing and harvesting all day in the hot sun.

When they were going inside for the evening Adrian stood with Cerini on the path beside the long beds of crimson-flowered cannas. Adrian looked across the gently sloping paddocks towards the town of Blenheim. He said to Cerini, 'In the Charlerois' vocations pamphlet they had a photo of this side of the building with Blenheim in the distance. That picture was the only thing that persuaded me to join the Charlerois.'

The afternoon sun picked out a few windows in Blenheim. The town was not all that far away. With a pair of binoculars he might have seen people in their backyards. Or someone in Blenheim could have seen him and Cerini beside the cannas.

Adrian said, 'I suppose the Cistercian monastery is pretty remote.'

Cerini said, 'Miles from anywhere. Would you like to see some photos of it?'

Adrian wondered why he hadn't thought of this before. He clutched Cerini's arm out of gratitude. The bell rang for showers. While they hurried inside Cerini promised to smuggle the photos to him as soon as he could.

Fifteen minutes later when Adrian was leaving the showers in his shorts and singlet, he saw Cerini making signs to him near the door to the toilets. Adrian understood. The two of them walked over and stood at neighbouring urinals. Each of them held his hands in front of him as if to open his flies. But Adrian saw the folder of photos in Cerini's hand. He edged his own hand across, took the folder and palmed it into his pocket—all without moving his head sideways. He pretended to shake the last water out of himself and then washed his hands at the handbasins.

Two or three fellows were hanging round but none of them had noticed anything.

Adrian almost ran back to his room. He shut the door and leaned against it. He opened the folder and dragged the photos out and pored over them. They were the first pictures he had ever seen of a Cistercian monastery.

Adrian knew he had to make a momentous decision. He did not intend to make it lightly. He put three pictures back in the folder and hid it under the lining of his bottom drawer. He put the fourth photo in the pocket of his shorts. Then he pulled on his soutane and put on his shoes and socks and walked down to the chapel as usual for meditation.

He made sure he was last to leave the chapel after meditation. While the others climbed the stairs towards the study hall, he slipped out of the cloisters through a side door and stood on the steps overlooking the beds of cannas.

It was almost dusk. There was just enough light for what he had to do. He took out the photo of the Cistercian monastery and held it at arm's length in front of him. He stared at it for perhaps half a minute. In the fading light he made out a building that looked like a farmhouse with wings and a tower built onto it. Beyond the building was a wide paddock ending in a belt of dark trees. Beyond the trees there seemed still more paddocks. And the whole landscape was surrounded by forested hills.

He looked away from the photo to the vista of farmland in front of him, with Blenheim in the distance. He looked briefly at the photo again and then compared it once more with the country before him. Then he put the photo away and went inside and bounded up the stairs.

He caught up with the last stragglers at the door of the

study hall. His troubles were over. He had made his decision. He actually looked forward to an hour of study. It was easy to throw himself into the Charleroi life now he knew he was leaving at the end of the year to join the Cistercians.

Next day Adrian returned the photos to Cerini and told him his plan. Cerini promised to keep it to himself, and from then on they seldom talked about the Cistercians for fear of being overheard.

But the next time they met in the corridor, Cerini pretended to talk to Adrian in sign language like the Cistercians'. And when Adrian caught Cerini's eye in chapel he put his hands to his neck and ducked his head. Anyone else would have thought he was loosening the collar of his soutane, but Cerini knew he was pretending to pull his monk's cowl over his head.

Often at sport or recreation when no one was looking they mimed the manual work of the Cistercians—pulling on a crosscut saw, milking a cow by hand, driving a tractor, or simply dashing the sweat from the face with a sleeve.

Once, at the midday meal, Cerini made as if to eat his chops and vegetables with a soup spoon. Adrian nodded at him and grinned—the Cistercians had only soup and bread at midday.

A few hours later in the chapel Adrian made a show of knocking over the statues of Our Lady and the Sacred Heart and painting over the ornate Stations of the Cross because Cistercian chapels were supposed to be bare of decoration. But Cerini didn't seem to understand. He looked alarmed—as if Adrian was desecrating the whole chapel and giving up his vocation. Adrian had to explain later what he had meant.

Each morning before mass Adrian performed a simple spiritual exercise. By an effort of willpower he caused his fellow students and the inessential details of his surroundings to disappear, and in their place he put the chapel at Yarra Glen filled with white-robed monks. After this he prayed as devoutly as any Cistercian. Many times during the day he worked a similar transformation. He was praying and working and studying harder than ever before to meet the challenge of the Cistercian life.

In the month of May the nights were frosty on the Southern Tablelands. In the mornings at the washbasins Adrian's fingers were too numb to feel the difference between the hot and cold water. He tried to ignore the cold and offer it up like a true Cistercian. But one morning before mass he could think of nothing but his fingers and toes and his ribs that cringed when he hugged them under his soutane. He could not even begin the exercise that changed him to a Cistercian. He had to spend the whole of mass in the unwelcome surroundings of the Charleroi junior seminary among boys in black soutanes who were almost strangers.

That afternoon the sun was bright and warm. The students played tennis and handball in their sports period. Adrian sat beside the tennis court waiting for his turn and hoping it would never come. He was trying to reach an important decision.

He could last the whole year at Blenheim as a Cistercian but not as a Charleroi. If the winter was too cold for him to live like a Cistercian he would go home to Melbourne.

But if he was going home he would have to do it soon because he must pass the matriculation exam before he could join the Cistercians. He was smart enough to coach himself in English and Latin and History if he bought all the books and stayed home all day at Accrington to study. But he would need something more than studies to sustain him during the long months before he went off to the Cistercians.

He leaned back and stretched himself in the sunshine and looked out past the tennis courts. It was the same view of grazing paddocks and distant bush that he saw every day from the upstairs windows. Usually it made him vaguely uncomfortable. It was all part of the world that a Charleroi was supposed to convert to the kingdom of Christ. But the yellow-brown undulating paddocks, the scattered roofs of farmhouses, the subtly folding forested hills seemed always to be drifting slowly out of his reach. By the time he was ordained, the whole of Australia might have been beyond saving. It would lie forever, a lost country, under a sunny pagan sky.

Now, when he thought of leaving the seminary, a glimpse of a secretive roof or a tantalising pattern of paddocks no longer troubled him. Somewhere out there, he knew, were thousands of people who would never be fitted into God's plan for the world. But Adrian would never have to rescue them or alter their obstinate landscapes. He was free to sit back and admire the fragile beauty of the land in the autumn sunlight. And in a few months' time, as a monk of the Cistercian order, he would contemplate his own private landscape—a few miles of grass and timber in the ranges above Melbourne.

He recalled in detail the vista of paddocks in Cerini's photograph. Already it had started him thinking lofty thoughts. And then he remembered that Thomas Merton was a poet as well as a monk.

Adrian himself loved poetry. Each year at St Carthage's, while other boys read only the few poems set by their English teacher, Adrian had searched his anthology for poems about remote and beautiful landscapes. His three favourites from his last year at school were 'The Lotos-Eaters' by Alfred Tennyson, 'The Hunter' by W. J. Turner and 'Kubla Khan' by Samuel Taylor Coleridge—in that order.

He half-closed his eyes and tried to recite 'The Lotos-Eaters' as though its setting was the Southern Tablelands of New South Wales on an autumn afternoon. But he could not remember more than the first ten or twelve lines. He realised it was the fault of the Charleroi life. There was no time for contemplating poetic landscapes in the frantic routine of the seminary.

The Cistercians were much more reasonable. Thomas Merton had taken his poetry notebooks with him into the monastery, and his superiors had let him go on writing as a monk. Adrian would start writing poetry as soon as he got back to Melbourne. When he joined the Cistercians he would show them his works and ask could he keep on writing. He would explain that he drew his inspiration from landscapes and had already admired photographs of their farm. They would almost certainly encourage him to keep up his poetry.

It was all settled. Someone called him onto the tennis court. He played a set. He threw himself into it. He played for the Cistercians against the Charlerois and wasn't surprised when he won. All the omens were urging him forward.

After showers he went with the others to meditation in the chapel. He spent the time preparing what he would say to Father Camillus that very evening. He would not trouble the priest with the whole story of how he had finally discovered his true vocation. He would say just enough to convince him that his motives for leaving were purely spiritual.

Adrian remembered the words of the Charlerois' vocations pamphlet: 'If, during his stay at the junior seminary, a boy decides that he is not called to the religious life, he is *free to leave at any time*. No one will put any pressure on him to stay.' He would quote these words to Father Camillus if the priest tried to win him back from the Cistercians.

As soon as evening study had started, Adrian left his seat and asked the Dean for permission to see Father Master. He knocked at the priest's door. A Charleroi always called out, '*Ave Maria*' instead of, 'Come in.' Adrian heard the priest's call and went in.

Father Camillus pointed to the visitors' chair and said, 'You're looking very solemn tonight, young Adrian. What is it?'

Adrian started talking. He was brief and blunt. He had tested his vocation rigorously and thrown himself wholeheartedly into the Charleroi life but now he found he was not called to it. He was keeping the story of his Cistercian vocation to the end, but before he got to it the priest stopped him.

Father Camillus lit a cigarette. (The Charleroi priests were allowed two packets a week. They said it was permitted by the Rule—their founder had written that a bowl of snuff could be placed at the disposal of the community in the recreation room. The Cistercians would never have allowed such a luxury.)

He said softly to Adrian, 'First of all, there's no need

to get so worked up about things. Just sit back and let me get a word in.

'In my job I've learned to be a pretty good judge of character and what it takes to be a good religious. Every year I see young fellows come in from all over Australia to test themselves for the Charleroi life. And every year a proportion of them come and knock on my door one afternoon and tell me they want to go home.

'Roughly speaking, there are two sorts who want to leave. The first sort of fellow takes me by surprise. Whenever I've seen him around the seminary he's fitted in well. He studies hard and enjoys his sport and takes his mass and his prayers seriously. But one day, without me noticing it, he's begun to worry about something. He thinks and prays and worries a bit more until suddenly he comes rushing in here and says, "Father, I realise I haven't got a vocation to the Charleroi life after all and I want to go home."

'Well, after I've got over my surprise I tell him what a tragedy it would be if he rushed off home without being absolutely sure he had no vocation. So he usually agrees to stay another ten days or so to be sure he really does want to give it all up. And during those ten days we sit down and try to sort out what's been worrying him.'

Adrian realised the Charlerois had lied in their pamphlet. A boy was not free to leave at any time. They were going to force him to stay for ten more days. He got ready to argue with the priest.

Father Camillus was saying, 'Then, Adrian, there's another kind of fellow. Now, don't get me wrong. No priest or brother of this order has ever thought worse of a fellow because he came and made an honest effort to test his vocation. There are fine Catholic laymen all over Australia who tried out with us until they found it was not what God wanted of them.

'Well, this other fellow usually catches my eye in the first few weeks after he's arrived here. He just doesn't fit in. He goes through the motions of following our rules but he can't settle down. In study periods he stares out at the paddocks and dreams about heaven knows what. Even during mass or spiritual reading he's thinking of something better he could be doing. At sport or recreation I often see him hanging back or moping on his own. Or else he forms a particular friendship with someone else who's a bit unsettled like himself and the two of them have a quiet grizzle together about why the seminary doesn't suit them.

'Well, one day this fellow comes in to me and says, "Father, I want to go home." Now, remember he's not a bad sort of fellow at all. He just wasn't called to the religious life. So I say I think he's making a very wise decision. Then I ring up the stationmaster at Blenheim and book his seat. And within twenty-four hours the fellow is sitting up happily in a window seat on the train home.'

The priest smiled broadly. 'Now, Adrian, would you like to wait here while I ring the stationmaster about your ticket? And while I'm gone you can compose a telegram for your parents. We'll send it tomorrow and you can be on the train to Melbourne the day after.'

Adrian wrote out the words for the telegram on the priest's notepad. His hands were so sweaty that he had to hold a handkerchief round the pen. Father Camillus was a long time away at the telephone. Adrian paced the room to stop his kneecaps from twitching.

361

Father Camillus came back and said, 'It's all fixed up. Tomorrow night I want you to knock on my door after night prayers to collect your tickets. You'll be leaving at nine the following morning. You know the rule here is "No Goodbyes". I'll take you quietly out to your taxi while morning classes are on. You're forbidden to tell any of the others you're leaving.'

Adrian interrupted him, 'Father, you've got the wrong story. I mean, I haven't told you the right story—the whole story.'

The priest said, 'Oh?' and lit another cigarette. Adrian wondered how he made his two packets last the whole week.

Adrian said, 'One of my main reasons for leaving—my only reason, really—is that I believe I have a vocation to the Cistercians. As soon as I get home I'm going to write to them and visit them. And at the end of the year I'll apply to enter their novitiate.'

Father Camillus looked out of the window for a long time. Adrian looked out too. He wished he could tell the priest how his love of poetry had influenced his decision. But the paddocks outside were almost invisible in the dusk. Poetic inspiration seemed a frail thing after all.

At last Father Camillus turned and said, 'Take a bit of good advice from me. Don't contact the Cistercians until you've given yourself a nice long holiday back in Melbourne. Then talk it over with your parents or your parish priest before you do it.'

He must have known Adrian wasn't convinced, because he said, 'You realise surely that if a fellow applies to join the Cistercians after he's already spent some time in a Charleroi junior seminary, the Cistercians are going to write to us

362

for some sort of reference. And we'd be bound to tell them truthfully how the fellow had measured up to our rules.' Father Camillus looked at his watch and drummed his fingers on his desk. 'And our rule of course is not much harder than a boarding school's, whereas the Cistercians'…'

He didn't have to finish. Adrian said, 'I see what you mean, Father. I'll give the matter a bit more thought—and prayer.' Then he left the room.

Adrian decided he would not be breaking the seminary's rule if he told Cerini he was leaving. He was not really leaving the religious life, anyway—only changing from one order to another. Next morning he took Cerini aside and told him his plans and said a taxi would be calling for him at nine the following morning.

Cerini said he was glad Adrian had chosen the order that suited him best. He even told Adrian not to be surprised if he (Cerini) turned up one day to join him at the Cistercian novitiate. He promised to leave class next morning, on the pretext of visiting the toilet, and try to wave to Adrian through the windows in the cloister.

PART FOUR

The train from Sydney stopped at Blenheim at mid-morning. It was due to reach Melbourne at nightfall.

Adrian was disappointed not to get a window seat. He had planned to sit in a corner brooding over the changing landscapes and making notes for a long poem called 'Pilgrimage to Yarra Glen'.

The poem was to begin with a description of the Southern Tablelands and the reasons (both geographical and spiritual) why that landscape could only provide an imperfect idea of the beauty and majesty of God. After that, the poet would muse in turn over the Riverina, a typical town of medium size in north-eastern Victoria, the hills of the Great Dividing Range and, finally, the outer suburbs of Melbourne. Certain features of each landscape would work on his deepest emotions and prompt him to praise one or other attribute of God. But in each district there would be some fault—a lack of proportion in the scenery, perhaps, or signs of rampant materialism among its inhabitants—that dissuaded the poet from making the place his spiritual home.

In the final section the poet would stand before the Cistercian monastery at Yarra Glen and look out across the farm where the monks worked all year. As he listed and praised the beauties of that place, there would steal over his soul at last an awareness of the true perfection of God.

The last stanza, the climax of the poem, would explain why this quiet valley was charged with the glory of God. It was because every soul in the valley was perfectly obedient to the Will of God. The devout Cistercians had transformed their little corner of Australia into a paradise on earth.

Adrian had the plan of the poem firmly in his mind before the train reached Goulburn. All he had to do was to put it into poetic language. He decided to use blank verse because of the scarcity of rhymes for key words such as triune, essence, attributes and evocative.

When the broad vistas of the Riverina opened up around him he took out paper and a pencil and worked at a rough draft of the first stanza. But whenever he wrote something, the man in the next seat stared at him. The same man had been fidgeting for a long time as though he wanted to start a conversation. Adrian wondered if the fellow had guessed he had just left a seminary. If he was a non-Catholic he might ask malicious questions. And if he realised the notes were for a poem he might think Adrian was one of those sentimental religious cranks like the authors of Protestant hymns or the nuns who wrote Christmas and Easter poems for Catholic magazines.

Adrian got up from his seat. Some of the best Riverina landscapes were slipping away behind the train. He stood in the open space near the main door of the carriage and tried to jot down his emotional response to a long bare hillside with a dam below it and a file of cattle coming down to the golden-brown water.

A young fellow in an army uniform came out of the men's toilet. When he saw Adrian writing he hung around and tried to look over his shoulder. Adrian stopped writing. The soldier might have thought he was drawing a map of the country around Yass or wherever they were. The fellow was still looking at him. It would be no joke if he was accused of collecting information about the terrain of the Riverina to hand on to an Unfriendly Power.

Adrian saw the sign VACANT on the toilet door and knew he could save himself from the Military Police or whoever dealt with suspected spies. He put his pencil in his pocket. He touched himself gingerly on the behind as though he was bursting to empty his bowels. Then he smoothed his notepaper between his fingers. He hoped the soldier knew that some people took their own paper into railway toilets for fear of germs. (Adrian's father had taught him this when he was a small boy.) He walked up to the toilet door and opened it with his left hand. Just as he entered the toilet he swept his right hand (with his notes for *Pilgrimage to Yarra Glen* lying flat against his palm) past his body in an extravagant gesture that was meant to look like a practice wipe. If the soldier was still looking he would have realised that Adrian was not acting suspiciously after all.

Adrian locked the toilet door behind him and felt safe. It was the only place where he could think clearly about his poem. He decided he would never finish it on the train. He had forgotten in the seminary how many distractions there were in the world.

He bent down and dropped his notes into the toilet. He held his head low over the bowl and listened to the rattle of the wheels and the roaring of the wind beneath the carriage. The wind would blow his poetic fragments into the shelter of some tussock in a lonely corner of the Riverina. The autumn sun would bleach his words and the winter rains would melt the paper to a sodden pulp. By the time his actual pilgrimage to Yarra Glen was over, his poetry would have dissolved into the land that had inspired it.

He still intended to finish the poem when he got back to Melbourne. But kneeling beside the toilet bowl he discovered something more wonderful than any poem. Near the bottom of the window was a small scratch in the whitish stuff that was supposed to coat the glass and keep the room private. So long as he stayed kneeling, the tiny ragged rectangle of clear glass was only a few inches from his eyes. And through this private window he saw a new country.

At any one moment he glimpsed no more than a splinter of landscape—a sweep of grass beyond a blur of foliage, a steep slope that might have led down to a river valley, a mass of coppery-green treetops below the level of his eye. But these baffling fragments might have been part of a whole land far more complex and variegated than Australia.

Adrian was perhaps the first to discover this new land. He verified this by sitting for a moment in the posture of someone straining on the toilet seat—the scratch on the window was too far from his eyes to reveal anything.

The land was almost certainly uninhabited. (If he had happened to glimpse anything like a roof or a fence he

370

could have blinked his eyes and never seen it again.) And he himself shared, in a sense, in its creation. It was he who assembled the fragments revealed to him and composed them into a pleasing whole.

Adrian had two or three minutes to enjoy his country before someone outside started to wonder why he was so long in the toilet. He kept his eye to the window. Now he saw irregular segments of sunlit grass that could have been fitted together into a noble plain. He wished he could have waited for a glimpse of tranquil brown water to mark his map with networks of rivers and streams. Even so, he had seen enough to prove that Australia could be rearranged into landscapes after his own heart.

Before he left the window he felt an urge to celebrate his discovery. One way would have been to throw himself down on a grassy bank far out in his own country and lie back and look from horizon to horizon and reflect that it was all reserved for him alone.

There was another way. With his eye still at the window he reached inside his trousers and took out a part of himself that had always responded to stirring landscapes. He did not even have to think of some girl or woman in his country. A peculiar cluster of vague golden hills, detached from all known continents, drifted past him. Before they were gone he had poured out his seed into the toilet bowl.

He got up quickly and buttoned his trousers. He washed his hand and flung some water into the toilet. Then he looked down into the tunnel that opened onto the roaring winds under the train. His poem had gone that way. Now the last blobs of his sperm would be dangling from the bottom rim of the metal until the wind tore them free. They

371

would never reach the new land he had discovered—only hang in tatters from some twig or grass-blade of the ordinary Australia.

Adrian went back to his seat and pretended to fall asleep. But all the way to Yass he considered the consequences of what he had done in the toilet under the influence of his private landscape. It was, of course, a mortal sin—his first since December 1953, when the sight of Denise McNamara had changed his life. All the spiritual merit he had earned in the eighteen months since then, including the value of his masses and communions and acts of self-denial in the seminary, had been wiped out. He was spiritually bankrupt until he made an act of perfect contrition or went to confession. As for his vocation to the Cistercians, God would almost certainly have withdrawn it as soon as he had unbuttoned his trousers.

The train stopped at Yass. On the platform, a few feet from his window, a woman and five or six children were saying goodbye to an elderly lady. The oldest child was a girl about sixteen. She wore a white uniform, as though she worked in a chemist's shop. (The kindly Catholic chemist had given her a half-hour off to farewell her grandma on the Melbourne train.) She was beautiful—short golden-brown curls, a sprinkling of faint freckles and the innocent quizzical expression that only Catholic girls had. He wondered what she would do if the stationmaster suddenly broadcast through the loudspeakers: 'Your attention, please. The foreman of a repair gang has just reported evidence that an unnatural act was committed on the Melbourne train some miles out of Yass. The train will be delayed briefly while railway detectives conduct a search of all carriages for the male passenger responsible. Thank you!' Adrian saw her rushing to drag her grandma back from the contaminated train. But her grandma was in no danger. And even if the girl herself boarded the train and sat in the seat beside him he would have behaved like a Catholic gentleman.

He stared at the girl's face until the train pulled away from the platform. The mere sight of her lips parting in a half-smile was enough to make him a changed man. He hated himself for committing a sordid sin only a few miles out of her home town. She could rescue him just as Denise had done long before. In the next Christmas holidays he would come back to Yass and stay at a hotel and go into every chemist's shop in town until he found her. He would buy a packet of some innocent medicine (throat pastilles or scalp lotion—nothing to do with the intimate parts of the body!) and ask her the times of Sunday masses at the Catholic church. He would sit through every mass until he saw her. Outside the church afterwards he would walk past her. She would greet him and introduce him to her parents. When they learned he was alone in Yass they would invite him home to Sunday dinner. The rest would follow naturally. He knew exactly what to do—he had done it all before with Denise McNamara.

But there were thousands of beautiful young Catholic girls in Melbourne. He might even meet one of them on the following Saturday evening when he went to confession to get rid of his mortal sin. It was even possible that the girl who was meant to save him was on the train with him at that moment. (God might have intended him to meet her on the very day he left the seminary.) He should have searched the train at Blenheim and found her and then thought of her all the way through the Riverina instead of crouching in the toilet and sinning like a common pervert.

He got up and walked the length of the train. He glanced at every female passenger and even at the young women behind the counter in the dining car. (God sometimes worked in mysterious ways.) There were no young women of his own age with Catholic faces—unless they were in one of the toilets, but he would not have dared to look at a girl on her way back from the ladies' room.

The most inspiring Catholic face on the train belonged to a young mother of three. He went back to his seat and thought of himself as the father of a young family. The children were all in bed. He and his wife were sitting by the fire confiding some of their dreams and ambitions to each other. Late in the evening he showed her some old photographs of himself. He started with a snap taken in the backyard at Accrington. While she marvelled at the dreariness of his early environment, a photo fell from the bundle in his lap and lay on the floor face up. His wife picked it up and said, 'What on earth is this?'

It was one of the pictures that Cerini had given him years before at Blenheim—a view of the Cistercian monastery at Yarra Glen. While he tried to explain what the photo had once meant to him, his voice quavered. He realised he had wasted his life. He had a lovely young wife and several children and it was years since he had committed a mortal sin. But far away under the night sky, in a lonely valley in the Warburton Ranges, the white-robed Cistercians in their dark choir stalls were chanting the office of Compline, and he should have been among them.

The train was pulling in to Gundagai. Adrian thanked

God he had remembered his true vocation before he was bound for life by the sacrament of matrimony. Luckily the girl at Yass had barely noticed him looking at her, so she wouldn't be disappointed if he made no effort to meet her again. He kept his eyes closed while the train was stopped at Gundagai in case some other girl was seeing her grand-mother off.

Past Gundagai he went over his plans to pass his matric exam and join the Cistercians. The only problem was his mortal sin. He would confess it the very next Saturday. After that he would regard himself as a Cistercian postulant and regulate his life as though he was already in the monastery—mass every morning, special prayers eight times a day, frugal meals, silence (unless his parents spoke to him) and solid work for the rest of the time (his studies, of course, but after the exams he could try a bit of manual labour in the backyard).

Late in the afternoon when the train reached Albury, Adrian still considered himself a Cistercian. Across the Murray and into Victoria he thought of the great monastic revival sweeping America. If it had spread to Australia there might not be room for him at Yarra Glen. But then he remembered from *Elected Silence* that the monks always made a new foundation whenever an existing monastery became too crowded.

Adrian suddenly realised what this meant. He might not spend the rest of his life in those few paddocks at Yarra Glen. Somewhere else in Australia was a landscape that would one day belong to the Cistercians. Adrian himself might be sent by his abbot to choose the site of his new monastery. How would he decide on a fitting landscape?

The train was somewhere near Wangaratta. He would practise assessing landscapes according to the spiritual uplift they provided. It was the sort of task he could never grow tired of. And to do it in the service of God made it doubly satisfying.

He tried to contemplate a dry hillside lightly strewn with granite boulders. But he was not being entirely honest with himself. He knew now that looking at landscapes and observing their effect on his emotions was what he really wanted for his life's work. Why, then, was he planning to join an enclosed order? As a Cistercian he would probably spend the rest of his life looking at only one landscape. There was only a slender chance that the abbot would send him out to prospect for the site of a new foundation. (If the abbot learned of his passion for landscapes he would probably keep him locked up at Yarra Glen, away from temptation.)

The train was slowing down, although there was no sign of a town. Adrian saw a sign beside the track: TWENTY MILE CREEK. He whispered the name aloud like a prayer and thought of a broad shining stream. It was a fitting place to discover his true vocation at last.

The train was barely moving. There were men beside the track. A bridge was under repair. Adrian was looking at things honestly for the first time in his life. What he had been searching for was not the perfect religious order but the perfect landscape. He was not called to be a priest. From that moment on he was a poet in search of his ideal landscape.

The ground fell away beside the train. Adrian's carriage crossed a small bridge. Beneath the bridge was a dried-up watercourse a few yards wide with eroded banks. This was

Twenty Mile Creek. Its dry runnels wandered away across a parched paddock. Adrian saw clumps of grass growing from its bed and decided that whoever named the creek must have been seeing things.

Adrian's parents and his two brothers met him at Spencer Street station and told him how much they had missed him. He was irritated by the fuss they made. They seemed to think it was homesickness that had persuaded him to leave the seminary. Yet he had told them clearly in his last letter that he was only leaving because it was God's Will that he should serve Him in some other vocation rather than as a Charleroi priest.

Adrian's mother served his breakfast in bed on his first morning at home. He enjoyed it, but he let her know that the students ate huge breakfasts at Blenheim, in case she thought he had come home half-starved.

Mrs Corcoran from down the street popped in to see him after breakfast. She said, 'I know the Charlerois are a very strict order. Was their rule just too hard for you, Adrian?'

Adrian said, 'No, Mrs Corcoran. I was surprised how easy it was to live the Charleroi life. I only left for private spiritual reasons.' The woman nodded solemnly, but he knew she was puzzled.

That evening his father asked him what he was going to do with his life. Adrian said he wanted to pass his matriculation exam. His father said he was mad to attempt a whole year's study in six months after all the strain he had been under. Adrian agreed to apply for a clerical position in the Victorian public service and to study one matric subject in the evenings. The following year he could study the remaining subjects full-time at a coaching college. He could pay his fees from the money he saved during his six months in the public service. If he passed his exams he could go to the university.

Adrian asked how his parents could support him while he did his degree. His father said he would have to apply for a teaching studentship. The Education Department would pay his university fees and a living allowance as well. Mr Sherd said, 'You'll have to teach in a state high school for three years after you graduate. That's not too much to put up with, is it, in return for a free degree?'

Adrian had never thought of teaching. He said, 'Would they let me teach in a country town?'

His father said, 'From what I've heard, they'll send you to the country for three years without even asking you.'

Adrian agreed to the scheme. His father said he could resign from teaching at the end of his three compulsory years, but Adrian planned a lifelong career as a teacher. He could teach English by day and write poetry in the evenings. The school would be a rambling brick building with ivy round its chimneys. From his desk in the upstairs classroom he could see past the leafy streets of his provincial town to the fertile farmland and the far ranges. Whenever he or his students needed inspiration during his English periods they only had to look through the windows at the great arc of rural landscapes beyond. With his matriculation students he formed a poetry society. He advised them on poetic techniques and read them some of his less personal works.

Adrian's father advanced him the money for his text-books for matriculation English Literature. He bought the books in Melbourne a few days later and sat up until midnight looking for outstanding poems.

By far the best was 'The Scholar Gipsy' by Matthew Arnold. Adrian had always thought of England as a crowded country, but the poem allowed him to hope that in rural counties such as Oxfordshire there were hills and meadows so remote that a man could wander there for years meditating on mysterious subjects or striving for a secret ambition beyond the understanding of ordinary people.

He was getting ready next morning to visit the State Library to study a detailed map of Oxfordshire when his father reminded him that he had to be interviewed that morning for a position in the Administrative Division of the Public Service of Victoria.

On the train into Melbourne Adrian started to learn 'The Scholar Gipsy' by heart. When he saw the strained faces of the people around him he realised there was something fateful in his discovery of the poem just when he had come back from the seminary to the secular world. Many a young man in his position would have been so dazzled by the attractions of modern living that he would have forgotten his high ideals and plunged into a life of pleasure. 'The Scholar Gipsy' was a reminder to Adrian that even though he had put aside his ambition to be a priest or a monk, he was still called to a special vocation and marked out from other men.

Walking from Flinders Street Station to the State Government offices, he bent his head low and gripped the lapels of his suit coat in one hand as though he wore an antique cloak that flapped around him in the English wind. Whenever he caught sight of himself in a mirror or a shop window he adjusted his expression to give himself the vague abstracted air of the Gipsy.

He walked so fast that he arrived early at the State Offices. He was pleased to see that the building overlooked a large park with plenty of English trees. There was time for a short walk under the elms. He avoided the paths and kept to the shelter of the tree trunks like a man who did not want others to grow curious about his great secret.

On the lawns of the Treasury Gardens he realised he wasn't taking 'The Scholar Gipsy' seriously enough. He had been too anxious about the outward appearance of the Gipsy when he should have been adjusting his own inner life to follow the example of that dedicated solitary. Walking towards the main door of the State Offices, Adrian tried to sum up the Gipsy's philosophy of life. But then he saw he had been confused all along—he had been too impressed by the similarities between the Gipsy and himself to realise that the Gipsy was not in fact a poet. It was all right to admire the zeal of the fellow as he journeyed through beautiful Oxfordshire landscapes with his head bent low and his thoughts on higher things. But the proper model for a young poet in Adrian's position was Matthew Arnold himself.

Adrian sat down quickly on a seat in the main hall of the State Offices and turned up the Biographical Notes in his poetry book. Unfortunately there was nothing inspiring about Arnold's life. The man who wrote such magnificent poetry had ended up as an Inspector of Schools.

Adrian walked up the massive stone stairway with his poetry book in his hand. It was almost time for his interview. He had less than two minutes to make up his mind on an issue that could affect his whole future. There was a strange significance in his finding out, just as he was applying to join the public service, that one of the greatest English poets had worked for the government as an Inspector of Schools. Work in the public service was supposed to be easy. A public servant's mind would still be fresh at the end of the day. He could read and write until late at night. At weekends and during his fifteen days' annual recreation leave he could travel around Victoria in search of poetic landscapes.

Adrian considered giving up his studies for the matric exam and his career as a teacher, and becoming a public servant by day and a poet by night—the Matthew Arnold of the Victorian public service. Yet this would be a dreary life compared with the Scholar Gipsy's. On warm afternoons he would be hunched over a desk instead of leaning on a gate watching the harvesters or lying on his back in a boat.

He stood outside the room where he was due for his interview and asked himself bluntly was he going to be the Scholar Gipsy or Matthew Arnold. He looked up and down the enormous corridor. A public servant was walking towards him—a young fellow in his twenties. Adrian looked hard at him. The knees of his sports trousers were shiny, and his grey cardigan had grease spots down its front. The fellow carried a sheaf of papers. They looked important, but he held them carelessly as if to show he was not in awe of them.

What decided the issue for Adrian was the way the young public servant walked. He was in no hurry. He dragged his feet a little; several times he veered slightly to one side for no apparent reason; and he stared slowly and thoughtfully all round him. Of course he wasn't looking at the drab walls and ceiling of the State Offices. He was thinking of his real life in his quiet room at nights and weekends. He was probably not a poet, but he had a mysterious other vocation, and all day he saved his energy for it.

Adrian knocked on the door, relaxed and confident. He could spend his life in the public service and still be a Matthew Arnold or a Scholar Gipsy or any other poet or hero of a poem.

The interview didn't bother him. His father had warned him that most of the top men in the public service were Freemasons. When he was asked what he had been doing since he left St Carthage's College, he said he had been at a boarding school in New South Wales. He answered the other questions honestly and saw that the interviewer was impressed with his results in the Leaving Certificate examination.

At the end of the interview the man said, 'You'll be advised by mail of the result of today's interview. If you're appointed, you'll probably start on probation in the Education Department—we're understaffed there at the moment.'

Adrian thought the interview had been a little too impersonal. He wanted to end it on a friendly, informal note. He said, 'The Education Department? That's a coincidence. A man I admire very much spent many years as an Inspector of Schools.'

The public servant was ushering Adrian to the door. He said, 'Oh? And what was his name?'

Adrian said, 'Arnold. Matthew Arnold. But he lived in the nineteenth century.'

The public servant looked hard at Adrian. It was the first sign of interest he had shown since the start of the interview. Adrian went away wondering whether the fellow read poetry in his lunch hour or at home in the evening.

Adrian didn't tell his parents that he planned to give up study and spend the rest of his life as a public servant and poet. He spent the last of his money for textbooks on a book called *The English Countryside in Colour*, a railway map of the British Isles, a loose-leaf folder and a ream of foolscap paper.

A week after his interview he received a letter advising him of his appointment on probation to the Administrative Division of the Public Service of Victoria. On the following Monday he caught a train to Flinders Street station and walked through the city streets towards the Treasury Gardens and the State Offices. The footpaths were crowded with office workers and shop assistants. Adrian saw they were no better than the city dwellers of the nineteenth century who had made Arnold so unhappy.

He knew much of 'The Scholar Gipsy' by heart. Along Flinders Street he recited appropriate passages under his breath. He hissed:

> ...this strange disease of modern life,
> With its sick hurry, its divided aims

at a young fellow who was thumping his leg with his rolled-up newspaper as he walked, and staring through the locked glass doors of a cinema. He murmured:

> And then we suffer; and amongst us One,
> Who most has suffer'd, takes dejectedly
> His seat upon the intellectual throne

when he saw an old fellow in a gaberdine raincoat sitting at a tram stop with his lunch in a brown paper bag in his lap.

When he rounded the corner into Spring Street, he almost broke into a run. Ahead of him were the Treasury Gardens—a walk of five hundred yards between trees and shrubs before he reached the State Offices. Because it was winter and the elms were bare, he recited the stanza describing the Scholar Gipsy's winter journeys.

He said the words aloud quietly until a fellow with rubber-soled golf shoes came up quietly behind him. When he saw the fellow beside him, Adrian started singing the words as though they were part of some sentimental ballad from the hit parade. But the fellow still looked at him suspiciously. He had a small brown leather case and he was heading for the State Offices. If he turned out to be one of Adrian's immediate superiors, Adrian would have to start singing whenever he passed his desk or met him in the corridor to convince the fellow that he hadn't really been talking to himself in the Treasury Gardens.

Adrian began work in the Teachers' Branch of the Education Department. The officer in charge of the branch said, 'We're up to our eyes in work and we haven't even got a proper desk for you yet. If you wouldn't mind taking that table and chair we've pulled up beside young Stewie's desk and giving him a hand. He's your Section Leader. He'll show you what to do.'

The officer in charge left Adrian with a man in his twenties named Stewart Coldbeck. Coldbeck put a few bundles of papers in front of Adrian and gave him some instructions. Adrian obeyed without knowing what it was all about. He spent the rest of the morning finding names of teachers or telephone numbers of schools or going to a big cabinet and reading details from teachers' record cards.

In the afternoon Adrian began to understand what was going on. Coldbeck and the fellows in his section were arranging temporary appointments of teachers to primary schools. The second term of school had just begun, and many teachers had transferred from one school to another. The Teachers' Branch was supposed to fill the vacancies that had arisen as a result of these hundreds of voluntary transfers. The branch couldn't send just any teacher to fill a vacancy—only a teacher whose present appointment was a temporary one.

Coldbeck explained: 'They're at our mercy, the temporaries. We just ring up the headmasters of their present schools and bung these forms into the mail and they go wherever we tell them to. Most of them are young—the experience does them good.'

Adrian looked at the form that Coldbeck bunged into the mail. It was headed in bold capitals:

EDUCATION DEPARTMENT OF VICTORIA
NOTICE OF APPOINTMENT
(TEMPORARY)

He had never dreamed he would handle anything so powerful on his first day in the public service. He put the form carefully back on its pile and said to Coldbeck, 'You mean, even if a teacher had lived all his life in Melbourne you can use one of these forms to send him to Portland or Mildura?'

Coldbeck said, 'If they've only got a temporary appointment we can give them another appointment anywhere in the state. Mind you, we're supposed to be reasonable. If Ouyen or Sea Lake needs a temp we sometimes try to

385

find someone who's already in that area. The trouble is we hardly ever have time to search through our lists for someone like that. We're usually so busy we just grab the first temp we can lay our hands on.'

After a few days Adrian began to understand the work of the Teachers' Branch. On the Friday afternoon he found himself with nothing to do. (Coldbeck was out of the room organising the weekly tipping competitions for the races and football.) He studied the list of state primary schools in Victoria. There were hundreds he had never heard of. Teddywaddy, Tempy, Traynors Lagoon—most of their names were uninviting by comparison with the places he studied each night on his map of England.

Yet on each page of the Education Department's list he found a few names straight from England. Macclesfield, Malmsbury, Mortlake—their green fields and leafy hedge-rows promised peace and poetic inspiration far from the dust and scrub of the Mallee and the Wimmera.

Suddenly there was work to do. Adrian sharpened a green pencil from Coldbeck's desk and turned to the first page of his list of schools. When he found a name from England he put a tiny green dot beside it. He worked through page after page until five o'clock. Then he took the list home in his leather satchel and spent most of the weekend with it.

On the Monday morning Coldbeck came in and threw his newspaper on his desk and said, 'Now, young Adrian, let's get cracking and shift some more of those temps.'

Adrian grinned at him. He was looking forward to his day's work. His life in the public service would not be drudgery after all.

The headmaster at Horsham needed a temporary assistant urgently. Coldbeck told Adrian to find someone for Horsham from the list of temporary teachers. Adrian paused a moment and thought of the little village of Horsham. Someone from his list was about to be transferred to the green fertile countryside of Sussex.

The first name on the list was Rosalie G. Mentiplay. She had a pleasant name that would have sounded well among the farmlands of Horsham. But she was already in England—at Blackburn, a well-situated town in the northeast, if he remembered correctly.

Adrian left Miss Mentiplay at Blackburn and considered the next name—Rodney W. Louch. Mr Louch was at present in a temporary position at Warragul. This was just what Adrian had been looking for. He would move the young man from the uninspiring haunt of Gippsland Aborigines to Horsham. With any sort of imagination, Rodney W. Louch could turn his temporary transfer into a spiritual pilgrimage from the harsh landscapes of Australia to a greener country.

Adrian made a note of Louch's journey on his blotting pad. He wanted to think of the fellow during the next few days while he was actually travelling to Horsham. Then he took all the necessary details across the room to the typist so that Louch's Notice of Appointment would be in the mail that afternoon. He didn't ask Coldbeck for his approval. He planned to present Coldbeck with the notice already typed and pretend he had forgotten to show it earlier.

The next few vacancies were at schools with names unconnected with England. Adrian chose temporaries to fill them without much interest and passed the names to

Coldbeck's desk for his approval. Then the school at Penshurst required a temporary teacher.

Adrian was ready. Penshurst, he knew, was buried among the hopfields and green swards of Kent. It was a worthy destination for any traveller. Brenda Y. Epworth would welcome the chance to set out from grim-sounding Black Rock for the rural peace of Penshurst.

At the end of the morning, when Coldbeck was approving Adrian's transfers he frowned at the two that were already typed. But then he shrugged his shoulders and initialled them and took them with the others to the officer in charge. Adrian kept a straight face, but he was overjoyed. He realised he need not have taken special precautions to get his English transfers past Coldbeck. All temporary teachers were a nuisance to Coldbeck. So long as Adrian filled the vacancies, no one would query them. Every day he could send two or three young men and women on long arduous journeys that would bring them at last to idyllic English landscapes. It was about as satisfying as planning poems or studying maps of England at night. In his poetry he was trying to describe spiritual journeys from everyday drabness to serene landscapes of the imagination. At work he was sending people to places whose very names evoked poetic imagery—but they were real people and real places.

He remembered a term at St Carthage's when his class had spent their Christian Doctrine classes studying Catholic Social Justice. Afterwards he had written an essay on the rights of the worker. Every worker should be free to work at a task that gave him a sense of fulfilment. Adrian had written that without fully understanding it. Now, in the

Victorian public service, he knew what it meant and fully agreed with it.

During the next week Adrian sent nine young teachers on pilgrimages from colourless Australian places to destinations in rural England. When the demand for temporary teachers was over, Coldbeck gave him other work to do. But in his spare time he prepared for the transfers in the third term. He prepared a list of the most deserving cases—the temporaries in suburbs of Melbourne such as Brunswick, Coburg and Maribyrnong—and made a note to give them first priority when vacancies occurred at places on the map of England.

Each day at lunchtime he walked in the Treasury Gardens. Many other public servants were there—middle-aged men strolling in threes and fours around the paths, groups of young women on seats around the lily pond, young fellows playing football with a bundle of newspapers. But Adrian avoided them all. He walked fast, backwards and forwards over the least-frequented stretches of lawn and in the shadows of thickets and beds of shrubbery. He was looking for places where he could stand and see nothing but lawns and trees in any direction, with no sight of a city building or an asphalt pathway.

His method was to find first a secluded spot where a mass of bushes hid the whole facade of the State Offices to the north. Then he would pace a little way in different directions trying to bring other foliage between himself and the city skyline to the west. Sometimes when he had got rid of the city, he looked back and found that a corner of the State Offices had come into view again. When this happened he had to move slowly backwards, one foot at a time, trying to watch the city and the State Offices until both had disappeared again. When the north and west were filled with greenery he turned to the south and tried to eliminate the Jolimont railway yards.

During his first week in the public service he found two spots from which he could see only trees and lawns and sky. He carefully noted their bearings on a piece of paper and decided they were enough for his purposes for the time being.

On the following morning before he left home he took his book *The English Countryside in Colour* and let the pages fall open. They opened at a picture of Symonds Yat, Monmouthshire. He read the text and looked once more at the picture to get the mood of the scene. At lunchtime that day he went to the first of his chosen spots in the gardens. He stood on the lawn and moved his feet by inches until he had turned a complete circle. He did this several times with his eyes fixed on the slowly changing vistas of greenery. And all the time he tried to see around him the landscape of Symonds Yat, Monmouthshire.

Next day he stood at the second of his spots and performed a similar mental exercise that took him to Wicken Fen, Cambridgeshire. The day after, he contemplated Poynings, Sussex, from the Devil's Dyke. There were only forty coloured scenes in his book, but if he found more of the right spots in the gardens he could combine each of them with each of the forty illustrations and provide himself with hundreds of poetic landscapes to savour.

In the evenings he drew up plans and tried to devise a title for a long poem about a man who discovered early in life that every landscape gave rise to a distinctly different mood in his heart (or soul—Adrian had not decided which of these words to use). There were sensual landscapes, landscapes suited to romantic love, religious landscapes and purely poetic landscapes. After viewing all four kinds, the man decided to dedicate his life to the fourth—the poetic. But then he made a tragic discovery—the landscapes that for him were most poetic were all in a distant country. Because it was impossible for him to visit that country he had to make a supreme effort of the imagination to recreate its landscapes in his everyday world. He tried various ways of doing this, but he realised in the end that the best way was to delineate them in his poems.

Here Adrian's rough drafts became so complex that he seriously considered abandoning rhyme and metre and using free verse to express himself more easily. Even so, he saw it would be hard to write a poem about poems containing landscapes that inspired poems. Sometimes he thought it would be easier to save up his public-service salary for a few years and travel to England and take his poetry notebook to a shady spot in Oxfordshire or Gloucestershire and look out at the hills and hedgerows and let the verses roll off his pen.

One morning when Adrian was coming down from the warm, green-muffled Cumnor hills towards the State Offices, someone behind called his name and ran to catch up with him.

It was Terry O'Mullane, dressed in a public servant's sports clothes and carrying a rolled-up *Sporting Globe*. They walked together into the State Offices. O'Mullane said he had been working in the State Rivers Department since the beginning of the year. Cornthwaite and Seskis were still at St Carthage's doing their matric.

They stopped in the corridor outside the lift. O'Mullane moved close to Adrian and said, 'And what's all this I hear about you running away from the monastery? Stan Seskis rang me up a few weeks ago and said he'd heard you were back in Melbourne, and you know what I told him? I said the priests probably found the poor bastard sticking up pictures of film stars in his room and kicked him out. Those were the days. We were only kids then. It doesn't hurt to look back and have a good laugh at some of the silly things we talked about. Listen, I'll meet you outside the building at one o'clock and we'll have a good yarn in the Treasury Gardens. I've joined the Young Catholic Workers in my parish and we've got this colossal dance going every fortnight. There's Catholic sheilas from miles around.'

Adrian said he would meet O'Mullane at lunchtime. Then, all morning at his desk, he worked at shifting his precious landscapes from their sites in the Treasury Gardens back to the pages of *The English Countryside in Colour*. By lunchtime the gardens were just a place where oafish public servants dreamed of YCW football and dances.

Adrian did not keep his appointment with O'Mullane in the gardens. He ate his lunch at his desk with his list of Victorian schools open in front of him. He wondered how to avoid O'Mullane on the way to work and in the corridors of the State Offices. He didn't want to hear about YCW activities and he knew O'Mullane had never enjoyed a poem in his life. But it was not only O'Mullane that he had to avoid. He realised he ought to keep away from anyone who might strike up a conversation and disturb his thoughts of poetry and landscapes.

He would have to model himself more closely on the Scholar Gipsy. Each morning when he left home he would recite some of the lines that described the Gipsy fleeing from farmers or travellers whose chatter might have distracted him from his high purpose. He would look up and down the street to make sure no neighbours were in their front yards. On the way to the station, if he saw some friend of his parents he would walk slowly to avoid catching up and having to pass the time of day. He would look carefully into the train before he chose a compartment. (The train to the city passed through Swindon, and there were several boys from St Carthage's still travelling on his line.) After he left the train at Flinders Street Station he would follow a different route through the city each day. There were lanes and arcades that he could use to dodge O'Mullane and the public servants from his own office. He would soon know the back streets of Melbourne as well as the Scholar Gipsy knew the lanes and byways of Oxfordshire.

That night Adrian recited stanzas of 'The Scholar Gipsy' aloud slowly while he turned the pages of *The English Countryside in Colour*. He paused over each line that seemed to describe his own situation or to justify his behaviour. 'But mid their drink and clatter he would fly.'

Twice each day Coldbeck and the clerks in the Teachers' Branch crowded together over cups of tea and chattered about football or horse races. Adrian did well to stay away from them. A poet of landscapes could learn nothing in such company. 'For most I know thou lov'st retired ground.'

This was an encouragement to Adrian to keep to his room or the shed in his backyard after working hours.

On his new routes through the city Adrian passed

several picture theatres. The Scholar Gipsy or Matthew Arnold would have scorned such diversions, but he found himself staring at the posters and the framed stills as he passed. Now that he had money in his pocket it would be easy to buy a ticket and sit through the intermediate session, which began at five in the afternoon. He could see again, after nearly two years, the American landscapes that had once ruled his life. He could even see, in the flesh, some of the women he had once known only from photographs in *Pix* or the *Argus*.

He had always kept on walking past the theatres, but a faint doubt was beginning to trouble him. Would he always be fully satisfied by poetic landscapes? Or would he have to struggle soon against the temptation that had made his life a misery for a whole year at St Carthage's?

He looked to the Scholar Gipsy for guidance. What was the Gipsy's attitude to women and sexuality? Adrian was struck for the first time by a passage that had previously meant little to him.

> Maidens who from the distant hamlets come
> To dance around the Fyfield elm in May,
> Oft thou hast given them store
> Of flowers...
> But none has words she can report of thee.

These lines suggested that the Gipsy was unable, or even unwilling, to forgo all contact with women. It was even likely that he admired them from a distance, although he prudently declined to press his attentions on them. The important question was whether he was troubled by thoughts of female charms afterwards in the long hours while he brooded alone in the countryside.

Adrian went back to the text. If he could find some hint that the Scholar Gipsy had had difficulties with purity he would engrave the poem on his heart. It would prove beyond doubt the value of literature—that a poem written in England a hundred years before could reach across the years with a personal message for a young man in Melbourne, Australia, in the 1950s.

He pored over the poem. He drew on all the skills he had once used to find double meanings in his parents' library books or magazines in barbers' shops, or to supply the details in guarded reports in the *Argus* of serious offences against women. But he had hoped for too much. There was only one passage in 'The Scholar Gipsy' that could have been a veiled reference to some kind of solitary temptation:

> And leaning backwards in a pensive dream
> And fostering in thy lap a heap of flowers.

Adrian had to admit that his favourite poem could not guide him in all of life's problems. It was all very well for Matthew Arnold to describe his hero brooding over scenes of natural beauty. But he was apparently incapable of explaining how the Scholar Gipsy coped with the demands of his animal nature. Nevertheless, somewhere in the vast treasure house of English literature there must have been a poet or a character in a poem whose situation was like Adrian's—some fellow whose poetic ambitions were endangered by memories of a sordid past.

Adrian remembered a book called *Anthology of Catholic Poets* in the POETRY section of Cheshire's Bookshop. The next day after work he called at Cheshire's and leafed through the anthology. It was there that he discovered 'The Hound of Heaven' by Francis Thompson.

While he was still standing at the poetry counter in Cheshire's, Adrian promoted 'The Hound of Heaven' to a higher place than 'The Scholar Gipsy' because Thompson's hero was more thoroughly human—he had sinned seriously in his youth. And Francis Thompson himself, whoever he was, became the model for Adrian's future development as a poet.

In the LITERATURE shelves Adrian found a thick history of English literature and looked up Francis Thompson.

> Born at Preston, 1859; spent some time in a Roman Catholic seminary; later studied medicine without success; moved to London and lived in extreme poverty.

Adrian wanted to shout aloud some triumphant cry, or preferably some great line from 'The Hound of Heaven'. Thompson and he were fellow souls. For one thing, they were perhaps the only two English poets who were also failed priests.

He read on. Thompson had been so incapable of coping with the simplest requirements of daily living as to be reduced to lying for days on benches in public parks and scribbling his poems on scraps of paper that chanced to come his way. It was almost too good to be true. Thompson, like Adrian, saw that poetry was the only thing that mattered in life.

Adrian wondered if he would be courageous enough to model himself completely on Thompson. He was already incapable of coping with many of the requirements of daily living. But would he be game to lie for days on park benches? Certainly not in the Treasury Gardens but perhaps for a few hours in some small suburban park in a part of Melbourne where no one knew him.

There was still much that he needed to know about Thompson. What sins had made him flee from the 'The Hound of Heaven'? Adrian felt instinctively that they were sins of impurity. And did Thompson love landscapes? The evidence here was not promising. Thompson had moved to London when he might have spent his life in the countryside around Preston. But perhaps, like Adrian, he ignored the distractions of the city and meditated on ideal landscapes among the thickets of parks and gardens. The setting of 'The Hound of Heaven' was a landscape more vast and affecting than any English scene.

Adrian walked to the shelves marked TRAVEL. Instead of looking vague and abstracted like the Scholar Gipsy, he practised walking like a man incapable of coping with the simplest requirements of daily living.

The travel books had pictures of landscapes all over the world. There was no obligation to confine himself to the gentle fields of England. He needed a wider, more savage landscape in keeping with the troubles his soul had endured. And it had to be as far as possible from Australia to emphasise his renunciation of his dreary outward life in Melbourne. He looked at four or five books before he chose *Views of the USSR*. The book itself was badly bound. The typefaces looked old-fashioned and the illustrations had a greenish-brown tint that blurred their finer details. But there was one picture that was worth the price of the whole book. Its title was simply *In the Steppes of Buryat Mongolia*. It showed a man, two horses and the largest expanse of empty grassland that Adrian had ever seen.

Adrian bought the book. While it was being wrapped, he asked the young woman behind the counter did they have a copy of the works of the poet Francis Thompson. She said 'Francis Thompson' as though it was the name of some obscure minor poet, and asked Adrian had he looked in the POETRY shelves. He said he had. The young woman said, 'Well, if it's not there we probably don't have it in stock.'

Adrian was almost glad. He could feel more sympathy with a neglected genius than with some popular poet whose works were in every bookshop for people to paw at. He went back to the POETRY section and took a copy of *An Anthology of Catholic Poets* to buy. It would be enough for the present to have Thompson's masterpiece.

That night Adrian began the notes for an epic poem set in a country so vast that the hero could make a solitary journey through fifty miles of desolate plains whenever he wanted to brood alone over his troubled past. Adrian kept the picture *In the Steppes of Buryat Mongolia* in front of him. But although the picture provided him with a perfect setting for his poem, he needed a little information about the customs of Buryat Mongolians to fill out the details in his narrative.

He found a useful article, 'Life in a Tent of Horses' Hair', in the junior encyclopedia his mother had once given him. But there were too many pictures of smiling children and not enough of worried adults. He wondered whether he dared write to the Russian embassy for an illustrated booklet about life in the steppes. He looked for the embassy in the telephone directory and found instead the Russian Catholic Church. The following Saturday he went to confession and asked the priest would a Catholic commit a mortal sin if he heard mass in a Russian Catholic Church. The priest wasn't sure. He asked Adrian why he wanted to attend strange places of worship. Adrian thought quickly and said he had a friend who admired Russian customs and scenery and kept inviting him to the Russian Catholic Church. The priest told Adrian to speak to someone at the cathedral if he was really interested.

Adrian went to a public telephone box and rang the number of the Melbourne Archdiocese. A priest told him at once that the Russian Catholic Church celebrated a valid mass because it acknowledged the supreme authority of the Pope, and any Catholic of the archdiocese was permitted to attend its ceremonies.

Adrian rang the Russian Catholic Church. A woman with a foreign accent told him the service began at ten each Sunday morning.

On the following Sunday be travelled by train and tram to the Russian Catholic Church. He planned to sneak into one of the back seats. When the priest started chanting in Russian, Adrian would close his eyes and hear the wind sweeping across the steppes of Buryat Mongolia. When the people were coming back from communion he would observe them closely, searching for a face for the hero of his epic poem. It would be the face of a man who had known sorrows like Francis Thompson's, but in a remote, mournful landscape.

He travelled deep into the garden suburbs. When he reached the address of the church he found himself in front of a large brick house set among lawns and shrubbery. While he wondered how he might sneak in without attracting attention, a man and a woman walked up to the gate and pushed it open and walked through. He followed them to the front door of the house and then inside the building.

Twenty or thirty people were gathered in a large carpeted room opening off the main hallway. They were all standing—no seats were provided. No one seemed curious about Adrian's being there, and he stood against the rear wall, trying to look as though he was praying.

The service began. The altar was hidden behind an ornate screen. A priest and two acolytes went in and out through two doorways in the screen, singing and chanting. The congregation sang in reply. The outlandish language and the tantalising melodies had the very blend of grief and heroic resolve that Adrian hoped would permeate his poem. If he could have taken notes of the thoughts that came to him during the service, he would have gone home with the complete plan of a poem about a man who wandered across endless steppes, trying to escape from his past.

The hero would have looked exactly like the taller of the two acolytes. He was a man in, perhaps, his late twenties with a face lined by melancholy and resignation. His eyes were a peculiar shade of blue—the colour of a wintry sky over the steppes. When he joined in the singing, it was as if he poured out a lament for a distant land. Adrian watched the man closely and even suspected he had seen him somewhere before.

The service lasted for nearly two hours. At the end, Adrian tried to get away quietly but a man stopped him and asked would he like to stay for the meal to celebrate the feast of St George. Adrian felt obliged to stay. He followed the man across the hallway, wondering what strange Russian customs he might soon witness.

The congregation sat down at several long tables set with plates of savouries and sandwiches and cakes. They chatted in Russian while they waited for the priest and the acolytes. The priest came in, dressed in an ordinary black clerical suit, and blessed the food and the people. The meal began. A man in casual clothes drew up a chair beside Adrian. It was the acolyte whose appearance had so affected Adrian.

Adrian nodded at the man and wondered if he understood English. The man said, 'I don't believe you've been to our church before.' He had no trace of an accent. Adrian said that he had come just this once because he was interested in the Russian liturgy.

The man said, 'We certainly hope you come again. I wish more Catholics in Melbourne realised this church is not just for Russian people. Anyway, my name is Brendan McQuillan.' Adrian shook the man's hand and introduced himself.

During the meal Adrian learned that McQuillan had been passionately interested for many years in what he called the Eastern Rite. He had learned to read and speak Russian and the Old Slavonic language of the liturgy. He hoped one day to visit the great Russian churches overseas. He was a bachelor and lived in a bungalow behind his parents' home in East Burwood. He earned his living as a clerk in the Public Works Department, on the floor below the Education Department.

Some of the Russian people began to sing. The melodies sounded mournful to Adrian but the people seemed to sing cheerfully. Adrian excused himself to McQuillan and left quietly.

On the way home, Adrian began to doubt whether his poetry would benefit from his visit to the Russian church. Some of the hymns had moved him, but he had learned nothing from the people. The acolyte who had taken his eye was not even a Russian and had told him that most of the congregation had never seen Russia—they had been born in China or Manchuria, after their parents had fled overland in the years after the Revolution. Adrian still intended to set his poem in a landscape like Russia's but he would draw his inspiration from his picture of a windy steppe where a nameless man on horseback prepared for a long, arduous journey.

Adrian thought the best result of his visit to the Russian service was his having learned that he was not the only member of the state public service who was leading a double life. He began to keep a lookout for other young public servants who might have pursued unusual interests in the evenings behind the drawn blinds of suburban houses.

In the following weeks, he found two such men not far from his own desk in the Education Department. One confided to Adrian that he was an actor. He had played several parts with a theatre company in his suburb but he wanted to play Shakespearean roles. He was saving up to travel to England, where he would find more opportunities. The other man built complicated models from dead matches. He brought Adrian a cutting from the *Sun News-Pictorial* showing a photo of himself with a scale model of a Melbourne tram made from twelve thousand matches. He told Adrian he was working on his most ambitious project yet—a model of the Melbourne Cricket Ground that would use more than thirty thousand matches.

Adrian had to acknowledge that the actor and the

model-maker had so far achieved more in their respective fields than he had achieved with his poetry, but he felt no sense of kinship with them. He had little hope that he would find another poet like himself in all of the state public service. He went back to spending his lunch hours and tea breaks alone at his desk. He consulted his list of Victorian schools, putting a tiny grey dot beside the name of any school that was surrounded by plains.

Victoria had nothing to equal the steppes of Russia, but Adrian knew that the Western District, beyond his uncle's farm at Orford, was mostly level land with few trees. And in his father's collection of *Walkabout* magazines were pictures of flat country in the Wimmera and Mallee districts. Not many temporary teachers were being transferred just then, but Adrian worked out a scheme for the third term, when more vacancies would need to be filled. If a teacher was needed at a school with plains around it—in the Western District, say—Adrian would try to obtain a teacher from another such school—in the Mallee or the Wimmera, for example. If the teacher thus transferred was at all sensitive or imaginative, he or she could savour the experience of seeming to move from place to place on the one vast plain or steppe.

In the evenings Adrian worked hard at the preliminary draft of his latest poem. It was to be called *Ivan Veliki*, after the main character. When the outline of the narrative had been noted down, Adrian became concerned that *Ivan Veliki* might be banned and he, its author, prosecuted under the Australian laws concerning obscene publications. If this happened, his name and photograph would be in the newspapers for his Aunt Kathleen and Denise McNamara and the brothers at St Carthage's and the Charleroi Fathers to see.

He would use a nom de plume. He first tried anagrams of his own name (Nash Radride; Dan E. Drishar; Anders Haird) but it occurred to him that anyone skilled at codes might easily work out his true name. He decided on a name inspired by his admired poet Francis Thompson. The seminary where Thompson had studied was called Ushaw College. Adrian adopted the literary name of U. Shaw, thinking that the U could stand for Ulrich or Umberto or Ulysses. On the cover of his folder of notes he wrote:

IVAN VELIKI
An Epic Poem in Two Cantos
by U. Shaw

Ivan Veliki lived on the steppes of Buryat Mongolia. At the beginning of the poem he was a young man but his face was already lined and he walked with head bowed and a slight stoop. He was a bachelor, whereas the other men of his own age were already married. His tribespeople wondered what flaw in his character, or dark secret from his past, had made him so reserved and thoughtful.

Whenever the tribe gathered to consult with one another or to celebrate some festival, someone would always call on Ivan Veliki for a song. He would always oblige with one of his own compositions. They were his own original poems set to music. Their poignant melodies and haunting images brought tears to the eyes of many of the men and women as they sat under the vast skies of Buryat Mongolia. But not even the eloquent lyrics of the songs revealed the cause of Veliki's melancholy.

The next section of the poem was going to call on all of Adrian's skill as a poet. In that section, he had to explain Veliki's secret. Adrian did not want to offend against Australian standards of decency, but he wanted his meaning to be clear to all male readers. (There was the separate problem of how female readers could be helped to understand this section. Married women could probably have their husbands explain it to them. Other women might have to remain baffled.)

For almost a year as a young man, Ivan Veliki had been a slave to the solitary sin. During that year, the sight of an empty steppe stretching away to a remote horizon would arouse him to a frenzy of lust. He would imagine himself taking some good-looking young woman of his tribe out into the windswept grasses and having his way with her.

One evening towards the end of the year just mentioned, Ivan Veliki was sitting by a campfire and listening to some of the songs of his tribe. One of the singers burst out with a ballad that Ivan Veliki had never heard. The ballad celebrated the beauty of the steppes and the inspiration they had provided to the poets of old. From that moment Ivan Veliki was a changed man. He foreswore his lust for women and dedicated himself to a higher form of beauty. From then onwards, whenever he was on the steppes alone, Ivan Veliki strove to express the beauty and power of the landscape in poetry.

One day during this period of his life, Ivan Veliki heard about a vast uninhabited steppe far beyond the boundaries of his tribal lands. He announced that he would travel there to start a new life with anyone willing to accompany him. A considerable number of his tribesmen and their families offered to go with him. They swore to follow him to the last steppe on earth and to obey him as their leader. (Canto One ended at this point.)

Years had passed. Ivan Veliki and his followers had prospered in their new homeland. Every day, Ivan Veliki rode around his vast herds and contemplated the endless-seeming steppes and composed superb poetry. He was known to his tribe as the Poet-Chieftain. He was still a bachelor, although any family from among his people would willingly have given him their most comely daughter in marriage.

One day, far out on a remote steppe, Ivan Veliki came in sight of a vista so striking and so rich in meaning that even his notable poetic power could not put into words its effect on him. He returned to his encampment and asked the parents of the most beautiful girl among his people to allow their daughter to ride out with him into the steppes on the following day. The parents agreed readily. They supposed that their chieftain was going to propose marriage to their daughter.

Next morning, Ivan Veliki took the girl to the place he had discovered. While he was away, a party of horsemen rode up to the encampment where Ivan Veliki lived among his leading tribesmen. The horsemen were from the tribe that Ivan Veliki and his followers had left years earlier. They had been sent by their chieftain to visit the new settlement and to see that Ivan Veliki was ruling his followers justly.

The visiting horsemen asked at once to see Ivan Veliki. When they learned that he had ridden out into the steppes with a young woman, the horsemen exchanged glances and said they would wait for him.

When the red glow of sunset had begun to overspread the far-reaching folds of grasslands, Ivan Veliki returned alone to the encampment. The horsemen rode up and demanded to know the whereabouts of the young woman who had ridden with him that day.

Ivan Veliki answered that he believed she was safe, although he could not say precisely where she was.

His questioners were clearly suspicious. Was she, perhaps, his betrothed, they asked.

Ivan Veliki answered mildly that she was not.

The horsemen became impatient. What kind of tyrant was he, to carry off the daughters of his subjects and force them to yield to him on the deserted steppes?

Ivan Veliki scorned to answer them. He wheeled his horse and made for his solitary tent at the edge of the encampment. The boldest of the horsemen rode up to Ivan Veliki and tried to knock him from his horse. Ivan Veliki flung the man from him, but a moment later the others were at him. When he saw that he was surrounded, Ivan Veliki made no effort to resist. He was led to the centre of the encampment and bound with thongs to a tall pole.

To the people who gathered around, demanding to know what crime their leader had committed, the visitors said, 'A despoiler of virgins is no fit leader of men. Ivan Veliki must die!'

There were surly mutterings from the crowd, but the spears of the horsemen held them in check. Then the boldest-seeming of the visitors stepped towards the pole and drove his spear into the heart of Ivan Veliki.

At that moment the cries of a young woman were heard from the rear of the onlookers. She who had ridden out onto the steppes that morning with Ivan Veliki had returned at last. On learning from the bystanders what had happened, the young woman rushed forward to confront the executioners.

'Fools! Murderers!' she cried. 'You have killed Ivan Veliki for no reason!'

The leader of the horsemen asked her sneeringly, 'Are we to believe that a virile young man spends a day in the steppes with a nubile young woman and does not try her virtue? What, then, did your unworthy leader want from you?'

The young woman lowered her eyes. She began to speak softly, and the people behind her pressed forward to hear. Even the horsemen were so intent on what she said that they lowered their spears and seemed not to notice that the crowd was slowly encircling them.

The young woman said, 'Ivan Veliki led me away from our tents soon after sunrise. We rode all morning, he only speaking to ask me was I hungry or thirsty or was my horse weary. Towards noon we stopped in a place overgrown by lush grasses and flowering herbs—a place, I believe, never yet visited by any of our people. After we had eaten a frugal meal, Ivan Veliki began to walk to and fro in great agitation. Not long afterwards he commanded me—or, rather, he requested me—to recline on a grassy bank in such a way that he could observe both my reclining body and, behind me, the distant prospect of steppes. When I hesitated, he swore on his honour as my chieftain that no harm would come to me. I trusted his word and hurried to oblige him. The sun was warm, and I had removed my cape and bared my arms. Otherwise, I was dressed as you see me now.

'While I lay among the grasses, I saw Ivan Veliki cast

a sweeping look about him at the wide steppes and then glance downwards in my direction. Ten times, perhaps, he repeated these motions. Sometimes he paused to strike his fists against his forehead. Once, he even drew out his silver-handled dagger and made as if to hack off his right hand with the sharp blade. Finally, he looked once more at me and then turned away and stumbled towards…not, I believe, the steppe after steppe surrounding us both but something that he alone could see…something that beckoned to him. Abruptly, he stopped. With not a word to me he leaped onto his horse and rode back to our encampment. I followed him soon afterwards but arrived long after him—too long.'

The young woman fell silent. Around her, the men of the settlement looked from one to another and then at the lifeless body of Ivan Veliki, still slumped and bleeding in sight of his killers and his former subjects. The young woman, in her innocence, had not grasped the full import of what she had told, but the men who had heard her out knew now something of the torment that their dead leader had for long endured—the same torment that had given rise to his best poems. Far from wondering at his frailty, his loyal followers felt urged to praise the man who had turned his sufferings into exquisite verse.

A voice rose from among those who had heard the young woman's report. 'Vengeance for Ivan Veliki! We will avenge our lonely leader!'

'Vengeance!' The cry was repeated from a hundred throats.

The visiting horsemen drew back, their hands on their weapons. The followers of Ivan Veliki soon surrounded them.

A man rushed forward from the throng. A sword slashed. The executioners were themselves dealt a rough justice.

The poem ended with the visiting horsemen all dead and the body of Ivan Veliki being carried at the head of a procession of all his subjects. Over his heart rested the manuscripts of all the poems he had ever composed.

The plan of *Ivan Veliki: An Epic Poem in Two Cantos* was finished. The poem would be written in blank verse, with stanzas of eight or ten lines each. Adrian spent a weekend working on the first two stanzas, which were to describe some of the main features of the steppes of Buryat Mongolia. On the Sunday night he put aside his working sheets to calculate when the poem would be completed and published.

Soon after its publication, *Ivan Veliki*, by U. Shaw, would be reviewed in the Literary Supplement of the *Age*. All over Melbourne, people who had known Adrian Sherd would read the review but probably none of them would guess the identity of the author. He would be spared such embarrassing questions as whether the poem was based on his own life and whether he himself had once dreamed of being alone with young women in scenic landscapes.

But what if Denise McNamara read *Ivan Veliki*? If the work was not completed and published until some years later, Denise might have been married in the meantime. She would show the book to her husband.

DENISE: There's something that puzzles me in this book, darling. (Shows her husband a passage in Canto Two.) What on earth was troubling that poor fellow when he went through that agony on the steppes?

410

HUSBAND: (Reads a little, then thrusts the book from him in anger.) What sort of smut is this? And how the hell did it get past the censor?

DENISE: You're misjudging it completely. It's a very moving story with some wonderful descriptive passages. But I wish I could understand that section I showed you.

HUSBAND: Well, it seems as if this hero of yours was having some sort of impure temptation. Wait on! (Looks closely at the text.) Yes, he's staring at that girl as though he might go away afterwards and commit what we call a sin of impurity by himself. And from the way he's behaving I'd say it wouldn't be his first sin of that sort, either. (Glances hesitantly at his wife.) I'm sure I told you about that sin after we were married, didn't I?

DENISE: Yes, but you told me only poor unfortunates did it. This man is a hero. He dies a tragic death.

HUSBAND: The way I read it, the author is only trying to trick you into feeling sorry for that kind of sinner. Who wrote the confounded thing anyway? (Looks at title page.) U. Shaw. Sounds like a pseudonym. I'll bet he's done it a few times himself, whoever he is.

Denise would read again and again the stanzas describing Ivan Veliki alone with the girl on the steppes. When Ivan Veliki turned abruptly away from the girl, Denise would be troubled by a vague recollection that she herself had once witnessed something similar. And at last she would remember the intense young man—Adrian was his name, Adrian Sherd—who had courted her silently on the Coroke

411

train for almost a year. One night, without any warning, he had disappeared from her life.

She had always supposed he must have had grave reasons for abandoning her as he did. Now, years later, *Ivan Veliki* offered an explanation. She was not rash enough to conclude that Adrian Sherd and Ivan Veliki suffered identical troubles. But U. Shaw's poem made her aware for the first time of the torments that could afflict a young man trying to reconcile spiritual or literary ideals with the demonic urgings of the flesh.

She felt a deep gratitude to U. Shaw for enlarging her understanding of the male soul and shedding light on a puzzling episode in her own life. She looked at the dust jacket of the book for some information about him, but there was none. She imagined him as a man who had read and loved poetry all his life.

It would be some days later, perhaps, before she recalled one of the many afternoons on the Coroke train when Adrian Sherd had read books of poetry with obvious delight. And then the thought would strike her like a lightning flash—could U. Shaw and Adrian Sherd be the same person? The strange and moving poem of Ivan Veliki—was it a message for her after all these years from the mysterious young man who was once so attracted to her but had been forced to desert her?

Adrian Sherd, with his notes for *Ivan Veliki* in front of him, wondered again how long it would be before the poem was published. If Denise was already married before she read it, she could do no more than admire his success and wish she had understood him better in the old days. But if she read it while she was still unattached, he might one day receive a letter (forwarded through his publishers) beginning:

> Dear U. Shaw,
> I trust you will not think it impertinent of me to send you this account of my reaction to your epic poem...

Adrian put aside his drafts of Ivan Veliki for two nights while he considered a problem that concerned his whole future as a poet. He saw he had been too hasty in assuming that a great poet had to live like Francis Thompson. He had overlooked the possibility that he might one day meet a young woman sensitive and intelligent enough to understand him and his work. Could he be the husband of such a woman and still write poetry?

There were sound arguments for and against. The happiness and contentment of married life might make it hard for him to compose poems of grief and spiritual suffering. On the other hand his work would benefit from being read aloud each evening to his wife for her sympathetic criticism. Adrian decided to postpone a final decision until he had learned whether any great poets had also been happily married and the fathers of large Catholic families.

He consulted his *Anthology of Catholic Poets*. The man he had been searching for was only a few pages away from Francis Thompson. And Thompson himself had described him as the greatest genius of the century. The name of this remarkable poet was Coventry Patmore.

Adrian had to admit he had never heard of Patmore, but the editor of the anthology lavished praise on him. His work was the high-water mark of English Catholic poetry.

He had brought English religious poetry to unsurpassable heights. His masterpiece was *The Unknown Eros*, a poem which praised married love as the means by which the soul might experience a foretaste of union with God.

Unfortunately the anthology contained no extracts from *The Unknown Eros* or Patmore's other great work, *The Angel in the House*. The editor had chosen only some exquisite shorter poems. Adrian planned to read Patmore's major works in the State Library. In the meantime he discovered from a history of English literature in Cheshire's Bookshop that Patmore had been married three times (his first two wives predeceased him), and that he had embraced Catholicism after the death of his first wife. In his last years he had lived at a quiet place in Hampshire.

That night Adrian did not open his folder of notes for *Ivan Veliki*. He sat thinking of the time when he turned his back on Denise McNamara and aspired to be a priest. If he had known of Patmore's poetry in those days he would have realised that a pure marriage was just as sure a path to God as a life in Holy Orders. His dreams of Triabunna, the bush near Hepburn Springs and the settlement in the Otways could have led him towards the mystic's goal if only he had taken them more seriously. He had turned away from Denise because he seemed in danger of lapsing into impurity. What he should have done was to elevate his love for her to a poetic emotion. But of course he had not heard of *The Unknown Eros* then.

Adrian took out a new folder. He would not discard *Ivan Veliki* entirely. It would be of interest to literary critics as an example of his early work. But all his poetic energy would now be devoted to a work on married love.

He tried for several days to compose a good introduction to his poem. On the following Sunday he attended the nine o'clock mass at Our Lady of Good Counsel's. This was known as the Family Mass. Most of the congregation were parents with young children. Ten minutes after the mass had begun a young couple with four small children crowded into the seat in front of Adrian.

Adrian inspected the woman. She was perhaps twenty-five, with short blonde hair and a rather pretty face. Her oldest child was about five. The second and third children were toddlers of different sizes, and the youngest was a baby, struggling to sit up. The husband was a colourless fellow in sports trousers and a shawl-neck pullover. He yawned instead of praying, and kept fingering the crust of dried blood on a shaving cut near his Adam's apple.

Adrian did some quick calculations. The couple had been married about six years. They had produced a child every sixteen months or so. On one of those very nights when he was mistakenly searching for happiness in America, somewhere in his own suburb of Accrington the couple had been engaged in the marriage act that gave rise to their third child. And one night in 1954 while he was using his numbered tickets to determine the moods of his wife, Denise, the pert, pretty face (it was only a few feet from his own as he knelt behind her) looked up at the colourless one (he was yawning again) in an invitation to the embrace that produced their fourth.

These people had actually experienced what Adrian was about to celebrate in his poetry—the blissful union of bodies and souls in the sacrament of matrimony. If they had abandoned themselves properly they might already

415

have felt, however briefly, that oneness with the Divine that Patmore had written of.

But had they? They were sitting back now, waiting for the sermon to start. The man had a toddler on each knee. The woman held the baby in her arms while the oldest child sat leaning against her. Adrian looked hard at them. There was no evidence that they had achieved anything by their marriage. They had probably never heard of Coventry Patmore, let alone read *The Unknown Eros* or reflected on the true significance of conjugal affection.

If anything, marriage had dulled them. The young woman was already neglecting her appearance. Adrian noticed on her neck, below her ear, haphazard blotches of powder. She had dabbed the stuff on hurriedly instead of giving her skin the uniform delicate texture that would inspire tender thoughts in a husband. There was a small spot on the front of her linen coat, as if a child had touched it with a greasy finger days before and she had not even noticed it. She was beginning to forget the importance of dress as a means of maintaining a husband's interest.

As for the man, he seemed almost asleep. He only opened his eyes when one of the children clutched at him or threatened to fall from his knee. He was apparently unaware that one of the greatest joys of a Catholic marriage was to worship with your spouse beside you and to sense that you and she were bound inseparably together and to God.

Adrian suddenly knew how to start his poem. The opening stanzas would describe a man and his wife who complained after five years of marriage that they still had not experienced true bliss. The poet would question them, and it would emerge that the couple had been too preoccupied with worldly things and not sufficiently aware of the spiritual opportunities in marriage.

It was strange to think that one day, when the poem had been reviewed in the *Advocate*, the young woman and her husband might buy a copy and read it and say to each other, 'If only someone had pointed out these things to us years ago when we used to slump in our seats every Sunday in Our Lady of Good Counsel's and wonder why our marriage seemed to have gone stale,' and never suspect that the author they admired could have leaned forward one Sunday and whispered his message in their ears if he had been sure they were ready for it.

Coventry Patmore had been married three times. Adrian realised that before he could execute the finer details of a poem on the divine qualities of love he would need to have a Catholic girlfriend.

He remembered O'Mullane's talk about the YCW dances and picnics. The YCW branch in Our Lady of Good Counsel's parish met every Wednesday night in the basement of the school building. On the following Wednesday, as soon as he had eaten his tea, Adrian told his parents he was walking to the school to join the YCW.

It was the first time Adrian had been out of the house (apart from his work and his Sunday mass) since coming back from Blenheim. His mother said she was so pleased he was going to mix with young people his own age instead of studying every night of the week. He realised he still hadn't told his parents he had given up his studies in favour of poetry, but he wasn't going to tell them about it just then.

It was midwinter. Darkness had come hours before. Adrian picked his way through the unmade streets towards the school. He knew he would meet no girls at a YCW meeting but he expected to hear the boys talking about some dance in the district where there were plenty of Catholic girls. (He had never learned to dance, but his mother might teach him some steps if he gave up his poetry for a few nights.) Or he might learn about some picnic arranged jointly by the YCW and the NCGM.

About a dozen young fellows were sitting round a ping-pong table in the school basement. There was no heating, and most of them had kept their overcoats on. Adrian felt the chill reaching through his shoes from the concrete floor. The president came over and asked Adrian his name and where he worked. The president said his own name was Barry Goonan and he worked as a moulder at Plasdip Products.

Goonan turned to the other fellows and said, 'A new member tonight, men. Adrian Sherd. He's a clerk in the public service. Let's make him welcome.' Three or four fellows moved along their bench, and Adrian sat down. Then the meeting began.

It was very brief. The only business they had to discuss was whether they should ask the parish priest again to install a heater in their meeting room. But Goonan ended the discussion by reminding them that the parish was deeply in debt and the priest had promised to buy them a heater as soon as he could afford it.

Adrian sat quietly and watched them. He guessed from the rough way they spoke that none of them had got far at secondary school. It would be easy for him to win the affection of a girl from the NCGM if these moulders and grinders and apprentice toolmakers were his only rivals.

As soon as the meeting was over the YCW boys stripped

off their overcoats and clothes. Underneath they were all wearing black shorts and gold singlets with OUR LADY'S in dark-green lettering across their chests. They got sand-shoes and gym boots out of their Gladstone bags and pulled them on. Someone opened a locker and three basketballs tumbled out. The fellows fought over the balls and ran outside yelping and grunting and calling to each other, 'Macca, Macca!' 'Titch, Titch!'

The president saw Adrian still in his street clothes and said, 'Here. Grab some spares, mate.' Adrian went to a locker and picked out a singlet and shorts and a pair of sandshoes. The singlet had the last two of the dark-green letters missing but he wore it anyway. When he was changed he walked outside.

The school basketball court had a floodlight at each end. The night was freezing cold and the fellows' breath rose in clouds against the lights. They were all dodging and passing and shooting for goal. Adrian jogged on the spot and rubbed his bare arms. A ball flew at him. It bounced off the court with a cruel metallic sound and hit him in the stomach like a huge ball bearing. The fellows called out, 'Mate! Mate!' or 'Sport! Sport!' Most of them had forgotten his name. But one voice said, 'Shirt! Shirt!' and Adrian passed the ball in that direction, although he couldn't see the fellow because his eyes had filled with water from the cold and the blow of the ball against his stomach.

They stayed on the court for more than an hour. Adrian chased them and called out to them and took some of their passes and tried to learn the tactics of the game. When they were all dressing afterwards, the president read out the teams for their match against St Kevin's, Luton, on the following night. Adrian was an emergency in the Seconds. The president said, 'We all meet at Accrington station tomorrow night at seven. Anyone can't make it?' No one spoke.

Adrian walked home thinking he could spare one more night from his poetry. He expected some of the NCGM girls to turn up as supporters at Luton. He would look them over and make a preliminary selection of three or four.

He sat with the YCW basketballers on the train to Luton. One of the older fellows had his fiancée with him. She sat knitting in a corner. Adrian wondered where the other female supporters were. He tried to join in the conversation. The YCW fellows talked and joked continually. Adrian understood each word they said, but when they gasped or chuckled or threw their heads back he realised they saw some deeper meaning that was hidden from him. He wondered if they were using some elaborate code, but they looked too honest and simple to invent such a thing. In the end, he sat back with a grin fixed on his face so that whenever they laughed and looked round at each other he would seem to be in on their joke. And he thought he would probably not include in his poem any dialogue between rough uneducated people for fear of getting it wrong.

At the Luton basketball court a group of girls sat on a bench under the scoreboard, but they were all supporters of the home side. The Second teams played their game first. Adrian sat beside the court with his sweater over his gold singlet. (His mother had stitched a Y and an S into place for him. They were the wrong shade of green but he thought no one would notice in the glare of the lights.) Close beside him, the Luton girls clapped and cheered whenever their team scored. Adrian was sure Patmore would have approved. The young people of Luton seemed instinctively aware of his doctrine. They relied on the power of love between the sexes to bring out the best in their players.

After ten minutes of play, Luton held a narrow lead. The Accrington captain asked for 'Time Out', and called Adrian and the other reserve onto the court.

Adrian was tense and excited. He was sure Luton must win with their girls watching them, but he was glad to be out on the court where the forces of love were at work. When the game resumed he was still trying to think of some line of poetry or some beautiful image that would do for him what the cries of the girls did for the Luton players.

He had discovered on the previous night that he was not entirely useless at basketball. He could not bear to compete for the ball in a pack, but he was quick enough sometimes to lead into an open space and take a pass on his own. On the Luton court he kept a few yards away from the packs and waited for the ball to dribble his way or for a teammate in trouble to knock the ball out to him.

He was alone near the goal with the ball rolling towards him. He grabbed it and took aim. A big Luton fellow knocked him off balance and he found himself in a pack of players with the ball gone from his hands. But the whistle blew and someone handed the ball to him. He was allowed two free shots at goal.

The first shot missed. He aimed a second time. And then, while his eyes were on the goal and the players of both teams stood poised around him (and the girls on the bench, no doubt, watched every move he made), he thought of the words to inspire him. As the ball left his hands he uttered them, discreetly disguised as grunts and gasps: 'The Unknown Eros!'

The ball hung on the edge of the basket. It started to roll around the rim. It travelled almost the whole distance around. Then it fell in. Someone clapped briefly. One of Adrian's teammates slapped him on the shoulder. Adrian trotted away from the goal hissing to himself, 'The Unknown Eros!'

It became his private war cry. He scored no more goals, but his teammates seemed to pass to him a little more. Each time he took the ball and sent it nearer Our Lady's goal he muttered again, 'The Unknown Eros!' When his captain asked for 'Time Out' and sent Adrian off the court he whispered his slogan as he walked past the girls on their bench. He didn't want them to hear the actual words (they would have been needlessly puzzled), but he wanted them to see that the thoughtful-looking fellow from Accrington, who flashed into the play whenever his team needed him, had some private source of inspiration. The more perceptive girls might even secretly prefer him to their supposed heroes from St Kevin's Luton, who enjoyed the luxury of having actual girls to smile on them.

For six weeks Adrian went to the YCW meeting and basketball training on Tuesday night and played in the Seconds on Wednesday night. On other nights he added to his notes for his poem on the sublimity of married love. During those weeks the only girls who turned up to watch Our Lady's team were the fiancée with the knitting and two girlfriends of fellows in the Firsts. As soon as Adrian saw these girls holding the fellows' hands and looking into their eyes he realised they were going steady. After that he was careful not to look directly at them in case they or their boyfriends thought he was interested in them.

In every match he followed the packs or dropped back into empty areas of the court. At least once each night he found himself alone with the ball close to the goal. At the instant he threw for goal he whispered his battle cry. Sometimes as he jogged away after the ball had rolled in, he chanted softly, 'Pat-more, Pat-more,' which was easy to fit to the rhythm of his feet.

At work in the Education Department he spent his spare time studying the lists of teachers who were newly out of teachers' colleges. He was working on a scheme for the third term when another batch of temporaries would have to be moved around the state. Now that he believed the most ennobling experience in life was married love (rather than the contemplation of English landscapes or of immense plains) he was going to arrange his temporaries so that single women with attractive names would arrive at schools where young men with heroic names were waiting for them.

At East Bendigo was a young teacher named Roland V. Marston-Cobb. As soon as a vacancy occurred for a temporary at East Bendigo or any nearby school, Adrian would send one of a pool of young women temporaries he had listed from schools around Melbourne. They were Priscilla J. Silk, Trudy H. Ravenswood, Virginia D. A. Honeychurch and Naomi Rosenbloom.

Adrian had other groups of women with appealing names ready for Marcus V. Treadwell at Yarram, Ralph Drum at Mooroopna and several others. If his schemes worked, exceptional young men and women in all parts of Victoria would have the opportunity to experience the truth of Patmore's doctrine.

Our Lady's First and Second teams reached the semi-finals of the YCW competition. On the Sunday before the semi-final, among the notices read out at each mass was a request for supporters to turn up and cheer Our Lady's boys.

While Adrian was in the dressing room before the big match he heard a sound that started his heart racing. It was the babble of young women beside the basketball court. The NCGM had come at last.

Adrian watched them while he warmed up for his match. There were four of them. One was ruled out because she was lightly touching hands with a fellow in Our Lady's Firsts. Of the other three, one hung back a little and only smiled when the others laughed loudly at a joke that some fellow had made. She was pretty, but not in the conventional way that would attract loutish boyfriends. The basketballers spoke familiarly with the other girls but kept their distance from her. She looked reserved and thoughtful—she knew there were more important things in life than flirting with YCW boys. Adrian saw the smile of wonderment on her face as he explained to her one day the teachings of Coventry Patmore. He saw the two of them on rainy Saturday mornings searching the shelves of Melbourne's second-hand bookshops for the copy of *The Unknown Eros* that he would buy her as an engagement present.

The basketball game had started, and Adrian's most urgent task was to attract her attention. He abandoned his usual style of play and rushed into packs. He leaped for the ball against fellows six inches taller. He saw she was following the game closely, but she seemed unaware of him as an individual.

He decided there was only one sure way to make her notice him. It might bring about his team's defeat, but it was absurd to weigh the outcome of a parish basketball game against the vindication of a major religious poet. When the ball came near him he pretended to trip. He stood up and hobbled towards the edge of the court. His captain saw him and called for 'Time Out'.

Adrian limped off the court and saw her look his way at last. He felt the same elation that he had once got from standing near Denise McNamara on the Coroke train. But whereas in those days there was only his boyish ardour to prompt him, now he was following in the footsteps of an eminent poet-philosopher, thrice married.

The following Sunday at mass, Adrian heard about a bus trip organised by the YCW and the NCGM to the snow at Mount Donna Buang. Adrian bought a ticket and thought how appropriate it was that he would first speak to his future wife in a snowy landscape such as Patmore must have admired while he courted one or other of his wives.

On the Sunday of the picnic, the bus pulled up at the church gate and Adrian was one of the first aboard. He took a seat at the very back because he wanted to watch his girl all the way and observe how the changing scenery affected her.

As the young fellows and girls filed into the bus Adrian realised they were dividing themselves into distinct groups. At the rear were the fellows who had no girlfriends and, from the look of them, no hope of winning any. On either side of the aisle, in the seats for two, were the steady couples—the girl usually in the window seat as if her boyfriend wanted her safe from marauders. In the longer, less-private seats at the front was an indeterminate group of young fellows and girls. None of them belonged to one another as the steadies did in their cosy seats. But behind their jokes and loud laughter and exaggerated gestures, the YCW fellows were all anxious to win a girl before the picnic was over. Adrian's girl, the one he had marked out at the basketball, was sitting quietly in a front seat.

On the way to Mount Donna Buang Adrian came two stages nearer his goal. He asked the fellow next to him the names of several girls in the bus and learned that his chosen one was named Clare Keating. And a little later, at the front of the bus, Clare herself pulled a face at a fellow who was paying attention to her, and looked as if she meant it.

The bus stopped at a picnic ground halfway up the mountain. During lunch the young people mostly kept to the three divisions they had formed in the bus. After lunch, on the steep path up to the summit, the groups were mixed together as some people stopped to rest or scoop up handfuls of snow and others scrambled past them.

Adrian adjusted his pace up the mountain until he was close behind Clare Keating. He wondered how he could let her know he was near her. Two or three times he said something funny, but no one turned round. He supposed his voice was not carrying as far as usual in the thin mountain air.

One of the fellows from the back of the bus picked up a branch with wet feathery foliage. Before Adrian could stop him, the fellow touched the dripping leaves first against the neck of the girl beside Clare and then lightly against a pink ear of Clare herself. The girls squealed, although not as angrily as Adrian had expected. Adrian was ashamed to be seen near the fellow. When the girls turned around he stood frowning into the distance so Clare would realise he disapproved of the childish prank.

A little later, when Clare and her friends slowed down and said they were puffed out, two fellows from near Adrian got behind the girls and tried to push them up the path. The fellow behind Clare put his hands on her ribs in such a way that the tips of his outstretched fingers reached towards the forbidden area of her breasts. It was the sort of familiarity that Adrian would not have dared until after the engagement (or certainly not before a mutual declaration of affection). If Clare had called for help he would have fallen on the fellow and torn his fingers away (although without himself touching her body). But she only laughed and leaned her weight backwards until the fellow gave up trying to push her.

Near the top of the mountain they came out of the haze or cloud that had surrounded them and into bright sunshine. Adrian hurried past the girls. He had never climbed a mountain before, and he wanted Clare to notice how deeply he was affected by a wild landscape.

The summit was grassy and treeless with hard-packed snow lying in its hollows. Adrian stood alone looking towards the east. From Donna Buang to the horizon it was all mountains—hazy ridges rising one after the other out of shadowy dark-blue valleys. The scene affected him as profoundly as *Near Parracombe, Devon*, the wildest landscape in *The English Countryside in Colour*. He saw he had been too hasty in abandoning Australia for England and the steppes of Buryat Mongolia. He wondered how many Australian poets before him had discovered landscapes like the one he looked on, and had made their spiritual home in them. The next time he was in Cheshire's he would spend a half-hour at the shelves marked AUSTRALIAN LITERATURE.

There was a blow on the back of his neck and the feel of icy water trickling down his skin. People were laughing and shouting not far behind him. He reached his hand to his neck and touched a dripping mass of snow.

He turned around. All the young people from the bus were pelting each other with handfuls of hard snow. Someone must have aimed one at him while he was staring at his landscape. Clare Keating and three young fellows were looking at him meaningfully. No doubt one of them had hit him. It was their way of inviting him to join their fun instead of moping over distant mountains. Perhaps even Clare herself had thrown the snow. On the way up the mountain she had noticed his interest in her, and now she was making it easier for him to speak to her without a formal introduction. He picked up some snow and tossed it aimlessly into the air. If he had thrown it at Clare or her group they might have thought he couldn't take a joke.

On the way back to the bus Adrian said a few words to one of the fellows hanging around Clare. The fellow answered him politely and Adrian considered himself one of the group from the front of the bus.

He waited outside the bus while the fellows from the back seat and the couples from the private seats found their places. If he had rushed in and grabbed a seat at the front he might have alarmed Clare by his forwardness. Instead, he was going to stroll in and sit down nonchalantly at the front and seize the first opportunity to join the conversation of her group.

As he climbed aboard, it occurred to him that all the front seats might be taken, and he had a moment of panic. In fact, there were two or three empty spaces. He sat down and looked out of the window. When the bus started to move he looked around for Clare Keating. He turned his head slowly to conceal his eagerness.

He discovered that the people at the front were not all the same ones who had sat there during the morning. There seemed to be fewer girls. There were even a few of the fellows who had begun the day in the back seat. And Clare Keating was missing.

For the next mile or so, Adrian looked briefly in turn at each of the seats where the steady couples sat. He kept fairly calm. She was probably with a girl friend in one of the dual seats—she had noticed Adrian preparing to court her and had decided to resist him a little while longer. She was probably tired after climbing the mountain or more reserved than he had suspected.

It was almost dark before Adrian found her. She was next to the window in one of the steadies' seats. Beside her was the same fellow who had thought it clever to tickle girls' faces with wet branches.

The driver turned on the radio. The sound of *Hit Parade* music carried all through the bus. Some of the YCW boys and NCGM girls joined in the words of the best-known songs. Adrian realised he hadn't heard a *Hit Parade* for some time—he had been too busy with his poetry on Sunday afternoons. As soon as he reached home he would throw himself once more into his poetry to stifle his grief at losing Clare Keating to an unworthy rival. But in the bus he had only the hit tunes to distract him.

The disc jockey announced a song that was sweeping America. Adrian sat back and let it sweep across him too. Its words were commonplace—an invitation to young people to involve themselves in a whirl of gaiety and pleasure. But the melody appealed to Adrian. A sensitive listener could discern something forlorn behind the insistent phrases—as if the composer recognised that for every young couple dancing together there was, inevitably, a young fellow with no other solace than the sight of distant landscapes. The tune was even more poignant because Adrian thought he would probably never hear it again. Even if he listened sometimes to a *Hit Parade* after he had gone back to his poetry, the song would have been forgotten long since, like so many others that had swept America.

He risked one last look at Clare. She and the oaf beside her were singing the words of the song. But for them there was no hint of sadness in its plaintive notes. They leaned their shoulders easily together and even looked occasionally into each other's eyes as they gave out the words of 'Rock Around the Clock'.

After the picnic at Mount Donna Buang, Adrian could not go on with his poem about married love. He put his notes carefully away—they could wait until he had found a steady girlfriend. Some of the couples in the bus on the way home from Donna Buang had rested their heads together and dozed off with looks of perfect contentment. When he reached that degree of intimacy with a young woman he would finish his poem about the mystical joys of love.

He intended to be more careful in his choice of girls in future. The best place to meet a girl with similar interests to

430

his was surely Cheshire's Bookshop in Little Collins Street, in the heart of Melbourne, and the best place in Cheshire's was the seldom-used space between POETRY and DRAMA. Adrian remembered occasions when he had been bending over a poetry book and some young woman had passed him so closely that her skirt had almost brushed against him. When this next happened he would start a conversation, but first he needed to acquire an expert knowledge of poetry. Then he could answer any enquiry a girl might make about a poet or his works.

Every afternoon after work, Adrian hurried to the POETRY section of Cheshire's. In the fifteen minutes that remained before closing time he studied the spines of the books on a given section of the shelves. His aim was to know the whereabouts of every poet represented in Cheshire's. When he had achieved this aim, he would station himself near the POETRY sign each afternoon, and each Saturday morning, until a suitable young female person came along. He would wait until she was trapped in the cul de sac of POETRY and DRAMA and would then walk up quietly behind her and ask was she looking for any poet in particular. He would have to act swiftly. His boldness might frighten her away before he could put an appropriate book into her hands. His aim was to have a suitable book in her hands within thirty seconds, after which she could hardly refuse to speak to him.

He trained himself for three weeks. Then he took up his position and waited. He was not so foolish as to make himself conspicuous by simply standing. He tested his newly acquired skills. In his coat pocket he had dozens of slips of paper, each marked with the name of a poet. While he waited, he would pull out a slip and hurry to find the works of the poet named.

On the first two afternoons no suitable person turned up. The only person he was able to help was a young salesman who was surprisingly ignorant about his own stock-in-trade. On the third afternoon Adrian set himself to learn an additional skill. Instead of merely handing a book to a young female, he would make a comment on the poet whose work it was. Even the most reticent young woman would feel obliged to say something in these circumstances, especially if the comments he made went against conventional opinions of the poet concerned.

Adrian was surprised at how few poets he could comment on readily. He began to improve his knowledge by reading dust jackets and introductions in the less-familiar titles. One of the first books that he looked into had on its cover a sketch of a young man brooding over an English landscape. The book was the *Collected Poems of A. E. Housman.* Adrian read two or three poems. Then he took the book to the front counter and bought it. Inside its sombre green cover he had found poems describing his own state of mind so accurately that he might have written them himself.

That evening, Adrian read every poem in the green-covered book and then began a new section in his notes under the heading 'Thoughts on First Reading a Poet of Genius'. The new section began thus.

> Surely a special Providence guides A. S.: For some time now he has been preparing to make the acquaintance of a young woman of similar interests among the poetry

shelves of Cheshire's. If such a person had come his way, he would now be writing her a long, heartfelt letter or talking to her by telephone or even accompanying her on some social outing. Thanks to his Blessed Providence he is still unattached and free to spend all his evenings in the company of a true soulmate.

Before one can write great poetry, one must have experienced powerful emotions. Of all the emotions, grief and a sense of loss are the most powerful. And grief and loss are what A. S. has experienced since a certain day on Mount Donna Buang. All that remains is for him to express these emotions in metre and rhyme.

Farewell to the shallow emotions of Arnold and Thompson and Patmore! Henceforth A. S. will seek to experience, and to express in his poetry, the profound sadness of Housman.

Now Adrian went from work each afternoon not to Cheshire's but to the State Library. He wanted to learn what calamitous loss Housman had suffered: what were the events from which had sprung his exquisite poems. After a long search, Adrian found a book about Housman by a man who had published an early edition of *A Shropshire Lad*. The book was a revelation. Housman was not a young farmer from near Ludlow whose heart had been broken by some Shropshire Clare Keating. He was a professor of Latin at Cambridge, a stern bachelor and almost a recluse. Unfortunately he had died nearly two years before Adrian's birth.

After learning these facts, Adrian wondered whether he was equal to the challenge that Housman's life presented.

The great poet seemed to have lived only for his studies and his poetry. He was a worthy but a daunting model. Adrian spent most evenings now in the State Library. His parents seemed to be hoping that he was preparing to enrol as a part-time student at university, but he was busy compiling a list of Housman's mannerisms and eccentricities. Afterwards, at home, he filed his list among the pages of one of his poetry notebooks. He meditated often on Housman's way of life in an effort to understand the source of his poetry, which was just the sort of poetry that he, Adrian, had been trying for years to write.

Housman had revealed little about his early life, but it was clear to Adrian that the poet, in his youth, had loved a young woman who had not returned his affection. The poet had then resolved, so Adrian believed, to prolong his melancholy indefinitely for the sake of the poetic inspiration that it gave rise to. He turned away forever from the petty consolations of marriage and family and even disdained to seek for friends, although he sometimes mixed with solitary males like himself at university dinners.

After he had absorbed all the known details of Housman's way of life, Adrian drew up a list of resolutions for turning himself into an aloof, unapproachable bachelor who wrote poems charged with emotion in his solitary room. One of these resolutions was to travel to England as soon as he had saved his fare. He would visit Shropshire and make pilgrimages to all the places named in Housman's poems. He would take lodgings in Cambridge as near as possible to the university where Housman had spent his later life. He would search libraries and bookshops for printed references to Housman and would call on people who had known the great poet during his lifetime.

At last, when he had learned even the least details of Housman's life, he, Adrian Sherd, the promising young lyric poet, would dedicate himself to following that life exactly. There would be adjustments and compromises, of course. Housman had worn, till the end of his life, Edwardian-style clothing. Adrian was not going to make himself an object of ridicule by strolling around Cambridge in the fashions of his grandparents' time. Housman had dressed as he had because he remained attached to the fashions of his youth. Adrian would follow the spirit of Housman's way of life by wearing always what a young man of the south-eastern suburbs of Melbourne had worn during the 1950s. He would take with him overseas a stock of Stamina brand sports trousers and some sports jackets sold by Hattams menswear stores.

Living in austere lodgings, taking solitary strolls in the semi-rural surroundings of Cambridge and rebuffing anyone, male or female, who intruded on his privacy, Adrian could preserve for years in their original intensity the emotions of his youth—not just the pain inflicted on him by Clare Keating but his regret for all his lost land-scapes in America, near Hepburn Springs, around the Cistercian monastery at Yarra Glen and on the steppes of Buryat Mongolia.

Before Adrian had finished his plans and resolutions, it occurred to him that he would be following Housman more faithfully by staying away from England. Housman had left the West Country as a young man. For the rest of his life he lived in London or Cambridge, far from the green landscapes that inspired his best poems. In fact, one of the themes of his poetry was the contrast between his hard and lonely life in the city and the rural satisfactions that he had left behind. Adrian was moving to England in order to achieve fulfilment and his own peculiar sort of happiness. Instead, he should have been planning to move to a place where he would have to endure solitude and the pain of being separated from the places where he might have found some vestige of consolation. When his annual salary had increased sufficiently to permit it, he would move to a respectable boarding house in one of the older suburbs of Melbourne. In the meanwhile he would model himself on Housman as far as was possible.

Adrian quietly dropped out of the YCW. One of his basketball teammates met him on Accrington station one morning and asked why Adrian had gone missing. Adrian said he had to study every evening, and his teammate said no more. Adrian was not only unwilling to mix any further with the young men of the YCW—as long as he stayed in their organisation there was the danger that he might meet a girl from the NCGM and fall in love with her. There was no evidence that Adrian was aware of for Housman's having belonged to any sort of organisation, even in his youth. He had dined occasionally with groups of his colleagues in later life, but no women had been present.

Every morning on the train to the city, Adrian found at least one typist or female shop assistant in his crowded compartment. He hoped his drab clothes told these young women that he scorned the trivialities of their generation and was not in the least interested in impressing the opposite sex. On his train journeys, Adrian read either a volume of Housman's poetry (he had bought several by now—both new and second-hand) or a novel by Thomas Hardy. (Adrian had learned that Housman once commented favourably on Hardy.) He tried to keep a faintly troubled expression on his face. If a young woman looked at him, as sometimes happened, he trusted that she wondered about him. When he felt her eyes on him, his first impulse was to exchange glances with her as though he was just another young public servant anxious to find a girlfriend. He almost always checked himself in time. Sometimes he had to recite under his breath some powerful couplet from *A Shropshire Lad* to keep himself from looking up. If the temptation was strong he often saved himself by repeating in his mind 'Housman, strengthen me!' or 'Great poet, preserve me!'

Adrian would go on reading until the young woman seemed to have understood that he had dedicated himself to something higher than romantic love and went back to her knitting or stared out of the window. He did not despise her. He wished her well in her small world of dances and films and picnics to the hills. He even hoped she had a steady boyfriend whose attentions gratified her. Sometimes he recited mentally some lines by Housman in which the poet expressed envy for those who could take love lightly and not see the terrible sadness of it all.

When the train reached Flinders Street, Adrian would try to catch the young woman's eye with a last look full of meaning. It was meant to tell her he was not unappreciative of her interest in him, but he was not free to respond to her as an ordinary young man would have been. She could not be expected to know that she was dealing with a poet, and not even an ordinary sort of poet but one who had to guard and foster his unhappiness and his sense of grief and deprivation. But at least she must have suspected that he was prevented from responding to her by some grave responsibility.

At lunchtimes he began to walk in the Treasury Gardens again. He was no longer afraid of meeting O'Mullane again. He had read how Housman had once rebuffed an American man who admired his poetry. The American had waylaid Housman on his regular afternoon walk through Cambridge. Housman fixed him with a stern gaze and dismissed him with a few monosyllables. If O'Mullane were to approach him, babbling about dances and NCGM girls, Adrian would use Housman's technique to get rid of him.

The season was early spring. The English trees in the Treasury Gardens were putting out leaves. It was the season in which Housman had composed some of his best poetry. After months of work on his Latin texts he would notice a tree in flower or a pair of young lovers strolling under a blue sky. His usual low-grade misery would intensify. Once more he would feel keenly his separation from the joys of common people. He would open his poetic notebooks again and would jot down the beginnings of some exquisite lament.

On his lunchtime walks, Adrian deliberately looked for couples strolling hand in hand or sitting on secluded benches or, in fine weather, lounging on the grass with heads close together. Whenever he saw such a couple he turned aside and walked towards them. He always coughed or scraped his feet to warn them. He was not interested in spying on them. As he passed, he glanced just once at their faces and then strode on with the measured gait of a man who knew that life was to be endured rather than enjoyed, and he waited for some memory of Denise or Clare to trouble him and to bring to his mind the first lines of a poem.

Not many public servants used their lunchtimes for courting, so Adrian discovered in time. After a week of striding past lovers, Adrian understood that he was looking at the same two couples every day. The young men had begun to look at him suspiciously.

On Sunday afternoons Adrian took long strolls around Accrington. He wore the jacket and tie that he had worn to mass that morning. His mother tried to tell him that young people nowadays preferred casual clothes at weekends and that he looked odd in a tie, but he could not even begin to imagine Housman in a shirt open at the collar. He walked beside main roads, where the traffic was heaviest. He stared resolutely ahead of him and stopped only to look at some shrub or tree that might have been found in an English garden.

He was sometimes aware of people looking at him through car windows. Driving on Sundays seemed increasingly popular. (Several families in Riviera Grove were now car owners, and the street had recently been turned from a sandy track into a bitumen thoroughfare.) The older persons who looked out at him he assumed to be married couples; the younger couples he assumed were going steady. They were of no interest to him as individuals, but flitting past him continually they provided a backdrop of romantic and domestic contentment for the springtime walks of a solitary poet.

The third school term had begun. The clerks in the Teachers' Branch were moving their temporaries again. Adrian discarded his earlier plans for bringing young teachers together with a view to marriage. His new scheme was much easier to arrange. He was no longer interested in the young women. They would have to form their romantic attachments with no help from him. He was going to give some of the young men a taste of the solitude and hardship that Housman had endured.

Some young male temporaries had spent all of their time since graduation in suburban schools. They would have been able to telephone their girlfriends every evening and take them to the pictures on Saturdays and drive them to the hills on Sundays. It would do them good to have to spend their weekends brooding alone in some remote landscape. At best, one or two might discover, as Housman and Sherd had discovered, the peculiar satisfaction of forgoing the beguilements of romance; they might even decide on a life of bachelorhood. In any case, their months of isolation would strengthen their characters.

Adrian sent a few complacent young men to one-teacher schools with names that seemed the Australian equivalents of the remote places mentioned in *A Shropshire Lad*: Peppers Plain, Big Hill, Clear Lake, The Cove, Mosquito Flat. On fine spring days when he crossed the crowded lawns of the Treasury Gardens, he envied the young temporaries in their distant schools, surrounded by the raw material for whole volumes of poignant lyric poetry.

One Friday in late September, the first north wind of the spring blew over Melbourne. Adrian's office was so warm after lunch that the public servants worked in their shirtsleeves. Adrian paused in the middle of moving a young temporary man from Kensington to Icy Creek. He watched the passage of the warm wind through the treetops outside and felt a strange urge. It was almost certainly the same urge that had made Housman look up from his Latin texts each year and wonder how the spring was progressing in his lost Shropshire. Adrian would have liked to observe the signs of spring at Icy Creek or Peppers Plain.

Housman, after a moment of musing, would have gone on resolutely with the task in front of him, but Adrian was not yet as strong-willed as his master. On his way through the city after work he bought a map titled 'Fifty Miles Around Melbourne'. Before tea that night he oiled his old bike and pumped up the tyres. He studied the map. Fifteen miles past the last of the south-eastern suburbs was an isolated township or hamlet where he could sit undisturbed with his poetry notebook on his knees and a pencil in hand. The place was called Stepney.

Next morning Adrian packed his lunch in a haversack. He wondered what Housman would have eaten and drunk on a trip through the countryside. He knew from his reading that the poet had been something of a gourmet. He used to meet his publisher at a place called the Café Royal and would always read carefully through menus and wine lists. On his holidays in France he liked to eat a dish called bouillabaisse. Adrian had cut the crusts from both ends of a high-tin loaf and had folded them in a lunch wrap with half a packet of Kraft Cheddar Cheese. At the first milk bar that he passed on his trip, he bought a bottle of sarsaparilla because it was the colour of wine.

He reached Stepney at about noon. He had hoped for a quiet village with a few shady seats or even a small park. He found only a school and a shabby hall and a store with a petrol bowser at the front. The countryside around was flat

441

and mostly treeless and given over to vegetable-growing. Adrian turned into a side road and made for a few cypress trees. When he reached the trees, he found they were ranged around the driveway to a distant farmhouse.

Adrian got off his bike. A cool wind was blowing across the bare paddocks. He needed a sheltered spot to eat his lunch and jot down some notes for a poem. The most suitable place was among the cypresses, but they were on someone's farm.

Adrian felt cheated and out of place in the Australian countryside. In Shropshire he would have had acres of common land to roam across, or he could have had access to farm after farm according to some ancient charter of rights. He sat against a fencepost, as near as he could get to the shelter of the tree. He finished his bread and cheese and opened his sarsaparilla. The drink spurted all over his hands and legs. He supposed he had shaken it while it rested against his back on the long ride to Stepney. He wiped himself with his handkerchief, but his skin remained sticky and uncomfortable.

He could not bring himself to take his pencil and notebook out of his haversack. He was in no mood for poetry. He leaned back against the fencepost and closed his eyes. The sound of the wind among the trees gave him an idea. The wind in Australia could hardly have sounded very differently from the wind in Shropshire. If he kept his eyes closed and recited vivid lines from Housman, he could convince himself that the wind passing his ears had come towards him from beyond the Welsh Marches. Better still, the feel of the grass at Stepney was surely not all that different from the feel of English grasses. He could touch the grass around him while his eyes were closed and persuade himself that he was in sight of Wenlock Edge.

Adrian got up and measured with his eyes a walk of twenty yards through the grass between the fence and the road. He closed his eyes and held his hand well away from his sides—partly so as to feel the tall grass but also to warn him if he strayed too near the barbed-wire fence. He waited until he heard a particularly strong gust of wind straining the cypress branches and then he stepped forward.

He had never seen an English landscape so clearly or felt so close to the countryside that was now his spiritual home. He was within sight of Bredon Hill when he lost his footing and fell. Even then, he still kept his eyes closed. The feel of the earth close to his face made the whole experience more lifelike. He got to his feet and stepped forward again. Now, however, he was unsure of his bearings. He veered deliberately to left and right, feeling with his hands for the fence and with his feet for the gravel at the edge of the roadside.

Adrian heard the noise of a car far away in the Australian countryside. He opened his eyes. He was pleased to see that he was still heading in the right direction despite his fall and his subsequent zigzags. He looked for the car. It was not in sight on the road. He listened carefully. The car was coming down the driveway of the farm behind him. The driver might even have seen Adrian performing his Shropshire-in-Australia exercise. That was all he had been doing—trying to transport himself in mind—but the driver of the car may have misinterpreted the matter.

Adrian walked back to his bike. The car was almost at the gate. Adrian refused to look in that direction. By rights, he should have been in an overgrown lane so narrow and leafy that no car could have approached him. The car stopped at the gate. Adrian stood beside his bike and began to strap his haversack onto his back.

'You got any sort of firearm on you, son?'

The man sounded nasty. It was probably better to answer him, Adrian thought, but there was no reason to give him the satisfaction of looking at him.

'No! Of course not!' Adrian thought his voice sounded timid and childish.

Adrian became suddenly aware of a strange incongruity. In himself, he felt like a middle-aged, formally dressed classical scholar, but in the eyes of the angry farmer he was a mere boy in shorts and shirt and sandshoes.

The man came nearer. 'You're still going to tell me what you're doing here near my property. I saw you doing something funny in the grass just now.'

The only way to be free of this fool was to tell him the truth. Adrian looked briefly at the man and then stared into the distance across the uncongenial Australian landscape. 'If you must know, I was composing poetry.'

Would the man believe him? Adrian could have shown him the pencil and the notebook in his haversack except that nothing was written on any of the pages. He dragged his bike to the road and mounted it. The man was still silent.

Adrian was pedalling away before the man called out, 'Poetry...'

It might have been a question or an exclamation or even a cry of derision. Adrian rode on. The man called out again, 'Poetry...' By now the wind had blown away any malice or contempt that might have been intended. The word sounded almost like a cry for help. Someone was lost among the paddocks and cypresses of Australia and and was calling on poetry to save him.

Adrian was fifty yards away from the man. Once more he shouted, 'Poetry...' This time, the word was hardly distinguishable. The man might have been calling Adrian by name. He was poetry personified, and from far away a frail human voice was trying vainly to call him back to the world of commonplace men.

Adrian had a hard ride home from Stepney. The wind that had been behind him in the morning was blowing into his face. His stomach ached. He wished he had packed a more substantial lunch instead of what he had thought was a snack suitable for a poet. Every few miles, he had to rest beside the road. He took no notice of the farmland around him. He saw how wise Housman had been to compose his nature poetry in London or Cambridge. When Adrian reached home he let the air out of his tyres and hung his bike in the shed. He would never visit the Australian countryside again.

He ate his tea with the Literary Supplement of the *Age* spread out beside him. (The *Argus* had ceased publication a few months before. Adrian supposed the Catholic men of Melbourne had succeeded in their campaign. But he was indifferent now to the passing of the *Argus*, which had never given much space to literature.) On the last page of the Supplement was a headline: 'A. E. Housman— New Light on a Secretive Poet'. Underneath were long columns of print—more than Adrian had ever read about his exemplar. A scholarly American had written the first complete biography of the poet. The author could never have dreamed that news of the book would reach a certain young Australian poet on the very day when he was most in need of something to confirm the standing of poetry and to sustain him in his dedication to it.

Adrian read the review several times. Most of the facts in it he already knew from his reading in the State Library, but the new biography offered an intriguing explanation for the poet's lifelong reticence and secretiveness. What was this explanation? The review did not disclose it.

On the following Monday, Adrian asked for the book in Cheshire's. No, it was not yet available, but it could be ordered from the local distributors if he wished. Adrian ordered two copies in case one of them was defective in some small way or was damaged while being sent from England. He called at the bookshop every week to ask whether the books had arrived. In the meanwhile he excused himself from trying to write poetry until he knew the truth about the poet he was modelling himself on.

One night, the salesman in Cheshire's came out from a back room with the two books in his hand. Adrian waited until he was alone in his room after tea before he even opened the parcel. One of the books was in mint condition. Adrian wrapped this copy in the brown paper supplied by Cheshire's and stored it safely in his wardrobe. The other book had a corner of its dust-jacket folded over. Adrian propped himself up in bed and opened the volume that would be his working copy.

At the front was a photograph of A. E. Housman at the age of fifty-two. It was the first picture that Adrian had seen of the great man. He was posed formally, with his chin resting on a hand. He seemed at first sight stern and forbidding, but Adrian could not believe he was unapproachable. If their lifetimes had coincided and if Adrian had written to Housman explaining how he, Adrian, venerated the poet's works and was trying to imitate his way of life, the proud severe face would surely have relaxed into a look of approval at their first meeting. The rigid mouth might even have twisted itself into a faint smile. Perhaps at their second or third meeting the carefully posed right hand might have been thrust forward in a gesture of unmistakable friendship.

Unfortunately, Housman had not looked directly at the camera. No matter how he positioned his own face, Adrian could not feel as though the eyes were directed at him. It was almost impossible to imagine the look of bluff affection from Housman that Adrian would dearly liked to have visualised.

At three o'clock next morning Adrian finished the book. He left the light on and sat thinking. Housman had proved to be a fraud. None of his poems would be of any more use to Adrian, who had wasted his money buying two copies of a book he would never read again. He would keep the books, but only to remind himself of how foolish he had been to make a hero of a poet without knowing the full story of his life.

According to the biography, the outline of Housman's life was as Adrian had supposed—a troubled but undocumented childhood in the west of England, years of solitude in London and later in Cambridge. Housman had no close friends and discouraged anyone who seemed likely to violate his privacy. However, his reason for living as he did was not as Adrian had imagined it.

The review in the *Age* had mentioned an intriguing explanation for Housman's eremitic way of life. Adrian had hoped for a love story set among the blossoming hawthorn hedgerows of Shropshire in early spring—Housman at twenty with his acutely sensitive heart broken and the girl he loved walking off among the masses of blossom with an uncouth farm lad. There was a love story, but not of the kind that Adrian had expected. As an undergraduate in the clammy corridors and shadowy quadrangles of Oxford University, Housman had fallen in love with a young man.

It made no difference to Adrian that the affair had come to nothing. (Housman had hesitated to declare himself; the other young man had affected not to notice anything unusual and had later married and gone to India.) Adrian felt badly deceived. Before he turned out the light, he looked for the last time at Housman's photograph. When he remembered that he had wanted, only a few hours before, to win an approving glance from those averted eyes and a grip of friendship from that plump, pale hand, Adrian shook his head.

Adrian had already found in the State Library a book titled *Twentieth Century Authors*. It was filled with brief biographies and tiny photographs of hundreds of novelists and poets and playwrights, most of them unknown to Adrian. Having finished with Housman, Adrian resolved to search through the collection of authors page by page until he found a man who had lived a solitary, misanthropic life while his powerful emotions drove him to write moving poems or novels.

Twentieth Century Authors was arranged in alphabetical order. Adrian found his first two candidates among the As. They were both Russian nihilists—Leonid Andreyev and Mikhail Artsybashev. Andreyev's forehead was deeply creased. In his short stories and articles he had proclaimed the worthlessness of all human effort. He had died in despair. He was not exactly the man Adrian was looking for, but he ruled over Adrian for two days until he reached Artsybashev. On each of those two days Adrian chose not to make his bed or brush his teeth because such activities went against the principles of nihilism. On the train and during his walks in the Treasury Gardens, he kept his eyebrows raised in order to deepen the faint lines on his forehead. And each morning, under his usual sports jacket, he wore a black tie from the old clothes box in the back shed.

Artsybashev seemed a more cheerful nihilist than Andreyev. He had worn brightly coloured silk blouses as a means of self-expression and he had preached total disregard for all moral restraints. His novel *Sanine*, named for its robust, amoral hero, had been banned in Russia but had been popular among a generation of European youth before the Great War.

As a Catholic, Adrian could not subscribe to Artsybashev's doctrines. In fact, Adrian had no wish to believe in them, let alone practise them. He was not even sure that Artsybashev himself had practised them. If the famous Russian had been a true nihilist, he would not have advocated free love and worn coloured blouses but would have sat alone at his desk consumed by poetic sadness while he thought of all the young people of Europe reading *Sanine* and afterwards enjoying themselves as they followed his doctrines. The only clue to Artsybashev's private life was the tiny photograph in *Twentieth Century Authors*. Mostly, when Adrian looked at the face behind the dark beard he saw an expression of gloom and believed that the Russian was one of his own kind. It was only occasionally that he saw the coarse features of a man who actually enjoyed the sensual pleasures that he proclaimed as the greatest good.

Adrian adopted Artsybashev as his provisional patron until he could find a more suitable entry under the letters B to Z in *Twentieth Century Authors*. He borrowed a sleeveless pullover with a Fair Isle pattern from his father and wore it under his sports jacket. He spent a week's wages on a second-hand signet ring with a square of black onyx set in nine-carat gold and wore it in the cause of self-expression.

In the State Library each evening he read about hundreds of writers from B to L but all were disqualified for one reason or another. They had married or had taken part in public life or they belonged to some cosy little group of writers who praised each other's works or issued manifestos.

A few had nearly qualified. A Norwegian novelist had lived all his life as a bachelor in the village of his birth. His novels were described as gloomy and pessimistic, which was very much in his favour, but Adrian rejected the man on the grounds that his work as a postmaster would have provided him with a rich social life and would have obliged him to exchange gossip with everyone in his village.

A certain Dutchman had written several gloomy, despairing novels. He had not married until he was past fifty years, which impressed Adrian. But the novelist was eventually rejected because he had spent much of his life in the East Indies. This cast doubt on his celibacy. Even

450

a pessimistic bachelor might have been tempted beyond his endurance in a tropical climate, surrounded by brown-skinned women in flimsy clothing.

Nearly three weeks after his search had begun, Adrian had reached the letter M. Walking up to the State Library after work, he had a premonition that he was close to discovering a man after his own heart. The evening was warm. The month was still only October, but the young women going home from their work in city offices wore summer dresses. Adrian saw himself in the summer months ahead, walking to the station after work with the sun still high in the west. The windows and doors would be left open on the trains. Dry heads of spear grass would fly in from beside the railway tracks. Near Caulfield the elm plantation would remind him of the summer afternoons when he would look up from behind his book at Denise McNamara. (Where was she now? The relentless flow of time must always be a major theme in his poetry!) His keenest pleasure would be experienced on hot Friday evenings when groups of young women, with the satiny skin of their bare arms in his full view, would chatter about their trips to the beach on the coming weekend. He would sit for mile after mile with his eyes on the book he was reading. Whenever a young woman mentioned her boyfriend or her new bathers or gave a faint squeal of joy, he would derive *his* pleasure from the thought of himself sitting all Saturday and Sunday in his shed with the blind pulled down against the sun and his notebooks in front of him.

On the lawn in front of the State Library three women students from the university sat together over their textbooks. Adrian paused a few paces from them. It was an

451

opportunity for him to experience already the sort of pleasure he had just now been looking forward to. He reminded himself that he could have enrolled at the university if he had not given up his studies for a literary career. The bare legs on the grass, the one naked foot with the sandal dangling from it—sights such as these might have confronted him every day on the university lawns, but his was the vocation of the poet who turned his feelings of deprivation into literature.

Adrian sat at his usual seat in the reading room and began at the letter M. Five minutes later, he read the half-page entry for the Flemish playwright Adhémar Martens, who wrote under several other names but mainly Michel de Ghelderode. Adrian read the entry twice through and then took out pencil and paper and made a complete copy. Then he closed the book. He might still read from N to Z, but he could not believe he would find in the rest of the book any male writer who better suited his needs.

Adrian read his pencilled notes on the train homewards. Martens had spent his life in his native Belgium. There was no mention of his having had a wife or children. At the age of thirty, he had retired to a few rooms of his family home, where he wrote numerous plays with mediaeval themes and surrounded himself with an odd assortment of artefacts that were all he cared to know of the outside world. In later years he had confined himself to one room and mostly communicated with outsiders by means of written messages.

Adrian read again and again the sentences reporting Martens' withdrawal from the world and wondered if he himself could dare to follow the brave Belgian. Adrian had no interest in plays or the theatre, much less anything mediaeval, but he did not doubt that Martens' way of life was appropriate for a young poet wanting to avoid the distractions of the world and to distil his emotions into poetry.

That evening Adrian hinted to his parents that he might move his bed into the back shed so that he could have more privacy. His parents disapproved. They said he was too moody and stuck-up as it was without locking himself in the shed and away from everyone. Besides, the shed was only of fibrocement with unlined walls and no electricity.

Adrian made his own plans. He was eighteen years old. In little more than three years he would be legally entitled to withdraw from the world with or without his parents' consent. One of his father's friends was a carpenter. Adrian asked the man what would be the cost of lining the shed. (The man was not to tell Mr Sherd about it. Adrian said he was preparing a surprise for his father.)

When the carpenter had quoted him a figure, Adrian calculated that he could pay for the job if he saved most of his salary for the next nine months. In the meanwhile, he planned the furnishings. He was justified in fitting out the place comfortably—Martens had surrounded himself with an assortment of artefacts. Adrian would buy his own radio. He would have to listen to *Top Forty* programs in order to capture the atmosphere of the parties and picnics where people of his own age were enjoying themselves. Just to sit in his isolated room, hearing a mournful pop song playing and knowing that Denise McNamara or Clare Keating might be dancing to the tune somewhere—this would be enough to put him in the mood for hours of poetry writing.

He would have a special shelf stacked with recent copies of the *Australian Women's Weekly*. The pictures of young socialites sipping cocktails and the advertisements for girdles and acne lotions would provide authentic details for the descriptions in his writings of the world he had turned away from. And he would take out a subscription to *St Gerard's Monthly*. He could stare at the photos of young couples with their six or seven children when he wanted to remind himself of the joys of family life that he had forsworn.

He would eventually have to resign from the public service. The strain of leading a double life—an administrative clerk by day and a recluse after hours—would one day prove too much for him. Until he had published his poems he could earn a modest living by writing short stories for magazines. He consulted an advertisement that appeared in the *Age* Literary Supplement every Saturday and then sent a postal note for five shillings to a post office box in Melbourne. He received by return post a booklet titled *A Marketing Guide for Australian Writers*, from which he learned that the *Women's Weekly* paid as much for a single story as he could earn in six weeks as a public servant.

On the following Saturday Adrian locked himself in the back shed. He pinned to an upright in the wall a map of Belgium from his brother's school atlas. Over the city of Brussels (Martens' birthplace) he fixed with sticky tape a tiny picture of the Great Man. (Adrian had recently removed the picture from *Twentieth Century Authors* by means of a razor blade.) Pinned to another wall was a coloured picture from a recent edition of the *Women's Weekly*. It was part of an advertisement for a biscuit with a low calorie content. A vivacious young woman was waving goodbye to someone as she stepped into a sports car. A young man held the car door open for her. He wore casual clothes and his expression was confident, bordering on arrogant. He used women for his pleasure—he had never experienced a poetic emotion in all his life. (The pictures were attached to the wall only temporarily. When Adrian moved into the shed for good, they would be part of a permanent collection like Martens' assortment of artefacts.)

By mid-afternoon, Adrian had several pages of notes for a short story. A young woman has left Australia on an overseas tour. She wanted time to think over a marriage proposal from the brash young man who had courted her for months past in his sports car. She felt that life must have had more to offer her than an endless round of social outings and Sunday drives. Her travels took her to the Continent. In the suburb of Ixelles, in the city of Brussels, she took a job as a domestic servant. The house where she worked was large and rambling and gloomy. She was warned never to pass a certain doorway on an upper landing. She learned in time that an austere genius, a literary recluse, lived and worked beyond the forbidden door. A whole new world opened up for her. All day at her work she thought of the great man in his dim room high above her and wondered what could have sustained him in his exile and whence came his creative energy.

Adrian was unsure about the ending of his short story. His readers would surely want the young woman to meet the writer, however briefly. And he understood that every story published in the *Women's Weekly* had to have a so-called happy ending. He could meet these requirements only by inventing a preposterous turn of events: the celebrated recluse was not what he seemed. He had been secretly hoping for years that a fetching young woman would come to hear of him and would seek him out and violate his privacy.

Adrian put aside his notes for the time being.

It was nearly summer. After tea each night Adrian spent an hour or two in his shed before the daylight faded. His parents still thought he was studying for his matriculation exam. He knew he would have to tell them soon that he had given up his studies long before. He would have to tell them too that he intended to resign from the public service and live the life of a poet-recluse. But often, on warm bright evenings, he thought he should just furnish his shed quietly and spend more time there each day until they realised that was the life that suited him best.

He still had to wait twenty weeks until he could afford the renovations to his shed. In the meantime he looked for pictures from magazines to decorate his walls. He had a small stack of the *Women's Weekly* and the latest issue of *St Gerard's Monthly*, bought from the bookstall outside Our Lady of Good Counsel's after Sunday mass.

Mrs Patricia Gollogly was hanging out her weekly wash in her backyard at Blacktown, NSW. One of her four children was playing on his tricycle nearby. It was exactly the kind of scene Adrian needed for his walls. After an hour of hard writing in his solitary retreat he could look up at the young housewife posing beside her gleaming wash-day result. Her smile was not the vacant wide-mouthed expression so common in *Women's Weekly* advertisements. Mrs Gollogly was pleased with herself, but also faintly amused by the sudden fame that had descended on her. Her smile did not reveal all. She held something in reserve. She was almost certainly intelligent as well as being rather attractive.

Whenever Adrian looked at Mrs Gollogly he would allow himself for a moment to envy her husband. Mr Gollogly would come home in the evening and feast his eyes on the wavy hairstyle, the wry smile, the creamy-coloured V of bare skin above the open neck of his wife's blouse. While they embraced they would exchange news of the day's events—he telling her about some business deal he had arranged, she describing the visit of the washing powder people.

At this point Adrian would stop envying the husband and begin to despise him. Mr Gollogly was only a humble underling in an office. Stripped of his white shirt and tie he was a physical and emotional weakling. Without his wife to boost his self-confidence and gratify his passions he would never have had the strength to keep going. If he had to spend a week in the solitude that Adrian Sherd endured for year after year, Gollogly would have collapsed into tears of self-pity. And yet his wife admired him and listened patiently to his stories of the office and took pride in getting his shirts whiter than white.

Then would come the climax of the exercise. Adrian would stare hard at the pretty young housewife from Black-town, NSW, and laugh—a long mocking laugh, varying in pitch and intensity as it summed up all aspects of his situation. He would laugh at the folly of the woman in yielding her body to such a mediocre man; then at the injustice of a world which kept beautiful young women enslaved to Gologlies while the men who valued love most highly, the poets and writers, were locked up in solitary rooms or sheds in backyards; and last of all he would laugh at himself for wasting his time with such a woman while the great task of his literary compositions was waiting to consume his energies.

It would be a subtle, complex laugh. Adrian practised it. While he was still getting it right he noticed that Mrs Gollogly's pose was not really that of a shy housewife photographed by surprise and overcome by the amazing success of her weekly wash. It was a provocative pose. Her lips were slightly parted; one arm was lifted high as though to adjust a clothes peg but in fact to display the white skin above the elbow where the short sleeve of her blouse must have only just covered her underarm hair; and one leg was thrust forward and bent a little sideways to reveal the perfect curve of her calf muscle. Most significant of all, the expression that at first had seemed a modest, fetching half-smile was actually the beginning of a laugh just as scornful as his own.

Adrian moved slowly closer, keeping his eyes fixed on her face. He was daring her to utter the first syllable of her laugh. His right hand was poised near the front of his trousers.

The blame for what happened next was entirely hers. If she had been the shy young housewife she pretended to be, she would have checked her laugh and turned back to her washing or even told him discreetly that he was making a fool of himself. Instead she shook her dark curls and tilted her delicate chin and set her shapely breasts trembling and laughed at all the solitary poets and writers who had no wives to float away the grime from their shirts.

Adrian strode forward and kicked over the cane laundry basket. The great heap of newly dried washing tumbled onto the lawn. And in the sunlit backyard in Blacktown,

NSW, while she lay among her gleaming whites and gayest coloureds, he took his pleasure from Mrs Gollogly, mother of four.

When the sound of laughter had died away in the shed, Adrian wiped himself and fastened his trousers. Then he put away his magazines and sat down to finish the notes of the story he had planned for the *Women's Weekly*.

But the story as he now envisaged it would not be suitable for the *Women's Weekly*. In fact there was probably no magazine in Australia that would dare to publish a work so outspoken on sexual matters. The final scene would describe, with a wealth of physical detail, how a writer was enticed away from his desk by a young woman and discovered that the most powerful aid to imaginative writing was not solitude but the fullest possible expression of his sexual urge.

A few weeks before, Adrian had read in *Time* magazine about an American writer named Henry Miller who made a good living by writing of his sexual experiences. Adrian intended to find out the name of Miller's publishers. They might be interested in Australian stories with a predominantly sexual content. Adrian's stories would not follow Miller's in being straightforward accounts of his actual experiences. It would be too easy, for instance, to write a coldly realistic report of his adventure in the Blacktown backyard. What he had to do was to transform such events into works of fiction.

Next morning on the train Adrian looked boldly at the first young typist who took his fancy. She seemed aware of his interest, but she refused to meet his eyes. He wished he could have told her she was rejecting the chance to be the anonymous heroine of a story that left nothing to the imagination.

That same day he remembered a report of a criminal trial published by the *Argus* during its last days. He consulted the newspaper files in the State Library and read again the story of the photographer who took four attractive models into a lonely part of French's Forest near Sydney and criminally or indecently assaulted all four of them. What the Sydney photographer had done was by no means original. Adrian himself had planned similar adventures in America years before. (He was sure he had taken five or six women to a desert playground in Arizona on one occasion.) But the story of the fellow's trial had made headlines in the *Argus* for days on end. The reading public wanted to hear about these things. Adrian would find a keen demand for his stories.

That night in his shed he decided to broaden the range of experiences that he would draw on for his writing. He took his *St Gerard's Monthly* and turned to the centre-page photographs of large Catholic families. The most attractive of the mothers was Mrs P. Driscoll of Deniliquin. There was nothing provocative about her pose. But Adrian was inflamed by her expression of demure virtuousness. It seemed to imply that she and her husband (and perhaps a few other Catholic parents) were the only ones privileged to know why God had implanted a sexual urge in the human male.

Adrian tore Mrs Driscoll away from her family and showed her that a solitary writer could be just as passionate as a Catholic husband.

It was after his experience with Mrs Driscoll that Adrian realised his way of life was not soundly based on a consistent theory. He still believed himself a recluse but in fact he was spending most of his spare time locked in his back shed with pictures of women. He needed a doctrine that would justify his thoroughgoing sensuality.

He remembered Mikhail Petrovich Artsybashev. The great Russian was no recluse. He strode out to meet the world with his coloured silk blouses blazing in the sunlight. As a true nihilist he took his pleasure where he found it.

On the following night Adrian approached his shed with the air of a nihilist. He wore no coloured silk, but he tousled the hair on his head and undid the two top buttons of his shirt in keeping with his repudiation of all social responsibility.

He picked up a *Women's Weekly* and turned the pages idly. He disregarded its moral exhortations. All he wanted was a brief encounter with one of the chic young women in its full-colour illustrations. If she tried to resist he would let her know he was a nihilist. She would realise it was no use arguing with a man who believed in nothing and had no illusions.

A certain young miss was boasting that her skin stayed soft and smooth under all circumstances. She ran down a glaring sand dune in her onepiece bathers. She stood so close to a waterfall that its cold droplets settled on her hair. And in the evening she wore an off-the-shoulder ballerina frock and sat close beside a young man in a restaurant. Wherever she was, her pretty face had the same smug look, because her skin could bear the closest inspection.

Before he took her for his pleasure, Adrian asked her questions such as Artsybashev would have used to convert people to nihilism. She was forced to admit that she kept her skin silky-soft for no other reason than to make her attractive to men. And since men, under their veneer of good manners, were only preparing to gratify their passions with her, the way of life she followed was no better than a harlot's. The young woman was amazed to see how nihilism could expose the emptiness beneath the complications of modern life. She was ready to be converted. She urged Adrian to enjoy her body to the full in the spirit of true nihilism. In his enthusiasm, Adrian ripped off the corner of the page showing the product that kept a woman's skin soft to the touch. He felt like Artsybashev tearing away all the pretence and hypocrisy from society.

For several nights afterwards Adrian read the *Women's Weekly* as a Russian nihilist would have done. Yet even while he stripped the advertisements and illustrations to their essentials he knew in his heart there was still one body of doctrines that nihilism might never shake. And he knew that eventually he would have to face the problem of how a writer could publish stories with a prurient appeal and still be a practising Catholic.

He had hoped he wouldn't find anything in the *Women's Weekly* to remind him of his religion. But one evening when he was gloating over a bridal group in the social pages he learned from the caption that the wedding had been celebrated in the Catholic church in the most exclusive of Melbourne's garden suburbs. And sure enough, behind the bride and her attendants was a steeple surmounted by a cross.

The cross, stark against the blue sky of a Melbourne spring, challenged him to oppose his nihilism against it, and he knew he could not. The ravings of a black-bearded Russian anarchist could not stand against a creed that had endured for twenty centuries.

In his confusion and humiliation he needed the help of a young Catholic woman. The bride in the picture already belonged to another. The bridesmaids were more likely single and heart-whole. Two of them were looking away from him towards the happy couple. But the third was smiling at the camera as if she knew that weeks later someone would search the *Women's Weekly* for the inspiration to amend his life.

According to the caption, the bridesmaid's name was Jenny Windebank. It was not a Catholic name, but the wedding had been celebrated with a nuptial mass and a papal blessing. And the sweetness and serenity of her smile could only have come from a soul that was in the state of grace. A groomsman from the wedding party stood beside her, but only for the sake of ceremony. The faint hint of eagerness with which she surveyed the world suggested she had not yet found a man worthy of her love and trust.

Adrian used scissors to separate Jenny Windebank from the rest of the wedding group. Then he mounted her photograph on a small piece of cardboard. He printed her name on the back and fitted the card into his shirt pocket. He meant to carry it wherever he went. If he was knocked down by a car and taken to hospital it would be all he had to identify him. The police would contact all the Windebanks in the telephone directory, asking for Jenny. When they found her, and she heard about the mysterious fellow with her photograph in his pocket, she would have to come to the hospital to see if it was anyone she knew. It was probably his surest way of starting a conversation with her.

But he wasn't at all anxious to get to know her. His

affairs with Denise McNamara and Clare Keating had ended badly because of his urge to hurry things along. With Jenny Windebank the spiritual element would be paramount. He would be content to know that somewhere in Melbourne a beautiful Catholic girl was still waiting for the love of her life. Not that he would go to the opposite extreme and languish for an imaginary woman. Jenny Windebank would be closer to him than Denise or Clare had ever been. Her photograph, in full colour, would be with him always.

Already she had made a marvellous difference to his life. He was no longer a nihilist. He belonged once more to the great multitude of normal people who found happiness in simple human affection. And he was not so anxious to write. The notes he had prepared in the past few months seemed a little too fanciful. He would do better to base his plays or stories or poems on his actual experiences. If he observed himself closely for a few weeks and noted the effects of love on his character, he would have all the material he needed. He might be surprised to find that after all his efforts to imagine plots and characters, his own life was full of material for a realistic work of literature.

On the following Saturday he went to confession. He had to ride his bike to a neighbouring parish. The priests at Our Lady of Good Counsel's might have remembered that he was the same fellow who had gone off to join the Charleroi Fathers a year before. If he confessed sins of impurity to any of them, he would seem to be going backwards spiritually.

But the priest he confessed to was not going to let him off lightly. He asked Adrian how old he was and how long he had been committing that sin.

Adrian was not frightened. He said, 'I'm eighteen, Father, and these few sins I've confessed today were the first for two years. And I'm confident I won't fall again because I've just become very interested in a wonderful girl.'

'Is she a Catholic, this girl?'

'Yes, Father.' He was not lying. He genuinely believed Jenny to be a Catholic.

The priest was not impressed. He said, 'I want you to come back here in a fortnight. And see if you can keep your hands off yourself—and off the girl too.'

Adrian sang all the way home. He would not go back to the irritable priest—not because he was going to sin again, but only to avoid awkward questions about Jenny.

No priest could have understood how it was between them. He smiled at the priest's suspicions and the idea that he might touch Jenny Windebank improperly.

That same Saturday afternoon, Adrian sat in his shed looking through *Women's Weekly* magazines for any other picture of Jenny that might have appeared in the social pages. The magazines seemed different. In the past he had turned page after page of pictures that meant nothing to him. They were pictures of a world he was shut out of—a world where tables were elaborately set and dishes were served with sprigs of green parsley around their edges, where smiling hostesses carried trays of strange drinks towards guests in suits and long frocks, where a fishpond or a fernery could turn a neglected garden corner into a centre of interest. But now he was anxious to study these scenes, and he wondered why.

Trying to live as a recluse without the love of a woman, he had been preoccupied with remote or abstract subjects such as poetic styles or the lives of long-dead authors or the philosophy of nihilism. He had been cut off from the everyday world where husbands and wives enjoyed the simple pleasures—dining together by candlelight or entertaining old friends or beautifying their garden. Poetic emotion was all right in its place, but too much of it could be unhealthy. It was a joy to be in touch with real life again. Adrian settled down to enjoy every page of his *Women's Weekly*.

Magi-Bake Instant Dessert came in four flavours—Vanilla Whip, Chocolate Foam, Lemon Snow and Strawberry Treat. The most attractive way to serve them was in glass goblets very different from the coarse china bowls that the Sherds called 'pudding plates'. A cultured woman like Jenny Windebank would know where to buy properly shaped goblets. Each night for four nights she would serve her husband a different Magi-Bake flavour. When he had decided which appealed to him most, she would make sure there was always a goblet or two in the fridge.

The contents of a tin of Rosella sausages and vegetables had been photographed close-up on a plate to show the tempting lilac colour of the plump sausages, the delicate pale green of the peas and the vivid orange of the diced carrot. It was the sort of snack a man could expect his wife to serve on a nippy autumn day when he came in from the garden.

As for the garden, Adrian read an article entitled 'Creepers for All Positions'. It would have seemed like gibberish to a solitary man, but knowing his wife would expect him one day to lay out a garden, he took a keen pleasure in learning the preferences of plants, their whims and peculiarities and feeding habits.

It was the same with advertisements for furniture and floor coverings and bathroom fittings. As a married man, Adrian would be entitled to stand silently weighing up the merits of different floral patterns or plastics while his wife and a respectful salesman waited patiently for his decision.

The world would hold no mysteries for a married man. With his wife on his arm, Adrian could stride boldly past the cosmetics counters in department stores and into the mysterious feminine areas he had always detoured around as a single man. Even the most baffling questions of all would be answered at last. His wife would explain the whole story behind the pictures of bejewelled women in evening gowns who gazed haughtily at the camera and said only the cryptic words, 'Modess because...' And one day he would solve the mystery that had bothered him since he had first read the *Women's Weekly* as a boy. He would put the question frankly to his wife: 'Those tall slender women looking gravely into the distance with their lower bodies encased in taut skin-coloured girdles—do they wear some further garment beneath their girdles, or is there nothing but air between their most private parts and the outside world, so that only the angle at which they hold their legs distinguishes the *Women's Weekly* from the most shameless of pornographic magazines?'

After a day with the *Women's Weekly*, Adrian was eager to do something a little more practical.

As far as he knew, the post-war housing shortage was over. But many young couples around Accrington still spent their first years after marriage in backyard bungalows or converted garages. Adrian had thought before of having his shed lined and floored and fitted with plumbing. Now he would definitely arrange for his father's carpenter friend to begin work on it. Afterwards Adrian himself would paint and furnish it. He would make it a cosy little nest fit to bring a bride into. They could live there while they paid off their own block of land in one of the newer parts of Springvale or Noble Park. On winter nights they would sit together over plans for houses and want for nothing. He would see a plumber about fitting a little sink and a shower recess, perhaps even a toilet bowl concealed in a cupboard. On Sunday Adrian measured the shed carefully and drew a floor plan to scale on a large sheet of paper. He sat in his room until midnight deciding where the pieces of furniture would go.

Next morning when he looked into the shed before leaving for work he was shocked to see how much rubbish his parents and young brothers had stored there. If he started to remove it openly they would ask embarrassing questions. He could bury a small amount each night in the long grass near the fowl yard. Or he could ride his bike to the Accrington tip at weekends with a sugar bag of rubbish on his back. Better still, he could carry a small amount to the Teachers' Branch each day and empty it into his wastepaper basket.

He opened his leather satchel and popped in one of his father's worn-out shoes. There was room for more in the satchel. He took an old torn woollen elephant from the box that his brothers used to call their treasure chest. He could still fit something into the hollow of the shoe. The bottom of the treasure chest was littered with broken seashells. He put a handful into the shoe and packed them in securely with some of the stuffing from the toy elephant.

On the train to the city he sat opposite a row of girls about his own age. Two of them were quite pretty. He almost smiled when he remembered how agitated he used to be in such situations. In his lustful period he had tried to look at girls' breasts or knees or bare shoulders without the girls catching him at it. As a recluse he had sternly refused to glance at even the most beautiful girl. But he had often worried whether the girls he never looked at had thought there was something wrong with him. Sometimes he had been concerned that the girls might think they were losing their charm when they saw him ignoring them.

Now his worries were over. With his picture of Jenny Windebank in his shirt pocket he could relax. He gave each girl in the carriage one glance to reassure her that she was still attractive to men, and to let her see that he himself was socially as well developed as she was. But by limiting them to one glance each he made it clear that he was not a candidate for their affections. They would then realise that he already enjoyed a special relationship with another.

He had never felt so comfortable in the presence of the opposite sex. He saw how all his anxieties in the past had been caused by his shame at having no girlfriend to show off to the world. He felt such goodwill towards the girls in the train that he wished he could have handed them Jenny Windebank's photo to admire.

He remembered pictures in the *Women's Weekly* of young people of both sexes enjoying themselves together. Dressed in expensive casual clothes and with clear unblemished skins, they smiled into each other's eyes or gestured exuberantly or leaned on the shoulders of their steady boyfriends or girlfriends. He had sometimes wanted to belong to such a group and experience that boisterous happiness, but he could never have joined in without a girlfriend of his own. As his train approached the city he felt he belonged at last in the world he had admired in *Women's Weekly* pictures.

He sprawled back in his seat and revelled in his innocent companionship with the girls opposite. He wanted to make one of those extravagant gestures that young people used to express their happiness. He stood up to get his satchel from the luggage rack. He lifted it down with a flourish. An odd rattling noise came from inside it. The satchel was upside down and the seashells were tumbling out of his father's old shoe. The noise was hardly loud enough for the girls to hear, but a thin stream of dust and fragments of shell had spilled out through the crack at the end of the zip fastener. Some of it settled on the skirt of the nearest girl. She shuddered and drew back her knees and tried to brush it off. She muttered something to the girl beside her and the two of them glared at Adrian. He kept his eyes down and was thankful that Jenny Windebank would never know how he had made a fool of himself in a suburban train.

Each day he emptied more rubbish out of the shed and made it a little more like a home for a married couple. He gave a lot of thought to the position of his desk and bookshelf. He wanted to look up from his writing of an evening and exchange smiles with his wife while she worked contentedly in the kitchen area. When he had settled on a place for the desk he considered the problem of what he would write.

He was not surprised to find that he could no longer write like Martens or Artsybashev or Andreyev. But he was concerned at his lack of enthusiasm for Coventry Patmore's themes. *The Unknown Eros* was the story of a man's ascent to a mystical experience through his intense devotion to his wife. Whenever Adrian tried to think of the most elevated spiritual joys of marriage he only saw himself sitting beside the kerosene heater in his cosy shed on winter nights holding hands with Jenny Windebank. He knew that the joys of human love were only a pale reflection of the bliss that came from union with God. But his perverse human nature seemed to want nothing higher than the contentment of sharing a home (or even a shed—properly lined and furnished) with a pretty, uncomplicated marriage partner.

When he remembered all his troubles of the past year, he thought of writing his autobiography. He made several pages of notes for the story of a man who tried to find happiness first in unbridled sensuality, then in a strict religious order, and then as a poet-recluse who experimented with nihilism and pessimism.

The story should have ended with the man's discovery that the most lasting contentment came from the simple domestic pleasures of a happy marriage. But the book seemed to deserve a grander climax. Adrian kept remembering *Elected Silence*, with its magnificent last chapters describing Thomas Merton's flight from the chaos of modern life to the peace of a Cistercian monastery. Adrian himself had been moved to tears when Merton recounted his arrival at the monastery late at night after a journey across hundreds of miles of America. But how many readers would weep when Adrian Sherd described his discovery of a picture in a *Women's Weekly* or his first months of marriage in a shed behind his parents' house?

Adrian paced the floor of his shed. He knew that marriage was good in itself and a worthy goal for ordinary people. But it was hardly a suitable ending for his autobiography.

What he needed was an act of renunciation. He had to turn away from the highest form of earthly happiness just when it was within his grasp. But what could he turn to? He had already tried to live in a religious order and failed. He had not made a fair trial of the Cistercians, though. It would make a superb scene—the former poet of the emotions, the ex-nihilist, the man who had turned his back on all the Jenny Windebanks of Melbourne, knocking on the monastery door at Yarra Glen and creeping into his true home at last.

But the reader would have known already about his interest in the Cistercians. The perfect ending would be for him to turn suddenly to something totally unexpected—to dedicate himself to an ideal that was utterly heroic and extraordinary.

Thomas Merton had written with awe of an order called the Carthusians who were even stricter than the Cistercians. They had a house in England where the monks lived as hermits. A life as a hermit in an English landscape would recall some of Adrian's earlier quests as well as being a fitting end to his story.

Adrian took his picture of Jenny Windebank from his pocket. He slipped it somewhere into his stack of magazines and carried them outside to the incinerator. He started a fire. One after another the pages curled at their edges and were scorched to a uniform dark brown before he eased them into the heart of the flames, where they shrivelled to wisps of ash. Even with their rich colours scorched, he could still recognise many of the illustrations. Rooms thickly carpeted with Feltex, beautiful women sheathed in Hickory foundation garments, tempting desserts prepared with Foster Clark's custard powder, gardens where zinnias made a colourful showing—all the creature comforts of modern life appeared to him one last time, trembling at the edge of the fire. But he remained unmoved and went on stoking the flames.

Adrian did not know the address of the Carthusians in England. He intended to write to them in care of the Catholic Archbishop of London. As the strictest of all monastic orders, they probably received letters every week from unhappy young men wanting to escape from the frantic secular world to the peace of a monastery. Adrian's letter was carefully composed to convince the Carthusian abbot that the writer was a genuine case. He wrote the simple truth: that he had several promising careers to choose from and took a normal, healthy interest in the opposite sex but had always felt that something was missing from his life and had lately realised what it was: his life in the busy world did not allow him enough time to meditate and reflect on what truly mattered. The letter ended with a request for detailed information about the monastery and an application form for admission as a novice to the Carthusian Order.

Before he posted the letter, Adrian decided to test his suitability by living a modified version of the Carthusian rule.

As far as he knew, each monk spent the day alone in his cell, reading and meditating, except for intervals when he cultivated the vegetables and herbs in his own walled garden. The cells and their adjoining gardens were scattered around the monastery grounds. The monks saw each other only in the chapel each morning for mass and once each week when they strolled and chatted together for recreation. During the rest of the time, they lived as hermits.

Adrian marked out an unused corner of the backyard for his plot of herbs and vegetables. When his first crops matured he would ask his mother to serve them to him for meals. Later, when his brothers would have stopped jeering at him and his parents would have come to understand that his new life was more than a passing fad, he would wash his salads outside at the gully trap and eat them alone in his cell with a devotional book propped open in front of him.

He inspected the inside of his shed. He could hardly believe he had once hoped to convert it into a home for a married couple. He had got rid of a few handfuls of rubbish every day without anyone noticing him, but it would have taken him years to empty the place at that rate. Now he could simply clear a space at one end for his cell. Most of the furniture he needed was already in the shed. He already had an old kitchen chair. A few planks resting together made a table. His few books could rest in a pile on a corner of the table. A disused ice chest could store his toiletries. He looked around for a bed. He wanted something crude and uncomfortable that he could lie on for his six hours of sleep between the offices of compline in the evening and matins in the early morning.

A year before, when he was leaving for Blenheim, he had given his model railway to his young brothers. The old door that had once been the base for the railway was lying against a wall. He recalled that his brothers had traded the railway for the model aeroplanes that he sometimes saw them with. The door was marked with the holes where the railway tracks had been fixed, but the thing would make an ideal bed. He fetched four logs from the woodheap and rested his timber bed on top. He lay down. It was just as uncomfortable as he had hoped for. He would have to lie on his back all night, but it would be good for his spine.

He remembered the map of the USA that had been faintly sketched on the timber beneath him. He sat up and looked for traces of the map. Only a few marks remained. Perhaps his brothers had erased the map for some reason, or perhaps the outline had simply faded. He could still recall how the whole map had looked.

He lay down again. His head was where New England had once been. Where his heart thumped softly, the great blue folds of Appalachia had once lain. His feet rested on the last traces of Texas, and his groin was in one of the Great Plains states. But America would never trouble him again. As a Carthusian monk, he would stretch himself peacefully on his simple bed with no thought of the land-scapes that had tempted him long before. He would sleep with his arms folded on his chest in the shape of a cross, and the tall wind-blown grasses of some remote prairie would wave above his slack genitals.

Adrian had fitted out his cell within a few hours. (He called it his study so as not to alarm his parents.) He felt so cosy sitting at his planks, with his spiritual reading within reach and his vegetable plot a few yards from his door, that he wondered why he had to go to the trouble of writing to England and humbly asking the Carthusians to accept him when he could lead a strict monastic life in the comfort and privacy of his own home.

He decided to write his own religious rule. It would be even stricter than that of the Carthusians but adapted to suit the special circumstances of a hermit who had to live in a backyard in Accrington, Victoria, and had to earn his living in the state public service.

He read parts of *The Imitation of Christ*, by Thomas à Kempis, looking for ideas, and got much encouragement from much that he read.

> Thou must be contented for Christ's sake to be esteemed as a fool in this world, if thou desire to lead a religious life.
>
> If thou desirest true contrition of heart, enter into thy secret chamber, and shut out the tumults of the world.
>
> It is meet that thou remove thyself far away from acquaintance and dear friends and keep thy mind void of all temporal comfort.

Adrian wanted his rule to be simple and easily remembered. He would rise at 4.00 a.m. and spend an hour reading from Sacred Scripture. At 5.00 a.m. he would begin an hour's meditation. At 6.00 a.m. he would be ready for mass.

It seemed inappropriate for a monk of an enclosed order to have to ride a bike more than a mile to attend mass at a humble parish church. A true eremite offered his own mass each morning at his own private altar. All the great saints of old who withdrew to the desert had been ordained priests beforehand.

Adrian devised two alternative plans for obtaining the power to celebrate mass. He could, perhaps, travel to Europe and seek ordination from one of the so-called Wandering Bishops—men who were not in communion with the Holy See but possessed valid episcopal powers that they could trace back through a long line of unofficial bishops, some of them excommunicated generations earlier.

Or he could attend the next ordination ceremony in Melbourne's St Patrick's Cathedral and sit as close to the altar as possible. Before the ceremony, he could offer up a silent prayer, presenting himself as an ordinand along with the young men in the sanctuary, who would have studied in the diocesan seminary or in some or another religious order for seven years past. He would whisper the same prayers that the candidates uttered aloud and would copy as many of their gestures as he could manage without alarming the congregation around him. Then, at the moment when the Archbishop laid his hands on the head of the first of the official ordinands, Adrian would pray that his own head might attract a few stray beams of the enormous spiritual force radiating through the sanctuary.

If only he were brave enough, he could leap the sanctuary rails at the right moment and butt his own head against the Archbishop's outstretched hands and then flee for his life down the main aisle and out across the Cathedral grounds and into the Fitzroy Gardens with the powers of the priesthood safe inside him. The men who passed around the collection plates and perhaps even some of the young priests might give chase, but what could they do to him? Could a team of bishops exorcise his priestly faculties? Could he be tried in some sort of ecclesiastical court? But he need not go to these lengths. The mass was a spiritual event. The visible ceremony was only an outward sign of the inner process. There was nothing to stop him from celebrating a spiritual mass alone in his cell. He would train his imagination thoroughly. Then, each morning at six, he would enact an entire mass in his mind. He would thereby gain all the spiritual benefits of a conventual mass.

If he could celebrate a mass in his mind, he could use the same method to perform the more difficult items in his rule. Instead of scourging himself with an actual leather thong, he could inflict on himself a spiritual pain at least as keen as anything that his fleshly buttocks might otherwise have endured.

But every single deed in the life of a monk was performed for its spiritual effect. He could enjoy all the spiritual benefits of the monastic life without lifting a finger. Instead of actually cultivating a garden, he could meditate for the appropriate length of time on tasks such as digging and weeding and could enjoy the spiritual fruits of his invisible vegetable garden.

Not only was his garden unnecessary—he could do without his chair and table and bed. He shoved his few pieces of furniture back to their old places in the shed. He would never again be confined by the material world. His monastery was wherever he willed it to be.

Adrian felt a sense of boundless freedom. All he needed was a reasonably quiet spot where he could close his eyes and meditate on his new life. In a corner of the shed was an old wardrobe that he had shared with his brothers years before. The door hung slightly open because the lock was broken. He hammered a nail into the inner side of the wardrobe door and then attached a length of string to the nail.

He made a cluster of nail holes in the roof of the wardrobe for ventilation. Then he stepped inside and sat down with the string around his wrist and pulled the door shut.

Adrian Sherd meditated on the life of a hermit. His cell was remote from the world. He could have followed his rule unhindered through all the seasons of the year, climatic and liturgical. But it occurred to him that most of the daily activities of a hermit—his manual work, his penances, even his mass and his formal prayers—were only a preparation for the climax of his day, which was his wordless meditation.

Adrian abolished his hermit's rule and gave himself entirely to meditation. He resolved not to engage in any other activity unless it was absolutely necessary for his survival.

The aim of his meditation was nothing less than the union of his soul with God. It was called by the church the Mystical Union. Only a few saints had been known to achieve it. One of them, St John of the Cross, had written exquisite lyric poetry to describe it. Adrian would allow himself to jot down a few stanzas if inspiration came to him.

He closed his eyes and saw a landscape. He was impressed by its sunlit grasslands and broad watercourses. But it reminded him a little of America and he dismissed it from his mind.

He meditated again and saw scenery vaguely like the places in Australia where he had once hoped to live as a Catholic husband and father.

He tried several times more. He whispered the most awesome words he knew—'Godhead, Deity, Eternity, Apocalypse'—and closed his eyes. The landscapes he saw

479

were from literature—green English settings from Arnold and Housman, Francis Thompson's forbidding country, even a place that could have been the mediaeval world of Martens' plays. They were more vivid and radiant than he had ever imagined them, but there was nothing spiritual about them.

Adrian opened his eyes in the darkness of the wardrobe and saw he was as far away as ever from the Mystical Union. He remembered that some of the great mystics had described a state of misery and near-despair that often afflicted the soul in search of God. He too was experiencing it. His vision of shining landscapes was his Dark Night of the Soul.

He interrupted his meditation to eat his evening meal and sleep in his bed under his parents' roof and spend a day in the Teachers' Branch. Before resuming his spiritual tasks he visited Cheshire's Bookshop to look in the RELIGION shelves for a book on mental prayer. He caught sight of a title that seemed to refer to the plight of mystics like himself—*A Season in Hell*. He picked up the book before he realised it came from POETRY and not RELIGION.

Out of habit he searched for information about the poet's life before looking at the poems. He read about a Frenchman named Arthur Rimbaud who was described as a visionary. Rimbaud had given up poetry at the age of nineteen and set out on a mysterious journey that took him at last to Abyssinia.

Adrian looked wildly round him, but no one had witnessed his fateful discovery. He took the book to the counter. While the young man was wrapping it, Adrian tried to compose a sentence to let the fellow know what the book meant to him. He wanted to say, 'Funny, isn't it, but I'm nearly the same age as Rimbaud was when he gave up poetry for good and went on his travels.'

But it was the same fellow who had wrapped up *An Anthology of Catholic Poets*, and he might have said, 'But you only took up poetry a few months ago.'

Adrian did not meditate that night. He thought about Rimbaud abandoning poetry and ending his visionary's quest in a remote part of Africa. Adrian himself was ready at last to give up searching for something remarkable in poetry or religion.

He knew it would not be easy to forsake his old life and set out for a place like Abyssinia. At work in the Education Department, Coldbeck and grey-haired Mr Armitage, the officer in charge of the Teachers' Branch, seemed to have got wind of his plan. He heard them talking quietly at Coldbeck's desk.

Armitage said, 'He probably did it for some kind of joke. But I agree with you it's not all that funny. Where is the place, anyway? Addis Ababa—it's not on our list of state schools, is it? Africa? Christ Almighty, it's hard enough to get our temps to the Mallee without sending them to Africa. And what was that business about the shoe in your wastepaper basket? Full of what? Shell grit? Well, it's no worse than the practical jokes the young clerks used to get up to when I was head of the Papers Branch. I'll have a talk to him just the same. We're shorthanded, as you know, Stewart. I wouldn't want to lose him unless we can get a replacement straightaway.'

Adrian pretended to be surprised when Mr Armitage called him to his room. The officer in charge of the

Teachers' Branch looked very tired after a lifetime in the public service. Adrian felt sorry for him. He had probably never travelled beyond the garden suburbs of Melbourne. He asked Adrian polite questions about his future. Adrian thought that if he told Armitage about his true destination the poor old fellow would have a nervous breakdown.

In the end they agreed that the public service was expanding rapidly and prospects had never been brighter for young fellows like Adrian so long as they took life seriously. When Adrian left, Mr Armitage looked quite reassured.

Adrian hinted to his parents that he felt like going on a long journey. They were not as surprised as he had expected, but they didn't fully understand him. They said they wouldn't be too upset if he failed his exams even though he had put so much effort into his studies lately. They suggested he ought to take a week's leave just before Christmas and visit his uncle's farm in the Western District and get out in the fresh air.

As soon as they mentioned the Western District he stopped listening. Anyone who thought a few miles of closely settled dairying country could satisfy a man like Rimbaud was mad.

Adrian went outside to the shed and looked round carefully. After he had gone there must be no clues to tell anyone where he was. It was most important to hide any sign that he had used the shed for meditation. If his parents called in the parish priest he might know just enough about the soul to guess where Adrian was heading for.

He took his father's axe and quietly smashed the chair he had sat on so often. He climbed up on a box and gathered cobwebs from the rafters. Then he smeared the dusty strands across the front of the old wardrobe to make it look as though no one had ever meditated inside.

He gathered the notes of plays and poems and short stories he had once planned to write. They made a smaller stack than he had expected but they blazed up high in the incinerator.

Last of all he looked over his collection of books. Most of them could stay where they were—there was nothing in them to suggest where he was going. Some would even mislead anyone looking for clues. If his parents picked up Housman's poems, for instance, they might think he was somewhere in the west of England. He smiled when he noticed *Views of the USSR*. He saw his parents praying for their son who had fallen into the hands of the Communists.

The only book he could not leave was *A Season in Hell*. Anyone who read the Introduction would know at once where he was going and who had inspired him to go there. He would carry the slender volume hidden about his person. No one would see it while he travelled, but if he was injured or killed they would find it on him. His name in the front would identify him and the book itself would explain the meaning of his last years.

He took a roll of strong adhesive tape from among his father's tools. He unbuttoned his shirt and lifted his singlet and bound the book to his chest with long strips of tape. When his clothes were in position again he lay on his back on the cement floor of the shed and visualised the discovery of the book on his body.

The only words visible among the intersecting bands of black tape were those of the title, *A Season in Hell*. Adrian realised at once that this did not look well. If the doctor or priest who saw it looked no further than the cover, Adrian might be supposed to have spent his last years in misery or even in mortal sin. He had to ensure that people knew the truth about him—that he had discovered at last a land after his own heart.

He got up and fetched a ballpoint pen and neatly crossed out the last word of the title without loosening the book from its tapes. There was space on the orange paper of the cover to write in a more suitable word, but Adrian hesitated.

He asked himself bluntly where he was going after all. He knew it was not to Abyssinia. Apart from minor practical difficulties, Africa was no longer the Dark Continent of sixty years earlier when Rimbaud had hidden himself there. By now Addis Ababa might have as many miles of dreary outer suburbs as Melbourne had.

He had never intended to follow Rimbaud literally. He was going, like Rimbaud, to a place where poetry was no longer necessary, to the most satisfying of all landscapes, a region that lay on the far side of literature.

But he had to name his destination for the sake of posterity. The nearer he came to it, the more it resembled a place that theologians had speculated about—the earth itself, transformed into an abode of perfect natural happiness whose inhabitants enjoyed as their right what Adrian Sherd had failed to find in dreams of America, of married life near Hepburn Springs, of the priesthood, of a poet's calling.

He lay down again on the floor and bared his chest with the book still taped to it. With his right hand he drew another line through HELL and wrote beneath it LIMBO.

But he knew that he was still deceiving himself. He was a baptised Catholic, and Limbo was only for those who had never heard of the true Church and had never been baptised.

He lay for some time with the pen in his hand. Even with his eyes open, he could see the place that he was hoping to reach. But he knew no name for it.

He felt close to exhaustion. If he could not name his hoped-for place, he might at least name the district or region that encompassed it. Yes, he had still enough strength and perceptiveness to do that. Weary as he was, he recognised that his longed-for destination had been called into being solely by his own wants and yearnings. He crossed out LIMBO and amended his last words for anyone interested.

He tossed the pen away. His skin was still bare with the book still securely in place and on its cover the amended inscription A SEASON ON EARTH.

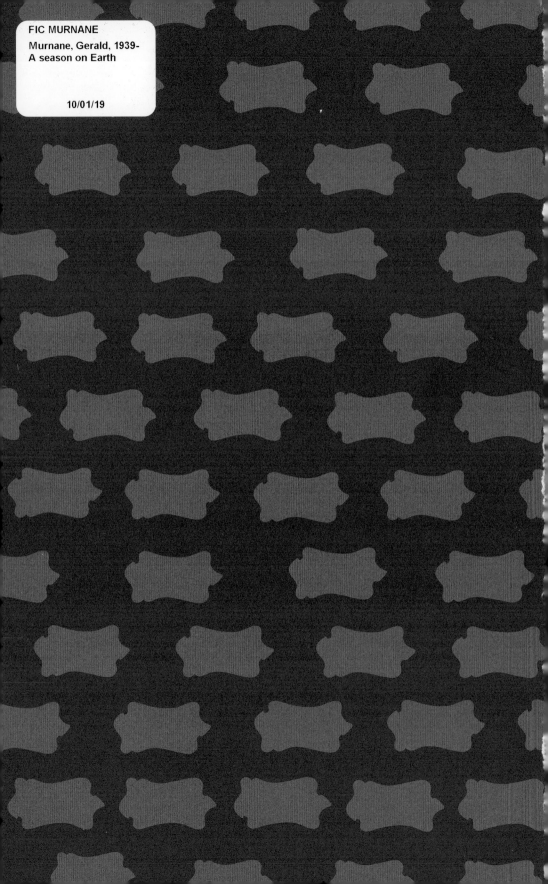